Sara Banerji

is married to an Indian, and lived in India for many years, bringing up her family there. She now lives in Oxford where, as well as being an artist and sculptress, she teaches in the E............ .... .t Oxford University.

From the reviews of *Shining Hero*:

'An unsentimental yet extremel............. .... sibling rivalry. Banerji's success is in the creation of two heroes who, despite their glaring flaws, are sympathetic. This is a stunning novel, rich in human experience and fascinating mythology, but beautifully written too, with flashes of irony and humour to lighten the deeper pathos.' *Tablet*

'Banerji handles set pieces ranging from the Calcutta underworld to the heights of the Himalayas, but she is best at the small significant detail – Karna, introduced to luxury by his success in commercials, sitting by his gleaming new telephone, stroking it and waiting for it to ring.' *The Times*

'A quite remarkable book that takes the reader through the various layers of Indian society, stopping at the mighty river that rules all lives, the squalid city rubbish dumps, the lavish home of the local landowner, the drug dealer's den and eventually the snow-capped Himalayan mountains, which feature in the final battle scene of so many Bollywood films.' *Oxford Times*

'Sara Banerji is a natural-born storyteller. *Shining Hero* enthrals with its punchy, exciting narrative. It is a gripping read, the kind of book that is impossible to put down. Banerji has a wonderful prose style – her writing is fluid and confident and extremely imaginative. She knows how to meld shimmering prose with rollicking, high-powered adventure, making *Shining Hero* vivid, dramatic and entertaining.' *Sunday Business Post*

SARA BANERJI

Shining Hero

Flamingo

An Imprint of HarperCollins*Publishers*

Flamingo
An imprint of HarperCollins*Publishers*
77–85 Fulham Palace Road,
Hammersmith, London W6 8JB

Flamingo is a registered trade mark of
HarperCollins*Publishers* Limited

www.**fire**and**water**.com

Published by Flamingo 2003
9 8 7 6 5 4 3 2 1

First published in Great Britain by Flamingo 2002

Copyright © Sara Banerji 2002

Sara Banerji asserts the moral right to be
identified as the author of this work

Photograph of Sara Banerji © Simon James 2002

This novel is entirely a work of fiction. The names, characters
and incidents portrayed in it are the work of the author's
imagination. Any resemblance to actual persons, living or
dead, events or localities, is entirely coincidental.

The quotations from the Mahabharata were translated and
condensed by Romesh C. Dutt (published by J.M Dent, 1972).

ISBN 0 00 713568 8

Typeset in Bembo by Palimpsest Book Production Limited,
Polmont, Stirlingshire

Printed and bound in Great Britain by Clays Ltd, St Ives plc

Dedicated to Matthew Kneale, mentor and friend

I would like to thank the Arts Council of England whose award gave me the encouragement, at a crucial moment, to complete the book. A thousand thanks to Barbara Trapido. Also to my daughter, Sabita, my husband Ranjit and Justine Burley.

THE MAHABHARATA IS AN EPIC POEM eight times longer than the *Iliad*, written in the third or fourth century B.C. It tells the story of a great war between two sets of cousins, the five Pandavas, the third of whom was Arjuna, and the hundred Kauravas, the eldest of whom was Dhuriodhana.

They fought for the kingdom whose capital city was Hastina-pura, which means city of the elephant, and to which the brave, heroic Pandavas were entitled. They had however been tricked out of their inheritance by the treacherous and devious Kauravas.

This poem is more than a story or a history. It describes the moral and ethical standards of the day and makes value judgements which are valid even in modern times. Anger, fear, hatred, jealousy, greed, lust, envy, pride and arrogance are all experienced by the protagonists of the *Mahabharata*. Heroes are capable of acting badly. One of Arjuna's brothers, the heroic Yudhistra, loses everything he owns including his wife and children as well as his kingdom, in a game of dice. Arjuna himself suffers weakness at the start of the battle. His chariot is driven by the god Krishna who instructs and advises him when Arjuna becomes filled with doubt because he realises he will have to kill uncles, cousins and even his old teacher.

In the *Bhagavad Gita*, meaning 'The Song Of God', Krishna, during the battle, reminds Arjuna that because he is a kshatriya, or of the warrior caste, he has a greater duty to fight than he has towards his relatives.

In the course of the song Krishna gives Arjuna precise instructions on how to silence his mind and reach the Absolute so that to this day those learning to meditate can find the instructions for transcending thought in the *Bhagavad Gita*.

I

SEDUCTION BY SURIYA

Pritha, yet unwedded, bore him,
peerless archer on the earth,
Portion of the solar radiance
for the sun inspired his birth.

The river, Koonty thought, was like Soma, the liquid god. A limpid
animal to whom she came for comfort and to be freed of pain, though
now, as she let the sacred water tickle against her ankles she wondered
if she had imagined the interior gnawing. Or perhaps this holy river,
annually stocked with melting goddesses, had cured her. Half an hour
ago she had been certain she was dying but now she was well again.
She stirred the water with her toes, started to feel happy. When she
was little she would never have touched the water in this way. Then
she had been afraid, for she had been told the story of the elephant
who was snared by water serpents. As it was dragged, drowning, to
the bottom of the river, the elephant implored the high gods for
help. Vishnu had heard its prayer and, riding on his vehicle, the angel
bird Garuda, appeared at the waterside. The great god, four-armed,
crowned with a diadem, did not need to act. His mere presence
had been enough. The serpent king and queen rose to the surface
of the river and balanced in the water, their great and weighty victim
struggled out of their tendrils and the Nagas folded their hands and
bowed to the Lord Ruler of the Universe. But Koonty had feared
that, in her case Vishnu might not think her sufficiently important
to be saved and it was several years before she would believe that this
tale was only a myth.

The stones of the riverbank had been smoothed by the slaps and caresses of ancient currents until they had become like dull jewels studding a water bangle. Even when the river lost control and drowned its own banks as though it no longer loved them, its stones stayed warm. But the river was not only a magic water woman bestowing wet kisses that grew rice. It killed as well.

Every year since Koonty was born she had seen it spread its transparent and reflective body over the land till houses were flattened, fields vanished and cuddled banks were lost utterly.

That was when Koonty and the zamindar's children got a new playground. Sitting astride floating banana logs they bounced over the lost fields shouting, leaping and splashing on their banana ponies and trying to shove each other off into the drowning rice crop, while the peasant farmers mourned the loss of their livelihood. Paddling with their hands or punting with passing bamboo poles, pretending to be walking on water like yogis or crossing the ocean like foreigners, the children explored a new, wet world that, yesterday, had been paddy fields, cabbage crops, the road to Calcutta. A mirror world where an enormous yellow sky shone on the ground and only the tips of plants were visible. Sometimes their rubber chappals got sucked off and were bobbed away like rubber boats to be captured in the spring, while Boodi Ayah, wheedling, threatening, urging, would try to wade through the slush to get at them. But the watery ayah had closed her extended world to adults.

Koonty's mother would rush out shouting, 'What is this crazy behaviour? Who will marry a girl who is seen acting like a peasant child? You will end up like your sister if you go on like this.' Shivarani, Koonty's older sister, would never get married because she was too tall and was a Communist.

'Me. I will marry Koonty,' whispered Pandu, the zamindar's oldest son, while Koonty's dry mother, the lady of the land, the un-magical woman, was telling her husband, 'You must do something about that wild girl before it is too late.'

'What harm can come?' murmured Koonty's father. He did not look up from his book.

'She might lose her virginity, sitting astride like that. Raped by a banana tree. What a waste,' wailed Meena, Koonty's mother.

But this river, thought Koonty, is not only a woman. It is a man as well. A husband. Every year his wife, Durga, is thrown into his body, to mingle with his substance in a million muddy forms, re-emerging later in little bits, a manicured finger here, a nose ring there.

Koonty and Pandu dived for her earrings and came up with the goddess' arm.

'I bet you don't dare keep that,' said Pandu. 'I bet you are afraid she'll put a curse on you.' He was always testing Koonty, trying to find out how far she would go. Her daringness excited him. Rolling the arm inside the hem of her blouse, she carried it to the rose garden and hid it there.

Several days later her mother saw the curling fingers beckoning from behind a Queen Elizabeth.

'This will bring trouble upon you,' she raged and beat Koonty about the ears with her supari cutters. Koonty leapt around the veranda to avoid the whacking scissors, while her mother shouted, 'Now for certain the goddess will put a curse upon you.' Now the fear came to Koonty. Was that what the pains had been? Durga's late curse? Her mother had gone down to the river bank, and, ululating, had thrown the sacred arm back into the water then waited for long minutes in case celestial retribution was to follow.

Koonty could hear the sound of hymns coming from the village over the loudspeaker. They were worshipping the Durga there and this time tomorrow would be immersing the goddesses here. This time tomorrow the river will be filled with new goddesses, she was thinking, when the pain gripped Koonty again so that instantly she could not think of anything else but it. IT. Big IT pain hurling through her stomach as though she, like the deep parts of the river, had inside her body sharp stones and a tumbling current.

Her bare feet curled, her hands clenched. 'Ouch, ouch,' wailed Koonty and she tried to get away from the pain by squatting down into the water. She arched her back against it. Tried to duck out from under the burden of agony. But the pain was inside her, she could not escape it.

She had started feeling ill during the monsoon. She had been very sick and her mother had taken her to the doctor. But though he examined her all over he had found nothing wrong and said it must have been something she had eaten.

'Keep her on rice and dahi for a day or two and she'll be all right.'

But the sickness had continued.

'Perhaps she is allergic to fish,' the doctor said.

Koonty's mother agreed. 'I have noticed that it is after taking maacher jhal that she gets the worst nausea. But it is a very great pity because here in Hatipur village we get the best fish of all India. There is nothing to surpass the hilsa taken out of our own Jummuna river.'

Koonty gave up fish and sure enough after a month and a half of abstinence she suddenly became perfectly well again.

But now she was feeling worse than sick and the pain was so intense that she could not walk, but had to crouch, waiting for it to recede. She was desperate to get home but each time she tried to start on the half mile back, the pain grabbed again. She wished she had listened to her mother who was always warning her of the wrongness of wandering so far away from home.

'What of it that the Hatibari estate is well guarded,' her mother told her. 'Even though there are tall brick walls all round and a stockade in the water, even though the people from the village are forbidden to come inside, yet still there are cobras in the jungly bits. And who knows, when the watchman is sleeping, dacoits might slip in from the river. You are to be married soon and a certain behaviour is expected of you. What a mess you are. It was bad enough when you were a little girl and went round with tattered clothes and untidy hair, but at the age of fifteen one expects something neater and more modest.

You are a woman, Koonty, soon to be married, and it is time you began to behave like one.'

Koonty was betrothed to Pandu, the zamindar's son. Pandu had given her a gold chain with a medal on it for her last birthday. 'Don't tell my father,' he had laughed. 'I should not even be talking to you now that we are betrothed, let alone giving you presents. But look.'

On the golden disc he had had inscribed, 'Koonty Pandava of the Hatibari of Hatipur.' She had giggled and felt thrilled at the words, for this was the first time she had fully taken in the full fact of what it would mean to be the lady of Hatibari.

'To be married to the eldest son of the zamindar of Hatipur village is a tremendous honour and triumph,' her mother would tell her at frequent intervals. 'You must not let any breath of scandal taint your reputation or the Pandava family will call the marriage off.' The zamindar had been very reluctant at first to allow his eldest son to marry the daughter of his estate manager.

The river flowed through land belonging to the zamindar, whose estate covered several miles in all directions and Koonty's father lived in one of the estate houses.

That river. It ruled all their lives and even the zamindar was sometimes conquered by it. Koonty remembered the last monsoon when the golden, killing waters had lapped right up to the steps of her parents' house and had even reached the Hatibari mansion. River had seeped into the beds of canna lilies and gaudy zinnias, softening their grip upon the soil till their roots broke free and floated away to join the garlands of the pauper dead. Koonty's father had had to call the Hatibari servants out at midnight and get them to construct a mini dam of straw and clay to prevent the water entering the house. But in spite of all his precautions the water managed to mount the Hatibari steps and the wife of the zamindar, coming down to view the disaster, had to raise her sari above her ankles.

'How stupid of the grandfather to have built this grand house so near the river,' she told Koonty's father, as he summoned yet more servants with mops and pails.

After the flood receded, the Hatibari garden was covered with river mementos; lotus leaves, boat bits, stranded fish, while the river bobbed with the memory of its recent association with land – parts of houses, drowned goats, ripped-out bits of trees. The liquid god left brown stains upon the purity of the Hatibari marble that took the servants, under Koonty's father's supervision, weeks of scouring, rubbing ferociously with twists of coconut rope and handfuls of sand, to eradicate.

Koonty tried to remember what she had eaten for the midday meal. Perhaps a chingdi maach had fallen into her dhall by mistake. Perhaps the cook had used fish stock when he made the mutton with kumro. It must be the fish allergy, for Durga was a mother goddess and no mother would punish so severely for the small offence of carrying away a single arm.

'Oh, Ma, Oh, Ma,' Koonty wailed. But the house was too far away. Her mother could not hear her though her cries were so loud that buffaloes lounging lazily, up to their shoulders in water across the river, stirred and opened their eyes and some of the mynahs, tick-picking on the buffalo backs, winged off.

She was only fifteen, she was engaged to be married and she was going to die at any moment.

Round the bend of the river and out of sight, she could hear village boys playing. From the sudden splash and laughing shriek she thought they must be hanging from the branch of an overhanging tree and dropping feet first, head first, bottom first, into the water as she and Pandu had done as recently as two years ago. The water buffaloes did not mind the boys' shouts. They only flinched from Koonty's screams.

Squatting low in the water, because this position seemed the least agonising, she gripped her arms around her knees and braced her body. Tilting her head back she could just see through the mango orchards and beyond the lake the great house that would have been hers if she had lived to be married. The Hatibari. Fifty windows reflecting the river. Stone lions larger than life-size on each corner of the roof. Her father was inside at this moment, preparing lists of wedding guests with the zamindar. He would never hear Koonty. The boys round the corner heard her. Laughed and shouted back. They thought she was laughing too, joining with them in their fun.

Ever since she was little she had kept coming here, though since she was soon to marry him and become a respectable wife, she no longer played on the water with Pandu. Koonty had been sitting here earlier in the year when she had first seen Suriya, the Sun God.

'Keep away from the waterside,' her mother kept warning. 'That is the place from which trouble can come.' For who can control water, who can put an impenetrable fence through a sacred river? The rest of the property was almost unassailable. The river was its only weakness in spite of the watchman who patrolled its banks. In the old days they had put up a brick wall seven feet high all along the bank but the first monsoon had washed it away so that not a brick was left standing and the bamboo water fence had to be replaced several times a year.

Koonty always sent the watchman away when she wanted to sit here. 'If I see someone coming I will shout for you.' She was going to be the new young mistress of the Hatibari. He did as she told him. But when she had seen a man come swimming into the Hatibari water she had not shouted for the watchman. She had kept perfectly silent the evening the Sun God came.

Koonty had first heard he was visiting their village from Boodi Ayah. Boodi had returned with the day's food shopping, gasping and babbling with the excitement.

'Dilip Baswani has come to the village.'

When the family looked blank she said, 'The actor who plays the part of the Sun God in the film of the Mahabharata.'

Koonty had stared at the young woman in disbelief. 'Dilip the glorious? There in our village? I must go and see him.' With her parents she had seen the film five times in Calcutta.

'He is making speeches in the tea shop. He is standing for the election,' said Boodi Ayah. 'I saw him with my own eyes.'

★   ★   ★

Dilip Baswani, dressed entirely in gold, had ridden into the village on a golden motorbike. His goggles were golden, he shone with gold leather and wore a plastic golden helmet.

'He is even more beautiful than in the film, Koonty Missie. His skin looks soft as silk and his eyes are the colour of honey.' The ayah's excitement became so great that a cone of fresh ladies' fingers fell from her arms and she nearly dropped the eggs.

'Take that stuff on to the big house where they are waiting for it and stop filling my daughter's mind with ideas,' said Koonty's mother sternly.

'When can I go to hear him?' cried Koonty. 'I think we should go this very minute in case it is too late and he is gone.'

Koonty's mother became stern. 'You are only fifteen years old and about to become the wife of the young zamindar. How can you be seen among the ordinary people? A girl in your situation must stay modestly at home.'

'What harm can it do for me only to go there and listen?' Koonty had begged. 'Boodi Ayah could come with me.'

'That silly woman will be useless in such a mob,' snapped the mother. 'It is all her fault, with her foolish chatter, that you are so eager to see this man who is nothing but a C-grade film actor. Also a thousand people from fifty villages will be there to hear him. What will your husband-to-be's family think if they hear you have been mingling amongst all kinds of untouchable people and gawping at a trashy film star?'

So Koonty had sat by the river instead, felt sad, cross, wished she was there among the village crowd which she could hear faintly from down the water. She imagined how impressed the girls at school would have been if she had told them she had actually seen Dilip Baswani with her own eyes like Boodi Ayah. His voice, drifting over the water, did not even sound the same as it did at the cinema.

All the girls at her school were deeply in love with one Mahabharata character or another. Koonty's passion was Arjuna and she had a lurid poster of the actor in her bedroom.

'Is this all you modern girls have to talk about? Cheap films and their cheaper stars. If you want to know these stories you should read the original texts,' Koonty's mother would reprimand.

'Oh, Ma, what an old fuddy-duddy you are.'

In the evening she had gone back to the river just in case the Sun God started talking to the villagers again. As she sat there she had heard a commotion on the water, excited shouts, cries of awe, as though a thousand people were gathered there watching something wonderful.

'Come and look, brother,' she could hear one person cry to another. 'It is the Sun God himself, here in our river.'

She heard later how the shout had spread over the countryside. People had leapt from bullock carts and run to see. Buses stopped and disgorged their passengers. The village streets emptied, shopkeepers hastily boarded up and ran to the waterside, labourers dropped their spades and rushed. Children flooded out of the school and raced their excited teacher to the river.

As the Sun God swam, he became surrounded by a hundred boys, dog-paddling alongside, and the crowds that gathered on the banks became ten deep. Trees on the waterside began cracking under the weight of people who had climbed them to catch a sight of the swimming film star and every house and hut that overlooked the water had people scrambling to the rooftops, trying to see him. Only the people of the Hatibari had remained inside, though from its upper windows could be seen the faces of the zamindar's servants craning there, trying to get a peep but not wanting to risk the wrath of their employers by gawping openly.

Dilip Baswani swam as fast as he could, trying, hopelessly, to shake off the mob of village boys, till ahead of him he saw the bamboo barricade cutting into the water like a fence, beyond which were trees and a domed roof. This must be the border of the Hatibari estate, he thought, the great house the villagers had told him about. Private property onto which they would not dare follow him, but onto which he, the zamindar's future MLA, would surely be welcome. He entered the stockade and felt gratified to see the mob of boys fall back. Inside he found himself gratefully alone.

He turned a bend and looked with pleasure onto groomed grassy banks planted with flowering shrubs and free of crowds. Then he saw one lone figure sitting, feet in the water, watching him, a young girl with untidy hair and a muddy sari.

She stared with sparkling eyes, her mouth rounded in an O of amazement.

'Hello,' he said, but the girl just stared at him in silence.

A servant girl from the Hatibari, but pretty enough, he thought. And the age he liked.

'What's your name, dear?' he asked as he scrambled out of the water. But Koonty's lips seemed to have got stuck in their gasp of surprise.

'I need a little rest,' he said. 'There are such crowds everywhere else. I don't expect the zamindar will mind if I get my breath back here.' He stood looking down at her, smiling. Charming, he thought.

He was not wearing a golden helmet, a gold leather jacket, gleaming goggles. He wore nothing but golden swimming shorts slung just below his small corpulence. But all the same Koonty knew exactly who he was for she had seen his face at the cinema five times.

'I always like to take a swim in the evening,' he said, as he sat down at Koonty's side. 'It is good for my digestion.'

Koonty tried to say something, opened her mouth, moved her lips, but only a sort of croaking squeak came out.

River water dripped from the Sun God's arms and ran down his chest in rivulets.

'Well, my dear, haven't you got a tongue?' He touched her arm. Gently. A shiver ran through her as though a stream of gold swished down her veins.

* * *

The crowds that were packed so thickly round the bend peered and craned, but the film star had become lost to sight. They waited for a long long time, but he did not come back. After an hour and a half they began to move away.

Now the pains were following each other so fast Koonty scarcely had time to breathe between them. She squatted lower into the water, braced herself tighter as a great racking spasm seized her. A sudden warmth gushed out of her and the water round her ankles turned red. A second spasm, huger than the first, overtook her and she could feel something heavy thrusting between her thighs as though she was being torn apart. Spreading her knees she saw, emerging into the water, something round and hazed with dark wet fur. Then another surge and the rest was there. Arms, legs, a stomach to which was attached a long twisted cord.

It lay under the water for a moment then floated up, eyes closed, lips moving.

Koonty let out a little scream of shock and darkness came over her eyes as though she was about to faint. Through the daze she reached out a hand and touched the little creature that lay half submerged in water. Its limbs began to move, tiny desperate thrashings. Its mouth began twisting, pouting. Koonty ran her hand over the child's face and felt the movement of its lips against her fingers. As she passed her hand along its arm, a minute and wrinkled finger clutched around hers.

She was not having some terrible dream. This was true. She had had a baby. She had given birth to the Sun God's child. She was finished now. Truly finished.

She had been worried at first. The things he asked her to do, the things he was doing to her did not seem modest. But he had reassured her.

'You trust me, don't you, my dear? You need not be afraid of me.'
He had spoken in his deep and husky voice and it had not come into
her mind for a single moment not to trust him, any more than she
would have mistrusted her father.

'Lie like that, there, let me pull up your sari. Now open your legs
a little. Good, good, that's right.' The doctor had talked to her like
that when she had jumped out of the banyan tree, missed the river
and sprained her ankle.

'Are you sure?' she had whispered and felt dazed with the deli-
ciousness of his nearness, the feel of his skin, the smell of his foreign
toilet water.

'Yes, yes, my sweet. Quite sure. Now close your eyes.' He had
told her, 'You needn't worry about anything I do, for after all I am
a god, aren't I?' Then he had laughed as though he had made a joke.
His voice had been very rich and loving.

That evening she had taken down the poster of Arjuna and put up
one of the Sun God instead.

He had told her not to worry, to trust him, but all the same she
had given birth to his baby and now the young zamindar would not
marry her. No one would. She would live lonely and ashamed for
the rest of her life. Her parents would feel such shame that they
would forbid her to go on living with them. She would not be
able to live in the village either, for everyone would know. Koonty
had earlier feared that she was dying. Now she was even more afraid
of living.

As the water surged round her clothes and legs, carrying the blood
away, she crouched numbly, gazed at the baby and felt chills of terror
running through her. Her mother might have heard her earlier cries
and at any moment come here to find her. She listened, her heart
cracking against her ribs, for the sound of Boodi Ayah's bare feet,
Boodi sent to look for her.

'The queen so pleased a rishi that he gave her a mantra which
would evoke any god she wanted who would then, by his grace,

produce in her a child.' Koonty remembered that verse from the Mahabharata. She understood. She had pleased some rishi and her life was now destroyed because of it.

The baby began to let out little mewing cries and she hastily picked it up, the umbilical cord trailing, and tried to silence it. Its skin felt soft as silk. Softer than the Sun God's skin. She pressed her knuckle against its mouth and at once, like the grip of a leech, its lips began sucking.

But after a moment it let go of the knuckle and began mewling again. She held it closer to her body and the baby started writhing. Her breasts had become tight and were spilling milk. She could feel it running warm down her ribs, over the place where her heart kept so loudly pounding.

To silence the baby, to stop the sound that would at any moment betray her, she pulled back her choli and held the child close. In a moment the baby had clamped upon the nipple and the only sound was a high-pitched grunt at every suck.

'Hello, Baby God,' she whispered, then pressing her face against the top of the head felt the soft fluff of newborn hair against her lips.

After a while the baby fell asleep. Koonty could not move. Her body was raw. Her legs felt weak. She sat there, the baby in her arms, and did not know what to do next, while the rose-ringed parakeets swooped among the trees, screaming. One extra loud bird cry startled the baby. It opened its eyes and Koonty saw that they were the colour of honey.

After that, sometimes the baby slept and sometimes fed but Koonty did not know what to do.

Night fell suddenly, the sun extinguished in a few fiery minutes. The bats came out. Fireflies began to dance among the silhouettes of trees. Behind her the lights came on in the Hatibari. She began to hear people calling her from the house. Never before had she stayed here after dark. Footsteps running over the paths. People calling, calling.

She held the baby tightly to her body, kept quite still and waited. She did not know what to do.

Her mother and Boodi Ayah were coming closer, shouting, 'Koonty, Koonty, Koonty.' Her mother was saying, 'Sometimes she goes down there by the river, but she surely wouldn't be there now, in the dark, when you have no idea who might be on the water.'

The household had been so absorbed in the news they had heard on the radio that they had not realised that Koonty was still outside. There was a fear of all-out war with Pakistan who had, that day, made an illegal military attempt to grab the Indian state of Kashmir. But now the worry about Koonty had made them forget about war and rush panicking around the estate, searching for the missing daughter.

Their voices came closer and Koonty gripped the child and felt dazed with fear. Then they began to move off again, their voices growing distant. 'Perhaps she's in the rose garden. Go and look there, Boodi.'

A little later, hurricane lamps and men's voices. Her mother talking too loudly because she was afraid. 'The only place left is the river. I am terrified that she has fallen in. Even though she can swim, this river is deceptive. The current can be very strong even for a healthy girl.'

The voice of the young zamindar. 'Give me the lamp. I will go and look there.' Her husband-to-be coming to where she sat with the Sun God's baby in her lap. She could see, reflected in the river water, the swinging light approaching.

'Koonty, Koonty,' called the young man who was to marry her. He was getting very close. She could tell them that she had found the baby at the river's edge. She could tell them it was a villager's baby and she was only holding it for a moment. He was quite near now. At any moment he would see her sitting here. She could hear his panting breath. She could see his face gleaming in the lamplight. The young zamindar found her there, standing knee-deep in the river.

*   *   *

'Why are you crying, Koonty? What's the matter?' Pandu kept asking her as he helped her back to the house. 'You are shivering all over and wet from head to toe. Whatever have you been doing all this time? We have all been worried sick about you.' He tried to hug her but she shook his arms off. 'Come on, Miss Koonty,' he whispered. 'Tell your Pandu what's the matter.'

After a while, when she only wept and would not speak he became angry. 'You are hiding something. It's those village boys, isn't it? I heard them shouting. Have you been talking to them? I should have listened to your mother. She always said it was not proper for you to be roaming round the estate without a chaperone. She always said you'd turn out like your sister.' All the way back to the Hatibari and even after they got inside, he kept on, sometimes trying to console her incomprehensible grief, sometimes raging against the suspected deception or infidelity. 'You are going to be my wife. You should have some consideration. Don't cry, my sweet. Here, wipe your face on the corner of my shawl.'

Later he told her mother, 'She was trying to rescue a kitten, I think, though I can't get her to talk about it.' He felt he was doing well, impressing the mother with what an understanding husband he was going to be. 'I heard something. A sound of mewing in the water.'

'She was always very kind to animals,' said Koonty's mother and secretly thought that perhaps the zamindar's family would be satisfied with a smaller dowry, now that they had discovered what a compassionate bride they were getting. 'She would sacrifice herself for some small creature.'

Later the young zamindar presented Koonty with a kitten, but at the sight of the furry mewling thing she began to cry and thrust it from her. 'Take it away. I don't even want to look at it.'

2

A LITTLE SUIT OF SHINING ARMOUR

Bowed with drops of toil and languor, low, a chariot driver came,
Loosely held his scanty garment and a staff upheld his frame.
Karna now a crowned monarch to the humble Suta fled,
As a son unto a father reverentially bowed his head.

The Emperor Aurangzeb suffered from a carbuncle until an East India Company official called Job Charnock found a physician who managed to cure it. As a reward, Job was granted a tract of land eighty miles up the Hoogly river by the Nawab of Bengal and there he founded the city of Calcutta.

By the end of the eighteenth century Calcutta was the capital of the East India Company's government, with an opulent and lively social life and opportunities for making a quick fortune for a lucky few. To this day, throughout the town, grand Western-style buildings, now crumbling, point back to its imperial past.

Dolly, her impoverished parents' eleventh child, was born in the house where once William Hickey had dined with his face covered with blood, because he had become 'sadly intoxicated' at a previous get-together and had fallen while dismounting from his phaeton.

At the time of Dolly's birth, more than a hundred families were living in considerable squalor and poverty in Hickey's one-time grand residence. But because the new baby was born in the year of India's independence her parents said, 'Perhaps the goddess is going to bless us at last even though this is only a female child.' For this reason, when she was old enough, they sent Dolly to the local school although their other daughters had never been give such an opportunity.

Each evening Dolly would come home and as she helped her mother pick through the rice for stones or roll the chupatties she would chatter joyfully about the things she had learnt that day. 'We did fractions,' she would announce, as she crushed the spices on the great thick slab of stone. Splashing water from the brass jar onto the seeds and pods and barks, she would heave the heavy stone roller over the top. Rolling, splashing, crushing she would tell her mother, 'Did you know that the Moguls ruled India before the British and that this is the first time for ages that we Indians have been free?' Or, as she stirred the great pan of simmering milk, keeping the iron spoon going to stop the milk boiling over or burning at the bottom, she would tell her mother about trade winds, or magnetism.

Sometimes the father would say worriedly, 'Do you think all this education is spoiling her? Perhaps she is getting too much of it and won't be able to find a husband.'

'She is not neglecting her domestic duties,' said the mother.

Later, after her parents and her ten siblings slept, Dolly sat by the light of a kerosene lamp and did her homework. She was determined to do well. She planned one day to live in a proper house, not a room in the bustee. If she passed her exams and got a good job, when she was grown up her children would have a bed each and they would eat mutton curry every day. Sometimes one of the babies would wake and cry, disturbing her. Then she would take it on her knee and joggle it on one arm while going on with her writing.

'My teacher says I will certainly get into university. He is sure I will get a scholarship,' she told her parents.

Her father's face was stern, her mother's anxious. 'What? What?' cried Dolly, suddenly afraid.

'All this education is not needed for a woman,' said her father.

'There are better things for a woman to do with her life than to study,' said her mother.

They had found Dolly a husband.

'But I don't want a husband,' wailed the girl. 'I am only thirteen. I'm too young to get married.'

'I was married at ten,' said her mother.

Dolly pinched lips and refrained from saying, 'I don't want my life to be like yours.' Instead she said, 'Baba, Ma, please. I am doing so well at school and if I get into university I will get a good job. I will become a teacher, maybe.'

'How long will this take?' asked her father.

'Four years. Five years.' Dolly was shivering.

'We cannot go on feeding so many,' said Dolly's father. 'We cannot spend all this on one when there are so many others who have a need. Anyway you are only a girl and the money must be spent on the boys.'

'I could earn some money from teaching now, maybe,' pleaded Dolly.

'Teach who? In this village?' Her father was scornful. 'Who can afford to pay a young ignorant girl to teach them? Anyway there is a school that costs nothing already. And after you have finished university you will be too old for marriage.'

'You can go on studying after you are married. There will be nothing to stop you then. You will be living in a company compound with all kinds of facilities. There will be many opportunities open to you there,' her mother consoled her. 'As it is we have to make a great sacrifice for your marriage. There is the big expense of the wedding feast and also the dowry. A large amount of our savings will have to be spent.'

Cheered by the thought of going on with her schooling after marriage, and eventually going to university after all, Dolly agreed.

The young bridegroom, Adhiratha, was twenty-seven years old and a company car driver. 'He even has a pension,' her father told Dolly. 'You are very lucky for you will be provided for all your life. Even after he retires. You will not be poor when you are old like your mother and me.'

'In fact we need a daughter with such a husband or how will we survive in our old age?' said Dolly's mother.

Dolly laughed at the thought of caring for her parents, not being able to imagine such a role reversal.

'He is everything nice,' said Dolly's mother, showing her daughter a photo of Adhiratha. She was happy to see the girl smiling again.

The picture showed a pleasant-looking young man with a thin face, a large moustache and glasses.

'He looks clever,' said Dolly. She was quite excited now, longing to meet the man, with whom she thought she had fallen in love already. As a Hindu wife-to-be, and therefore required to respect the husband, as was the tradition she did not use his name even in her mind.

'He has a sensitive face,' she thought and the 'He' to which she referred was now the central person of her life. All other 'he's' she thought, must go by some other name from this day on.

Adhiratha looked like the kind of person who would appreciate education and Dolly visualised the two of them discussing books together, or even both attending night school. After all he would not be wearing glasses if he was not an intellectual.

If Dolly had known then the real reason for the glasses, would her parents have continued to insist on the marriage? Would Dolly have felt afraid?

Dolly fell wildly in love with Adhiratha the moment she set eyes on him.

'How glad I am,' she thought after their wedding, as they sat together in a proper electric-lit room to eat their meal. The company bungalow was a pukka stone and mortar affair with running water and glass in the windows.

They could not stop smiling at each other across the table. Sometimes before the meal was eaten, with only a smile for a signal, the two of them would leap up, overturning chairs, spilling misti and rush for their bed with its new sheet and dunlopillo mattress that had been kept wrapped in its cellophane for protection.

In bed they would lie naked, sweating under the slow turning fan, and explore each other's beautiful bodies all over again. Adhiratha would bury his face in Dolly's thick black hair that smelled of the spices she had been cooking. He would kiss the softness of her neck and whisper, 'I love you, Dolly, I love you Dolly, I love you Dolly.'

He went to work each day wearing his smart chauffeur cap and a pristine white uniform with the company logo embroidered on the pocket that had been lovingly starched and pressed by his little new wife.

After he had gone Dolly would sing as she dusted her house, washed up the dishes, and swept her yard. She remembered how she had quarrelled with her parents when they had tried to arrange her marriage but now she was so happy. Her heart sang with joy because she loved Adhiratha so much and because everything she wanted in the world had been given to her. A hundred times a day, as she swept and polished their bungalow and made special delicious things for her husband's evening meal, Dolly would say to herself, 'How lucky my parents insisted I got married to Adhiratha.' They even had a little garden and Dolly would pick hibiscus, zinnias and canna lilies and arrange them in a jug, then blush with delight when Adhiratha came home and praised her artistry.

Dolly was invited to continue her education at the company school and when term began, each day she would walk across the compound to her class, crossing shady yards, under trees planted by the company, past beds of flowers. There she revelled in the company of girls of her own age and she and her friends would sometimes get a chance to go to the bioscope, then later imitate the accents and behaviour of Ashok Kumar, or swank around pretending to be Meena Kumari.

But no matter how much studying she did, nor how much fun she had with her friends in the day, when Adhiratha got home in the evening she was always there, ready with his evening meal. Her mother had taught her to cook. Her chupatties puffed out like footballs, her parathas were as thin and fine as silk, her kheers and paish the best on the company compound. When Adhiratha invited fellow workers to a meal they would marvel that so young a wife should turn out to be such a marvellous cook. Pulling her sari over her head in deference, she would serve out the food for them, while the young men teased her until she blushed. 'Hey, Dolly, those chupatties will float up like balloons if you make them any lighter.' 'Hey, Dolly. I think I will throw away my own wife and take you home with me instead so that I can eat sag like you make every day.'

'No you won't, you swine,' Adhiratha would josh back. 'She's mine. She's the best thing in my life and I'm not giving her up for anyone.'

'But when are you starting the baby?' Dolly's mother kept asking and patted Dolly's stomach, which sounded hollowly empty.

'We are waiting for a year. Till I take my exams,' Dolly told her parents.

'How modern,' said the father. 'Let us hope that the gods will not take offence.'

'What do you mean?' Dolly was startled.

'They give us children when they decide. It is not up to you to make such decisions.' He spoke fiercely. 'Exams are not an excuse for delaying children.'

'Oh, Baba, you don't know anything,' laughed the modern Dolly, amused by her parents' silly superstitious and old-fashioned attitudes. 'These days women don't just have to fill the house with babies like they did when you and Ma were young.'

'But why take such risks?' said the mother, trying to soothe the situation. 'What difference will it make? Have the baby and when it comes, God will look after you. And look after the baby.'

'I plan to look after my baby, myself,' said the blasphemous, proud Dolly.

Soon after their marriage it was the time of the Durga Puja.

Goddess Durga is the giver of rice. She is the mother. But she is also yellow and terrible. She is Devi, one of the female aspects of the Absolute, that infinite, inert and creative Silence. Her serene and aloof expression does not change as she slays the demon who is trying to destroy the world. She shows no trace of rage or emotion because, for her, the deed, the Cosmos and her self are only illusions, only parts of the Cosmic dream. She rides a lion, holds weapons in her many arms, is cool as a dream and calm as an untroubled river. She is the inaccessible, the inevitable, for she knows that all this is an illusion. All this is Maya. And Durga is responsible for the illusion, she is the illusion and she is only playing at creation. Creation is the play of the gods, nothing to be really taken seriously. That is what her calm face says.

Each year great images are made of her all over Bengal. Wood armatures fifteen feet high are wrapped with straw, then covered with clay, which is modelled into the smallest detail. Lips rich with scarlet gloss, eyelids dark with lamp khol, fingernails manicured with crimson lacquer, her tiny waist belted in gold, her human hair glossed with resin. Her tinsel-trimmed sari glitters and her cut-glass jewels sparkle.

The puja lasts for four days, during which the images, which have taken so many months to sculpt, are worshipped by the rich and the poor, the educated and the illiterate, who present the goddesses with flowers, fruit, garlands and sweets. For Durga is very powerful and has it in her power to grant life to the dying, health to the sick, children to the infertile and husbands to the hideous. There is no one so rich and privileged that they never need her help.

There was much competition, at Durga Puja, among neighbour-hoods and companies, but year after year Adhiratha's employers always came out with the most beautiful image of the goddess and the most impressive shrine. The company shrine was an exact replica of a Hindu temple and as large. It was made of cotton material stretched over a bamboo frame which in the dark glowed with the light of a thousand multi-coloured electric bulbs. It was painted so realistically that people who saw it from a distance thought a new temple of brick and stone had sprung up overnight.

On the first Durga Puja after her marriage, Dolly made a dish of the milky sweets called shandesh. They were the shape of little fishes and she decorated them with foil of purest gold. When they were ready she put on her best sari and decorated her forehead with scarlet kumkum, then she walked across the compound to the shrine. There, many other people were making offerings to Durga. Some were prostrate on the ground before the goddess. Even the directors of this company had come with gifts for their goddess, for the company was thriving.

Dolly put the plate at the feet of the austere towering image, then, placing her palms together, knelt and bowed till her head touched the ground and said, 'Thank you, thank you, thank you.'

After the period of worship was over, Adhiratha was one of those given the honour of carrying the goddess to the holy river, where she would be ritually immersed. People cried out Durga's praises as the gigantic figure, with her calm face and ornate attire, was jogged along the roads. Some people ran ahead of the procession and threw themselves in the goddess's path as though she was the Juggernaut and they wished to be crushed to death by her.

At the river other Durgas were arriving, though none as large and lovely as that which Dolly's new young husband and the other men were carrying.

The company had two long boats waiting, boards lashed between them to form a platform for the statue. It was hauled onto this, then held in place and steadied with poles and ropes.

Dolly and Adhiratha stood on the bank watching while the boat was punted to the centre of the river which was already bobbing with a hundred little boats and rafts carrying Durgas of every size.

There, with the lookers-on ululating and shouting holy praises, the goddess was tipped into the river. As she sank, people scooped up handfuls of water, that had become further blessed by contact with the deity, and threw it over their heads. And as the goddess disappeared from sight, men filled their mouths with petrol and, setting fire to it with cigarette lighters, blew great arcs of flame over the water.

Firecrackers were hurled from the banks and bridges. Little clay lamps burning oil were set bobbing away on the water like luminous ducklings. For a while the whole bubbling river was spattered with bursts and crackles of fire and the wild cries of the people calling out to the vanishing goddess.

Dolly took her exams and did well. She had been married for a year. In the evening when Adhiratha got home he told her, 'They have promoted me. I am to become head driver and will get a raise of a hundred and fifty rupees a month.'

Dolly put her arms round him and hugged. She felt so happy she could not speak. Then she whispered something.

'What? I couldn't hear.' Adhiratha was teasing her. Although he had not heard, he knew quite well what she had said.

Her eyes down and whispering a little louder, she said, 'We can start our family this year.'

'Did you ask for Durga's blessing?' he asked, laughing, as he hung his chauffeur's hat on the rack. His wife's devotion to Durga always amused him. 'It's only a statue,' he would say. 'I'm the one who does all the hard work, while she just stands there. It's me you should be thanking.'

'Oh, you,' Dolly chided. 'You must not talk like that about the goddess. She might put a curse on us.'

That night Adhiratha made love to her without using a condom and afterwards they laughed and embraced each other, certain that the baby was already made.

After three months when Dolly had still not become pregnant, the first little flicker of worry began to set in. Dolly, only half joking, told Adhiratha, 'I said you should not have spoken disrespectfully about the goddess.'

'Silly girl,' said Adhiratha. 'It is early days. Look how well everything is turning out for us.' His new job had earned them a bigger bungalow and the allowance for a couple of servants. There was only one little trouble to shade their lives – Adhiratha's eyes often ached.

He had always had trouble with his eyes and his glasses were not a sign that he was educated or particularly literate as Dolly had presumed from looking at his photo. He had worn them since childhood.

'Don't keep rubbing them,' Dolly urged and made eye-washes for him out of herbs and spices, remedies that the people in the village used when they could not afford a doctor.

Dolly woke in the night sometimes, to hear him moaning softly. She would gently massage his forehead with her thumbs till the pain ebbed away.

'You have to see the doctor,' she demanded and went on insisting in spite of his protests.

'I am a driver. If this company finds out that I have problems with my sight they may sack me.' He tried to soothe her, 'My eyes have given trouble all my life. I know how to cope with it,' but she would not be calmed. She felt sure his eyes were getting worse.

In the end, at her insistence, and with many misgivings, he agreed.

The company doctor gave Adhiratha painkillers and made an appointment for him to see a specialist.

Dolly had still not conceived a child by the third Durga Puja after their marriage. She was getting worried, no longer soothed by Adhiratha's assurance that 'it's early days'. Her mother had been pregnant with her third child at this stage. Dolly felt ashamed to go and visit her parents these days.

'What is the matter with you? Are you infertile or something?' Dolly's usually gentle mother became quite angry at the idea. And worried. Would Adhiratha's family take revenge on her daughter, if they began to think she was infertile? There were stories of such failed brides having kerosene thrown over them then being set alight by the parents-in-law.

At this year's Durga Puja, Dolly prostrated herself before the haughty goddess and instead of saying, 'thank you' said, 'please, please, please'. She rose at last, speckled with grit from the ground, having only implored, 'Make me a baby, make my husband's eyes better.'

The specialist diagnosed Adhiratha's problem as glaucoma, a build-up of fluid within the eyeball. He gave the young chauffeur drops to put in his eyes that might, over time, reduce the pressure.

'How much time?' asked Adhiratha.

'One or two years. This medicine retracts the pupils, affecting your sight, so you must not drive a car for a couple of hours after application.' Adhiratha had to get up two hours earlier each morning to get rid of the effects of the medicine in time for his day's work and he lived in a constant state of anxiety in case he was called upon for emergency jobs, when his vision was still blurred.

'It is preying on your mind, my husband,' Dolly said. 'Isn't there another job the company can give you that does not need good sight?' Secretly she began to think that part of the reason for her failing to conceive was because her husband was so worried and tired.

Six months later Adhiratha crashed a company car.

'We are sorry to see you go,' said the manager. 'You have been an excellent driver.'

'Is there no other job you can give me?' pleaded Adhiratha.

The man bowed his head and looked sad. 'If this had happened a year ago, yes, we might have found some place for you in the packing department. But last year we made a loss. We are getting rid of staff. I am so sorry, Adhiratha, but there is nothing I can offer you.'

Adhiratha was given a farewell party and a lump sum.

Dolly cried the day she and Adhiratha had to leave their bungalow in the company compound. She moved in with her parents while Adhiratha dossed down with friends and hunted for a place to live that they could afford. Because he had only been working for the company for five years, although they had been as generous as they could, the severance payment was not enough for him to rent anything better than a short-term lease of a room in the bustee.

'It's home, though,' he told Dolly when she arrived to join him. 'And knowing you, you'll make it nice.'

Dolly cried again when she saw the sordid room.

'I'll get a job, don't worry, don't be afraid,' Adhiratha tried to reassure her, but she could hear the fear in his voice too.

Adhiratha had no skills apart from driving and for a while worked as a taxi driver. But a smashed taxi put a stop to that.

'Don't worry, my darling,' soothed Dolly. 'We still have a little money left, and something is sure to turn up.' By now he had to accept that his driving days were over. No longer treated by the free medical service of the company and without enough money to pay for the expensive drugs, his eyes rapidly deteriorated. He could hardly see six feet ahead of him. And what work can an almost blind man find in a city with so much unemployment?

'Don't be sad, darling husband,' sobbed Dolly. 'I have got my school cert so I should be able to get a job while you are looking for something. I might become a hotel receptionist.' She felt quite excited at the idea and visualised herself seated behind a smart desk, wearing a uniform, and meeting all kinds of interesting people.

But when she went out in response to adverts in the *Statesman* she found that she was competing for humble jobs with people much more qualified than she was. Men and women who had left university with first-class degrees were clamouring to become shop assistants, bus conductors, railway clerks and company secretaries. Dolly didn't stand a chance.

After six months the severance payment was nearly finished. Soon, not only would they have nowhere to live, they would have nothing to eat either.

'We will have to go to the village and live with your parents,' wept Dolly.

Adhiratha shivered at the idea. 'They have ten other children and are trying so desperately to raise enough money for the dowries so that my two sisters can marry. If there is no work in the city there is certainly none in the village. How can we possibly inflict ourselves upon them?' He felt sick with shame.

Next day Dolly went back to the company where she and Adhiratha had once been so happy. She went from bungalow to bungalow offering to do the washing for the families there. At the end of the day she had the promise of five households of washing.

She came home and told him, saying, 'We will have to buy a charcoal steam iron.'

Adhiratha was aghast.

'Suggest something else then,' said Dolly. 'At least I will be able to make just enough so that we have shelter and do not starve.' She added with deepening bitterness, 'Now I understand why Ma Durga never gave us a child. Because she knew we would not be able to afford to give it a decent life.'

Adhiratha held her tight against him, hugged and hugged her till her miserable shivering stopped.

Later he said, 'We haven't even got running water. How are you going to wash all these clothes?'

'In the river. Like the other dhobis,' said Dolly firmly.

'Oh God.' Adhiratha groaned and put his hands over his eyes. 'But you don't know anything about being a dhobi.'

'Don't know anything?' she mocked. 'Darling husband, who has been washing your clothes these last three years, since your mother stopped doing them? Have you ever complained? Weren't your collars and cuffs always crisp with starch? Didn't I always get the last grimy traces off them? Didn't I starch your uniforms and dhotis with boiled rice water till they were so stiff they could have stood up on their own? How can you say I don't know how to be a dhobi?'

'But that was different,' said Adhiratha. 'In the bungalow we had hot running water from the tap. A clothesline in the garden. Electricity for the iron. Here you have none of those things.' In the bustee room the only light was from oil lamps and lanterns. Water came from a ruptured pipe along the road.

But Dolly was undaunted. 'There is no other way. I will manage.'

She washed endless piles of clothes, all day long, standing ankle-deep in the shallow part of the river, among a line of other dhobis. Daily at dawn she would be at the riverside wetting the garments, rubbing them with strong yellow soap, then beating them against a stone already rubbed smooth and shiny by hundreds, perhaps thousands of years of dhobi wear. From the time the sun rose until it sunk again Dolly beat the washing then laid it to dry on the riverbank. At night, carrying the vast heap of dry, clean washing on her head, she would return home. There she would prepare the evening meal for her husband and herself on a chula, a stove made in a pierced bucket that had been lined with mud and which burned the cow-dung fuel that Adhiratha collected and dried each day. Their morning meal was only rice water from the previous night's cooking.

During the weeks that followed Adhiratha tried to help Dolly in every way he could. He struggled behind her carrying the heaps of dirty clothes. Went round the bungalows collecting the washing in a basket. Even tried to assist his wife in beating the clothes against the stones. In the end she told him, 'It is not your dharma to be a dhobi. Try to find some work that is more suited to you.'

'I am no good at it, you mean,' he said humbly.

'That is what I mean,' she laughed.

Adhiratha found a job at last. Pulling a rickshaw.

It was Dolly's turn to be aghast. 'You are to become a rickshaw wallah? I am to be the wife of a rickshaw wallah?'

'Well, I am the husband of a dhobi woman,' he laughed. 'We are coming down in the world. That is all.' Then he gave her a hug and said, 'We have still got each other. We are still young. Who knows what will turn up.' He picked up her hand, and caressed it. It was wrinkled like the hand of a dead person from so much immersion in water.

'We would be better off if we had never had the good period in the company compound,' she thought. Their present situation, a home surrounded by stinking drains and a single daily meal of rice and dhall, would have been easier to bear, she thought, if she had not experienced those happy days in the leafy compound, where they ate chingri and hilsa and bathed their rice in ghee.

That year, on the first day of the Durga Puja, as Dolly passed the company shrine on her way to collect the dirty washing, she turned her head the other way. And hoped the goddess noticed and felt ashamed, for by this time Dolly and Adhiratha had been married for five years and, in spite of all her prayers, there was still no child. In fact Adhiratha had begun to say that it would be a disaster if Dolly became pregnant now.

Dolly was tempted not to offer homage to the goddess that year. She wanted to punish Durga who had given her a happy life for a very short time, so as to be able to take it away and let Dolly see what she was missing.

But all the same, after she had gone round all the houses, and her basket was full, she made her way back to the shrine.

She had gone without her meal the previous evening and bought a small milk sweet with the money she had saved. As she unwrapped this, her stomach let out a rumble of hunger. She became seized with a strong temptation to eat the sweet instead of giving it to a goddess who was never going to listen to her prayer. All the same she put the sweet down on its peepul leaf and prostrating herself, begged aloud, 'Oh Mother Durga hear my prayer and make me a mother too.' She did not mention Adhiratha's eyes. Perhaps she had been presumptuous, the last four years, in asking the goddess for two favours at once.

She reached the river late because of her visit to the goddess. The other dhobis were already laying their clothes out on the rocks to dry.

Dolly waded out into the water and, wetting the first of her sheets, rubbed the harsh yellow soap over it. All afternoon, up to her thighs in water, she beat the cloth against the smooth rocks.

'You had better hurry,' said the other dhobis in the evening, as they folded their already dried clothes and stacked them in the baskets. 'They will be bringing the Durga down here for immersion soon and you mustn't still be in the water.' Dolly had to bite back tears remembering the previous years when she had been celebrating the company puja with her husband. Now she was not even allowed to stand in the water when the goddess came.

Frantically Dolly worked but the pile was huge and the clothes

33

filthy. By the time the sun began to set the other dhobis were leaving and she had still not finished.

She would have to take the wet washing home, ten times as heavy, to dry in the tiny apartment.

She heard the shouts. People were yelling, 'Oi, Ma, get out of the water. The goddess is coming.'

She looked up and saw the procession approaching. Men in fresh white carrying the gigantic figure of Durga on a palanquin on their shoulders. Not Adhiratha this year. Rickshaw wallahs don't carry the goddess.

They were coming to this part of the river to immerse the Durga.

'Out of the water, out, out,' they cried as they approached. To immerse the goddess in water polluted by an untouchable dhobi woman would be a terrible sacrilege.

Desperately Dolly began to gather up her pile of washing, pulling still wet sheets and saris, shirts and pajamas out of the water, hurrying because the Devi was very close.

Something bumped her knee as she scrabbled up her wet washing.

It was a hand of last year's Durga, huge, the arms of clay long since melted away. It lay palm up, its beautiful fingers curled round something sharply gleaming. Dolly bent to take a closer look and felt amazed that the nail polish should still be intact after so long in the water, thrilled because the knuckles and finger rings were almost unblemished. She was thinking to herself, this must be a miracle, when the shining thing lying on the palm began to move as though it was alive. For a moment the light reflected off the holy hand became so bright that Dolly had to look away, dazzled.

When she could open her eyes, she bent to take a closer look and saw, cuddled among the goddess' fingers, some creature with tinsel twisted round it. A puppy perhaps, that had got tangled in the remains of Durga's marigold garlands.

The shouts of the approaching Durga worshippers were growing ever nearer and more furious.

Dolly was the only one still in the water but instead of hurrying, she bent, staring fascinated at what lay in the palm of last year's goddess. The glittering thing let out a sound like the mewing cry of a cat. The hand began to twirl as the current caught it again.

Dolly's arms were full of washing. It was only a half-dead kitten, then. Round the weighty bundle she did a namaskar of respect to the hand of Durga then turned away as the current caught the hand with its living glittering burden and started to twirl it off.

Then Dolly realised what the sparkling mewling thing was, dropped her armful of clean washing into the water and grabbed. Snatched the shining thing from out of the middle of the hand just a moment before it was carried out of reach.

She held a newborn child, still attached to its placenta and tangled up in sparkling tinsel. The hand that had prevented the baby from sinking went speeding off along the river.

Dolly stood thigh-deep in water, dazed with joy, because the goddess Durga had, after all these years, answered her prayer. Everybody knew that goddesses do not do things like ordinary people. This child had been sent to her in an unusual way, but all the same it was what she had asked for and what the goddess had given.

Grabbing up the once again filthy and now dripping washing and thrusting it into her basket, pressing the holy child against her breast and ignoring the furious outcry from the Durga worshippers, she waded out of the river and began to stagger home.

She arrived ages late. Adhiratha was home already and shocked at the sight of Dolly's catch.

'How are we going to feed this child?' he demanded as Dolly began unravelling the baby from the twists of tinsel. 'Put it back where it came from. We have hardly enough for ourselves. Wait till we get a child of our own then it will be able to drink milk from your breast and will cost us nothing.'

Dolly was furious. 'How dare you speak in such a way of the gift of the goddess?'

'Well, she should have provided some food for the child. How can she expect us to feed it?' All the same he could not help creeping over and peeping curiously into the face of the little newborn baby.

'Getting things from the gods is not like going shopping,' Dolly ranted on. 'You don't just go and say "I would like two kilos of baby" as though you were buying onions. You don't say "I want a couple of breastfuls of milk as well as a baby". You just take what you get.' The last of the tinsel was unravelled and then Dolly let out a scream of surprise for hanging round the little boy's neck she had found a golden chain from which hung a disc. Taking it to the window she read the words 'Koonty Pandava of the Hatibari of Hatipur'.

She turned to her husband, her eyes filled with amazement, and repeated the words to him. Her surprise now became touched with a tiny chill of fear which Adhiratha echoed by saying, 'That is some other woman's child.'

'It is not. It is mine,' cried Dolly hugging the baby against her body, and wishing the disc had been washed away in the water.

As she carried the new child to the water spurt, she felt terribly tempted to sell the piece of gold and then pretend it had never existed. She felt a scald of conflict. Without the disc the baby would have no identity but the one that she and Adhiratha gave it. Without that disc she and her husband were the baby's parents. But on the other hand this piece of gold and the information it gave were the baby's only possessions. She had no right to take them from him and one day the little child might need to know who he was.

She shook her head and tried to dash away the worrying thoughts that the disc aroused in her as she rubbed the mud from the baby's body. When she got back into the room with the now spotless baby, Adhiratha was rushing round, hunting for something. He looked up, laughing, at the sight of her holding the child against her chest. The baby was making little whimpering sounds and nuzzling its lips into Dolly's choli.

'What have you lost?' asked Dolly. The desperation of the baby was troubling her.

Triumphantly he held out his hands. 'I knew I had some paise hidden in this pocket. I'll go out now and buy some milk for her.'

'For him,' laughed Dolly. Happy tears began to run down her cheeks because she knew everything would be all right from now on. Holding the now howling baby in one arm, she reached up and kissed Adhiratha.

'You don't know how much I love you,' she said. 'You just don't.'

'I won't be long,' he said as he rushed out. 'I expect there will be some left over at the khatal.'

The cattle stall in the centre of their area was owned by the landlord and his tenants bought milk for their households and businesses from there as well as using the dung for fuel.

Dolly stood at the open door looking down into the darkness of the stairway, till she heard at last the sound of his footsteps receding.

The baby went on crying for a little while and then, exhausted, fell asleep.

Dolly waited, thinking, 'He is being a very long time. Perhaps there was no milk left at the khatal. Perhaps he has had to go to the house of the Gwala.'

An hour later she was still waiting. The baby woke up again and once more began crying. Where could Adhiratha be?

After another hour, in which Dolly started to panic and the baby's desperation was unendurable, she decided the only hope was to go from room to room, and hut to hut begging milk from someone.

Adhiratha never came back. He was hit by a lorry and died on the spot. It was two days of numbing dread and misery before Dolly found out.

3

WARLIKE GESTURES

Sankha's voice, Gandhiva's accents, and the chariot's booming sound,
Filled the air like distant thunder, shook the firm and solid ground.
Kuru's soldiers fled in terror or they slumbered with the dead,
And the rescued lowing cattle with their tails uplifted fled.

Shivarani Gupta, Koonty's eldest sister, was so tall by the time she
was thirteen that her father began to worry that she might never find
a husband.

Shivarani laughed, called him an old silly and accused him of
knowing nothing about the modern world in which, she said, tall
women were the fashion.

By the time Shivarani was sixteen she was taller than
ever and her father's anxiety was greatly increased. As was her
mother's.

The Guptas lived on a modern bungalow on the Hatibari estate that
had been built ten years earlier to house the estate manager. Meena
Gupta, Shivarani's mother, went once a week to Calcutta to meet
her friends at the Calcutta Club where they ate miniature samosas,
drank flowery orange pekoe and played mahjong. And there Meena
Gupta poured out her worries.

'Shivarani is growing like this sort of giraffe because of the genes
of my husband's family. My sister-in-law is nearly six feet tall and
if my mother had known about her, she would have forbidden the
marriage for everyone knows what difficulties come to families whose
daughters are too large.'

Mrs Gupta's Calcutta Club friends smiled with sympathy, thinking how dreadful it must be for someone as fair and small as Mrs Gupta to have a dark giantess for a daughter.

The Guptas began to approach suitable families, hoping for a match for their lanky daughter while she still possessed one marriageable asset, the bloom of youth.

Three times Shivarani was paraded, wearing her prettiest sari and Meena Gupta's most costly jewels, before the parents of suitable boys. Three times the Gupta family heard no more of the matter until receiving an invitation to a wedding. The suitable boy was marrying a shorter fairer girl.

'So many boys wanting to marry Shivarani,' lied Mrs Gupta to her Cal Club friends. 'Boy after boy, from good family after good family brought before her for approval and like princess in fairy tale, she rejects them. Eeny meeny miney mo.'

There followed insincere commiseration on the unreasonableness of nubile daughters. 'We all have such a girl at home, don't we know it.' They knew that in reality it was the boy, or his family, who was rejecting Shivarani. But then what good family would marry a girl like that?

Someone said helpfully, 'I have seen a product for lightening the skin being advertised. Perhaps you can purchase it in Sahib Singh's.'

The suggestion made Mrs Gupta unreasonably cross. 'And why should I require such stuff? Are you saying my daughter is black, Leela?'

'Have another little samosa, Meena. Don't pay attention to silly Leela,' the friends tried to soothe.

Meena Gupta, silently blaming her husband for his outsize sister, nibbled her samosa through a veil of tears and vowed, though there was nothing to be done about the height, she would try to lighten Shivarani's complexion the moment she got home.

After the third rejection Shivarani, her face red with her humiliation, her eyes red with tears, said she would not allow herself to be paraded any more. Her parents, frantic with worry, because what sort of life was there for a woman without marriage, begged Shivarani to give the process just one more chance. Reluctantly the girl agreed.

'But on condition, no jewels and no pretty sari. They must see me as I am.' Shivarani's parents shuddered. What hope was there for the girl, unless she was disguised in opulence and glamour? But those were Shivarani's terms and she appeared before the aunts and mother of the prospective bridegroom wearing a plain handloom sari in beige and, 'Oh no, my God,' whimpered Meena, a pair of high-heeled shoes. 'You said they must see you as you are, but you are not as high as that,' mourned Meena Gupta but Shivarani insisted. Either she would appear thus dressed or not at all.

There came a little gasp from the assembled family of the prospective bridegroom that Meena knew was not of admiration. But all the same they continued with their questioning as though, in spite of everything, they were still interested.

A photo of the boy was produced. Meena accepted it with caution and for a moment hardly dared focus her eyes on it. There was sure to be something dreadfully wrong with the fellow or why was his family, even after seeing Shivarani in her khadi sari and high heels, still considering her? When Meena at last dared to look, she thought he was quite handsome.

When Shivarani saw the photo, for the first time in the husband-choosing process, she actually smiled. 'He looks nice,' she said.

At last Meena Gupta felt it was safe to tell her club friends. She was unable to keep the triumph out of her voice as she said, 'He is good-looking, of high intelligence, from excellent family, and what more can any mother want for their daughter?' Meena thought she saw a quick glance flash between two of her friends. 'What?' she asked. 'I there something I don't know?'

'Of course not,' said Leela hastily. 'I have never seen the fellow and I am sure he is a very good match.' She had been on the rough end of Meena's temper once already and did not want to risk it again.

Meena went to have tea with the boy's parents and to meet the boy himself while Shivarani waited anxiously at home. But when Meena, usually the most garrulous of women, returned, she hung her shawl on the hook and removed her outdoor slippers in silence.

Shivarani clenched her hands till her knuckles went white, and waited. After a long silent moment she asked, 'What was he like?'

'Very nice,' said Meena. 'Just as good-looking as in the photo. And he is clever too.'

'Yes, but,' pressed Shivarani.

Meena turned her back to her eldest daughter and looking into the hall mirror, began patting down her hair.

'There is something wrong with him?'

Meena, her gaze on her reflection, shook her head.

'But I know there is something,' Shivarani pursued.

'Well . . .' said Meena.

'What, yes? What?' Shivarani could hardly bear it.

Meena shrugged gently and said, 'He is young. Perhaps he will grow a little more.'

Shivarani, frowning, said, 'Young? How young? I thought you said he was nearly thirty.'

'That is young,' said Meena stiffly.

'What are you telling me?' cried Shivarani. 'That you are hoping a man of nearly thirty will keep on growing?'

'But you never know. That's what I am thinking,' murmured Meena Gupta and winked a tear away.

Shivarani stared at her mother's back and the colour drained from her face. 'He's a midget, you mean?'

'Hush hush,' soothed her mother. 'Size is not all. He comes from a prosperous family. He looks like a very nice person. He has doctorates in three subjects. And most important of all, you are so tall and so if you have a short husband your children will come out the right size.'

Shivarani burst out in fury. 'You want me to marry a dwarf so that your grandchildren come out the right size? That's really amazing,' she roared. 'That is the end,' she said. 'No more bridegrooms. I will make my own way in the world.'

Meena Gupta knew then that the battle was lost and that Shivarani might never marry.

Her consolation became her youngest child, Koonty. Meena drew a pencil line on the frame of the door, measured the child weekly and each time felt reassured that Koonty was growing at a normal speed. Meena was not sure what she would do if her youngest child started sprouting too. Perhaps there were things she could do if the fault was discovered early enough. Maybe Sahib Singh's, the Park Street chemist, had a medicine for slowing human growth. Meena was watchful of Koonty's complexion too. She kept a photo of Shivarani at the same age, and at regular intervals held it up against Koonty's cheeks, comparing for darkness although it is difficult to see skin colour properly in a black and white photo.

Shivarani's parents began to feel despondent about the future of their big dark daughter. Meena, who could not think of anything more dreadful for a woman than to remain unmarried, said hopeful things like, 'Perhaps your Papa could find the cash to send you to UK. I have heard that the men there are not all that fussy about what kind of woman they are married to,' and could not understand why Shivarani suddenly burst out weeping.

'What are you saying, Meena?' cried Shivarani's father, outraged. 'That our darling should be shipped off to marry some undiscriminating gora?' And to Shivarani, 'Marriage is not all, my darling, no matter what your mother says. Perhaps you could join some religious community and devote your life to love of God. Mahadevi did so and she experienced constant holy bliss in spite of being without husband.' Mahadevi was a Tamil saint of the middle ages who, abandoning all aspects of society, including clothes, wandered South India clad only in her long hair, devoting her life to Shiva and singing hymns to him. Shivarani's father adored his eldest child, but felt he could not properly understand her because of the way her weeping intensified at his suggestion.

Shivarani went to college, put all her attention on her work and tried not to notice the way the young male students responded gently to other girls but not to her. She had friends, even among the men, but they treated her as though she was a friend, and like one of them. How else could have they been to a woman who was an inch or so higher than the tallest guy?

One of the young men was a joker. No matter how serious the conversation he would always spoil everything by some silliness or other. In the evenings when the young men and women gathered in the dark and grimy coffee house and were in the midst of a serious discussion about the fear of war with Pakistan, Bhima would ruin it all by making a funny face then chanting, 'When I kiss a little Hindu I'm careful not to smudge her bindu. When I kiss a Pakistani I hold her tight and call her "jani".' The others, unable to stop laughing at such nonsense, would all the same get cross. 'That rubbish has spoiled the important tone of our conversation.'

The students would talk for hours over a single bitter brew of dirt-cheap coffee-flavoured chicory, discussing the problems of India. There were those who said things would only be solved by a revolution after which corruption would be rooted out, education made available for all and equality created for Indians of every caste and either sex. To destroy the present society and rebuild it better was considered by some the only solution to the present problems of corruption and inequality. Others though disagreed, and felt that change could only come by building on what was already there and that killing people and destroying property would never solve anything. The arguments would grow increasingly heated as the night wore on and in the end they always seemed to turn to Shivarani for arbitration as if, though the same age as the rest, she was perceived as older and wiser. One evening it was only she and Bhima still left, still arguing. Darkness had fallen, fireflies started to sparkle in the trees and the mosquitoes started to bite. Bhima, instead of listening to her ideas on education for all, began trying to balance a glass of water on his head, an experiment ending with water gushing over his nose. 'You look like Shiva catching the Ganges on his head,' said Shivarani strictly. 'And you have not been listening.' She did not approve of such frivolity.

'Your beautiful hair is on fire,' said Bhima, wiping his face. He gently took a firefly from her head, and held out the little flashing light to her in his palm. Shivarani suddenly could not remember what she had been about to say.

★   ★   ★

When she came home for her vacation Shivarani was shocked at the frivolity of her younger sister, Koonty, who rampaged round the Hatibari estate playing with the local children as though she was one of them and whose bedroom walls were covered in posters of film stars. 'Even here, in the village of Hatipur, there are children who don't have enough to eat,' said Shivarani. 'You should be thinking about things like that instead of getting swoony over some film star. Tomorrow I am going to the village to see what help I can give the people there. You should come with me.'

'Don't get cross with me so soon,' begged Koonty. 'Tell me about the people in college? Did you fall in love?'

Shivarani hesitated for the smallest moment before saying, 'No.'

Koonty could not come with Shivarani to the village. She had been invited to the Hatibari by the young zamindar. 'I will come with you next time, I swear, Didi,' she said.

Shivarani jumped, startled at the creaking stirring of a bush, thinking that a snake was about to emerge, and had told herself that if the brain-fever bird did not shut up, she would be driven mad. When she was halfway to Hatipur the bird did fall silent for a while, and then all she could hear were the squawks of mynahs, the high screams of the rose-ringed parakeets robbing the guava trees and the river slapping its banks like an arrogant hero beating his thighs. The air was peppery and stung a little, as though the leathery trees and the bushes with their dangerous-looking speckled leaves were gasping spice. She wished her parents had not chosen to live in such an out-of-the-way place.

As Shivarani arrived a cry went round for someone to bring a chair for the Hatibari manager's daughter. Ignoring their protests and refusing the battered plastic seat she told the gathering crowd, 'I have been studying for the past three years, learning about the problems faced by the villagers of India. Now that I am back, please tell me what has been going on here.'

At once a great babble of excitement rose. People, packing tightly round her, began to talk all at once. They waved their arms, beat their breasts and dramatically pulled at their hair as they told of the things they needed – a well so they would not have to go so far for water, a bus service, a health clinic and most of all electricity. 'Also we would like our own cinema,' they told her. 'At present we must travel to Dattapukur three miles away to see the films and because we are from outside, we have to sit at the back while those from Dattapukur get all the good places. And also when it is raining there is only a small tarpaulin for shelter and we of Hatipur are forced to sit outside of it till we become completely wetted. Even those with umbrellas become wetted underneath because of the water running over the earth.'

Shivarani quickly turned the conversation to drains, school books, clean water and medical care but every now and again one or another of the young men would let out an ear-splitting yell of 'yahoo.' 'They have been to see the film of *Jungly*,' a woman explained. 'Have you seen this wonderful film, Memsahib Shivarani? In this Shamee Kapoor is this wild man, who is constantly shouting in such a way.'

'But although hanging from trees and such like he is of a very handsome type,' said another. 'Like the gopis and their passion for the blue god, Krishna, all the women of Hatipur are in love with this fellow though the married ones do not mention it to their husbands.' The surrounding girls giggled protests and hid their faces in their hands while the men of their families looked at them accusingly.

Shivarani brought the conversation back to tangible problems that she might have a chance of solving.

A woman spoke up, 'My name is Laxshmi. If you wish to be helpful then you should do something for me. I have three daughters already . . .' she gestured to three little girls wearing starched frocks, with bows in their hair. 'I am pregnant again. If this child is a girl as well, my husband has said he will leave me. So can you make this child into a male?'

Shivarani sighed.

Others began to pour out their problems. They began to tell

Shivarani of the paralysed grandmother who had to be carried everywhere, the threatening mother-in-law, the child that did not thrive, the cow that had dried up too soon, the virus in the tomatoes. One man described his happiness because his cow had given birth to a female calf. Another expressed his dismay because his wife had given birth to a female child. And then there were the widows. There were fourteen of them. 'Perhaps you can find some work for us, Shivarani Memsahib,' they said. 'For these days we hardly get enough to eat for even if the families of our husbands wanted to, they would be unable to spare enough for us after the children have eaten.'

'The wife of the misti wallah has a trouble and needs your help,' someone told her. Shivarani followed him.

The misti wallah's wife was sitting on bolsters in the room at the back of the shop, pressing shandesh into little wooden moulds in the shape of fishes. The room smelled of sugar and buzzed heavily with bees and flies and the misti wallah's back was visible through the bamboo curtain, as he sat cross-legged behind his piles of sweets.

'I want my eldest sons, Rahul and Ravi, to go to school, but instead they are thieving around the village and their father does nothing to stop them,' said the woman. 'Ravi is the leader, and Rahul, though the eldest, follows him. I want the best for our children and my husband says he does too, but it costs money and the attention of the father to bring up children properly.'

The misti wallah's back flinched as though he heard or guessed what his wife was saying about him. He worked very hard, getting up before sunrise to separate the curds and set the dahis. For hours, even on the hottest days he would be toiling over a vat of hot oil, dribbling in the batter to make jellabies, then dropping the hot crisp squirls into simmering sugar syrup. After his stall opened he would be sitting there all day long, serving customers with rosogullas, Lady Kennies, gulab jamans, shandesh. Spooning almond-spiked paishes and rose-flavoured kheers into terracotta pots. Packing jellabies into banana leaf and tying the bundle with thread. Even after the stall was closed his work would still not be finished. He would still have to seal the jars of warm curd with muslin and waxed paper before carrying them to the river to cool all night in the shallows there. The evenings in the drink shop were his relaxation. He looked forward all day to the hour when he would be able to sit in silence in the little concrete room of the arrak shop and down a few tumblers of arrak. Then, fully drunk, his worries about his out-of-control sons and his wife's complaints forgotten, he would stagger home and sleep.

The misti wallah, on his way to the arrak shop, would sometimes pass the bullock cart on which his wife and children were squashed among the other villagers, on their way to see the film at Dattapukur. His wife, like the other women, wearing her brightest sari and with jasmine in her hair, his sons wearing oversized shorts, with their hair greased down and behaving properly for once, crammed among little girls in frocks embroidered with glittering thread and men in starched pyjamas. 'Why don't you come with us instead of getting drunk,' his wife would cry as he squeezed onto the verge to let the cart rumble by. 'The cinema will not give a headache and tonight is one very good film.'

Later, at the arrak shop, the misti wallah would settle onto the cool cement seat, glass in hand, and hear the shrill excited laughter and the creaking of the axle receding, as the cart made its way out of the village, and feel grateful for the silence that followed the departure of his family.

'My children are getting a bad example,' said the wife as she began to shake the shandesh fishes from their moulds and decorate them with silver leaf. 'That must be the reason for their bad behaviour but I am hoping that, since you are college returned and therefore of a great cleverness, you will speak with my husband and ask him to desist from the drinking of arrak, and come instead to the cinema with us.'

The zamindar's son, Pandu, had taken Koonty all down the long gallery, telling her about the family portraits. And now they sat on the verandah drinking nimbu pani with ice. Although he was so much older he talked to Koonty as though she was as grown-up as him, telling her of his plans to bring the Hatibari back to its former glory. 'In the days of my grandfather there were fifty servants, and all the land you see in every direction belonged to our family.' He was planning to buy a herd of Jersey cows, he told Koonty. 'There are all these stables that my grandfather used for his pig-sticking horses and they will make good byres.' He brought out photo albums. 'Look how pretty my great-grandmother was. And this aunt, see her. Isn't she beautiful? Though not as beautiful as you.'

Koonty felt a heat in her cheeks and, unable to work out how a modest woman was supposed to respond to such a compliment, said nothing. Kuru Dadoo, who was Pandu's father, joined them and, pointing to a faded sepia photo, said, 'That is me on the day I saved the life of a Calcutta box wallah. I was a hero in my time though you wouldn't believe it now.' Then he laughed till his big stomach shook, pinched Koonty's cheek till it was sore and popped a sweetie in her mouth as though she was a little girl and not a woman of thirteen and said, 'I hope you will be visiting us often because I need a pretty little girl around.'

Meena Gupta became very excited and hopeful when she heard of the visit. And a few days later when Koonty was invited round again Meena went nearly hysterical with hope. Kuru Dadoo had talked of Koonty's marriage with Pandu.

'Tell me word for word what he said.'

'I've told you twenty times and I'm not going to say it any more,' cried an exasperated Koonty.

'Once more,' pleaded the mother. These words were music to her after the dreadful business of Shivarani.

'He said, "If she was a little less jungly and a bit more modest Koonty would make a suitable bride for you, Pandu," but he might have been only joking. I don't think he really meant it. And anyway I don't want to be married. I want to go on being as I am.' Being as she was consisted of swimming in the river with Pandu and his boy cousins or even going with them into the village and playing games of cricket with the village boys in the main street.

'All this must stop instantly,' said Meena, who felt as though

Koonty had grown up into a young woman in a moment, and without anyone noticing. Whatever could she have been thinking of to let things come to such a pass? She forbade all further visits to the village, and put a stop to meetings with the Pandava and Kaurava boys unless there was a chaperone present. Koonty cried and begged, but Meena was filled with terror mixed with a marvellous hope.

Shivarani had managed to solve a few of the village's problems. She had got money from Oxfam to dig a tube well, and had started a little industry for the fourteen widows. They now made blue-eyed, yellow-haired dolls which Shivarani sold to a Calcutta toyshop. But Meena was not impressed. 'What is this, going around all day among those dirty people? I think that you are stirring up trouble where no trouble was before, and sooner or later it will come to the ears of the zamindar. Do you want your father to lose his work here? Then you will be in the state of these poor people of Hatipur that you are so sorry about.'

'Don't listen to Ma,' Koonty tried to console. 'I think it's wonderful, all the things you are doing. I wish I was a good person like you but I just couldn't do it. I know I couldn't.'

When Koonty was nearly fifteen Pandu's mother formally requested the union in marriage of Koonty with her son Pandu. Meena, nearly fainting with joy, reflected that the last year of Koonty's sulks and rows had been a small price to pay for this wonderful reward.

Koonty now spent her days moping alone in the garden while the boys rushed around on their bicycles or went swimming in the river. 'Of course you may not swim. Have you forgotten you are to be the wife of the young zamindar?' 'Certainly you may not go on a bicycle. That is not at all a suitable behaviour for a bride-to-be.'

Sometimes Shivarani, feeling sorry for her lonely sister, would sit with her and brush Koonty's hair or rub mustard oil into her fingers, while Koonty told her sister the story of the latest film she had seen. 'The Mahabharata. And the Sun God is absolutely gorgeous, though the one I like best of all is Arjuna. I've got a poster of him on my wall.'

Shivarani would tell Koonty about the things that were happening in the village, how Ravi, the misti wallah's son, had broken the darjee's sewing machine, how Laxshmi had given birth to a daughter and her husband had left her and how she was having difficulties in getting the doll shop to pay up. 'The widows need the money so badly. You have no idea how poor they are. It's not just a matter of having to wear white and being forbidden jewels. Their husbands' families treat them as though surviving their husbands is a punishable offence.'

'I would hate to be a widow,' said Koonty. 'I would kill myself if my husband died.' And she touched the gold medallion that Pandu had given her the day before.

'What a way to talk,' cried Shivarani. 'Here are you not even married and you are talking of your husband dying and you killing yourself. And you should not be accepting gifts from your husband-to-be at this time. Especially you should not accept something valuable like that so near to the wedding.'

Koonty crinkled her nose and hastily tucked the symbol of Pandu's love back into her blouse.

'Don't screw up your pretty face like that,' said Shivarani. 'I know you are going to look beautiful on your wedding day but all the same you must be careful not to get a wrinkle.'

Koonty laughed. 'And so will you look beautiful, Didi, because you'll have to wear nice clothes and jewels for my wedding instead of those ghastly drab old saris.'

Shivarani shook her head and smiled. 'It wouldn't matter how I was dressed. Nothing will make me pretty. I will always be ugly.'

Koonty was appalled. 'But Didi, how can you say such a thing? It's because you don't even try. Here. I'll show you how to do flirting things with your sari. You never know. Some gorgeous man might come to my wedding and fall in love with you.' Leaping up she demonstrated. 'Just flip the palu like this, as though by mistake.'

Shivarani did a reluctant tweak.

'Not like that,' protested Koonty. 'You've got to do it daintily and at the same time your eyes have to give a quick glance in his direction and then you have to look away.'

★   ★   ★

Shivarani was away during the months leading up to the wedding, travelling round the villages with her college friend Malti, seeing what could be done to help the villagers.

Villagers would instantly drop what they were doing when the two girls arrived, and stare, fascinated. Strangers were always exciting but the big one with the black face amazed them. Sometimes a whisper would go round among the children. 'Where are her other arms?' They thought that Shivarani was the goddess Kali. Malti was a type these villagers had encountered doing charity work at the health clinic or coming to instruct them on birth control. She was normal height, fair-skinned, wore gold earrings and her sari, though simple, was clearly expensive. They had never seen anyone like Shivarani before. It was not only her height and dark complexion. She wore no jewels and her wrists were bare, though even the poorest village woman wore at least a glass bangle. Her hair was short like a man's and, in fact, although she wore a cheap handloom sari, they could hardly tell if this was man or woman. Perhaps it is a hirja, they whispered to one another. Hirjas were people of indeterminate gender, who wore women's clothes and had the voices of men. They were frightening people, who appeared at the birth of a baby threatening to curse the child unless they were given payment. Shivarani's voice was nearly as gruff as a man's as she boomed out her party's promises of education, clean water, and food, housing and transport for all.

Meena was horrified, and when she met her eldest daughter would scold, 'Once more you are stirring up trouble where no trouble was before. You should be at home, in the Hatibari helping with the preparations for your sister's wedding, not rampaging round the countryside and hobnobbing with all these dirty villagers.'

As the day of her younger sister's wedding grew closer a letter from her mother persuaded Shivarani to return to Hatipur.

'Although I have never known you give way to envy, anyone might think you are jealous of your sister now, in her time of joy,' wrote Meena. 'The Kaurava family are already commenting on your absence. Please come back at once, Shivarani. The wedding takes place in two weeks and there is much to be done before that.'

Shivarani felt ashamed as she reluctantly made her arrangements to go home. She hoped she would be able to look at her sister, wearing the red sari of the bride, without her feelings showing.

She arrived in the village to find the whole place a buzz of action and expectation. All along the main street, silk, chiffon, gold zaree and shadow appliqué poured from the needles of the squatting darjees' ancient Singer sewing machines. The air steamed with the breath of garlic, chillies and palm tree jaggery as ingredients for the wedding feast arrived on lorries. The rickshaw wallah, who usually was unable to stand the sight of Shivarani walking, no matter how often she refused him, now trotted past her, his face hidden under banana fronds, his carriage laden with the potted trees purchased from Dattapukur that were to decorate the wedding pandal. He did not even notice the towering, striding figure of Shivarani Gupta in her dusty sari and her hacked-off hair. The pandal itself was arriving too, a lorryload of acres of gaudy cotton stitched with mirrors and fringed with little silver bells and fifteen-foot bamboo poles to form the frame. The great wedding tent, when erected, would tower above the Hatibari, be more brightly coloured than the cinema posters of Dattapukur. It was going to look more realistically like a glittering palace than the most voluptuous set from a Bollywood movie.

As Shivarani passed the Hatibari on her way to her parents' house, Pandu's brother's wife and Boodi Ayah were crouching on the verandah floor, arranging presentations for the bride. Gadhari looked up at Shivarani's greeting. 'I hope your sister is going to like these things, though in all the years that I have known her I have never seen her with a handbag once, let alone with fifty-three.' She told Shivarani bitterly that their task was to artistically arrange a matching set of blouse, petticoat, slippers and handbag onto each of fifty-three plastic trays. 'With no sides,' complained Gadhari. 'And the weather so hot that the sellotape will not stick.'

Shivarani stayed and helped for a while, struggling with the slippery plastic and the unruly silk and leather, while Gadhari muttered things like, 'They never gave anything like this to me when I was married.' And 'What woman can make use of fifty-three pairs of chappals?' And, 'Wait till she gets pregnant, then what use will these little blouses be to her? To me it is a perfect waste but Kuru Dadoo has insisted.'

Outside, Gadhari's sons shouted and laughed as they pedalled new trikes among the rose beds, while from an upstairs balcony their grandfather, Kuru Dadoo, watched them with pleasure. 'He gave them the trikes yesterday, but he is going to regret it when all his precious rose bushes have been destroyed,' said Gadhari.

When Shivarani left at last, Kuru Dadoo called out from his balcony, 'Good afternoon Shivarani, we have a great day to look forward to, have we not? And when are you getting married, my dear girl?' Shivarani felt her face grow hot as she hurried on.

Meena came running out. 'At least you are come at last. One would think that the unknown peasant women are more important to you than your own sister. And don't tell me you walked all the way here from the station.'

'Where is Koonty? She must be feeling terribly excited. Only a week to go,' said Shivarani.

'She's in her room. Go and see her. She's been a bit mopey lately.'

Shivarani found Koonty sitting, listless and pasty, on the edge of her bed. The wall was tattered with the remnants of ripped paper, as though the cinema posters had been dragged off wildly. 'I don't like the cinema any more,' said Koonty dully. Her hair was lank as though she had not brushed it. She did not get up. And Shivarani, instead of feeling pleased that her sister had grown out of the frivolous stage and might now be about to take an interest in more serious things, felt worried.

'What is wrong with her?' she asked Meena later. 'Has she been ill, or something?'

'There is nothing wrong at all,' said Meena. 'Koonty is, as is to be expected, feeling somewhat apprehensive about the coming ceremony, which is due to be quite the biggest event this village has seen since the marriage of the old zamindar and at which very much will be required of her. I myself was rendered unconscious several times over during my own wedding and I was only marrying into a middle-income family, though of unfortunately large genes. So you may imagine how it must be for your sister. Also she is behaving, at last, with the dignity of a woman who is about to become the bride of the zamindar though you, with your cavortings round the villages, would not know anything about proper behaviour.'

'Ma must be right,' thought Shivarani, but all the same could not get from her mind that there was something more wrong with Koonty than dignity or apprehension.

After a while Meena admitted that Koonty had been depressed ever since the day she lost the golden jewel that Pandu had given her. 'Even after I told her, don't worry about that, for at the wedding she will be given a hundred times as much gold and that I am sure the young zamindar will not be angry but will give her another if he comes to know of the loss, she has not been made happy.'

'Koonty is forever losing things. The last time I was here she had mislaid the sovereign piece that the zamindar had given her and she didn't seem to mind a bit. You were the one who was furious,' protested Shivarani.

'Then there was the episode at the river,' went on Meena. 'When you were away she tried to rescue a kitten, or so we think, though she will not talk about it. However, it seems that the creature was carried away by the current and it is from that time that Koonty seems to have suffered from a lowering of the spirits. Perhaps you can talk to her and see if you can find the source of the trouble.'

Shivarani managed to persuade Koonty to come out of her room and be measured for a blouse to go with her wedding sari. Koonty emerged unsteadily and stood passive while Shivarani wound the tape measure round her body. 'I think it's stupid to be making more blouses,' she said. 'Considering how you told me they are sending me fifty-three new ones, stuck to trays with sellotape, from the Hatibari.'

'Keep still,' said Shivarani, her mouth full of pins. 'Are you looking forward to the wedding?'

'Yes,' said Koonty in a voice that made it sound like 'no'. Her thoughts seemed far away.

'Why do you keep staring at the river? Can you see something there?'

'No reason,' said Koonty and looked down at her feet as though the question frightened her.

'Do you know what happens on the wedding night?' she asked. Koonty said nothing, but something wet touched Shivarani's bowed-over neck and when she looked up she saw that there were tears falling from Koonty's eyes.

Shivarani asked, 'Do you want me to tell you?' wondering how to phrase it if Koonty said yes.

'No,' said the girl. 'I do know. You needn't tell me.'

As the day of the wedding approached the activity of Hatipur reached fever pitch. From every side came the sound of hammering, as decorations were erected, the pandal completed, the ovens for cooking the feast erected. Meena had to take to her bed twice in the course of that last week, overcome by nervous exhaustion. Every man and woman and child in the village was occupied in some way with the preparations for the ceremony itself or purchasing or manufacturing gifts and overseeing the stitching of their own new outfits. The wedding was to last two weeks, and the richer people of the village planned to wear different clothes on every day. Goats, chickens and sheep were being fattened for slaughter and the flour for ten thousand chupatties purchased, for two thousand people would have been fed by the time this wedding was over.

These days every conversation in the village would sooner or later come to the subject of the wedding gifts. People tended to panic on hearing what someone else was giving, and would rush away and exchange what they had already bought for something more expensive. The widows were sewing a pair of three-foot-high dolls, dressed in UK bridal outfits, for their gift. Laxshmi was giving the bridal couple her best mother hen, who, when broody, had not left her eggs during the loudest fireworks of Diwali and had fought off a water buffalo that had come too near her chicks.

★   ★   ★

The misti wallah was creating a vast shandesh fish, big enough for five hundred people, and decorated with leaf of gold and pearls from Hyderabad. The rickshaw wallah, whose rickshaw had been painted gold, was going to transport guests free of charge.

A special tent was erected for the viewing of the bride and groom and on the day row upon row of guests poured into it, their eyes fixed on the two empty thrones which were soon to be occupied by the bridal couple. As they waited silver trays of sandal paste were circulated for the guests to ornament their foreheads, some Europeans among them eating this, mistaking it for a ritual snack.

There came gasps of delight when, at last, the bridegroom arrived. He had ridden from the Hatibari on a white Marwari horse, and had to be led to his chair, because the strings of jasmine flowers hanging from his pith helmet obscured his sight. Now all eyes were on the entrance for a first sight of the bride.

But she did not come. She could not be found. Though she had been kept inside her room and constantly surrounded by female relatives, when the moment arrived for her to be taken to the pandal in the golden rickshaw, she was not there. 'I left her for a moment to get a glass of water,' said an aunt. 'She was there two minutes ago. I dashed off to get a safety pin, in case she pulled out the sari folds,' said a cousin. The family wasted precious time beating on the locked door of Koonty's room and begging her to let them in.

The guests waited and wondered what was happening.

Eventually a carpenter was called, and managed to break the door lock. The room was empty. Koonty's wedding outfit that had taken such hours to arrange, was flung over the floor and the window was open.

Meena began to wail and accuse her husband, saying, 'I told you we should have bars put on her window. My friends from the Calcutta Club will be filled with malicious pleasure when they discover.'

They must find her quickly, the family knew, before the guests discovered that the bride, moments before her wedding, had ripped off all her clothes, climbed out of the window and run away.

The guests were growing restless and the bridegroom kept looking towards the pandal entrance like someone waiting for a bus. The Calcutta Club ladies began to whisper delightedly to each other, suspecting and hoping for a scandal. Meena, overwhelmed with self-pity, shame and fury, wanted to go to bed and lie in the dark with an iced sponge over her forehead but instead ran this way and that like a hen who had lost her chicks.

It was Shivarani who finally found Koonty. The girl, wearing only her petticoat and blouse, was sitting on the river bank, staring into the water as though she had lost something. Shivarani sat down beside her and putting an arm round her, said, 'Tell me what the matter is.'

Koonty stared into the water and was silent for ages. Then she said, 'Didi, if someone put a newborn baby onto a floating goddess' hand, how long do you think it would stay alive?'

'That's silly. Come back. All the guests are waiting, and Pandu is feeling very sad.'

'And do you think that if someone saw a hand of Durga floating by, with a little newborn baby lying in it, that they would rescue the baby? Do you think that, Didi?'

Shivarani sat silent, as something totally impossible and terrible began to seem possible. 'Tell me what happened,' she whispered, though she did not want to hear.

When Koonty had finished Shivarani tried to speak but words would not come.

'It was very dark and I do not know if it was a boy or a girl even though I held it in my arms for so long,' Koonty whispered at last. 'But I feel sure, from its gentle little movements, that it was a girl.'

'I see,' said Shivarani, and her mouth felt dry as though she had a fever.

'It is because of this I cannot face these wedding guests.'

'Why not?' asked Shivarani.

'Can't you see, can't you see?' cried Koonty. 'There are all those children coming to the feast and one of them might be mine, rescued from the hand of Durga. Suppose I saw my child, what should I do?'

'If anyone had found that floating baby, the whole village would have talked about it by now,' said Shivarani and thought to herself that the baby was surely dead.

'But anyway, I cannot marry Pandu,' said Koonty.

'Why can't you?'

'As soon as I have told him he will not want me,' said Koonty.

'Then don't tell him.'

'But how can I not? And even if I say nothing, he will find out tonight. My body will let him know.'

'Our young Indian men are so innocent that I think he will not know and you must never tell him,' said Shivarani.

Half an hour later Meena, nearly weeping with relief and fury, saw Shivarani returning with Koonty, who was walking stiffly as though she was ill. Shivarani's face was grim.

The wedding went smoothly after that. Koonty was put on display at last and sat silent and wilting under the weight of silk, gold and jewels. The villagers who thronged to see her were most impressed with the way this previously undignified girl had been rendered quiet and pale by the honour being done to her by the family of the zamindar.

Among the wedding guests were two Hatipur lads who, having returned from university, were unable to find jobs. Dressed in their best starched outfits they sat cross-legged on the ground to eat the splendid feast and said to all who would listen, 'Why should these zamindars have so much, when we have so little? At our weddings will we have a thousand guests? In fact will we have any wedding at all, for we may never find a job, and no parents will allow their daughter to marry a man who is unemployed. And if we did manage to marry, would we receive so many wedding gifts that they had to be brought in a bullock cart? We would be lucky to even receive some pots and pans and two saris for the bride. Is this Pandu any cleverer or better-looking than we are? It is by no effort of his that he is sitting up there, well fed and dressed in jewels. We would look just as good if we had the money.'

The older men and women shook their heads. 'Your problems are the consequence of your karma. Next time, if you do enough puja to Durga you will be zamindars yourselves and villagers will cook your food, plough your fields and clean your houses.' As they mopped up mango chutney with their fingers they told the youths, 'If you perform your dharma with regard to the zamindars, next time round it will be you who are living in a palace and driving through the countryside in petrol-driven vehicles.'

But the boys were not impressed. 'This is old-fashioned thinking,' they said. 'We have become Marxists and we want these things now.' Nitai Mandel, the village Communist leader, said, 'Equality does not come from making envious statements and the people of India will not become equal with the zamindars by such complaining.'

'You are saying we should sit in a small hut of mud, watching these rich people dining off maach and paish while we have only dhall with rice? I say that we should fight to destroy this corrupt and greedy society, so that a better, fairer one can be created. We should take away from the rich and redistribute to the poor and if they try to prevent us we should take violent action. That is the only way.'

'You are right to say that we must fight for justice,' said Nitai. 'But your battles must be fought at the polls and this talk of killing and robbing is not the way to go about it.'

One of the boys said scornfully, 'You say you are the leader of the local Communists and yet you continue to own half a hectare of paddy land with only a pair of baby bulls to plough it, while these zamindars own a thousand hectares. Your politics lack conviction.' And as the boys walked away they muttered to each other, 'Nitai Mandel is a dinosaur and people stopped thinking like him ten years ago. Now the Communist Party belongs to us who are young, disillusioned and determined.'

The younger boys of the village listened, thrilled and scared by the young Marxists. Ravi, the misti wallah's nine-year-old son, said, 'I am going to go up to Pandu Zamindar, while he is sitting there on his big gold chair and I am going to tell him that he's got a silly face.' The two older boys laughed kindly at the bravado.

Shivarani's college friend, Malti, said, 'What they say is true. The rich have too much and the poor too little and some of us from college are planning to do something positive about this.' Apparently the students had heard Mao Tse-tung on Radio Peking and had become inspired to start a revolution in a village in North Bengal where landlords had seized the crop of one of the sharecropper peasants leaving the man and his family without even food to eat. 'We have heard that this kind of thing is going on all the time,' Malti told Shivarani. 'Now several of us from college are going to Naxalbari to help the villagers get their due. Why don't you come too?'

There was so much food during the zamindar's wedding that even the pye-dogs thrived and hardly ever needed to be kicked. The village cows were garlanded with marigolds and for three weeks grazed from each other's necks and gave marigold-flavoured milk. During the day joss sticks were pierced into the trunks of the banana trees, where they smouldered and perfumed the air with sandalwood and musk and each night a thousand oil lamps were lit and sent bobbing down the river, till the water sparkled with just as much light as the firefly-glittering trees.

For years after, people measured time by that grand occasion. 'I was born in the year of the zamindar wedding.' 'My child ate his first rice in the month of the zamindar wedding.' 'My tube well was drilled the week after the zamindar wedding.'

Shivarani and Malti travelled by third-class train and even Shivarani, who was well used to squalor, gave a little shudder as they came into Naxalbari. Her first impression was of greyness. Everything, from the sore-ridden pye-dogs, the squatting children, to the rickety huts was filmed with a layer of dead grey dust. The place smelled of human faeces. There was only one adult in sight, a man so still and old that he looked dead already, sitting with his shrivelled legs stretched before him, leaning against a tree that had been robbed of all its branches and now consisted of only a single trunk pointing into the sky like a finger of accusation.

'The other students are in the fields teaching the local people how to use hand grenades,' the man told them. He had no teeth and his words were blurred. 'There, that is them returning now.' He pointed a wavering finger to the furthest horizon, and Shivarani made out through air that wobbled with heat, a group approaching, dark against the brightness of the fields. For a moment she thought she saw a man that was darker and taller than the rest but it was only a trick of the light. He was not among them.

Local men carrying bows and arrows, and a few with modern rifles accompanied the students as they arrived in the village at last. 'You look half starved and what has happened to your faces?' asked Shivarani, shocked.

The young men and women smiled mournfully. 'Wait till you've been here a week. Once you've had three goes of dysentery and been bitten all over at night by mosquitoes and in the day by lice you will be looking just like us.'

'For two months we have been helping the peasants seize cattle and rice from the jotedars and grab land for redistribution,' they told Shivarani and Malti as they led them through the village. 'We have raided the jotedars' homes and offices, threatened them into giving up the title deeds to the land. At last justice is being done. The rich are being forced to be fair to the landless.'

'And the police have done nothing to stop you?' asked Shivarani.

'Not till this morning,' she was told.

The police had been in a quandary. Whereas they were sympathetic to the cause of the peasants, indeed many of them had families in the village of Naxalbari, the jotedars were rich and ruthless and the law was being broken. So on the previous day the police had been forced into action and a jeep was sent into Naxalbari to put down the violence.

'There was a battle and we won,' the students cried jubilantly.

'You mean the police just gave in and went away?'

'We killed one of the policemen and then they realised that they were beaten.' The students laughed, punched each other trium- phantly and danced about, mimicking the events of the day before.

That night Shivarani lay awake for ages and it was not only because of the iron-hard of the mud floor or the endless buzz and bite of insects. The killing of the policeman had been, she felt sure, a terrible turning point. Police attitudes always changed in an instant once one of their own was killed.

She woke next morning before the sun had risen. The others lay sprawled around her. What fools, she thought, to be sleeping so calmly as if that was the end of the matter. She rose and with the heavy cloud of anxiety still pressing on her, walked through the still dark village to the small scummy doba at the further end. The sun was rising as she reached there and a blue mist of early-morning fires hung like a pashmina shawl over the fields. A man was walking, visible from the waist up, through an invisible field. A koel called. Macaque monkeys woke, yawning and scratching, on the roofs of huts and lower branches. She walked slowly towards the pond, glad that the grey dust was hidden, relieved to be away from the others. Perhaps after all they were right, and nothing more would happen.

She was bending over the green water when a voice behind her said, 'Shivarani?' She straightened, water dripping from her face and there stood Bhima. He wore a check lungi and a vest. She could see the dark hair under his armpits. He had not shaved and the newly risen sun glowed in the short black stubble. She stared at him for a long moment before the realisation came to her that she was only half dressed. Her petticoat was crumpled because she had slept in it, and her hair had not been combed since yesterday. Hastily she covered her breast which was only barely hidden by her blouse. He stood gazing at her, his lips twitching as though he was about to smile. Or worse, laugh . . .

'You've caught me at a bad moment,' she said, her voice chilled from shame. 'I'm a terrible mess.'

'Oh, no, I don't think so,' he laughed. 'I think you look beautiful.'

When the two returned to the hut and food was doled out, Shivarani hardly noticed the gritty rice and the hard floor because sitting opposite her was Bhima.

It was May, getting very hot. The students, used to fans and air conditioning, panted and sweated in the only shade, the airless hut. They lay inert and sweating, telling each other that there was now no doubt they had won. More than thirty hours had passed since the raid by the police and the killing of Inspector Soman Wangdi, and nothing more had happened. 'Your worries were for nothing,' they said to Shivarani.

At midday a lad rushed in and said the police were coming. The students were energised in a moment. Hotness and tummy upsets forgotten, they ran out to join the villagers who were already waiting with their bows and arrows. There was an air of excitement and expectation, as though having won once they could not fail to do so a second time.

'Let them come,' cried the villagers. 'This time we will not kill just one but twenty.'

For the first time the students became a little alarmed, and urged, 'No killing. Definitely no more killing.' But the men were eager, like hunters who had sighted a plump herd of sambar. They pranced around, arrows at the string, waiting, ready, fearless. They were expert bowmen for the only meat they could afford to eat was what they shot, the occasional deer or monkey. Usually wild birds and even mongeese.

In the midday silence the sound of the approaching police cars grew and soon even the hopeful hunters realised that this was not just a jeep and a handful of constables, but a whole retinue of armoured vehicles. Even they realised that bows and arrows would not work this time. 'Bring out the cows. Block the road with them,' went round the call. 'The policemen are Hindus. They will not hurt the cows.' Now the police procession could be seen as a cloud of dust approaching like a slow grey ball. Putting their bows aside, men went running to the stalls and byres. Women dashed for their milking cows. Children emerged from huts hauling little calves. Field workers unhitched their bullocks and by the time the police arrived the road to Naxalbari was blocked with cattle.

The police rounded the corner. The first vehicle, a large armoured lorry, paused briefly. The villagers, watching from behind their cattle herd, began to feel smug and look triumphant. There came a shouted order from the rear of the police column and with a clatter of rifle fire, the first vehicle plunged into the cattle herd. There followed dull thuds as the jeeps and lorries banged against cows. The cows began rushing, swerving, falling, howling, galloping tail high, squirting shit, until they burst the thorn fences and escaped into the surrounding paddy fields and stands of maize.

There fell a small shocked silence from the watching villagers then the cry went up, 'The women then. They will never dare to shoot women.' Wives, mothers, daughters, grannies, urged by the men, came rushing to fill the gap left by the fleeing cattle. Shivarani thrust her way through the women till she got to the front and stood there. The sight of her, tall and fearless at their head, filled the women with greater courage and determination. They pressed around Shivarani, defying the oncoming police lorries that rumbled towards them. When the first lorry halted, policemen leant from it and pointed weapons at the women. 'Stop this,' yelled Shivarani. 'Don't kill women. What are you thinking of?'

There came the crack of a shot and Shivarani staggered as she felt pain pierce her shoulder. There followed a hail of bullets. In agony, Shivarani ducked and dodged as behind her she heard people screaming. She felt her strength going but forced herself to stay standing so that she could shield the bodies of the smaller women at her back. The pain was terrible but she forced her body to stay upright. She could hear a young girl crying. The women were scrambling to get away, and the police were still firing.

Then something came between Shivarani and the steady and menacing approach of the police. Behind, above, ahead she could hear the sound of shooting and screaming, could feel the desperate struggling of people trying to escape as Bhima put himself between her and the bullets. His body gave a heave as a bullet struck it, and then he crashed backwards, knocking her to the ground and falling on top of her. She felt warm fluid – Bhima's blood – pour between her thighs.

The shooting stopped. The silence that followed was broken by screaming from the injured and the sobbing of women.

Koonty had joined a traditional Hindu joint family consisting of Pandu's father, Kuru Dadoo, and his younger son known as DR Uncle. There was also DR's wife, Gadhari, and their three sons.

Pandu told Koonty, 'It is OK for you to laugh and run even when my father is there. He is very modern and won't think you are being disrespectful.' And when she still seemed sad, he told her, 'Perhaps you don't like to live in a joint family situation. Would you like us to go somewhere else? To a house of our own?' The idea filled him with dismay, but he felt ready to do anything to make Koonty happy. She shook her head. It was not that. 'What is it then? What is it? What is it?' But he could not discover.

Kuru Dadoo was delighted that Koonty had joined his household and felt sure that he would be able to make her happy, even when her own husband could not. He had known her since she was little and continued to pinch her cheeks or pop sweetmeats into her mouth as though she was still a little girl. 'What is the matter with my little Koonty?' he would laugh. 'Why is she looking so sad?' He would pluck a flower from the hibiscus bush and hand it to her saying, 'For your hair, my pretty little daughter.' He had two sons and three grandsons. This was his first little girl and he was making the most of her. Gadhari watched with envy for Kuru Dadoo had never popped a dudh peda into her mouth. He had never given Gadhari flowers for her hair.

Koonty's longing for the baby to be rescued from the river was tinged with fear because they would see the gold chain round its neck and discover her shameful secret. But days, then weeks, passed and this did not happen, and a few months later she became pregnant. To the relief of her family, her sadness lifted. 'If this baby is a little girl,' she thought, 'I will know that the goddess has forgiven me. It will mean that Durga rescued my baby from the river and is giving her back to me in a miraculous way. I will not be the killer of my baby after all if this one is a little girl.' She stopped waiting for the baby lost in the river to be brought back to her because the goddess had replaced it in her womb. She decided to call her daughter 'Shobita' because that means 'Sun', for this baby was really the child of the Sun God, and not Pandu's at all.

When Koonty's baby was born everyone laughed because it was a boy and there were three in the household already but then, as Kuru Dadoo pointed out, 'You can never get too many boys.' But Koonty's dark mood returned. 'Postnatal depression,' Meena Gupta tried to console Pandu. 'She will get over it, don't worry,' but Pandu was not convinced. In the end, to take his mind off his young wife's gloom, Pandu, indulging in a lifelong dream, sold the Hatibari chandelier, took the money and travelled to South India, where he bought twelve pure-bred Jersey cows.

The villagers arrived in their hundreds to see the gold-haired, dark-eyed beauties being unloaded from the lorries. They laughed aloud at the sight of the wide, fair brows and hornless heads. They bent and giggled in wonder at the vastness of their bouncing udders.

'Beautiful, beautiful, beautiful,' was all Pandu seemed able to say, overcome with awe at the gracious appearance and prospective vast milk yields. 'We must all work hard to make sure these pretty creatures do not suffer in our heat.'

Ice, prepared in the fridge, was crushed, poured into hot-water bottles and tied on the heads of the twelve new Jerseys. They stood in a mournful row at the shady end of their byre, looking silly under their ice-water bottle hats, water trickling down their eyelashes, their tails whacking exhaustedly at the attacks of fierce flies that were quite new to them. The darjee was called and set to work on his pedal Singer, stitching hessian coats for the cows to stop the flies from pestering them and Pandu had them dressed up till they looked like European women in frocks and hats.

Kuru Dadoo was shocked by his son's new enthusiasm. 'A zamindar should be out there, shooting tigers and sticking pigs, not spending his day in the dairy like some gwala.'

'They are so beautiful, Papa. Look how they have dark round their eyes as if they have been painted with kajal. And don't you admire their golden colour?'

Kuru Dadoo snorted with scorn. 'If you wish for a beautiful golden creature with painted eyes why not go to Free School Street and find yourself a Nepali prostitute like I used to do.'

'I prefer the local girls. And these cows are like pets.'

'If you wish to keep pretty creatures you should go for cheetahs. My father had a hunting pair of great beauty and danger. Clever also. He never had such hunting luck when he was only accompanied with dogs. Shall I contact the zoo and see if they can obtain some for you?'

Gadhari was furious when she found out about the chandelier. 'It was family property and worth a fortune. Why did you let him do it? You should take legal action against him,' she raged at her husband. But DR Uncle, whose greatest joy in life was poetry, only smiled at his wife's outburst, and said, 'I'm sure it will be better cared for in its new home.'

A new-rich Parsee, called 'Sodawaterbottleopenerwallah' after the gadget he had so successfully marketed, had bought the chandelier. It now hung, pristine and resplendent in a brand new concrete and marble house in Alipore. No longer did sparrows perch and shit on its hand-cut Venetian pendants. No longer did pendants fall like leaves to be gathered up by the sweeper in the morning. No longer did it dangle sideways like a drunk going home from the foreign liquor shop.

The village gwala turned up at the Hatibari to give Pandu advice on how to care for the new cows and use the milk. 'You do not know how to make ghee, Sahib, so I will show you. First we make kheer, then we turn that into butter, then we turn that into purest ghee,' he said and began a demonstration on the Hatibari stove that took such hours that the cook was unable to prepare the midday meal.

The gwala brought milk from his own herd of desi cows and Pandu was forced to watch while the gwala and his daughter boiled it, stirring it till it was thick as heavy cream, and clotted with skin round the sides.

'Surely that's enough,' pleaded Pandu. But the old man was merciless. He had known Pandu as a little boy and was not the least in awe of him. 'We go on till the milk is solid,' he said. It happened at last and the crusty lump that had once been twenty litres of fresh milk was crushed on the spice grinding stone till it separated into butter.

'But I have read of butter being made in Western countries and it is not done like this at all,' said Pandu. 'There they take cream and beat it till it separates from its buttermilk. It is a much quicker process than this.'

The gwala roared with scoffing laughter. 'If we made butter by such careless techniques in this hot country our butter would be left with water in it and go bad in no time. Now we cook this butter, always stirring, slowly slowly, into purest golden ghee.' This took another hour of stirring. 'Now see how the solid has fallen to the bottom, Sahib, and on top the butter oil is gold and clear. We pour this off carefully and there we are.'

'Now I show you how to make channa,' he said, just when Pandu thought he was to be let off the hook. 'After that you can get cook to make it into all Bengal sweets, rossogulla, Lady Kenny, Gulab jaman and so on and also channa. We heat up the milk then curdle with alum.' Pandu remembered alum. His father had used it to stifle the bleeding of razor nicks.

The boiling milk swished into two parts almost at once, as the alum was poured in and the old man brandished a soft firm lump of snow-white curd. 'Now we grind again then mix with a little soojee. Roll in little balls then boil in syrup flavoured with cardamom pods till the jamans rise to the surface . . .'

'I am tired,' said Pandu. 'I never intended to become a sweet maker.'

Ignoring him the old man went on, 'Or we fry this with some of the ghee, rosewater, cardamom pods and jaggery till it goes thick and stiff and press it into moulds till we have shandesh . . .'

Pandu groaned.

'As a small boy you were somewhat lazy and I see this has still not altered,' said the gwala sternly. 'Now we come to the feeding and the milking of the animals.' He told Pandu that the animals must have hot feeds each evening of rice bran boiled with jaggery and that the cows would not let down their milk unless the calves were allowed first suck.

'You keep a little muzzle on her baby during the day and at milking time you let baby have a little suck. Then mummy lets down milk and you give a pull. After a while mummy will find out it is your fingers and not baby taking the milk and she will pull it up again. Then you let baby have another, and so on.'

Pandu looked bemused, 'But in the West they take the calves away from the cows at birth.'

The old man looked as though he was going to cry. 'This is a terrible cruel thing. These poor Billaty cows. How much they must suffer. But then how do these foolish Billaty people get milk?'

Pandu shrugged. 'I don't know how, but they do.'

The old man went off at last, bemused and mumbling at the extraordinary ways of foreign cows, the cruel ways of foreign people and the terrible ignorance of the zamindar.

Pandu was thrilled with his new son, and when Koonty breastfed her child, Pandu would sit at her side, stroke her hair and murmur, 'You two are the joys of my life,' and think that he was the happiest man in the world. He would come each evening to watch with delight as Boodi Ayah bathed the new baby and pressed whiskery kisses on his body. 'He is a big boy even now and when he is a man he will be magnificent like his Daddy,' Boodi Ayah told Pandu. She was a hill tribe woman from Bihar with limbs like charcoal sticks that looked very black against the pure white of her short blouse and dhoti that exposed her bandy legs and large cracked feet.

After Adhiratha died Dolly wrote a letter to her parents, telling them what had happened to her and explaining about Karna. After a very long time her father sent her back a letter, written by the local scribe, in which he said that she should only come back to them if there was absolutely no other way she could survive. 'For you are a widow and in this village such a person would, a generation ago, have been expected to perform suttee and even nowadays her being alive gives a certain offence in the villages. But as for this foundling child, we have barely enough food for our own stomachs and certainly not enough to feed another woman's brat.' He added, 'I am speaking for myself and not your mother.'

Dolly cried when she read this letter, then she tore it up.

In the months that followed she would wake in the morning and sometimes her mind would trick her into thinking that Adhiratha was still there. She would reach out for him, her hand feeling around in the dark and it would be long moments before she would be plunged back into the sadness. There were happy nights when she dreamt that he was still alive so that during the day she would long for sleep, where she could find him. She tried for a while to continue washing clothes, but the money was not enough and the day came when she could no longer afford the room.

It was May and very hot the day she stepped out of the room where she and Adhiratha had lived together. She stood in the road, baby Karna in her arms, and did not know what to do next, or where to go. And as she hesitated, dazzled with the heat, the brightness and the hopelessness of everything, the realisation came upon her that even her work as a dhobi could not continue, for now she lacked anywhere to keep or iron the clothes. She had no income or home.

Holding everything she owned, including the precious baby, she began to walk along the pavement, not going anywhere, but not knowing where to stop. She walked like this for two hours until at last she sank down on the spit- and urine-spotted pavement because she was so tired and because the baby had started crying. She squatted in the dust with her child across her knees, while people going past jostled against her or stepped over her, as though already she had ceased to be part of the human race.

In the weeks and months that followed she lived on that piece of pavement, eking out the little money she had left from her dhobi work to buy the cheapest food and wondering what she would do when it was finished. At night she slept on the hard ground with only her straw mat under her, and a bedsheet wrapped round her and Karna to keep them from the mosquitoes. Karna was the only thing that made her life worth living. If it had not been for him she would have killed herself, thrown herself under one of the new underground trains, for there did not seem anything else in her life worth staying alive for. Often during those sad months she would take out the little golden disc on which was written what she had decided was the name of Karna's mother. At first she had been tempted to take the baby back to this woman called Koonty of Hatibari, giving Karna back the life that was his right. Then, with Karna's life ensured she would do away with her own. But a woman who has thrown a baby away once might do it again. In the end Dolly decided that the baby would be better off with her, in spite of the poverty, than being sent to a woman who did not love it.

When Karna was four months old, a charitable organisation that specialised in getting work for pavement people found Dolly a place as a live-in maid. Dolly was given a small room in the compound where she and Karna slept, but during the day she was forced to leave the baby alone. Dolly's new employers did not allow children in their flat. 'You are lucky that we are giving you this chance of a job but we can easily take on someone else without children if you do not want it,' the wife said.

So whenever she had a little gap in her work during her fifteen-hour day, Dolly would race across the yard to feed the baby. As Dolly washed the cement floors with a piece of hessian, rubbed the utensils with charcoal or swept the beds with a short straw broom, her mind was always on her little boy. She would worry about him a thousand times as she scoured the dishes with coconut string, scrubbed the saucepans with sand in a tin bowl of cold water, or washed the floors with disinfectant. The moment her work was done she would run as though the goddess Kali was after her, to where her baby lay weeping in his cradle and only feel safe when she had him hugged tight inside her arms. And then, even though she was so tired that her legs shook, she would light her cow dung brazier, heat up water, and give her little boy his bath. It troubled her that the child was left so much alone, but at least she was earning a little money, they had a roof over their heads and as he grew older she would be able to give him decent food. Karna grew older, learnt to sit and then to walk. Dolly did everything she could to keep the toddler safe while she was out, but he was forever getting up to mischief and the room was not designed for a baby. Once Karna dragged a stool to the window, climbed up, fell out and had to be retrieved screaming and bleeding from the road. Another time he managed to find matches and nearly set their bedding alight. The final straw came when Dolly rushed in at midday to give him his meal and found the door open and the room empty. It was two hours before she found Karna toddling along on the main road. She seized him from the path of a lorry in the nick of time and sat sobbing, hugging and shivering, while nine-month-old Karna, thrilled to be back in his mother's arms, beamed and prattled triumphantly. It was half an hour before Dolly could find the strength to get up and go back to her employers, carrying her exuberant child.

Her mistress was waiting on the stairs, her expression thunderous. 'You are incapable of even looking after that single child, let alone performing domestic duties at the same time. Every day there is some new reason for you to abandon your work,' she shouted. 'And today, when my husband came home there was no midday meal for him. Now he has returned to his office with an empty stomach and a great anger. Things have gone too far. I do not want you in my service. I will pay you what I owe and you must be out of that room by tonight, because I have another maid coming already.' Dolly threw herself at the woman's feet, wept, begged, promised, but it was no good.

'You have made all these promises so many times already and you have never been able to keep them. It is the fault of that child. He is more trouble than three children put together and as long as you are burdened with him you will never find anyone to employ you.' Baby Karna beamed and chuckled as though he was being complimented.

Just having his mother holding him was all he ever wanted and if it meant that some woman shouted at them at the same time, what did it matter?

That night Dolly and Karna were back on the pavement again. In a way she felt relieved, for now, although they were poor once more, she could keep her child with her all the time. She became a rubbish-heap scavenger, specialising in flowers discarded from women's hair or from thrown away garlands that had been used for honouring gods or guests. She would also find overblown blooms that gardeners had discarded, or flower arrangements that householders had considered past their prime. There were usually a few blooms that could be salvaged from any bunch or garland, no matter how wilted and damaged they at first might seem. Dolly would sort through her finds and roll the good ones into a moistened piece of cloth, to be taken home later and woven into new garlands, a little more bedraggled than the originals, but cheaper.

Dolly scavenged among men, women, children, pye dogs, crows, cows, all making a living out of the filth of the rubbish heaps. There were people who collected string, carefully garnering the lengths then rolling them into tidy balls. Others worked with old tins, others with pieces of cloth, others gathered the tinsel from garlands. There were people searching for tin, for plastic, for paper. And there were the really desperate who relied on the heaps for nourishment, fighting with the crows, dogs and rats to eat some rotten discarded end of a banana or samosa. There would be a sudden scramble because a green coconut shell had been unearthed with a little flesh still adhering or someone had come upon a thrown out bread loaf. The little desi cows seemed to be the only creatures to thrive upon the heaps. They were plump and had shining coats as though old newspapers, in which greasy food had been wrapped, provided a better diet than all the care and scientific feeding that Arjuna's father gave to his pure-bred Jersey herd. Pandu's Jerseys would never look as fit at the little cows of Cal. The cows were rented from their owners by people in the bustees, who fed and milked them and used their dung for fuel. They were let loose all day to forage on the rubbish heaps or among the shops where shopkeepers and passers-by would give them fruit or a sweetmeat. In the evening the animals returned to the bustee for hot bran and jaggery.

The rubbish heaps, breathing out powerful odours of rot and gas, were cleared away a couple of times a year. The raw rubbish was carted in lorries to the wet lands on the outskirts of the town and there dumped on damp land where it acted as a fertiliser for fields of vegetables. Among the hectares and hectares of still stinking debris grew the largest whitest cauliflowers, enormous aubergines, cabbages nearly two feet wide and the best ladies' fingers in the whole of Bengal.

A new British Deputy Commissioner found one such stinking heap toppling near the High Commission and contacted the council, complaining of the health hazard, the smell and the flies and requested it be removed regularly, but was told there were insufficient funds. In the end he offered to pay for it himself, but this generous offer was greeted with fury by members of the ragpickers' union. They marched in vast and tattered numbers round and round the residency shouting that they were about to be deprived of their living until he was forced to withdraw his offer and had to continue to live in the proximity of the heap. Sometimes these heaps would grow to ten, fifteen feet high then suddenly topple. Several ragpickers had been killed or badly injured by being buried under a collapsing heap of rubbish.

In the evening Dolly would bathe Karna ferociously under the ruptured pipe till she had rubbed away every trace of stink and rot. To Karna's mother the sight of her frail son, shining with water in a muddy puddle, was the best sight of her whole day. When he was clean she would seat him on the ground and serve him whatever food she had managed to scrounge, for he was, after all, the man of the house. Sometimes she would manage to get enough fuel together to brew up a tiny fire on the pavement and cook her little man a hot meal of rice and lentils and on very good days even give him a spoonful of achaar to go with it. She always waited till Karna had finished before eating anything herself and as his appetite increased there would be very little left over for her. Often nothing.

When he was two she looked round and could not see him. She ran wildly up and down the road screaming and found him at last tugging at passing people's clothes, patting his stomach and lisping, 'No Mama, No Papa, very hungry,' copying a bigger beggar girl called Laika.

Dolly was furious. 'How dare you. We are not beggars. We still have our dignity.' But the moment her back was turned he was down in the street again, and the money he gave her was welcome. She could not deny that. But there came a day when she could not find Karna anywhere. She went to all the places where he might be, till someone told her he had seen Karna being carried away by a foreign lady.

'Which way did she go?' asked the weeping Dolly. 'Where did she take him?'

People pointed this way and that. Someone told her, 'The kid was screaming.' Dolly ran even faster and felt despair. She asked everyone she met, 'Have you seen my little boy? He's got golden eyes and a foreign lady has taken him.' Dolly kept running madly and shouting, 'Karna, Karna, Karna.' The idea even came to her as she ran that, though she longed for her child so dreadfully, he would be better off with this foreign lady who would be able to give him good food, nice clothes and a proper education. But all the same she could not stop hunting for Karna. Perhaps when she found the lady, she might agree to let her take Karna away.

She ran, sobbing, all up Park Street and along Free School Street. She raced, panting heavily by now, along New Market Street. She rushed along Chowringee, banging into porters with merchandise on their heads, ignoring the outraged cries of shopping memsahibs, crashing into sahibs with briefcases.

She found him outside the Grand Hotel. The foreign lady was looking discouraged.

'He told me he was an orphan,' she said to Dolly. 'Otherwise

I would never have carried him away. I was only hoping to help him.'

Dolly was afraid, after that. 'Don't beg from foreigners till you're older,' she warned. 'Stick to people from Bharat for now.' He, of course, did not listen to her but was more careful now.

Dolly, worried at her son's lack of education, began to teach him to decipher the words on the enormous cinema posters. The first words Karna learnt to read were the names of film stars and the titles of films. He began to watch out for new advertisements on his own and would come home, thrilled, to tell his mother he had managed to read 'Prem Pujari' or 'Johnny Mera Nam', all by himself. Concerned that his education was so one-sided she looked for other teaching tools. She encouraged him to recognise the letters on car number plates. She began to collect bits of newspaper off the rubbish heaps and instead of selling them on, wiped them clean of filth and grease and used them to teach Karna a wider range of reading. She even had a newspaper that she had kept from the good days and would bring it out on special occasions reading him the story of a man who had climbed the Himalayas without proper clothes and had survived because he was a yogi. 'If you are a yogi you can do anything,' Dolly told him. 'Yogis can make themselves hot or cold by willpower, and make their tummies full without eating any food.' Karna liked to read about Bollywood most of all. 'I am going to be a film star and then I will turn you into a Maharani,' he told his mother proudly.

She was afraid of pride, though, feared angering the gods with it. 'You must take care not get punished like Dhuriodhana,' she warned him. 'He was the eldest of the Kauravas. A powerful rishi warned him not to fight the Pandavas in the war of the Mahabharata, but Dhuriodhana was too proud to take advice and mocked the rishi by slapping his thighs in a show of strength. Later in the battle he was punished by having both his legs broken.'

'It's only a story,' said Karna. He began to bring back presents for her – shandesh, oranges, saffron, betel nut, little pots of warm dahi, a handful of lychees, telling her that he had earned the money carrying a lady's bag or showing a foreigner the way. 'You must be earning well, my son,' said Dolly with pride. 'But please don't spend so much of it on these luxury items. We need rice and another cloth to wrap round us at night.'

He did not tell her that the gifts he brought were really stolen. She had funny, old-fashioned notions about morality and he did not know what her reaction might be if she found out.

Cricket became the craze all over Calcutta and the streets were filled with boys and young men bowling, fielding, batting. Lorries, their drivers pretending they had broken down, blocked the entrances to streets, increased the traffic blocks, so as to allow cricket matches to take place in peace and untroubled by passing vehicles. Karna and other little pavement boys got great bowling practice and improved their batting skills, using rotten oranges for balls and an old box for a wicket just outside the New Market till they were shooed away by porters. For a short while Karna wondered if he would like to be a cricketer instead of a film star.

Dolly felt sad because, in spite of all her son's hopefulness, he would probably amount to nothing because of her. If he had gone to school, she thought, he would have been playing cricket with a proper ball instead of a bruised orange.

As Karna grew older he started to help Dolly pick through the Calcutta rubbish heaps for something saleable, hunting through the debris and competing with other ragged and emaciated men, women and children. And with crows, pye dogs and rats. He began to fight to claim some reusable item, even taking on adults and sometimes winning. Dolly thought he would have been killed ten times over if she was not always on the lookout, and ready to grab him and hold him back when he got into one of these one-sided tussles.

At the time of Koonty's engagement to Pandu it had been decided that Koonty's father would seek another job as Pandu would find it awkward to have his father-in-law working under him. Koonty's father had in fact long had plans to work in Canada, and now the chance had come and Meena and her husband were to emigrate. Shivarani, who had been touring the countryside for months, wrote to say that she would be coming to see her parents before they left and that she was bringing a male friend.

Shivarani arrived by car in the afternoon, and Meena, who had gone through every emotion possible since she woke in the morning, felt quite dizzy as she watched the young man emerge from Shivarani's car. Her joy was overtaken by fluster as Bhima fully revealed himself. She seemed hesitant and reluctant as she ushered the young man to take a seat on the verandah, and told her maid to bring sweets and tea.

Laxshmi, a stocky, sensible woman, who had been abandoned by her smuggler husband on giving birth to a fourth daughter, Bika, hurried off suppressing a smile and wondering how Mem was going to handle this.

Meena did her best to be polite, inviting Bhima to help himself to yet another misti from the salver when Laxshmi returned and then sending the maid to make cold nimbu pani, 'For I am sure, Mr Bhima, that you must be very hot after that dreadful journey from Calcutta.' But she told her husband later, 'I am really worried now. It will be worse if Shivarani marries this fellow than if she never gets married at all.'

'She has never even suggested marrying him,' protested the husband. 'I expect he is merely a college friend or fellow politician. She talks to him quite coldly, as though she does not even like him.'

'Are you blind, Ogo? She cannot keep her eyes from the fellow and when she looks at him it is as though there is not another person in the world. Of course she is thinking of marrying him.'

'I can't see there's all that much wrong with him,' the husband said. 'His face is rather scarred but Shivarani said he got the wound because he was saving her life in Naxalbari.'

'It's not the scar,' snapped Meena impatiently. 'That is not the problem though it is certainly unsightly.'

'I agree he's a big young fellow, but that's OK too, I should have thought. Till now the men have always been too short.'

'He's a dalit, Ogo. How is it possible that you could not see? He may be well-spoken and educated, but anyone can see from the blackness of his skin that he is an outcaste.'

The zamindar gave a farewell party for his departing manager during which he told Shivarani, 'Pandu will be managing the estate from now on and I will not be employing anyone so the bungalow will be empty. You are welcome to take it over as your home if you wish.'

Shivarani was touched. When her parents told her that they were leaving the country she had felt worried for she did not have enough money to rent a place in Calcutta. 'Thank you,' she said. 'That really takes a big weight from my mind.'

Pandu was so busy with his cows these days that he hardly noticed the matter of Shivarani's friend or even the departure to Canada of his parents-in-law. His Jersey herd were causing great excitement in Hatipur. The local cows were sharply horned and half the size. Daily crowds gathered at the byre to look at the new cows, asking each other, 'Are they buffaloes?' Bending to peer at the Jersey udders, which were four times bigger at least than those of the local cows, they would emit gasps of wordless wonder. They stared, stunned with awe, as the mighty steaming buckets of yellow milk given by these Billaty cows were carried from stall to dairy. They had never seen anything like it. 'We are lucky to get three cups a day from one of ours. These creatures are not of this world, but are provided by the gods,' came the eventual village pronouncement. Pindu feared that these compliments were bringing down curses from an envious deity for each month there came a new bovine disaster, sending Pandu dashing to the gwala for advice. But these foreign cows did not react to the local medicines of turmeric, tamarind, and mustard oil. They developed sicknesses that the gwala had never seen. Three cows died of redwater. The cowman passed cow pox from teat to teat till all were too sore and lumpy to be milked. The heaviest yielder got mastitis and was treated with antibiotics squeezed up into her teats from a tube after which her milk was undrinkable for two weeks. Three quarters of the calves were male and were distributed among local farmers to be used as plough-pullers, till no more were needed and still more male calves were born.

'In the West these surplus animals would be used for meat,' sighed Pandu, 'but here in our Hindu land I cannot think of an answer. There seems no end to the problems.'

At first it was difficult to sell the milk. The people of Bengal were used to pure white buffalo milk and looked on the golden cream of Jersey milk with suspicion. Eventually Arjuna's father found a dairy in Calcutta which catered to a sophisticated sort of Memsahib. But after only a month of the arrangement there was a blockade. The Naxalites closed the road for a week in protest at one of theirs being murdered. The blockade was lifted. Pandu tried to get the milk into town again but on the following day the group who had committed the murder closed the roads in retaliation for the retaliation.

Pandu lost the market in Calcutta.

Before he bought the cows, Pandu had gone to see his friend, the minister for dairy development.

'A government chilling tanker will collect your milk once it reaches a hundred litres,' he was told.

Day after day, as the quantity rose, the hope of government salvation drew closer. At last the day came. A hundred litres was in the tank. Pandu contacted his friend, the minister.

It took a week of lost milk for Pandu to discover that the chilling tanker had been a figment of the minister's hopeful imagination.

Pandu decided to deliver it to the chilling centre himself. This was at Barrackpur, on the outskirts of Calcutta, requiring the milk to be driven, unchilled, for four hours. They began milking the cows at three so as to get it to the centre before the sun rose and the weather grew hot.

At the end of the week Pandu went to collect his money. And found he had been fined for selling watered milk.

He protested, 'I am with the milk from the moment it is taken from the cows to the moment I deliver it to you. There is no way water could have got in.'

'Perhaps the cows are not of sufficient quality,' suggested the manager.

'These are Jersey cows. Their milk is the creamiest in Europe.'

'Ah, Billaty cows, I have heard of this being a problem. Their milk is very low in butterfat.'

A government official was sent to test the milk at the moment of milking. He pronounced it well within the desired range. 'Good for a Billaty cow,' he said. 'Though of course the milk of a desi cow is much higher in butterfat.'

Pandu returend to the chilling centre with his milk and once again was penalised.

This time the manager looked sympathetic. 'You see, the system is that there are fellows putting water into their milk and taking credit from others.'

'But I thought you had people overseeing,' protested Pandu.

The manager shrugged. 'But who is to oversee the overseer? These fellows are being bribed by those who are watering. This is our problem. So long as the bulk turns out sufficient butterfat content then this is OK. Your milk is taking the burden of many double-dealers.'

Pandu arrived next morning and approached the overseer. 'This is for you,' he said, pressing a bundle of notes into the man's hand. 'And from now on I hope my milk will be acceptable.' He did not like the idea of bribery but when it is a question of survival it must be done.

The man paused for a moment, surveyed the money bundle, then thrust it back into Pandu's hand. 'We do not take bribes from people like yourself, Sahib.'

'What is wrong with me?'

'You have a friendship with the dairy minister and know officers of the police. We take money only from the poor humble man, who stands in the corner wrapped in his blanket. It is dangerous to take bribes from people with such friends as yourself.'

Pandu returned to Hatibari, defeated. 'We will have to get rid of these cows,' he told Koonty sadly. 'I love them but we cannot afford to keep them if we can't sell the milk.'

'We should go in for cheese – it doesn't need to be sold so fast,' said Koonty. A few days later, Gadhari found her sister-in-law, her sari hitched up, pummelling curd in the dairy. 'You are letting down the dignity of this family,' she cried. 'Leave this kind of thing to the servants and other lower castes.'

The remaining cows began to acclimatise. The cheese was a success. Koonty took several large rounds of it in the jeep to Calcutta where the first shop she showed it to snapped it up. The Calcutta Club put in a big order. Tolley followed suit. Even when there was a blockade, things were not lost as the cheeses could wait till the roads re-opened.

The yields of the eleven remaining cows improved. Their daughters matured and though giving less milk, were proving hardier, less prone to disease. Things went well. They took on a head cowman. Planted more roses. Bought a new chandelier. Began work on building a bank to keep the flooding out. They put Arjuna's name down for Doon school, where his cousins already went but for now he went to the local school where, almost at once, he fell in love. 'She is Laxshmi's daughter, Bika, and she's bigger than me, and she's the most beautiful girl in the world.'

Boodi Ayah was shocked. 'It is not suitable for a child of his age to talk of love.'

The misti wallah's sons, Ravi and Rahul, joined a gang of young Marxists, among whose members were the two young men who had returned from college and never found jobs. The gang, wearing tight white trousers and dark glasses, would swagger around the village, snatching up a fruit from this stall, a sweet from that one, the shopkeepers making no protest, because these boys were trouble and had power. The one-eyed Communist leader, Nitai Mandel, began to worry about the excesses of the boys which he felt were giving Communism a bad name and turning people against them.

When Ravi was fifteen and Rahul sixteen, their sister became pregnant and the outraged brothers joined her parents in giving her a beating, but through her sobs she said that a wealthy local man had raped her. Raging with fury, the brothers ran to Nitai Mandel. 'You must send people to execute the rapist. It is your duty as the leader of our local Communists.'

Nitai Mandel sighed. 'How many times have I told you we must not fritter away our political advantages with acts of revenge. And also too much violence turns people from the cause.'

'But this is a question of justice,' raged Ravi.

Nitai would not give in. 'I forbid it,' he said. 'This is a matter for the law and the police and it will give our party a bad name. You must go and demand that the police take action in this matter.'

Even when Ravi said, 'They refuse to take action – they are saying that my sister has invented the charge out of shame,' Nitai would not give in.

'I have always told you he is a dinosaur,' said Ravi. 'He is in the pay of the zamindars and what can you expect? The responsibility is ours now.' Next day five young Marxists walked onto Hatipur railway station, where the accused rapist stood waiting for the Calcutta train. As the man tried to explain that the girl had come to him willingly and had said she was in love with him, Ravi stabbed him in the stomach. Then they hacked off their victim's head which was later found stuck on a pole in the village with a note saying, 'This is what happens to the rich men when they rape our women.' Although four hundred people were waiting on the station, no one admitted to witnessing the murder. When Ravi was questioned by the police, he had ten young men to swear he had been playing cards with them. After the episode, Ravi became hero-worshipped by the young Marxists who began following him instead of listening to Nitai Mandel. When Ravi said that something must be done about the price of rice, older boys including his brother, Rahul, eagerly went with him to the mill. The miller refused to lower the price and that night a home-made bomb was thrown into his house, killing the mill owner and his two-year-old daughter. Once again the police never found the killers. The gang became increasingly influential. If a Marxist was arrested in Calcutta or beaten up in Haringhata by members of another political party they would ignore Nitai Mandel's objections and shut down the village in protest, then smash up any shop that opened, beat anyone seen going to work or set fire to traffic that inadvertently blundered into their blockade. None of the boys had a job. Their income came from protection money from the Hatipur shops and businesses and when they needed anything, from a pair of shoes to a sack of rice, they simply took it. The owners never protested. It was not worth it. You could have your mill burnt to the ground and your legs broken if you stood up to the young Marxists. The fathers of these boys were shocked at this appropriation of other people's goods and accused their sons of stealing even when the boys maintained that they were merely taking payment for their work in providing the village with security and justice.

So when Ravi arrived with his gang at the Hatibari elephant gates, the two durwans only hesitated a moment before letting them in. The durwans lived in the village, had wives and children, and knew all about the ruthless Ravi, son of the misti wallah. Ravi and his followers shouted Communist slogans as they marched up the drive towards the Hatibari house.

'Oi, Dadoo,' they called when they reached the marble steps.

Kuru Dadoo came out of the house and greeted the young men with a courteous namaste. 'What do you want?' he asked. He recognised them. He recognised Ravi, son of his friend, the misti wallah, who had been a guest at Pandu's wedding.

'We have come to take the cows,' Ravi said. 'They are being requisitioned. Call your son. Tell him to give up his cattle for the cause.'

'My son is not here at the moment,' said Kuru Dadoo. 'But what you are doing is not right. I know all of you. You are like my family. I know your fathers. What will they say? This is theft, not requisition.'

'The day of the zamindar is over,' shouted Ravi. And to his followers, 'Go, take the cows since the old man will not give them up.'

But the other young men began to feel flustered. Kuru Dadoo was not the mill owner or some newcomer to the village. He was the heart of the village. Almost every one of them had benefited from him in some way. Kuru Dadoo had given dowries, had paid for weddings, had financed hospital bills. Kuru Dadoo was everybody's grandfather and however strongly these young men felt about their cause, they still felt respect for their elders. Gradually it became the voice of the zamindar which sounded the loudest and the longest while the voices of the rowdy Communists grew quieter and, eventually, silent.

They had respected him for too long. They could not challenge him. They departed silently, their heads a little low. For a while the only voice that could be heard was Ravi, shouting bitterly, accusing his followers of cowardice and disloyalty to the cause. It was only when they were once again outside the Hatibari grounds and on the road that the rest began chanting again.

'Next time they won't give up so easily,' said Pandu when he got back.

That evening a marigold garland was put round Daisy's neck and she was led through a delighted, fascinated village and offered to Nitai Mandel.

'Good cow, good cow,' Nitai Mandel said, patting Daisy lovingly on her blonde neck. 'And no more worry for you, Zamindar Sahib.' One bit of trouble from any of these young hotheads and I will have three hundred men out at your place to put a stop to it – for though the boys do not listen to me any more, their fathers and their uncles do.' Then, addressing the cow herself, he said, 'Welcome to our house, my daughter, and may you be happy here.'

'But his men could have taken all twelve cows from you,' said Arjuna that night. 'Why was he happy with only one?'

'Because we had honoured him,' Pandu said. 'This is something

you have to know. How much people will do for you if you
honour them.'

4

THE CURSE OF A YOGI

Pale before the unknown warrior,
gathered nations part in twain.
Conqueror of hostile cities,
lofty Karna treads the plain.

Dolly was often ill and gradually the fear grew in her that she would die and leave her little boy alone in the world. She had kept Karna's golden disc in a cloth bag round her waist all these years. Sometimes she would take it out and examine the decorative elephants round the edge; run her finger over the scrolled words, let the heavy gold of the links run through her hands, and work out ways in which this jewel might secure Karna's future if she should be taken from him.

When Karna was five she opened her eyes to find him standing over her, sobbing. He had, he said, been trying to wake her for an hour. She realised she must have lost consciousness and knew she must do something soon. She would take Karna to Hatipur, and show him the place, tell him that if she died he must go there and force these people to take responsibility for him. And when the little boy kept on crying she told him, 'You must be brave, Karna. You are called after a great hero and you must be like him.' She had told him the story often: how the Mahabharata Karna pretended to be a Brahmin and went to get teaching from the rishi, Parashumara, how the teacher fell asleep during a lesson with his head on Karna's lap and a worm began to burrow into the chela's thigh. The pain was terrible but the boy, not wishing to disturb his teacher, did not move and Parashumara only woke when Karna's blood began to flow. She had not yet told him the other half of Karna's story, though. She thought he was too young to hear how, when the teacher woke and understood what had happened, he realised Karna must have lied to him, for no Brahmin could have endured such pain. The teacher therefore cursed Karna so that, though the young man would know mantras to give him great mastery of body and spirit, when the battle moment came, he would be unable to recall them.

Dolly found out that Hatipur was a village forty miles away, only three hours by train. She began to save every paisa for the railway tickets, hardly eating anything herself and giving Karna so little that he would yowl with hunger at the end of his meal. For the first time in her life, on the days she felt well enough, she began to beg. There were days when she did not even have the strength for this but all the same, after a few weeks, she got together twelve rupees then went with Karna to the station and asked for two return tickets to Hatipur.

'Rupees forty,' said the man.

Suddenly Dolly felt she could not go on. She sank to the ground and sat there, overwhelmed with hopelessness.

'What's the matter, Ma?' begged Karna, tugging at the end of her sari. 'Come on. Let's get on the train.' He had been anticipating this moment for days, ever since his mother had told him that she nearly had enough money for the ticket. 'Come on, Ma. Get up or it will go without us.'

'We're not going,' said Dolly and she felt tears fill her eyes. 'We don't have enough money.'

Karna wilted with disappointment for a while. He had been looking forward to his first ride on a train. He said, 'Don't cry, Ma. I will get lots of money for the tickets. I will polish shoes all day long till I get enough.'

'It will take too long,' said Dolly. 'We need to go soon.'

'Then I will find a quicker way to make money.' Karna thought of all those foreign memsahibs who went shopping in New Market with their money-bags hanging over their shoulders. Everyone knew that such people carried huge amounts of rupees with them and he felt he could easily snatch a bag and run off before anyone was able to catch him.

Sadly Dolly shook her head. 'There might not be enough time for anything, my son,' she said. 'I might not be here by the time you earn enough money.'

'But where will you be?' He squatted beside her and looked into her face. 'Ma, Ma, where are you going?' but she did not answer.

She could not move. 'Don't cry,' she said. 'I'm just tired, that's why I said that. Leave me alone for a little while, son. Go and look round the station, see the trains, while I have a rest.' Her voice was so quiet that he could hardly hear her over the roar of trains coming and going.

He gave her a last look of worry before reluctantly going off.

Dolly was wondering if she would ever get up again and thinking that a lot of her weakness might be from lack of food, when a passing passenger dropped a banana. It fell at her feet as though the gods had sent it to her. If she ate that, who knows what strength might come to her? She was reaching out for it when she was struck a great blow on the side of her face and a clawlike hand snatched the food away. A man with a hideously scarred face, dressed in grey rags, was scowling down at her furiously. 'This is my part of the station and everything that falls on it belongs to me,' he told her. She pressed her hand against her smarting cheek and watched numbly as the man strode off, ripping away the banana skin and devouring the fruit with ravenous gulps.

Karna had found a standing train and examined it with delight. He was determined to make up for his disappointment at not travelling today. Looking from right to left, making sure the car attendant polishing the outside brass was not looking, he sneaked into the empty air-conditioned compartment and sat down on the soft plush seat. The springs gave way with a groan that filled his body with joy.

He had never sat on anything so soft in his life. He was breathing in the smell of cold rubber and foreign cigarette smoke when the car attendant burst in. The man grabbed Karna by the arm, dragged the child to the door and flung him out onto the platform where he fell heavily onto the concrete. As Karna struggled to his feet, wiping the dust out of his cuts, the man shouted, 'Next time you get a beating as well,' and picking up his duster, went on with his polishing.

A woman who lived on the railway line, in the ten-foot area between the buffers and where the trains actually stopped, looked up from her cooking and saw Karna crash onto the ground. 'He's only a little boy. Have you no pity?'

The car man gave a grunt of contempt and moved on to the next carriage.

'Are you hurt, little man?' the woman called to Karna. 'Come. Are you hungry?' Karna, enthralled by the smell coming from the clay pot bubbling over a fire of newspaper, edged towards her and looked down. 'Yes, I am hungry,' he said.

'Come, eat with us,' said the woman, smiling and she beckoned him down. 'Come on, don't just stand there.'

'But there is also my mother,' said Karna. And he pointed to the place, far along the platform, where Dolly was sitting.

'Bring her. There is enough for all, I am sure,' said the woman.

Nearby, squatting on the rail, sat a group of boys playing cards. At the woman's words, they looked up and said in outraged tones, 'Ma, there is hardly enough for us. How can you give any away?'

'Didn't you see the fellow throw the poor little boy onto the platform?' demanded the woman fiercely. 'People like us must stick together.' And to Karna, 'Go on, darling. Bring your mummy here and let her join the meal with us.'

'Come, sit down here with us,' said the woman when Dolly shakily arrived. 'You don't look very well at all. Let me help you.' It was quite a struggle for Dolly to clamber down onto the rails.

'My name is Savitri,' the woman said as Karna leapt down after his mother. 'These are my sons and this is my daughter.' A little girl with ribboned hair and glass bangles on her wrist, looked up from chillies that she was chopping on a bit of waste board and smiled.

As he ate, Karna could not take his eyes off the trains. This was the most exciting and terrifying place he had ever been. He was on a level with their wheels and every now and again a train would come roaring upon them and stop so late and close that it seemed certain to Karna and his mother that it could not fail to crush them.

'It's all right,' said Savitri, seeing them flinch. 'They always stop in time. We have been here for six months and not one of the hundreds of trains has ever hit the buffers.'

'I wish I could live here like you,' Karna said.

'There are better places.' Savitri smiled at his enthusiasm. 'The worst thing is the noise at night, with trains coming and going so much, though you do get used to it. And we have so little room. But we can get everything we need off the station. Fuel for our fire, even most of our food.'

Later, as Dolly and Karna made their way back into town, Dolly thought that the kindness had done as much to restore her as the hot meal of rice and spiced dhall.

In the days that followed she tried to get work as a maid again, but word of her ill health had gone round and no one would employ her. She began to think of other ways of getting to Hatipur. She considered trying to travel without a ticket but she had never stolen anything in her life and did not know how to begin.

She began to approach people selling goods – the fruit wallah, the khatal wallah, the seller of New Market flowers, offering to deliver their product to Hatipur. She offered to carry sweets for the misti wallah and mustard oil from the food store. Her proposal was always greeted with scornful laughter. 'Hatipur? Those illiterate peasants wouldn't know a rose if they saw one.' Or, 'How would you expect to get milk all that way without it going bad?' or 'Those villagers wouldn't be able to appreciate the sophisticated produce of Calcutta even if they had enough money to pay for it.'

She returned to the railway station, in case there was someone there wanting a delivery taken to Hatipur. 'I can't understand why you want to go to this place so much,' said Savitri. 'Still, if I hear of anything I'll tell you.' But no one at the station wanted Dolly's services.

Karna, too, was mystified by his mother's endless efforts to reach a place called Hatipur, and begged her, 'Couldn't we go on a train to somewhere else? Couldn't we go somewhere that doesn't cost so much?'

But she insisted it had to be Hatipur.

'Why? What's there?' he would demand.

But she only said, 'I'll tell you when you're bigger.'

She set off round the small industries, offering her services. After three weeks, when she had given up hope, a manufacturer of soap, swayed by the longing in Dolly's eyes and a need to expand his business, said he would pay her train fare and a little over to take his product to the village.

The soap factory owner had given her a little cash, saying, 'It will give our business a bad name if you are dressed in such rags so please be wearing a clean outfit when you deliver our goods.'

She had bought new clothes not only for herself but for Karna as well and there was even a little money left over which she kept by for emergencies.

On the morning of their departure Dolly washed Karna all over with one of the soap bars, massaging the foam over the little boy's squeezed-shut face and then rinsing him with water poured from her cupped hands. The loss of one won't even be noticed, she thought. She would pay for it herself.

Dolly had been tempted to spend the last of her money on a rickshaw to the station so that Karna's white socks would not get soiled, but in the end decided to keep it, and buy the two of them a hot meal in the village.

When they reached the station the train was already in.

Dolly gave her son a sandal-perfumed shove saying, 'Go on, Karna, get into that compartment there.'

Savitri saw Dolly getting onto the train and looked amazed.

'We're going to Hatipur,' Dolly called.

'I have never understood why you are always wanting to go to that place but all the same I am happy for you.' Everybody on the station had been laughing at Dolly's crazy desire.

Dolly, telling herself one more won't matter much either, prised a soap bar from her box and, shouting, 'Here is something for you,' threw it down to her friend. Savitri caught it and sniffed with delight before looking up at Dolly with a smile of gratitude. The scarred man who had grabbed the banana was picking through a pile of rubbish and did not recognise Dolly standing on the train, wearing her new clothes. But as Dolly stood at the train door and touched her cheek she wished she could have a banana to drop now. She would watch with her arms crossed like a memsahib while he grovelled and struggled at her feet. Already she felt like someone from another world altogether.

Karna was smiling and prancing with delight.

'Stand calmly like a rich boy,' Dolly kept urging him, but he could not. His legs were dancing on their own. Today nobody was going to throw Karna off the train because Dolly had bought tickets. The train gave a lurch. 'Hurry, Karna, now we must find a compartment,' said Dolly. She was shaking with nerves for she was finally getting to Hatipur and she didn't want to, any more.

As she pressed her way along the crowded corridor of the third-class compartment Dolly felt anxiety giving way to hope. She felt almost well. Perhaps, after all this time of hunger, rags and homelessness, she was going to have an income and she would not die after all. If things went well, she thought, the soap factory might go on employing her. She might be able to afford a little rented room in the bustee again after a year or two, with a window and some furniture. Her body ached for a charpoy bed. They might even manage to afford a mosquito net after she was given a salary.

In the days before Adhiratha lost his sight they had gone on holiday by train, travelling second class, not third like now. A waiter had come to their compartment and taken an order for their meal. At the next station, an hour or two later, another waiter had brought chicken curry, dhall, chupatties, saffron rice served in china plates on a metal tray, a white cloth over the steaming food to keep the flies off. Dolly's mouth watered at the memory as she gently shoved Karna onwards and lugged her boxes. They passed one full carriage after another until, by the time the train had begun to get up speed she came to one that seemed slightly less packed than the rest.

Struggling in, she wedged her boxes between a basket of noisy ducklings and another of mangoes. The compartment was packed with purchases; new shoes, sugarcane sticks, transistor radios, bales of cloth and kapok, five-gallon tins of mustard oil, pans of live fish, flopping. Dolly at last managed to squeeze Karna between two men on the seat and squatted on the floor herself, her bottom resting on cracked heels, holding the end of her new tinsel-trimmed sari out of the dirt.

Passengers were grumbling to each other, one man saying, 'I couldn't sell my milk and now my kujahs are returning even though they have crossed the holy river twice. You would expect the goddess to be more kind to people who respect her.'

'Hush, hush,' his wife urged. 'You are insulting the goddess and she will take revenge on us.'

'But he is right,' another man said. 'My cabbages have crossed six times in a week and still, in spite of so many blessings, failed to catch a market.'

People began to joke, saying, 'It is a kindness of the goddess to save people from having to eat those wrinkled things. That is why she would not let you sell them in Calcutta even though your train went over the river bridges.'

Dolly hardly heard them. Her attention was on Karna and she was feeling proud because he looked like any rich person's child in his yellow T-shirt and blue nylon shorts.

One of the women examined Karna's face then asked Dolly, 'Where did you get him?'

Dolly blinked. The question had always made her frightened. Once a policeman had tried to take Karna away from her saying she must have kidnapped him and she had had to run to escape.

'For he is a nice-looking child,' the woman added, as though it was unlikely that a true child of Dolly's would look nice.

A discussion followed. Karna was scrutinised from every side, different people making pronouncements, most agreeing that, in spite of his skinniness, Karna was a handsome boy.

Dolly wished they would not talk like that, fearing that such a compliment might make the gods jealous. If she had been able she would have burnt chillies now to ward off the evil eye. Karna gazed at his admirers with honey-coloured eyes and swung his legs ostentatiously, hoping they were noticing his new Bata sandals and tall white knee socks. Dolly had felt proud of Karna when she had finished dressing him in his new clothes but now she wished he was back in rags so that these people would not pay all this dangerous attention to him.

One of the women said, 'He reminds me somewhat of Dilip Baswani.' There came cries of horror.

'The face cut is entirely different,' said one.

'Also the ears are of another shape altogether.'

'And even the complexion of this child is of a deeper hue.'

'Our Dilip is of a pleasant plumpness and this is one skinny fellow. There is no likeness between them,' said one woman with indignation and she leant forwards and peered into Karna's face.

He stuck his tongue out at her.

Reeling back she gasped, 'See, see, how could anyone compare the divine Dilip to such a mannerless urchin.'

'Don't be so rude,' Dolly ordered her son.

But the first woman continued to insist she saw a likeness and turning on Dolly accusingly, said, 'With such a beautiful child you should be feeding him better.'

Dolly felt sad but asked, 'Who is Dilip Baswani?'

There rose a hubbub of amazement. 'But how can it be that you have not seen the Sun God of the cinema Mahabharata?'

Dolly had not been to the cinema for so long that she had forgotten

Dilip Baswani. Trying to make light of it all she gave a laugh and said, 'My little Karna is forever saying he wants to be a film star,' but thought to herself, 'It is because he is wearing good clothes. No one thought he looked like any film star when he was in his rags.'

'What do you think, little man?' asked one of the women and pinched Karna's cheek with a thumb and forefinger, leaving a red mark. 'Would you like to be a film star?'

'Oh yes,' cried Karna. 'That's exactly what I'm going to be. There will be great big posters of me all over Calcutta when I get famous.'

Everyone laughed indulgently.

When the train crossed the bridge that spanned the sacred river Jummuna, the women all rose from their seats and scattering thermos flasks, betel nuts, gaudily-clad babies and paper rolls of popcorn, folded their hands. Facing the frothing water that was dark as beaten cocoa, they bowed their heads in a namaste of respect. Even the sellers of the unsold milk and cabbages rose and salaamed, for who knows, next time the goddess might be kinder and to deny her respect might make matters much much worse.

Dolly too struggled up from the floor and bowed exceptionally low, for what she felt for this river was not only respect but an enormous gratitude as well. It had given her Karna.

The train chuntered on over the Indian countryside and Dolly swayed from side to side, her toes sliding among cigarette stubs, betel-scarlet spit, oily newspaper, the leaves of bananas in which curd rice had been rolled. Her feet were bare for there had not been enough money for her to buy shoes.

Karna sat awed and thrilled among the nicotine-flavoured husbands who cuddled goods too precious for the floor, breakable china, bottles of arrack and whisky and a new TV set still in its box. He would own a TV when he became a film star, he decided, and imagined himself and his mother sitting side by side, the blue light flickering on their faces, watching him acting the part of the Sun God. He had caught a glimpse of one once, in a shop display, showing a film of gods and goddess wearing white gowns with golden haloes. They were all nicely fat and were seated on a cloud, singing. One of the gods wore a wristwatch. Karna had stood enraptured till the shopkeeper came and drove him off. Remembering it, he decided that as well as a TV he would also find some way of owning a wristwatch like the god had worn, one with a big face and silver hands. The train passed slowly through narrow streets of towns and Karna was able to look into windows and see what the people were doing inside. He saw a woman crushing spices with a stone roller, schoolchildren facing a blackboard and reciting their lesson, a man sitting naked and cross-legged on his veranda massaging oil into his skin, a young boy and girl kissing each other as though they were Europeans. Many of the houses had TV aerials on their roofs, even in these rural towns. Roads of motorcars flowed by, lorries piled high, bullock carts dragging country produce and rice straw, a car fitted with giant posters from which a voice loud-hailed announcements of the latest film. Karna's eyes rushed swiftly from the delights outside to those inside – all these people who, any other day, would have refused to allow him near them. When he was a rich film star, he thought, he would always travel on trains.

At midday the people sitting opposite Karna, a stout bald man and his stouter wife, pulled out a tiffin carrier and took the sections apart. They began to ladle spoonfuls of rich mutton curry onto a couple of stainless steel plates till the compartment was filled with the strong smells of spices and the fats of meat. As though it was a signal the others began to bring out their food as well; banana leaves wrapped round rice and curds, small fat samosas in newspaper, parathas stuffed with mincemeat. Quite soon everyone's jaws were moving except for Karna's and his mother's.

Karna watched his mother's hands, and waited for the moment when she too would bring out some food but she only sat there, her head lowered, and would not look at him. After a long while, when nothing happened, he wriggled to the smallest edge of his seat and watched the fingers of the people opposite carrying the succulent food to their mouths, staring as though his eyes could eat.

After a while the woman, her mouth full, said, 'If you stare any harder your eyes will pop out,' but Karna was like someone hypnotised. Dolly pulled Karna's face against hers and whispered, 'I have kept a little money back in case there is an emergency during our journey. If there is some left over I will buy you a meal in the village. Be brave till then, son.'

But the boy could not take his eyes off the food until after a while the people became restless under the hot gaze of the longing eyes, their expressions petulant, their movements furtive. If it had been possible they would have gone somewhere else to eat, where a ravenous little boy could not see them.

The fat woman stopped eating suddenly, as though she could not bear it. Tipping some water into the cup of her thermos flask lid she rinsed her fingers and wiped them on a small lace hankie, then opening a bag took out an orange.

'Here,' she said, handing it to Karna.

He snatched at it wildly. But before he had time to start peeling, Dolly smacked it out of his hand. 'We are not beggars. Please don't give food to my child.'

People were still eating when the train stopped with a sudden scream of brakes and a ferocious jerk that sent kebabs and keemas, ghugni and begun bhaja shooting over the laps of the eaters and onto Dolly sitting on the floor. Luggage went flying from the racks. Ducklings went tumbling, crockery clattering, the TV thumped over, the cloth bales began unrolling. Karna was flung from his seat and landed, with a splat, onto the basket of mangoes.

The people in the compartment began craning through the window bars. 'Perhaps the train has hit a buffalo.' 'Perhaps the engine driver has been taken ill.' There came the sound of shouting but no one could hear what was being said. 'A customs check, perhaps,' said one man. 'A tree across the line,' suggested another. 'Yes, it must be that. A tree.' 'Sometimes after the monsoon the river floods the railway line and the trains can't proceed.' 'Or the driver has gone on strike. This often happens.' They waited, wondering. Someone opened the door and scrambled down onto the line.

'Come back inside,' commanded his wife. 'The train might suddenly start again and then what will you do?'

The mango basket was covered with a piece of hessian, attached with string. While the attention of the passengers was diverted by the sudden stopping of the train, Karna surreptitiously began to unpick the string and pull the cloth back. 'When I am rich,' thought Karna, sniffing deeply, filling his nostrils with mango scent, 'I am going to own a mango orchard and then my mother and I will eat mangoes all day long.'

The shouting was growing louder. Suddenly the man who had got down began scrambling up again. 'It is dacoits,' he gasped as he clambered back inside the compartment. People hurriedly pulled down the latches of the door and tried to thrust their purchases under the seats where they would not be seen. From further down the train there came a sudden howl. A girl's voice let out a shriek.

Karna found a mango that had split and, making sure no one was looking, dipped his fingers into the pulp. A man said, 'I am not waiting inside here to be killed,' and clutching his basket of Calcutta purchases, leapt over the mango basket, kicking Karna on the head. Ignoring the boy's outraged yowl and squelching mango pulp in his chappals, the man began to open the outer door.

At once the other passengers began screaming, 'Keep it shut, you fool, or they'll get in.'

The man continued to wrestle with the door latches and a woman hit him on the head with her thermos flask, shouting, 'Shut it, shut it, you salah, or all of us are dead.' He fell back, sparkling glass and water drips showering from his hair.

There came a banging on the door and angry men's voices roaring, 'You in there. Open up.'

Several people near the door put their shoulders to it as it began to heave. The bolt was bending. The women began pulling off their gold earrings and stuffing them down the front of their cholis. In terror Dolly pulled out the cloth bag that held Karna's inheritance.

Even as she hunted the foul heaps of rubbish, and had nothing at all to eat, she had never once been tempted to sell Karna's chain and without it now she would not be able to carry out her plan, and secure Karna's future. She clutched it tightly as the two dacoits burst the door bar.

The passengers cringed back into their seats. Karna sucked his fingers. The dacoits wore army boots and a sort of tattered khaki uniform, and grubby red bandanas.

One, smiling broadly over a luxuriant moustache, said, 'Salaam, Hello. Pass over jewels, money and watches.' He spoke as though he was the conductor asking to see tickets. 'Come on. No need to be afraid.' He leant over and pinched one of the cuddled babies on its cheek.

A woman mutely showed him her bare arms as evidence that she had no bangles and another gestured to her naked throat, while Dolly felt her heart beating heavily against the hidden chain in her palm.

'I have nothing, only this two rupees,' the people started saying. Men turned their pockets inside out to prove the truth of this, women shook open their handbags.

One dacoit reached out to the nearest woman and, taking her choli at the neck, gave it a yank. Money, a watch, earrings, a necklace and bangles tumbled to the floor.

The dacoit laughed and picked up the treasures. 'Come on, the rest of you. Let's have it. No more tricking.' But men and women had started pulling out their precious things even before he spoke, rootling in their underclothes, inside their saris, under their kurtas, groping down the back of the seats.

Soon the two dacoits had their pockets bulging and turned their attention to the things on the floor. One opened the outer door while the other peered into bales and bundles, finding one full of cabbages and tossing it, with a scoffing laugh, onto the rails, discovering the TV set and the radios and setting them outside carefully. They joked with each other as though they found the contents of the boxes and baskets hilarious, and stopped every now and again to give a child a tickle under the chin, or blow a joking kiss to a terrified young woman. The kujahs were hurled to explode on the rails in a spray of terracotta and souring milk. One dacoit, saying, 'Come on out and have a walk,' shattered the duckling basket with a kick and in a moment released ducklings were everywhere. Out went the shoes and the sugar cane, the melons and the bottles of arrak.

When they came to Dolly's soap they began to argue over whether it was worth saving or chucking and in the end it got the latter treatment. Dolly let out a sob as she saw her only hope for the future bursting open over the rails. The sound made a dacoit turn his attention onto her. Grinning, he jerked at her choli, ripping the cloth, while Karna watched from his basket, his eyes round with dismay. Now his hot dinner in the village would be gone. The dacoits were going to take away Dolly's money.

The dacoit tore the cloth away then pulled at her sari, jerking the folds out, but nothing fell from her body. Then the bandit saw her clenched hand and began to prise at her fingers with his, ordering her, 'Open it.'

Dolly clung frantically to Karna's chain.

'Give it to him,' urged the other passengers. 'He'll only hurt you if you don't.'

But they would have to kill her or chop her hand off to get possession of Karna's chain.

Karna suddenly emerged, orange faced, from his basket and shouted, 'Stop doing that to my mother.' Jumping up he caught at the bandit's hand and tried to pull it away. As though swatting off an insect, the dacoit whacked Karna aside and took out a heavy, curved-bladed knife.

'No, no, no,' screamed Dolly. 'Please, oh, please.'

Holding her arm tightly the man raised the knife.

Dolly was screaming, writhing, frantic, but could not get away. The knife came down and bit deep into Dolly's arm as Karna, yelling, launched himself at the man.

The dacoit dropped the knife, let go of Dolly and grabbed Karna by the hair. Dangling the kicking screaming child he called out, 'Look at this disgusting thing, Raj.' Karna tried to struggle free as he swiftly licked the last drops of mango pulp from his fingers.

'Eh, Mohun, throw it out of the door with the other rubbish,' laughed the second dacoit as he chucked a hessian bundle of bedding, but Karna, who had already been thrown from a train once and knew what it felt like, grabbed tightly at the fingers gripping his hair. 'Don't dare, you banchod,' he screeched.

'What a hero.' The dacoit swung Karna back, preparing to hurl him but the boy clung like a kitten with claws, gripping the man's ears, his fingers, the back of his shirt.

'He is only a little boy. He is only six. Let him go,' yelled Dolly, wrapping the sari end round her arm to staunch the bleeding. Her fingers were still gripping the precious medallion. Karna's jaws were chattering and his voice shrill. 'Put me down. My head is hurting.'

Mohun put his face close to Karna's, grinned and asked, 'Aren't you afraid of me? Everybody else on the train is.'

'No. I'm not afraid of anything,' the child yelled. But all the same his whole body was shaking like paddy in a monsoon storm and his teeth were clacking together so hard that they sounded like dice being shaken.

'Why aren't you afraid of me?' laughed the dacoit.

'Because I hate you,' screeched Karna. 'Because you hurt my mother. When I am grown up I shall never hurt people's mothers.'

Mohun gazed down at the tiny defiant figure and with a laugh, dropped the child onto the floor. Then, turning on Dolly, he grabbed her hand with both of his and jerked it open. He saw the gold she was holding, froze and stood staring.

'It's his,' Dolly whispered, gesturing to her son who was struggling from the floor. 'It is all he has.'

The bandit, whose eyes had not left the glittering treasure in Dolly's hand, suddenly seemed to come to some decision. Quickly folding Dolly's fingers over the chain again, he called out to his partner, 'This small fellow has defeated me. Come on, Raj. That's all we can get from here.'

As the dacoits reached the door Mohun called back to Karna, 'You can join us when you are older. We want brave men like you.'

'When I am old enough I shall find you to fight with you, not to join you,' shouted Karna, massaging his head.

'Hush hush,' implored the people in the compartment. 'They will come back and kill us all,' and Dolly put her hand over her son's mouth to stop him talking, but Mohun only laughed as he jumped down onto the lines.

As soon as they were gone Karna saw the blood on his mother's arm, and was all ready to go after the dacoits again. 'They cut you so I will kill them.' Dolly and other people in the compartment had to hold him back. They began saying, 'You can see that he is the son of the film star, Dilip Baswani. Only the child of the sun god would be strong and brave enough to fight off the dacoits.'

But Dolly slapped Karna, shouting, 'You stupid boy, do you want to be killed?' Tears shot down her cheeks.

'What were you holding?' Karna asked at last, when her fury began to subside. Wrenching himself out of her grip he demanded, 'Let me see it. Why wouldn't you let the dacoits have it?' And he too began to prise at his mother's fingers, trying to get them apart and to see.

'Stop that.' She pushed him away. 'I will show you soon. It is yours and that's why I didn't want them to have it. I would have given it to them if it was mine.'

'Mine,' breathed Karna, who until the new clothes had never before owned anything he had not stolen.

He craned this way and that, trying to see, as she smuggled the secret thing back into a bag at her waist. 'What is it? Why won't you let me see? I want to see it.'

'Be quiet.' He knew this voice. She really meant it this time. He sank back, silent and forlorn, a little boy again instead of a conqueror of dacoits.

She suddenly hugged him. 'As soon as we get to the village I will buy you a hot pilau.'

'But he took your money. I saw him pull your choli,' cried Karna.

She took hold of his hand and pressed it in the fold between her breasts. 'Here,' she whispered. Karna felt the hot damp of her skin under the ripped choli, the softness of her body, the thin hard fold of paper money. 'See.' She was not crying or angry anymore. She was smiling and Karna laughed too because he and his mother had both outwitted the dacoits.

People had already begun rootling among the shattered objects on the line. The owner of the milk found, miraculously, a single kujah unbroken. Dolly and Karna found some of the soap but the packets were soiled and torn.

The train did not leave for hours. The passengers, after they had gathered up whatever they could of their possessions, waited in long and whimpering silence, broken only by the constant piping of the ducklings.

During the night Dolly started to cough and put aside the soap tablets she was trying to clean. Karna struggled up and put his arms round her. He could feel her shivering. 'Are you cold?' When they got back to Calcutta he would get her a shawl, he thought. He would sneak past one of those New Market stalls, snatch one from the stand and rush off along the aisles with it, before the shopkeepers or the watchmen could catch up with him.

She shook her head. 'Just happy because I have you,' she said.

'I will get her pashmina,' he thought. 'Soft and warm. She will stop coughing once I have got the pashmina shawl for her. Or shahtoosh.' Shahtoosh was the wonderful soft wool that came only from the throat of a particular kind of wild mountain sheep and was so fine that a full shawl could be pulled through a finger ring. Maharajas were given shahtoosh shawls as wedding gifts. He was quicker than anyone. Surely he could steal such a shawl for his mother.

The fit at last over, Dolly went on wiping the tarnished bars.

They reached the village of Hatipur in the morning. Dolly felt very weak. She had lost a lot of blood, and the wound hurt. Karna was disappointed. He had expected the platform to be thronging with elephants for otherwise why should this place be called 'Village of Elephants'? He had even been slightly nervous, and wondered how he and his mother would cope among all the gigantic tuskers. But there was not an elephant to be seen anywhere.

He realised his mother was trembling.

'It's OK,' he told her. 'You needn't be afraid. The elephants have all gone.'

'Elephants, you silly. Why are you talking about elephants?' she laughed.

'If it's not the elephants, then why are you shivering?' he asked. 'It's not at all cold now.' Instead of answering, she caught him by the hand as though something urgent had come up. 'We have to go somewhere,' she said and began hurrying him, ignoring his demand for the hot pilau. 'Come, come, don't dawdle.' Lugging her bag of soap samples, she thrust herself and her son through the packed station crowd.

'I am looking for a house called the Hatibari,' she told the ticket collector.

'The Hatibari.' He repeated her question with a hushed tone of respect and, gesturing, told her, 'It is there. That way. Half a mile.'

Suddenly, showing Karna the house of Koonty seemed more important to Dolly than selling soap, eating food or even cleaning herself and her child. The events on the train and her coughing fit in the night had made her realise that she must act quickly. The dacoits would have taken the medallion if it had not been for Karna and then no one would ever believe he was the son of Koonty of Hatibari. Or they might have killed Dolly before she had time to tell Karna how she had found him. She gasped at her first sight of the Hatibari house with its domed roof and multitude of windows. Great trees surrounded it, and the drive leading up to it was flanked with an avenue of Asoka trees. The entrance was protected by high golden gates, the archway of which was formed from two rearing elephants, tusks jutting, trunks touching. At the side sat a durwan on a stool, wearing a pair of heavy spectacles and reading a newspaper.

Dolly had suspected, ever since she had found the baby in the river, that the place must be somewhere of importance, but this palatial home was far grander than anything she had expected. Even in Calcutta she had never seen such a large and awe-inspiring residence as this. Guilt and panic grabbed her because this was where

Karna should have spent his earliest years, not existing, hungry, on a stretch of dirty pavement.

'Does the Maharaja live here?' asked Karna, dancing with excitement, his eyes wide with wonder at the marvel of the place. And then with a shriek of joy, 'Look at the elephants, Ma, look at the elephants.' He felt happy again because, as well as the colossal gateway ones, there were four others, trunks raised, tusks thrusting, carved in pure white marble and vastly larger than life-size, flanking the corners of the roof. 'Or I bet it's the house of Diliswani,' said the little boy remembering the name of the film star to whom he had been compared on the train. 'I shouldn't think even a Maharaja could have enough money to live in a house like this. It must be a film star's house.'

'Dilip Baswani,' corrected his mother vaguely. Her mind was reeling with sorrowful thoughts.

'What is this place? Does Diliswani want to buy your soap?' Karna was asking. 'I want to see the film star.'

The grandly uniformed durwan thrust his glasses to the end of his nose and looked over them at Dolly and her child approaching the gates.

'Is there a lady called Koonty living in this house?' Dolly asked, trying to keep the tremble out of her tone.

'Koonty Memsahib is the wife of the zamindar. What do you want with her?' said the durwan in a tone of irritation.

For a moment Dolly felt as though she had been winded. She tried desperately to get her breathing level before asking her next question. 'Has she any children?'

'She has a son, yes. His name is Arjuna. But what is that to you? Please take your child and leave from here. They don't like to have people hanging around. Go.' He waved an imperious hand at her.

Dolly, still gripping the thrilled Karna by one hand, stood firm. 'Look at this house, Karna. If I am not here you must remember it and come back here because this Koonty must look after you when I am gone . . .'

'Go away and don't talk crazy,' said the man without looking up and returned to his reading. After a while he looked up. 'Why are you standing there? Go off with you.'

Dolly sat Karna at her side and showed him the medallion. 'Now look at this. You can read now, can't you?' For the first time Karna was able to examine the secret thing that his mother always kept inside the waist of her sari.

'This is what I would not let the dacoits take away. This is yours. Read what's written there.' She pointed to the word, 'Hatibari'.

Laboriously Karna struggled through the letters, then stared from the medallion to the elephant gates where this same word was written. He looked bewildered.

Dolly lifted the chain and hung it round the child's neck. 'From now on, because you are brave and because you are old enough, I do not need to keep it for you. You can wear it yourself, now, my son,' she said.

'But what does it mean?' asked Karna. 'Why is Hatibari written on the gates and on my medal too?'

'This chain was round your neck when I found you as a baby in this very river. You were lying in the hand of Durga, and must have floated forty miles downstream to Calcutta.' It took the little boy a long time to understand what Dolly was telling him.

Dolly tucked the medallion under Karna's shirt and went on, 'If anything ever happens to me you must come back here again. If I go away and can't come back to you again, you must bring it to this house. You must show it to Koonty and force her to understand that you are her son.'

'But you are my mother, not this Koonty person,' he wailed.

'Haven't you been listening to the things I told you?' asked Dolly. 'Anyway that is what you must say.'

Karna stared at her blankly.

'Do you hear me?' commanded Dolly.

'But where are you going, Ma? You keep saying you are going to go away but you mustn't leave me,' he wailed.

'I will try to stay with you, my son. But in case I am not able to, you must remember this place. Remember how we got here. Remember the name. Now do you promise me?'

'I promise, Ma,' Karna whispered.

Dolly, lugging her heavy load with one hand because the other arm hurt so much, cried as she and Karna walked along the road towards the village. She did not stop even when Karna told her, 'Don't be sad, Ma. You've still got me.'

In the village, the first shopkeeper glanced scornfully at the tattered soap packages. 'What do you think, that we villagers will buy any dirty thing that is not good enough for the town?' Then he scrutinised Karna with surprise and said, 'Apart from being so scrawny, your child is the very image of our Arjuna Baba from the Hatibari Zamindari. There is such a likeness that they might be brothers.'

5

THE DHARMA OF THE KSHATRIYA

But to save the pilfered cattle,
speeds he onward in his fear
While these warriors stay and tarry
to defend their monarch's rear.

Koonty's parents wrote frequent letters to their grandson, Arjuna, from their new home in Canada, describing cold that was so intense that it came right through, from the outside to the inside, so that blobs of ice appeared on the bolt heads inside the central-heated sitting-room. It was the hot weather when Arjuna got the letter, and, sweating under a slow-turning fan, he tried to imagine such a thing and could not.

He grew up by a river, with a playtime filled with cousins and friends, in a home smiled over by an ancient grandfather. He lived in a house where the doors were never locked and the children went free and wild. Meals were filled with family chatter, fragrant with saffron, Basmati rice, mutton in mustard oil. Milk from Pandu's herd provided the children with rich milk, dahi, ghee and trays of Bengal milk sweets. It was a world where tomatoes grow so big that one, stolen from his grandfather's garden and cut with Durio's secret knife, was shared, scarlet-dripping, among the six of them. Showered with petals and spotted leaves, the boys climbed the trees in the mango and lychee orchards where koels called and crystal-green parakeets with scarlet necks swooped, screaming.

Kuru Dadoo gave his older grandsons bikes and, their knees hitting their chins because they grew so fast and with Arjuna clinging to

Durio's carrier, they would escape to the village to challenge the local boys to a match. Or they would play tennis on the weedy, uneven court that had been built by Kuru Dadoo's father. Shivarani often came to stay in her parents' vacated bungalow and she and Koonty would sometimes challenge the boys while Gadhari watched scornfully from a window. Wearing white kurta pyjama, their hair in single long plaits which beat against their backs, the sisters, who did not have the advantage of school tennis teaching, would rush from one side of the court to the other and hardly ever manage to return a ball. For a while Koonty and Shivarani would behave like girls instead of two nearly middle-aged women while Pandu sat in the shade of a mango tree, a brandy soda in his hand and loved them both.

He never played himself. He was no longer the right shape and, these days, a long walk to him was a fifteen-minute stroll round the estate in the cool of the evening, a servant walking ahead whipping the falling dew from the grass tips so they would not wet the ends of his pyjama. He was amazed at the energy of his family and certain that his mother would not have dreamt of rushing round after tennis balls. Kuru Dadoo, who was over eighty, had to use a stick when he walked these days, and needed help when he rose from sitting. But sometimes he arranged for a chair to be brought to the side of the tennis court. Then, leaning on a servant's arm, he would stagger out to watch the tournament and delight in the way his grandsons always managed to beat the grown-up women. He felt increasingly pleased with his grandsons and most impressed of all with Arjuna, who did not yet go to school but because his older cousins had taught him to play was already showing talent. Though Arjuna was the youngest, thought Kuru Dadoo, in the end he might become the greatest hero of them all.

On the whole his cousins patronised little Arjuna, as he toddled patiently after them all day long, but he had one skill which they admired. He could pee an arc of six feet. The cousins had measured it, cheering at the sight of the golden bridge of urine spanning so much red earth, so many tufts and bushes. Arjuna greatly admired all his cousins, but in particular was impressed by the eldest, Durio, who walked in a swaggering way and had a habit of whacking at his inner thighs with open palm. Durio taught Arjuna to swim in the Jummuna river at the end of the garden, gripping him by the back of his pants, shouting, 'Kick can't yar. Flap your arms, idiot,' panic shooting Arjuna's skinny arms out of the water every time his cousin loosened his grip. 'Kick, you batcha. Don't dangle like a corpse.'

Encouraged, Arjuna tried again. During his third lesson something bumped into him and knocked him out of his cousin's grasp. Whatever had hit him seemed alive and Arjuna tried to scream, his cousin's mocking laughter lost in the splashing of his own flailing body. Choking water, Arjuna waited for the grab of last year's sunken goddess. A dark lump blotted everything out. The banana trees, the paddy crops, the glistening bodies of wallowing buffaloes all vanished so that Arjuna thought he had been dragged into the goddess's underwater kingdom. He tried to scream again, took in more mouthfuls of water and couldn't breathe.

It was a buffalo corpse, on its back, swollen with gas. The legs stuck out at each corner of the square bloat like four black sticks of sugar cane poked into an enormous puri, out of proportion because the legs had not swelled at all and the body swelled so much.

Durio jerked Arjuna up till breath returned, gave the corpse a casual shove with his free hand and as though it was Durio's toy boat, the gassy body settled back into the current and went bouncing away down the river.

'You're such a baby,' Durio scowled. 'Crying at the least little thing.'

'He's scared of being pulled to the bottom by the snake goddess like happened to the Mahabharata Arjuna when he swam in the Ganges. That's why our cousin can't learn swimming,' teased the cousins.

'Is it true? Arjuna wept to Koonty. 'Will I get grabbed by a snake?' In the Mahabharata, the goddess Ulupi had fallen in love with Arjuna and said she would kill herself if Arjuna did not return her passion so he spent one night with her and in exchange she granted him the boon. 'Ulupi made Arjuna invincible in water. He couldn't be drowned,' said Koonty. 'You tell your silly cousins that.' She tried to teach him to swim herself, holding him more gently than Durio, one hand cupped under his chin to stop him toppling, while the cousins stood on the bank and watched, scornfully. Her skirted bathing-suit frilled out on the water's surface as she struggled through the mud and, to horizontal Arjuna, her thighs looked like pillars and her breasts overhung him like a pair of cliffs.

'Ya. Baby,' shouted Durio from the bank.

Arjuna refused to let his mother teach him again.

'But your cousin makes you cry,' she persisted.

Arjuna was adamant and instead begged Durio.

'So long as you promise not to cry.'

'I swear. God's honour, yaar.' Arjuna held up scout's fingers while his mother stood on the verandah watching anxiously.

Durio tied a piece of coconut string round Arjuna's waist and striding up and down pulled Arjuna along like a wet puppy till he got the knack.

The river was the boys' playground. Their games that needed no more rules than those dealt out by unrelenting flora and strict and ruling currents were bounded and administered by its holy water. During the monsoon, when the river ran very fast and strong, Boodi Ayah would try to stop the children diving in, but could never catch them for the boys were fast and slippery as hilsa fish.

'Let them, let them,' smiled Kuru Dadoo. 'They are strong.'

The boys would use the bathing buffaloes as bridges, running barefoot over the submerged haunches, past the mynah birds tick-picking, till they reached the middle and found a good place to dive in.

Then they explored the watery darkness that glittered with the melting eyes of the goddess and glowed with the bones of sacred children and occasionally lost ones. They found clay fingers decorated with nail varnish, glittering with tinsel rings, joints tilting, cuticles twirling. Once they came across the face of the goddess, hair falling away from the dissolving clay as though she was suffering from some depilatory disease. But the grown-ups had told them to leave such sacred things alone and they never brought them out of the water.

Arjuna learnt to dive and, sometimes, as he slid through the weeds that waved like a woman's hair, he entered a new strange state in which thought was banished from his mind. When this happened he seemed to need less breath than usual and stayed under the water for so long that Boodi Ayah panicked and even the bigger boys were impressed.

Coming up to the surface the boys would grab passing puja coconuts and, treading water, scrabble out the flesh with their fingers. They would pull up lotus roots and catch in their fingers scaly fishes that tasted of mud, then roast the food over little fires. 'You boys always seem to be eating something,' laughed Kuru Dadoo.

The grandsons found other things in the water, a car tyre, a slipper, a fresh marigold garland, a child's plastic toy. They would speculate on how these things had got there, ghoulishly imagining corpses and disaster. Anything found floating denoted tragedy. People did not throw away a single chappal, a plastic cup, pieces of clothing. These meant a drowned person or flooded house. Babies, and sometimes older people, occasionally bobbed by, bellies puffed, sandal paste on the brow, marigold garland round the neck, hands and feet sticking out stiffly like doll limbs, ball people stuck with pin limbs. They had been let loose in the sacred current by those who could not afford the wood for a funeral pyre for their lost ones.

Bika, the child of Laxshmi, slipped off a buffalo's back and was sucked into the swirl of yellow water like a thin soap going down the water hole in the bathroom. The Kaurava boys and Arjuna reached out and offered sticks for her to grab, but the girl was too tumbled up in debris and grey froth and only twirled, choking, screaming, kicking.

Kuru Dadoo was watching from his window and later said, making Gadhari wince with hurt and fury, that it was sweet Koonty's son who had rescued the drowning child. 'As though he was the true Arjuna of the Mahabharata,' he said.

'Are you sure it was Arjuna?' asked Pandu. 'For you weren't even wearing your glasses.' But Kuru Dadoo felt certain and rewarded Arjuna with milky sweets, mango leather and sugar cane.

Arjuna munched amshotto and felt confused. He had not been aware that it was he who had done the rescuing, but if Kuru Dadoo said it was, then it must be so.

The ninety-year-old Pishi, who had the reputation of seeing into the future, heard about the rescue and, staggering along on twisted legs, her shrivelled breasts bare and swinging, came to see the little hero. She never wore a blouse, declaring that they had been imposed on the women of India by the prude Victorian British. Traditional Indian women, she maintained, wore only a sari with its end covering the breasts to a larger or smaller degree or not at all according to the stage of life. Pretty breasts were useful as flirtation tools but Pishi considered hers long past the flirting stage so therefore did not bother to cover them at all.

'I have known from the time this Arjuna was born,' she said in her creaking voice, 'that he would grow to greatness. This child will be famous all over India when he is grown-up.'

They made a bore hole in the Hatibari garden, drilling down into the middle of a rose bed, till water squirted up like a miniature oil well.

'Where did it come from?' asked Arjuna, thrilled.

'There is water under all the ground round here,' Pandu told him.

Arjuna told his cousins grandly, 'The Hatibari is floating on water,' and stamped on the ground, expecting to hear a slopping sound.

'Stupid,' said Durio.

'It's true. My father told me and he never tells lies. Our garden is like a boat.'

'Idiot,' sneered Durio.

Later Arjuna asked, 'Isn't it true, Ma? Baap? Why won't they believe me?'

Pandu laughed and gave his son a gentle smack on the bottom.

'Why doesn't our garden float away?' Arjuna persisted.

'Water, water, water. He is always thinking of water,' sighed Koonty. 'But when it comes to being bathed we have to haul him there.' Water made her sad. The thought of the river made something go tight in her stomach.

After the cousins went back to school Arjuna wandered round the Hatibari estate and felt lonely till he discovered you could tell what grown-up people were thinking from hiding under the garden chairs and, squatting among their dropped sandals, watch their naked toes. Shivarani's toes would twitch like the tail of a cat that is angry when anyone talked about marriage. His mother's toes curled like scorching paper when anyone mentioned the river and then his father's toes would clench like fists because Pandu was afraid of Koonty's sadness. If he saw it start to mist her eyes he would try to distract her. 'You should write poems. There is something very soothing about the writing of verse.' His mother's toes curled like cats being stroked, the day she read her poem. 'I walk in my lonely garden. Koels call. Why is my face smudged with dark in the daytime as though night has already fallen? Is it the kajal that I put on my eyes to make them large? It has fallen down my cheeks. It did not work.'

'Shabash,' cried Pandu clapping. 'Good, good. What does it mean exactly, though?'

'She cried,' said Shivarani tartly, raising one eyebrow. 'You must not discourage her.'

'No, no,' said Pandu and wished he had not suggested poetry.

His mother's toes had leapt like mongooses fighting with a nest of snakes when she told Shivarani, 'The only thing my husband thinks about is cows and girls. He is here, there and everywhere, doing love scenes. He started it the moment we were married. Of course he loves me too or there would be no Arjuna but the smell of other girls is always on him. He never tries to hide it. He laughs at me, tells me not to be jealous. Says that he has the right to make love with any of his tenant's daughters. Even wives.' Her toes had moved in a different way as she added, 'But I know that he loves me best.' She bent and saw Arjuna under the table. 'Are you down there again, you dirty boy? Chi, chi.'

Shivarani's doll industry was flourishing and dolls were being taken for sale to a posh shop in Park Street. On the three-hour journey to the town Koonty and Shivarani hid their jewels against their breasts and Shivarani told the driver not to stop for anything, for dacoits and highwaymen were robbing travellers all the time these days. In town Basu, their driver, edged the car past buses smothered under outside passengers, cyclists balancing a ten-foot-high pile of terracotta pots or three yards of sugar cane. He eased Shivarani's rusty Ambassador among food sellers, street musicians, shoppers, school kids, men in pristine white, swinging briefcases and hurrying to the office. Arjuna, squashed between his aunt and his mother on the back seat, reflected how Shivarani had her own special smell, different to Koonty's: chalk, supari, foreign and something metallic.

They reached New Market at last, and Koonty took Arjuna, protesting wildly all the way, to have his hair cut.

'What is the matter with this fellow?' laughed the barber. 'Why is he wriggling like a fish trying to get away from the net? Does he not know how a barber saved the world?'

Arjuna stopped howling and asked, 'How?'

'Some demons, long long ago, grabbed power of the earth,' said the barber, tying a bib round Arjuna's neck. 'Everywhere there was crying and sadness, and the Earth went to her father, the god Vishnu, and begged him to help her. So Vishnu got his barber to cut off two of his hairs, one light and one dark. The light hair became Balarama and the dark hair, his brother, Krishna, who later drove the chariot of Arjuna in the Mahabharata and these two great gods chased away the demons.'

At New Market, cool air spilling onto Arjuna's neck where his hair had been, Koonty said, 'I hope number ninety-eight is free otherwise we may have to make do with thirty-nine.'

Each authentic New Market porter wore a badge showing his number and you had to take one even if you only wanted to buy one packet of needles.

Luckily ninety-eight was there, squatting at the entrance, his basket at his feet. He rose smiling at the sight of Koonty and her son. He was a slim pockmarked man of indeterminate age and with surprisingly un-greyed hair. He had been carrying for Koonty ever since she could remember and he had carried for her mother too but to Koonty he looked just the same as he had when she had been a little girl.

'The barber cut off a lot of my hairs but none of them turned into gods,' Arjuna told the porter.

'Next time better luck, little man,' the porter smiled as he put his basket on his head.

As Arjuna and his mother followed number ninety-eight into the market, they saw ahead of them a foreign memsahib with several porters clustered round her, each urging her to hire him. Refusing them all she set off, the loudly exhorting porters following. Beggars began to join the crowd of imploring porters. Each time the woman passed a stall or shop, accompanied by her nagging mob, the owner sprang out, urging her, with terrible insistence, that she buy from him. Child beggars and legless people plucked at her clothes. A man crept alongside her, whispering, his lips so close they almost touched her ear. 'You like filthy, Memsahib? I take you to shop where you can buy very filthy.' On her other side another man whispered, 'You got dollars, Memsahib? I give you very good exchange. You come this way and I give you best in this town.'

Arjuna was fascinated as he and his mother walked serenely in the wake of number ninety-eight, perfectly unmolested. Once you had chosen your porter all the competition melted away. Your porter, basket on head, large number badge on his chest, protected you.

'Why don't you tell her, Ma,' Arjuna said.

'She will soon learn,' smiled Koonty.

Koonty bought Arjuna a camouflage suit, plastic helmet and tin machine gun. On their way back to the car, Arjuna asked, 'Where does number ninety-eight live, Ma?'

Koonty realised that though she had employed this man for so many years, she knew nothing about him. When she had been a little girl he had sometimes carried her in his basket among the shopping when she got tired, as later he had carried little Arjuna. And not only did she not know where he lived, with a flush of shame she realised she did not even know his real name. She thought of him, as her mother did, as ninety-eight. Pronounced Nunetyett. Like that it sounded like a real name but surely his wife, if he had one, must call him something else. Was he married? Did he have children? She did not know. As the driver opened the boot and the porter carefully loaded the shopping in, Koonty opened her mouth to ask her questions, but in the end she said nothing. It was too late for intimacy. Too many years had passed.

Kuru Dadoo and Nitai Mandel both died that year. When the monsoon came the river swelled and ripped its banks till the sound of thundering water was audible in every part of the village. Boodi Ayah in the bazaar, getting herself some more tobacco for her pipe, had to wade to her ankles in water when she saw the young Marxists, led by Ravi, marching towards the Hatibari. 'Power comes out of the barrel of a gun,' they were shouting. Ravi was sixteen now and his followers were more determined than the last time.

Arjuna's father had been making love with a girl called Shonali when he heard their shouts and understood what was happening. A huge man, bulky, soft-bodied, fair and fine-skinned, he was not made for running. His clothes, silken, floating, clasped with jewels, caught the wind and held him back. His shoes were curl-toed and embroidered in gold. As he lumbered past, people shouted, 'They are stealing your cows, Zamindar Sahib.'

He took off the hindering shoes and for the first time in many years tried to run barefoot. His body shuddered with its impact with the road as he tried to get home fast and put a stop to the disaster that had been building up there in the short time he had been caressing Shonali of the midnight-thick, queen-of-the-night perfumed hair. A mountain on the move, Pandu gripped the jewelled handle of the dagger that his father had left to him.

Ravi led his followers as they came chanting to the elephant gates and walked right through them. Durwans are not paid to get murdered. Durwans are not compensated for appearing to side with the zamindars and against the people. The Marxists entered the cow stalls where the men were milking. Koonty raced after them and tried wrestling with their hands as they untied the cow ropes. 'We are taking them for re-distribution,' said the youths as they led Pandu's cattle into the yard. 'The days of the zamindar are over. In these times of equality for all it is not right that one man should have so many cows when there are peasants in this village who have none, whose children starve for lack of milk.'

Pandu arrived, wheezing. 'You bastards,' he yelled, pulling out the dagger and trying to chop Buttercup free. It had been Pandu's fancy to name his herd after English wildflowers. He recognised the lad who led Buttercup. It was Rahul, Ravi's older brother. Only recently Pandu had given this boy money for his college fee.

'I thought we were friends,' Pandu said over the back of the bouncing Buttercup. 'I thought your family was grateful for the help I have given.'

'We want our rights, not charity,' said Rahul.

'These cows are not your right. They belong to me, not you or your party.'

'I am communist and all possessions are the property of all society,' said Rahul.

'I have always looked after your family. I have cared for you as though you were my own.' Pandu's tone was sad.

'My first loyalty is to the cause,' said Rahul, but he could not meet Pandu's eyes.

As they struggled, Buttercup began to panic, butting and kicking while the young man tried to jerk the rope out of reach. Around them people shouted, cows mooed, dogs barked, servants wailed.

There came the sound of cow hooves galloping and, in a splatter of mud, Arjuna, shouting with excitement at the adventure, went racing towards the river trying to capture Meadowsweet, who had broken free. She had been halfway through milking and her udder was still tight and spraying milk. She was wild with panic and heading for the swollen water.

'Leave her, son,' cried Koonty. 'She is only a cow.' There came a splash and Koonty started screaming. Arjuna had managed to grab at Meadowsweet's trailing rope at the moment the cow toppled into the water. He was jerked in after her and in a moment the wild current had sucked down the pair of them.

'Ogo, Ogo, come,' yelled Arjuna's mother.

People abandoned the cow seizure and began running to the waterside, trying to help rescue Arjuna who popped up suddenly in unexpected places and remained on the surface for a few short moments, his head bobbing on the water like a coconut. He was out-pacing them. He was vanishing fast down a speedy current. Koonty began screaming like a mad woman, 'You bitch, you filthy whore, you Durga, you murderess of children.'

Only later, when the red dust had settled, when Arjuna had been pulled from the water, did anyone notice that Rahul was lying on the ground and the dust under him was redder with his blood.

Rahul's father had been bailing in the water with a long bamboo, trying to halt the rich man's son in his rush to death at the very time his own son lay dying.

There followed long shocked moments, in which people tried to understand. There had been a lot of killing in this village over recent years but the people who had died had been the landowners, the greedy shopkeepers and moneylenders. The upper classes got killed nowadays, not the lower. It came as a shock to see one of their number, a village son, the son of the misti wallah, lying dead. What had happened? People pressed around to get a better look at the body. What killed him?

Someone remembered the flash of a knife. Someone else had seen the zamindar sahib take out a dagger. 'How did it happen?' people were asking over the sound of the misti wallah's weeping. 'Who did it?'

'Rahul is dead and the zamindar has killed him,' said Rahul's brother, Ravi. 'In the old days the landlords could do what they liked with us. Kill us, take our property, rape our wives and daughters. Now all that has changed and since the Communists came in we have got the power.'

The crowd was waiting, as the zamindar, his silken clothes streaked and dribbled with river mud, came walking back. The people of the village watched in silence as he came hauling his great body painfully towards them. There was blood on his kurta.

Pandu wanted to thank them for saving his son and felt muddled by the oddness of their behaviour. He could sense hostility as he approached the people but was too tired to sense danger.

The crowd waited for the zamindar with fists clenched round hastily gathered poles and stones. Shooting lights began flashing in the zamindar's eyes as the men tightened round him. He felt suddenly dizzy. He needed to sit down.

'Could someone bring me a glass of water,' he said. His heart was quivering painfully against his ribs. He looked round, into the faces of the men who had saved his son and saw hatred in their eyes. No one went to get water for him. The only movement was that of fists tightening round stones.

A lone police constable, on the outskirts of the crowd, not daring to enter it, tried to get a glimpse of what was going on.

What can one man do? Anyway it did not look good for the police to be seen siding with the landlords against the people in a Communist state. Softly he twisted his handlebars and pedalled away. He would put in a report. That is the most he would do.

6

GOLD AND SILVER

And she saw her sons in combat,
words of woe she uttered none,
Speechless wept, for none must fathom
Karna was her oldest son.

Dolly's arm never came right after the day the dacoit slashed it in the train. Even hunting the rubbish dumps was sometimes too hard for her and she began to worry constantly about Karna's future, so the day she found someone willing to teach her son a skill she was filled with gratitude. The beedi wallah offered to take the child and train him, as well as give him a small wage. 'I need children under the age of ten,' said the man. 'After that their fingers become too big to roll the leaf or tie the string.'

Dolly was jubilant. 'Everything will be all right now,' she told Karna as she spruced him up for his first day's work. 'Chacha will teach you and when you are grown up, you will become fat and rich and have gold stoppings in your teeth, just like him.' Her son had been saved from spending his life as a beggar or something worse.

Every morning, before the sun was up, Dolly would examine Karna to make sure he looked clean and tidy, then send the little boy off to a room in a bustee that had once belonged to Clive of India. The beedi wallah had taken this room by force, coming in with several of his brothers, all armed with lathis and throwing out several penniless families.

There, Karna and a dozen other ragged, emaciated children, sat cross-legged on a hard floor for fourteen hours a day, rolling raw tobacco leaves in thin sticks and then tying them with whiskery thread. The children, many of whom had developed harsh coughs from breathing tobacco dust, ranged in age from a peaky-faced child of three who sat in a constant puddle of his own urine, to a blind boy of nine. They were overseen by the pock-marked beedi wallah who leant on a bolster, smelled of imported aftershave and chain-smoked smuggled foreign cigarettes which further polluted the atmosphere of the already stifling room. Chacha kept a bamboo pole at his side for hitting the children if they paused, talked, or made a mistake. His business was doing well. His beedis were the finest in town because he used children and his profits high because he kept wages so low.

There came an evening when Karna, his long day of work finished, got back to find his mother lying where he had left her on the pavement in the morning. Full of panic he gave her water which revived her slightly. Deciding she needed food he tried to sneak up and grab a samosa from the stall in the next street, but he was too small and could not reach. Eventually the man became suspicious and batted Karna away with an oily ladle. 'My mother is ill. Will you give me one?' pleaded Karna. The smells of the frying pasties were filling his stomach with longing.

The man baled into the sizzling oil, said, 'Do I look like Mother Theresa?' then went on serving his gathering of late-night customers. But all the same Karna could not stop staring hopefully at the smoking golden triangles emerging from the hot dekshi. A young man, standing by the stall, gave Karna a smile and handing some more money to the samosa wallah, said, 'Fry the kid one as well.'

Karna went back to his mother tossing the scalding food from one hand to the other and dancing because the kindness had lifted a little of his weariness. But when he held the food to her mouth, though she moved her dry lips she did not bite it. He picked out a little of the soft potato filling and pressed it against her teeth, but she seemed unable to swallow. Putting the rest of the samosa into his pocket, Karna decided to try to get some milk for her instead. The small boy's legs were shaking with fear and weariness by the time he got to the khatal near where he and his mother had once lived. The gwala remembered Karna and, after much persuasion, gave him a little milk in a tin cup.

By the time he got back to his mother she had managed to sit up a little. When she saw him, she began to cry. 'I could not stand. I tried and tried but I could not get up so I have been unable to make you any food.'

'It's all right, it's all right,' soothed Karna as though he was the mother and she was the child. 'I will eat the samosa. You drink this.' He poured the milk, drop by drop, into her mouth.

'I want to say something, Karna,' said Dolly when she started to feel better. 'Now listen to me carefully.' Her voice was very low so he had to put his ear to her mouth.

'What, Ma? I am listening.'

'Do you remember giving me that promise, Karna?' Her voice was like a breath.

'What?' His heart was sinking. He did not want to do the thing she asked.

Dolly's words came out, slow, straining, and so quiet that Karna could hardly hear.

'You promised that if I am no longer here you will go back to Hatibari and show them the disc.'

'Don't go, Ma. Please don't go,' Karna begged. He put his arms round his small thin mother and pressed his head against her breast. He remembered the time the dacoits came, how she had hidden the money there. He wished she could hide him inside her bosom now. 'Stay with me, Ma.' But she did not answer and he knew. He could feel her heart tinkling quickly and unevenly against his ribs. A great cough began to rise in her and he held her tightly, trying to calm her racking convulsion.

'You must keep the promise you made to me, my son, because this is the last thing I will be able to ask of you,' she breathed.

'I promise, Ma,' whispered Karna and he gently kissed her head. Her hair that had once been so thick and luxuriant had turned grey and thin.

Next day he felt afraid to leave her but knew he must. His wages barely bought them the smallest amount of food. At the beedi factory he begged the owner to pay him more. 'I work all day and still don't have enough money to give my mother proper food,' he said.

The manager scowled. 'Take what I give you or get out,' he said. 'There are plenty of children who would value this job. If your mother wants money she should not be so idle but get some work, herself. If I go giving you more, all the others will be wanting it too. It's people like you that ruin the market.'

The day after that, Karna could not wake Dolly. Although he shook and called her, she lay there limp. After half-an-hour he began to feel afraid. He ran to the khatal, since milk had revived her once before. The khatal owner was not there. His wife was squatting before the chula, stirring a metal pot of boiling milk. She did not know where her husband was and she did not have any milk to spare.

'Some of that,' begged Karna, pointing into the steaming pot.

'This is for the kheer,' said the woman. 'We need it all. Move out of the way.'

'Just a little. A very little.' Karna stood firmly over her.

The milk was at the crucial stage. If the stirring was paused for a moment it would boil over. Without looking up the khatal wallah's wife turned her spoon in the rising heaving milk and ordered Karna to go.

'What will I do?' beseeched the child.

The khatal wallah's wife had always been irritated by her husband's enthusiasm for Dolly, who was prettier and younger than she was and now told him crossly, 'You will have to go and look elsewhere.'

'Please, oh please,' begged Karna.

In the end, because the child would not go away and the milk was past the boiling-over stage the woman took up an empty baked-bean tin with her free hand and impatiently ladled a few drops into it. She handed it to Karna, instructing him to bring the tin back then quickly went on stirring to stop it catching on the bottom.

Dolly was still not awake when Karna got back so he tried to feed it to her while she slept. He tilted the tin against her mouth but it trickled down her chin as though her lips had gone stiff. There was so little milk that he did not want to waste it so he tried dipping his fingers into it then putting them against her lips, but still she did not swallow. At last he managed to force her mouth open and pour some of the fluid into her throat. Then he sat back watching and waiting hopefully. But nothing happened and the milk only lay in a white pool at the back of her mouth.

For the rest of the morning he ran wildly from one place to another searching for someone who would help him, going back at intervals to his mother and always finding her unmoving and asleep. He ran to Sahib Singhs, the Park Street chemists and tried, in gasping breaths, to explain. The chemist asked Karna a series of questions and eventually, understanding that the boy's mother had once had a cough, took down a large bottle of syrup and poured some into a bottle. Karna watched the ruby-red liquid flow as though it was life pouring back into his mother.

'Fifty paise,' said the chemist and waited, wrapped bottle in hand.

When the man understood that Karna had no money he became furious, ordered Karna out of the shop and tilted the syrup back into the jar. Desperate Karna began stealing things which might cure his mother of her prolonged sleep. He ran till his chest began to hurt from so much panting and his feet became scalded from the rough pavements. He returned to Dolly with coconut, plantain bananas, a bottle of Thumbs Up, a Five Star chocolate bar and a bottle of something misty and black that he had seized from the Ayurvedic chemist. As he approached the place where his mother was, he began to feel hopeful, certain she would be awake and cross because he had been gone so long. He longed for her to be angry with him, to say with a frown and in a stern voice, 'Never go off without telling me again.' Then she would hug him and say, 'I love you really, Karna. It's just that I get so worried about you.'

His mother was sitting up. Relief and happiness rushed through him. He felt a great laugh burst from his stomach as he dashed towards her, holding out all his gifts.

But as he got closer his happiness vanished. The hunched form was not Dolly at all but a large pye dog sniffing over her as though it was about to bite into her cheek. Karna ran at the animal screaming and the dog slunk off.

Dolly was lying exactly as he had left her. She had not moved the smallest bit. A fly was walking over her lips. Putting down his burden he swatted the fly away then took her head in his arms and, rocking, began shouting, 'Ma, oh Ma, oh Ma,' as though it was only because he had not yelled loud enough that she was still asleep. He rocked her head and begged her to wake up. After an hour he stopped using words but, still rocking his mother's head, he started wailing, letting out short anguished howls that had no words in them, only misery.

The man who lived on the next bit of pavement looked up from plucking at his toes and said indifferently, 'No point in going on like that, son. She's dead and you won't bring her back.' Then he returned to his toes.

Karna sat beside the body of his dead mother all the rest of that day and all night too. Hunger began to grow in him, but for a long time he could not bring himself to eat the food he had stolen although he knew that Dolly would never need it now. Throughout the night he lay by her side and, at first, he would reach out his hand and touch her body for comfort. But after a while it stopped feeling like his mother for her limbs lost their warmth and became stiff.

In the morning he woke, knowing that, though he was only six years old, he was now completely alone in the world.

Sitting by Dolly's side for the last time, Karna ate the piece of coconut, the two plantains and the chocolate, pretending that it was the breakfast his mother had given him and she was now sitting with him while he ate. He drank the Thumbs Up. He ate the squashed samosa from his pocket. Then, putting the bottle of Ayurvedic medicine at his mother's side just in case she woke when he was away, and could be cured by the magic dose, he got up. He looked down at his mother for the last time then walked away.

Under his shirt he felt the golden disc on which was written the name of the woman who, his mother had told him, must look after him from now on.

It took Karna over two hours to get to the station but as he drew nearer he remembered Savitri and began to feel comforted. She was so wise and kind that she might even know how to bring his mother back to life again.

He sneaked under the barrier when the ticket collector was turned away and ran to the track. He peered down onto the rails. The area before the buffers was empty. Only a little debris wafted back and forth in the breeze of an arriving train. One small broken glass bangle lay between the lines. It must have fallen from the wrist of Savitri's little girl.

Karna dashed round the station, tackling people. 'Where are they? What's happened to them?' It seemed as though, if only he could find Savitri, everything would be all right again. He would not have to go to Hatipur and ask this unknown woman to be his mother and Dolly would wake up again. 'Where is Savitri?' he sobbed to the guard who had his flag up and his whistle in his mouth.

'Where are the people who lived on the rails?' he demanded of the man who sold plastic bottles of water.

The man with the scarred face, who had snatched the banana, looked up from a heap of debris which he was rummaging through and muttered what sounded to Karna like, 'Train got them in the end. I knew it would.' He seemed pleased. Karna caught the ticket collector by the sleeve and pulled at it as though he was ringing a temple bell.

'Stop that,' said the man, smacking Karna's hand away. 'They've been moved on. It's the new government policy. Now get out of here.'

Karna's heart was heavier than ever as he crept into the train to Hatipur when the guard was not looking.

He travelled to Hatipur crushed under the seat because he had no money for a ticket. He did not come out once the entire way, in case he was thrown off the train and was unable to fulfil the promise to his mother. He did not stir when people kicked their heels against him or allowed their bottles and bags to roll on him. He was very tired and fell asleep at last in the stifling airless heat of the under seat so that he nearly missed the station of Hatipur and had to scramble and leap from the train as it began to gather speed. Then he had to run again, and dive under the barrier, pursued by the ticket collector.

By now his mother would have been smoothing his hair with her fingers, making him bend down by a pond so that she could rinse his face, beating the dust out of his shorts with her palms. As he approached the mighty elephant gates, the only thing that gave him courage to keep going was the feel of the golden disc under his shirt. His mother had told him, 'They will know who you are when they see it.'

The uniformed durwan was scowling even before the filthy ragged child was within ten yards of the gates.

'I have to see . . .' Karna tried to remember how such a lady should be addressed. 'I have come to see Memsahib Koonty.' His voice came out very shrill.

'Clear off,' shouted the durwan. 'There has been a great tragedy in this house, the zamindar has been murdered and they do not want urchins like you coming in and troubling them.'

Karna felt his lips go dry at the news but all the same tried again, 'But I need to see her.'

'Her husband has just died,' shouted the durwan. 'So go away and stop making trouble.'

Karna looked back once as he went tramping down the road. The durwan was settled back with his paper. Karna was briefly tempted to try to dash back and make his way through when the man wasn't looking, but realised this would be hopeless. The man would catch him in moments, once he was inside the grounds. He would have to get in secretly. Although the place looked well guarded, with high tight fences, Karna felt sure that, because he was so little, there must be some gap somewhere that he could sneak through.

It took him an hour to circle the estate and in the end he decided that his best chance was the river that formed one border. There was a bamboo water fence designed to keep intruders out but he was small and thin, and he thought there must be a gap. He dived in, fully dressed and felt the water washing away the filth and dust of his journey. He had to swim alongside the bamboo water fence for quite some time before he found a gap big enough to get through.

As he approached the back of the Hatibari he kept a careful watch for more durwans. But there was no one except for one small boy who was swimming. The boy looked up, raised splashing hands and shouted, 'Go away.'

'You go away,' Karna shouted back and kept steadily on. 'I live here.'

The boy and Karna met mid-river and began treading water and glaring into each other's faces.

'Who said?' demanded Arjuna.

'My mother,' said Karna.

'Don't talk stupid,' scoffed Arjuna. 'This is my family's river and you are not allowed here. My uncle gets angry when village children swim onto our land.'

'I am not a village child,' said Karna grimly. 'And I don't know who your uncle is.'

The boy raised his eyebrows. 'You don't know? He is the zamindar of all the land round here.'

Karna scowled. 'Then you are Arjuna.'

Arjuna peered closely back. 'Yes. But who are you?'

'My name is Karna and I am your brother.'

'My name is Arjuna and you are a liar because my mother doesn't have any other child, and if you don't go away I will call the durwans. They are just around the corner. And when they catch you they will beat you up.'

'I bet there aren't any,' challenged Karna. 'You're just saying that because you're frightened of me.'

'Why should I be frightened of a kid like you?' scoffed Arjuna. 'Usually a durwan is watching by the river, but today they are all busy because a lot of people are coming for my father's . . . something. I can't remember the name.'

'What is it anyway?'

'A puja to tell his soul to go away and not come back,' said Arjuna.

'Why do they want his soul to go away? Is he wicked?'

'No of course not,' cried Arjuna hotly. 'He's the goodest person I know.'

'Then why do they want his soul to go away?'

'I don't know,' said Arjuna sadly.

'Won't your mother tell you? My mother told . . . would . . . tell me everything.'

Arjuna started laughing. 'I knew you were telling lies and that your mother and my mother are not the same person.'

'You are my stinking brother and I hate you and your stinking mother threw me in the river when I was a baby and I hate her too,' screamed Karna. 'And I love Dolly who found me and brought me up and she's really my mother now except that she is dead.'

Arjuna said, 'My father is dead too. He died last month.' He found this sentence awkward. In the early days he had kept saying, 'My father went to die,' as he would have said, 'Went to Calcutta,' but he had been corrected so often that he had now, apparently, got it right. Yet to Arjuna's ears it still sounded wrong.

Karna trod water and waited.

Arjuna added, 'But I expect he'll be back soon because he never goes away from us for very long.'

Karna asked scornfully, 'How old are you?'

'Five.'

Karna winced because this boy was a year younger and already taller. He said, 'When you are six like me you will know about deadness and then you will not be so stupid.' Then he thought of the bottle of Ayurveda medicine that he had left at his mother's side even though he knew she was really dead. Karna went on, 'And my mother who is Dolly and not Koonty said that because Koonty is my mother you've got to give me everything because I am the oldest.'

'Huh, I'm not going to give you anything except this.' Arjuna slapped his fist into Karna's face. Karna lay on his back and kicked his heels into Arjuna's stomach.

Arjuna gasped and took in a mouthful of water.

'And I hate you and hate you and hate you most of all and I wish I could kill you,' yelled Karna. Arjuna got Karna by the hair and pulled him under the water till the bubbles stopped rising. Karna came up with a gasping plop, took two breaths and went for Arjuna again.

Arjuna flung himself backwards and started to swim for the bank, Karna coming after him like a mongoose after a snake. Karna, dog-paddling behind Arjuna who was performing a polished crawl, battered the water wildly and felt his heart nearly cracking as he strove to catch up and hit Arjuna again.

Arjuna stopped at last and looked round, laughing and contemptuous at the sight of Karna struggling and panting, some yards behind. He said. 'You can't even swim properly and I think you are such a stupid boy that you couldn't possibly be my brother.' Karna grasped his head and pulled him under the water. Arjuna grabbed Karna by the ears. Clutched together, their limbs shaking with effort, they faced each other with magnified eyes through the green water. Silver bubbles rose from their noses. Their hair stood up on end and waved in the current like water weeds. Karna's lungs felt as if they were going to burst. Arjuna raised his underwater eyebrows, questioning, 'Are you giving in?' Karna slowly shook his head. 'No.' He wished desperately that Arjuna would die under the water, but was growing afraid that he was going to die himself. Then suddenly it was over. The pair popped up onto the surface together.

'I won,' shouted Arjuna jubilantly.

'One day I really am going to kill you,' yelled Karna.

Panting, they crawled out and lay side by side, gasping. Then Arjuna said, 'If you really are my older brother then you will be able to pee further than me.'

'I bet I can, too,' scowled Karna. He was renowned, on the pavements, for his long-distance peeing.

Arjuna won. Nothing Karna could say or pretend could change the fact that Arjuna's gold arc had dashed leaves at least a foot beyond where Karna's had fallen. Karna tried and tried, and that only made things worse.

'I told you,' chanted Arjuna in delight. 'That proves it. You are just a village boy who tells lies. Now go away. I don't want you in my garden.'

'It's my garden too,' shouted Karna as he buttoned back his dripping shorts. 'And I've got to see your mother because she is my mother too.'

'Stinking liar,' shouted Arjuna. 'She can't see anyone. I thought I told you.'

Karna leaped up and began to run towards the house. Arjuna raced after him. 'Don't you dare. You come back here.'

Karna reached a flower bed and leaping into it, began jumping up and down, stamping on the flowers and crushing them as though the zinnias and the canna lilies were responsible for his deprivation. Malis who were cutting the blue-grass lawn behind humped Haryana bulls yoked to an antiquated mower, raised their fists and shouted angrily at the sight of the urchin vandal. Karna screamed back at them and ran on past the mango trees, coconut palms, ashoka, grevillia, among which swoops of rose-ringed parakeets shrieked and dived for fruit. He raced over groomed lawns lashing out at statues as he passed, with Arjuna at his heels. This beautiful garden with tall trees hiding the lowly huts of villagers and their tatty fields was the birthright that he had been denied. Fury gave extra speed to his legs as he rushed towards the shining white house that sparkled like a polished tooth, because this was where he should have lived all his life, instead of on the pavements of Calcutta.

Karna leapt up the steps three at a time, Arjuna still following him. As he entered, mud and water dripping from his clothes, a small and black-skinned woman sprang at him, waving her arms ferociously and shouting, 'Get out of here, you dirty boy.' Then, turning to Arjuna she said, 'Look at you, Arjuna Baba, dropping water over the clean floors when all these people are coming at any moment and the servants have spent a whole week, polishing. Have you no thought for others at this sad time, Arjuna Baba? And who is this beggar boy you have brought with you?'

'His name is Karna, Boodi Ayah, and he wants to see my mother,' said Arjuna, apparently unperturbed by the indignation of the old woman. 'I told him he can't, but he won't go away.'

The ayah gave Karna a sharp shove on the shoulders. 'Get out of here.'

Karna pulled out his golden disc. 'Look, look,' he shouted. 'My mother said that when Koonty Ma sees this she will have to keep me.'

Boodi Ayah leapt at Karna. 'So that is where it was all this time.'

'It was round my neck when I was born,' gasped Karna, dodging out of reach.

'It belongs to Koonty Memsahib and she has been troubled by its loss for a very long time.'

There came a cry from upstairs. A sad-looking woman with untidy hair and a crumpled sari stood there. 'What is happening?' Koonty asked.

Boodi and Arjuna both spoke at once.

'It's this bad boy, Ma,' cried Arjuna. 'He says he is my brother.'

'This is the wicked boy who stole your golden disc, Ma,' said Boodi Ayah.

Karna flourished his medal, shouting, 'This.'

Koonty stared and said after a while, 'It is the very one.' Her voice was hollow as though something of her soul had already left her body. 'Where did you find it, boy? Did you see my baby? Was she still alive?'

'Ma has not been well,' the ayah said to Karna. 'And you are upsetting her. Give us that medal and get out of here.'

Karna screamed, 'I am that baby. You are my mother. It is your duty to give me education because I am your child.'

'You are my child?' said Koonty.

'Don't listen to him, Ma,' cried the ayah. 'Such a wicked boy saying such wicked things.'

'Come nearer so I can see you properly.' Karna moved into the light and stood waiting, while Koonty scrutinised him.

'My mother, Dolly, who found me in the river, told me to come to you,' Karna said.

'Can't you see how you are troubling her?' shouted the ayah and to Koonty, 'You are upsetting yourself, Ma.'

'This child is too small,' Koonty announced at last and turning prepared to mount the stairs again.

'It's because you have not given me food that I am small,' yelled Karna at her retreating figure.

'And he is ugly,' said Koonty without looking round. 'It is not possible that this is the child of the beautiful tall sun god. Also the child was a girl and this one is a boy. Get my medal back and throw him out.' Wearily she began to climb the stairs. Her shoulders were shaking as though she was weeping.

'I am that boy. I am your child,' Karna shrieked.

'Get my medal back,' she called again and then was gone from sight.

'My mother said I must come to you,' screamed Karna as the servants came at him. They almost got him as he rushed through the great double doors. He did not pause for thought. He ran for the river, dived in and was swimming away before any of his pursuers had even reached the bank.

Koonty was closing the door of her room when she realised. She came rushing out, shouting, 'He had golden eyes. Stop him. Stop him.' She was too late. The boy was gone.

Karna's journey back to Calcutta, cowering in the stinking dark of the under seat, was filled with despair. He thought with bitterness of Arjuna who wore white socks and lived in a house made of marble while he, Karna, had nothing and no one in the whole world. He was hungry and at this very moment Arjuna was probably eating a meat curry. Meat curry. Once there lived an indigestible demon who would disguise himself as a meat curry and get his brother to serve the dish up to his victim. When the victim had eaten the food the demon's brother would call, 'Come out, Brother' whereupon the demon would tear through the victim's stomach, ripping him to death. Karna would have liked to try this trick on Arjuna in that moment, though in the end the demon was outwitted and digested by the powerful stomach juices of Holy Agastaya. When the brother called the demon out, all that emerged was a little burp. Karna's own stomach juices rumbled as he travelled under the seat back to Calcutta. He got off the train at last, stiff and exhausted, and for a while stood in the middle of Howrah Station, not knowing what to do or where to go next. At last, summoning up courage, he crawled out under the barriers, and went plodding away along the road, heading for the place on the pavement where he and his mother had been living for the last two years.

When he arrived, another family had set up there. They had erected a canopy of bamboo sticks and plastic bags from the railings and the woman was lighting a little smokey fire of burning debris. Under any other circumstances Karna would have stood over them shouting demands for them to leave but now he felt too exhausted, despairing, and sorrowful to do anything more than sink down at the small area of pavement left free by this family of intruders.

At once the woman turned from her fire and began flapping her hands at Karna.

'Get away with you,' she shouted. 'What are you doing there? This is our family place.'

'Where is my mother?' muttered Karna. He felt dizzy.

'I don't know where your mother is but she's not here,' said the woman. She began breaking up an old basket and feeding the fire with it. 'So clear off.'

'She was here,' said Karna, but his voice was so low it was almost inaudible. 'She was dead and she was lying here.'

'We know nothing about her. Go away,' said the woman and turned her attention entirely back to the cooking of the evening meal.

The man in the next patch said, 'They took her body away on a rickshaw.'

'Where to?' whispered Karna.

The man shrugged.

When Karna continued to sit on the corner of the pavement, the woman, without looking up from her cooking, shot out her foot and gave Karna a shove. The little boy rolled softly into the gutter and lay there, sewage water and mud saturating into him. He had no fight left.

Karna lay there all night. The people who had taken his mother's pavement were still asleep, rolled up in their cloths like corpses, when Karna woke up in the morning.

He rose and walked away knowing that his mother's piece of pavement was lost to him as well as all the other things.

That day he went back to Chacha Khan. But Chacha flew into a rage at the sight of him. 'First you demand higher wages, then you walk out for two days and now you expect me to take you back again. Shoo, shoo, off with you. I have another child in your place now and also you were never any good at wrapping the beedis. You never had your mind on it and always seemed to be thinking of other things.'

Karna survived for a week, eating thrown-away scraps on rubbish heaps and crumbs from people eating round the food stalls. He slept wherever he happened to be when tiredness hit him and tried not to think about the days when he had slept cuddled against his mother and ate the food she made him while she looked on, smiling. If he allowed his thoughts to go to Dolly he found it difficult to keep back the tears.

When it seemed to Karna that all the options of life were now closed to him, he felt someone touch him on the shoulder. He looked up and saw a taller boy standing over him.

'What's the matter? Why are you crying?'

'My mother is dead,' whispered Karna.

'You had better come with us, then,' said the boy.

Karna entered a new life. He joined a little band of other orphan boys called 'kigalis'. Karna and the other kigalis guarded cars when their owners were shopping. This was a lucrative business, whether the owners paid or not, for those who refused to employ the gang would return to find all removable parts gone. Karna would have imaginary conversations with his mother as he squatted waiting for shoppers needing taxis. Karna felt happy among the kigalis though sometimes he would still go to the place where he and his mother had lived together. He would stand across the road and tell himself, that was where Ma cooked dhall for me. That was where she hung my clothes after she had washed them. He would be there so long that the people who had taken the place for their own would start to shout at him. 'Go away, boy. Why are you standing there staring at us?'

The boys earned money running for taxis and guarding cars. Sometimes a goonda would burst upon them, as they slept rolled up together in a park, or under some trees on the maidan. Kicking and threatening, they would rouse the children and send them off on some errand that an adult might fail at – stealing drugs, delivering stolen jewels, spying on someone marked out for a mugging.

'Today I am working for sahibs,' Karna would tell his mother. 'You needn't worry about me any more.' Or he would say, 'Now I am a car guardian, Ma,' as he looked after an Ambassador for a driver who had gone for a pee. And in his mind she would say she was proud of him. 'Who knows, one day you may be employed as a car-park attendant, wear a uniform, even get a pension. You must be very good at this car-minding job that so many people employ you.' He did not tell his lost mother of the other side of the business. She had funny old-fashioned ideas about morality. Sometimes Karna would feel guilty because he was making no more effort to keep his promise to his mother. But he could not see what else he could do. If he went back to the Hatibari the people there would only take away his piece of gold, and then he would lose all proof of who he was.

The kigalis had no expenses. They slept in parks or on the pavements and they didn't even pay for food, for there were restaurants and cafés that gave the boys whatever was left over in the evening. So they spent their money on foreign cigarettes and going to the cinema. After a month among them, Karna managed to see his first film. Sitting in the cheapest seat he watched, hypnotised with happiness, the heroes and heroines of Bollywood sing, fight and dance their way through a magic world of jewels, flowers, peacocks and snowy palaces. That night, instead of filth and chaos, all he could see were glittering dancers. Instead of the roar of traffic, his ears were filled with the sound of love songs. He went to every film he could afford after that and watched people winning through in the face of illness, poverty, and injustice. He revelled in the love scenes and became breathless with excitement when, in *Aradhana*, the lovers, Rajesh Khanna and Sharmilla Tagore, hide in a dark cave to try to stem their mounting passion. He began to learn the songs from the films he saw and would sing, 'Roop tera mastana', 'Your shape drives me mad' as he polished windscreens or made off with hubcaps. Soon he had assembled quite a repertoire. People would stop and listen affectionately to the humming of the ragged urchin and they paid him extra because they were amused that someone so small and grubby should be singing of glamorous adult passion. But after he saw the child star, Poopay Patalya, he had eyes only for her and lost interest in all the other film stars. He had been thrilled by her years ago, when he had seen her on the posters and his mother had been teaching him how to read. In fact the little film star's name was the first word he had managed to read all by himself. Now he went to see every film she acted in.

The first time, Poopay was a ten-year-old bride whose ancient husband had just died. His family and the village elders had persuaded the little girl to commit suttee, telling her that then she would become a saint. Karna wanted to murder the villagers, whose only motivation for allowing a child to die in agony, was to bring profitable pilgrims to their village and thus make them all prosperous. He wanted to dive into the cinema screen and rescue the screaming girl from the blazing funeral pyre.

In the next, Poopay was a street child like Karna himself. Her face was dirty, her clothes ragged. She slept on pavements and washed in gutters. And like Karna, she had dreams of growing rich. He wanted to shout out, 'I will make you rich, Poopay Patalya. I will give you jewels and beautiful saris as soon as I get money.'

His dreams became all about Poopay. He would imagine meeting her. He would plan the words of love he would say to her.

As Karna became better at catching taxis he began to earn more. But sometimes he would give away all that he had earned that day and be forced to miss the film. Once it had been an ill woman lying on the pavement. Karna had been reminded of his mother, and he bought milk for her. He bought popcorn for a little boy called Vijay before bringing him to where the kigalis were and all that night Karna had hugged the sobbing little boy. But most often he gave to Laika. The girl's face was so terribly scarred that she could not smile or close one of her eyelids and Karna had spent all his money on a jasmine garland for her hair once, because a man had cringed from her and she had looked so hurt. She was perhaps two years older than Karna. Even she did not know who her parents were – the first thing she could remember was standing on street corners begging. 'I must have been about two,' she said. 'I used to say, 'No Mama, no Papa, and because I was so little and pretty – for I had not got these scars then – people gave me money. Even at two I was alone.' People didn't give her much money anymore because she had grown older and become ugly. A man had tried to rape her when she was eight. She had resisted him and he had slashed her face then raped her all the same.

'I want to be a prostitute, but how can I with such a face?' Laika told Karna. The other kigalis would tease Karna for giving his money away. 'Buy yourself a new shirt instead,' his friend urged him. He still wore the one his mother had bought for him a year before. Each time he put it on, he would remember Dolly getting him ready for his job at the beedi factory, putting the shirt on, doing up the buttons, stroking his hair tidy with her fingers. Then she would look at him with her head a little on one side and her eyes squeezed up so that she got the whole impression. At last, with a smile of satisfaction, she would say, 'There, you look like the most handsome boy in the world, my darling Karna.' But she would not say that now, for the shirt was ripped and far too small for him. His skin was grimed, his nails broken, his hair dull and dirty. If his mother saw him now she would say sternly, 'What a mess you are in, Karna. We don't have to look like beggars even though we are poor.' Every now and again he would find he had enough money for a new shirt and determine to buy it so that he would not let her down, but whenever it came to it, he found himself unable to part with the old one which had buttons that her fingers had touched. When he felt sad or lonely he would caress those buttons and almost feel his mother's fingertips against his own.

'I was nearly mad with sorrow at the losing of my husband the day that boy came,' Koonty told Shivarani. 'That is why I did not realise about his eyes until it was too late but now I feel more and more sure that that really was the child.'

'You said it was a girl,' protested Shivarani.

Koonty was trembling as though her body was racked with fever, her dry eyes scalded. 'I never looked. I thought it was a girl because it moved so softly and gently.'

In the Hatipur arrak shop men said to one another, in the old days the Pandavas lost everything because of the malice of their cousins and this time they seem to be losing once again. 'It is not our fault that the zamindar Pandu died, but only the karma of his family,' they would say to each other and retell the tale, though everyone had heard it a hundred times, of how the Pandavas had been outwitted by the Kauravas. How, in the end, unable to defeat the Pandavas in open combat the Kauravas had resorted to trickery and invited their cousins to a friendly game of dice. How, in this loaded game the Pandavas had lost everything including their kingdom and Draupadi their wife, and were forced to hide in exile in the forest. 'In these modern days,' the old men said, 'such things do not so often happen but all the same there is much suffering and loss in the family of Pandava already.'

Koonty had Boodi Ayah cut off all her mistress' hair, then she took off her bangles and her earrings and put them away into her locked box, telling Arjuna, 'I will never wear these again because I am a widow, but when you marry your wife may have them.' Then she put on a plain white sari, and taking her son by the hand walked into the village.

'Where are we going, Ma?' asked Arjuna.

'We are going to find out who killed your father.'

When the people of the village had found the blood of Rahul on the horns of Buttercup and realised that the zamindar had been executed for a murder committed by the cow a horrified silence had fallen on them, so when Koonty arrived among them, they hid behind their doors and dared not come out. The rickshaw wallah saw Koonty walking and did not invite her to ride but instead sat cowering under his rickshaw and hoped she did not see him. People peeped at her from shops and windows but she saw only crows and pye dogs. She stopped when she came to a golden cow with dark-rimmed eyes that was tethered in one of the yards and told her son, 'That is Buttercup.' In the dark interior of the hut she could see the family watching and hoping they were unseen. After a while the man came out.

'That cow belonged to my husband and you have stolen it as well as murdering him,' said Koonty.

'It was not me. I was not there. I swear it, Memsahib,' he said and rushing to the cow undid the rope. 'Please take your cow, Koonty Ma. I wish I had not accepted it.'

'It is too late for that,' said Koonty. 'Who killed my husband then?'

'Ravi, son of the misti wallah. Everyone in the village knows it. Everyone in the village saw him strike the blow.'

'Where are the other cows?' asked Koonty.

'Ravi gave them to people in the other villages. There are three in Dattapukur. This is the only one in Hatipur,' said the man. He was very nervous.

'Please care for her as though she is your daughter,' Koonty said and grasping Arjuna by the hand, turned and went walking back to the Hatibari. On the way she told him, 'When you are old enough you must punish this Ravi.'

'I will kill him,' cried Arjuna, and looked forward eagerly to the moment. 'I will shoot him with my New Market gun.'

Koonty shook her head. 'You must not kill him for then you will be sent to prison and your life will be ruined too.'

'What shall I do then?' asked Arjuna.

'Perhaps you will find a way to humiliate him in front of all his followers,' suggested Koonty.

Though police continued to investigate the killing of Pandu they had not found a single suspect and in the end concluded that the crime had been committed by goondas from Calcutta. DR Uncle assured them that Ravi was responsible but the police said they were unable to arrest him without evidence and witnesses. 'Also he is becoming a big shot in Communist politics,' explained the police officer. 'You must understand our position. We are having to close this case since there seem to be no witnesses to the event.'

The misti wallah came to visit Koonty. He did not speak at all. He could not even tell her of his sorrow. He could not tell her anything. He could not ask her to forgive him because his son had killed her husband but only lay on the ground and grasping Koonty's feet, wept in silence. Then he laid a basket filled with fresh-made misti at Koonty's feet. One or two of the round white sweetmeats fell and went rolling through the scarlet dust and turned red as though they had been dipped in blood. But Koonty had lost her appetite for sweets.

Dishes of rice and milk sweetmeats arrived and a little cow with marigold garlands round her neck, bells tinkling on her horns, a new calf butting at her udder, was sent to Koonty as a gift. Her horns were as hooked as a pair of new moons. Her brindle coat shone like peanut toffee. The calf had a wide wet nose and it was so young it wobbled on its thick legs. But after the visit of the misti wallah, Koonty refused to come out to receive these things and the village knew that she could not forgive them. She would not buy anything in the village because it was the people there who had murdered Pandu.

'You must help me find that boy again,' Koonty begged her sister.

'Keep calm, Koonty. You must put the whole thing out of your mind, and concentrate on Arjuna, for he only has you now.'

'I am unable to caress Arjuna because I keep thinking that that boy might after all have been my child and that he has no mother loving him.' What woman would let her child wear a shirt that was full of holes and was too small for him? 'I have got to find him again. Because I am a widow now and must dress only in white, I must go to Calcutta to buy saris and have blouses made. Please come with me and help me look for him.'

'You can buy such things in Hatipur,' protested Shivarani.

But Koonty refused to allow the darjees in the village to sew for her because they might have been among the people who killed her husband.

Shivarani, protesting that she was absolutely certain that Karna could not possibly be Koonty's child, all the same agreed to embark on what was clearly a fruitless search. As they drove into Calcutta Koonty told her sister, 'Now I think of it he did look like Arjuna, I know he did.'

It was Durga Puja. The streets were tight with festivities. Shrines and cotton temples stood in every street. A hundred goddesses cast cool smiles of aloof disinterest on the excited worshippers. Koonty threw herself in front of every deity they encountered. 'Oh lead me to my child, most holy mother.' All day long they looked among the children before the market. They stopped porters, shoppers, stallholders, describing Karna, asking if anybody knew him. Shivarani looked around her in despair, though, because there were a hundred children fitting the boy's description; children grabbing taxis, polishing shoes, hunting through rubbish, selling shoelaces, guarding cars. None or all could have been Karna. 'Let's go home. I'm sure the child you saw is not the right one,' said Shivarani. 'From what Boodi told me he did not look at all like Arjuna.'

'I saw a likeness,' persisted Koonty. They drove into slums and up little alleys and through heavily packed markets. They thrust among sellers of spices and, sneezing with chillies, choking with ginger, questioned the pot bellied cross-legged merchants across their piles of powdered turmeric, cumin and ajwain. They moved among the prostrate Durga worshippers demanding information. They entered temples and asked the priest to inform the people of their search. They asked among the porters and the beggars, they stopped the goondas and offered to pay for information, 'These memsahibs must be mad,' the goondas told each other. 'For if there was such a little boy, his gold would have been stolen from him long ago.'

'Look at me, look at me,' cried Koonty to the beggars. 'Have you seen a boy with a face like mine?' 'Have you seen a boy who looks something like the Sun God from the Mahabharata?' she asked the trotting porters, as they went by with weighted baskets on their heads. She thought that if she could find the child and make life right for him, the goddess would take the curse from her and forgive her for her husband's death.

'It is not your fault that he died,' said Shivarani. 'I don't know why you keep saying it.'

But Koonty insisted. 'She cursed me by making me a widow because I threw my child away.' Several times during the day Koonty looked near to collapse, and would have to lie in the car to recover from dizziness. At the end of this day of fruitless hunting Koonty looked so ill that Shivarani knew she would have to put a stop to it. 'While you were waiting in the car an old man came up to me and told me that, six years ago, he found the body of a little baby girl lying dead in the floating hand of Durga,' she told her sister.

'I don't believe you,' said Koonty.

'Would you like to meet the man who saw it?' Shivarani would find some fellow and pay him to tell the story.

'It is true then? My baby was dead all the time?'

'It is true,' said Shivarani.

Later she began to fear that the lie had been a mistake for though Koonty never asked to search for her child again, her sorrow seemed to deepen.

When the day came for the immersion of the goddess Koonty would not let Arjuna go to the river but made him stay inside with her with the windows shuttered and the blinds pulled down. Even then she could hear the muffled sounds of people yelling joyfully and goddesses bursting into the water with a splash. Shivarani had gone away. She was giving speeches, persuading people to vote for her, from a place so remote that even letters never got there.

'Because our patron is not here it is we who must try to bring Koonty Memsahib comfort,' the widows who stitched the dolls told each other. But when they came to the Hatibari, Boodi Ayah told them, 'Memsahib is too upset and sad to see anyone.' The widows insisted. 'We have made a gift for her and it helps a suffering person to meet another with those same sorrows.' The seven widows squatted all day on the Hatibari verandah with the ends of their white saris pulled over their heads for respect while Boodi went to Koonty at intervals to say, 'Why don't you come? They will never go away otherwise.' By nightfall they were still there and Koonty peeped at them through the carved marble trellis. 'Come and talk to us, Koonty Ma,' they cried at the sight of her. 'We are widows too, like you are, and have much sorrow in our lives, but there are happy things as well.'

Even Gadhari was unable to persuade the women to leave. DR Uncle was sympathetic, saying, 'I'm sure it will be a good thing for Koonty to meet these other women. She will not feel so alone, for, although I grieve for my beloved brother, Koonty's suffering is so much deeper.' After dark Koonty came down reluctantly though she did not expect to find comfort anywhere and only met the widows because otherwise they might stay on the Hatibari verandah forever. 'Please come with us to the river,' the widows said. 'And when the goddess goes into the water we will all make prayers for the souls of our lost husbands and you can do one also for the Lord Pandu. And when Durga's body is dissolving into our holy river and returning to her husband after her holiday on earth it will be a sign that we will be with our lords again when our next lives come.' Then they gave her the present of a Pandu doll, complete with fat stomach, curl-toed shoes and a golden dagger at his waist. For a long moment she stared at the little moustachioed pompous toy without expression. Then a tiny smile touched her mouth.

Although her eyes were filled with tears as well, still the widows felt happy.

DR Uncle was pleased when Koonty agreed to come with them to the water. His sons and Arjuna, in spite of protest, were dressed in white starched kurta pajama, embroidered waistcoats and Gandhi caps for the occasion. 'The whole village will be there and it is expected of you,' Gadhari told her rebellious sons, who had hoped to go in jeans. Though the family was grieving, it was the puja and together they could do the final rites for Pandu's soul. It would be a meeting of forgiveness and of restoring relationships with the village. It would be a chance to lay the hate to rest. The children, who had thought they would have to miss it all because of Aunty's and their father's sorrow, now laughed and shouted because after all they would be there for when their Durga, the biggest and the best in the whole district, would go crashing into the water. Even Gadhari only pretended to be scornful but really looked forward to the crackle and thunder of fireworks, the arcs of spat burning petrol and the plunge of the mother goddess. Arjuna danced and laughed among his cousins and told his family, 'That is where the boy who said he was my brother squashed the flower bed.' 'This is where I learnt to swim with Durio holding me on a string.' DR Uncle laughed and petted him and he hardly noticed his mother's lonely silence. The widows were already at the waterside. 'Oh, the little lords, they are so like the zamindar, their grandfather.' They smiled at the sight of the four crisp-clad boys and because Arjuna was the youngest, they mussed his hair and pinched his cheeks lovingly. Shivarani's maid, Laxshmi, was waiting there with her four daughters each holding a little bunch of marigolds. 'And that is Bika, the little girl I rescued,' said Arjuna. 'Do you remember, Laxshmi, how I saved her?'

'Arre, you batcha,' scowled Durio crossly, still resentful that he had never received the credit.

'Hush, hush you boastful boy,' Boodi Ayah reprimanded Arjuna. 'The goddess will punish you for pride.'

Koonty had never dared come here till today. 'And this is where

I sat,' she thought, 'the day the Sun God came swimming through the water. And this is where I waded when I let his baby fall.'

The people from the village had already flooded in through the gates DR had made for them today. They were happy at the sight of Memsahib Koonty standing by the water and told each other, 'This means she now forgives us.'

The boatmen brought out the great Hatibari dugout, the carved and gilded boat the first zamindar had had made to visit neighbouring zamindars, rajas and European officers to play games of chess with them. The punt men holding the great boat steady, one by one the family stepped in and, when all were seated on the silk embroidered cushions, were rowed to the middle of the river. The widows watching on the bank waved and cheered to see Koonty sit among the others. Koonty, holding onto her Pandu doll, smiled a little but did not wave back at them.

When darkness fell, the floating families became unable to see each other's faces except in little flashes from explosions of a rocket or the glow of a passing flare or lamp. The water bobbed with lit clay lamps, the passing boats had torches flaming at their bows. Teeth would be abruptly illuminated and Arjuna, cuddled between his ayah and his cousins, felt excited to see so many faceless smiles flashing in the night. An air of expectation came upon the crowds when they heard the sound of running feet and panting and knew that soon the goddess would be there.

She appeared through the trees, bobbing on the shoulders of fifty invisible men, her own face glowing and bright because someone had fixed a hand torch to her bosom and four large flares burnt brightly at the corners of her palanquin. Among the men who carried her were those who had created her. The sculptor had the front pole because he had had the most responsibility. Behind him came the darjees who had made her clothes, the barber who had collected the long hair of new widows including Koonty's, for the goddess' head, the jeweller who had made her tinsel rings and necklaces, the artist who had painted in her eyes and lips and nails. A great cry rose from the throats of the people of Hatipur as their goddess reached the water and was loaded onto rafts. They shouted prayers and picking up handfuls of holy water, threw it over their heads till the boats tossed and rocked and the people in them grew wet.

Silence fell while Durga was rowed to the deep part of the river and everyone held out torches, flares and little lights to see her. There came a pause and then in she tilted, the biggest splash and crash that had ever been made by the biggest Durga anyone had ever seen. Her body made a hole in the water that was brief but deep and there came such a shouting screaming ululation that the people of Dattapukur heard it and felt jealous and all the little bobbing lights leapt with the wave of Durga's leaving. Arjuna and his cousins whacked each other over the head and shouted till their throats were sore. DR Uncle recited a poem from Tagore with much passion and emotion that was completely inaudible under the din. Gadhari forgot her dignity for a moment and clapped her hands The misti wallah tilted a whole jar of misti dahi into the water as an offering to Ma. Laxshmi told her daughters to throw their flowers and the orange heads went bobbing over the water among a rain of fireworks. The roar of farewells reached a crescendo as the goddess vanished. She paused briefly, halfway under, one hand outstretched as if in blessing, and then she slipped in totally and was gone. Moments later all that was left of her was bubbles rising from her hair and a little toss of blossoms that had escaped from her garland.

There is always a mood of sadness when Durga has departed, even though she will be back next year. When the boats turned and began punting back to shore, their occupants were quiet. Then someone shouted, 'Where is Koonty?'

The lights were going out now and in the increasing darkness they searched and hunted through the boat, feeling, groping, finding the knees of children and Boodi Ayah's feet. But they could not find Koonty. They began to hunt among the other boats and through the water. The puntsmen prodded mud with poles, people began shouting, calling, 'Koonty, Koonty.' Arjuna started crying. His cousins dived into the river and felt beneath them with their feet. People on the banks clambered through the water weeds and started feeling with their hands for the widow of the zamindar. At times they would think they had her then find that the handful of hair, the foot, the clutch of sari was that of the newly drowned Durga.

'Call the police,' DR Uncle shouted to people standing anxious on the banks and 'Go to the Hatibari and use the phone there.' They went running back across the gardens and dialled for Dattapukur. The widows squatted down, covered their heads and started weeping. Gadhari put her arms round Arjuna and tried to hug away his sobbing.

7

SATI

Jumna's dark and limpid waters
Laved Yudhisthra's palace walls.
And to hail him, Dharma raja,
Monarchs thronged the royal halls.

Shivarani's friend, Malti, was setting up a day centre for the street children of Calcutta and had asked Shivarani and Bhima to come and help her get it started. The chief minister had been asked to open it officially so when, in the middle of a thunderstorm, the phone rang, Shivarani thought it must be him agreeing to come. Through the cracks and crackles on the line at first she was unable to understand what Gadhari told her. It was as though her mind would not allow her to hear the words, 'Koonty is dead.'

'What happened? How did it happen,' she shouted over the dim line, when she realised at last what was being said. She heard, 'Durga Puja' 'the river' and 'only just found the body.'

'But when I left she seemed so much more calm,' yelled Shivarani, choking back sobbing. The opening was postponed and Shivarani returned to attend the sad occasion of Koonty's funeral. Bhima offered to come and give support but Shivarani refused. 'My parents are coming back from Canada for the funeral and I don't like the way they treat you.'

'It's not their fault,' he said. 'It's how they have been brought up. How the whole of India has been brought up. If I will be of comfort to you I will come in spite of their efforts at retaining ritual purity.' He did a little joking flapping of the hands, fingers spread, knuckles out, the age-old Indian gesture that high-caste people make to warn untouchables not to come too close. 'And you can understand it,' laughed Bhima. 'After touching me, your parents would have wash in cow's urine to clean away the pollution.'

'Oh, God, Bhima. Don't talk like that. They should adore you for the person that you are.' She had not seen her parents for three years and wondered if she could bear to talk to them. But when she arrived, Meena was so bowed with shock and sorrow that Shivarani could think of nothing but ways of comforting her. She even tried hugging her mother, a thing she had not done since she was six. But she was too tall and her arms were too long and boney. The contact was a failure, ending with Meena ducking and struggling to get free and saying, 'Your wristwatch has got caught in my hair and pulled my chignon out.' She had become slim, smart, fashionable and westernised in her Canadian exile. Shivarani did not try to hug the lonely little orphan boy and left caresses to Boodi Ayah, DR Uncle and even Gadhari, who, being a mother, was better at it than she was. But even Boodi Ayah's hugs could not comfort Arjuna. He stood straight and rigid, accepting the attention of these adults, his gaze distant and his thoughts elsewhere.

After the funeral the Kaurava cousins became reluctant to let Arjuna play with them because he did not concentrate on the games anymore. In their cricket matches he would miss the ball altogether. When term time came, and the cousins went back to school, Arjuna wandered listlessly round the garden for a while. DR Uncle, out of pity, offered to bowl tennis balls for him but the little boy had lost his appetite for play.

Boodi Ayah begged, 'Talk to me, Arjuna Baba,' but he would not say anything. He knew what Karna had meant now. He had grown older and understood what deadness was. It was not only his parents that he had lost. The happy silence that, ever since he was very small, had frequently filled him, now came no more. He had lost the knack of staying underwater without breathing. Because of sorrow he had gone beyond the range of magic.

Gadhari told her husband, 'Arjuna just mooches around all the time and I cannot cope with it anymore. Also I don't see why I should. He is not my child. All my children are away at school and I think he should go to his aunt for he is her responsibility now.'

'He is my brother's child,' said DR Uncle miserably. 'How can we send the child away from his own home just because he has lost his parents?'

But Gadhari was bitter that Arjuna had inherited the Hatibari estate and she could not bear to think that Koonty's son should be the owner of her house. She would have liked to take the case to court, showing the foolishness of the grandfather's will which had resulted in this miscarriage of justice. 'He would not have done it if he had known that Pandu was going to die so young,' raged Gadhari.

'All the same, because he is a minor child, he is still under your authority,' the lawyer told Gadhari. 'He must do as you say till he comes of age, though nothing can be done about the inheritance. When he comes of age his property must be made available to him.'

DR Uncle would have liked to sell the Hatibari and live somewhere else after all the sorrow there but Gadhari refused utterly. 'How will we buy another house? We will have to beg a seven-year-old to purchase one for us.'

No one knew how to comfort Arjuna. Gadhari eventually suggested that he go to live with his grandparents in Canada but Arjuna said, 'I want to stay here. Definitely.' This was his new word. He used it as much as possible.

'Won't you be lonely when the cousins are at school? What will you do all day?' said Shivarani.

'I will get my guns ready,' Arjuna said. 'Then I will learn how to do strangling.' Shivarani was taken aback. Arjuna had always seemed quite a gentle boy. 'And then I will learn how to shoot arrows. Then when I am ready I will poke little holes in Ravi, but not exactly kill him.'

'Oh, no, Arjuna,' cried Shivarani, alarmed.

Arjuna was adamant. 'My mother said I must, I forget what, humbelate him or something, in front of everyone because he killed my father – so that's what I'm going to do and that's why I'm going to stay here. Now I'm too little and he's nearly grown up but while I'm growing I'm going to work out how to do it.'

In the days that followed, Arjuna's anger mounted. Shivarani, who stayed in the Hatibari now because the bungalow had been taken over by the new manager of the estate, would watch her nephew throwing stones in the river and shouting 'I hate you because you killed my mother.' When Boodi Ayah tried to brush his hair he kicked her, when Gadhari tried to put her arm round him, he pushed her away, when DR Uncle came to bowl tennis balls for him he flung them back, trying to get his uncle in the face. He began to run round the garden yelling, 'I hate Durga, I hate Durga,' terrifying Boodi Ayah, who expected holy retribution every moment. He began to rush at the wall, hitting his head against it till he bruised himself. He bit into his own arm so deeply that it bled. Arjuna's anger was against everything and everyone, because everything and everyone had destroyed his parents. Before his mother died he had focused all his rage on Ravi but now it seemed to Arjuna that he had enemies on every side. The river, the boat, the family and the goddess were all responsible for his mother's death. And the person he blamed most of all was himself. He had been in the boat and had not even known that his mother had fallen in the water. He should have grabbed her as she fell, he should have dived in after her, his mind should have heard the sound of her dying so near to him, but he had been having fun and heard nothing but the fireworks and the happy shouts of worshippers. Somehow the heavy mooring chain had become wound around her body and he had not noticed. No one had noticed. She had drowned and her son who swam so well and who could stay underwater for three minutes on end, had failed to save her and had in fact been laughing when she died.

In the end the family decided to send Arjuna to stay with Shivarani in Malti's Calcutta house while Shivarani made arrangements for the opening of the children's centre. It would get Arjuna away from the Hatibari and the constant reminders of his parents for a little while and it was felt that it would be good for Arjuna to meet children so much worse off than him.

Malti had persuaded several Calcutta businesses to finance the centre, a large modern building comprising of a school and play room, and an adjoining kitchen and washroom. The latter, where the children would be able bathe themselves, consisted of a sloping concrete floor, with water outlets at the lower end, and a series of taps and buckets. Malti hoped in due course to be able to install a boiler but for the moment the children at least had running cold water and soap in which to wash themselves and their clothes. There was also a small dispensary where a chemist would be giving out basic medicine, and where once a week a doctor would be giving his services for free. The building was flanked by a large yard and a playground equipped with swings, seesaws and a slide. The centre was to be staffed by unpaid volunteers and the project had been so popular that money was still coming in and already Malti had people on the waiting list, hoping to do voluntary work there.

Although there had been much publicity already, Bhima fixed a loudspeaker to the roof of Shivarani's car, and Shivarani, Malti and Bhima, with Arjuna sitting silent and crushed between them and Boodi Ayah, were driven round Calcutta by Basu. Bhima used the speaker to announce their invitation to the children of the street to come for a day and be given a meal, clean clothes, a bath and an education in reading and writing. Even Arjuna could not stop himself from giggling as Bhima sang, 'Come to children's centre next week or I'll give your nose a nasty tweak.'

When the kigalis slept they often held each other for safety and for comfort and sometimes in Karna's dreams the arms that hugged him would be Dolly's and not those of another skinny boy. Instead of a child's ribby chest, Karna would dream that he leant against the soft breasts of his mother and when he woke, waves of grief would rock him and he would yearn for the feel of Dolly's hands caressing his face and her kisses on his cheek. It was a year since anyone had told him they loved him. Sometimes his grief would turn to shame as he realised how much he had let her down. She had always struggled to keep him smart and clean, scrubbing his skin with soap till it stung, then standing him under the water squirt with his eyes squeezed tight while she rinsed him. In the year since she had died he had not once washed with soap, for there was no one to care if he was clean or dirty. He went on trying to learn to read and write, though, because Dolly had thought that so important. When Karna found bits of newspaper he struggled to make sense of the words. Laboriously he would work out the sentences on hoardings, spelling out advertisements for butter, water pumps, tailored suits, condoms, farm machinery. Squatting in the dust he would trace out words he saw on the posters for films – Dilip Kumar, Hathi Mera Sathi, Ganga Jummuna Saraswati, not knowing what they meant but practising the letters all the same. He could read the name of 'Poopay Patalya' though, and write it too. And the word he wrote the most often of all was his mother's name, Dolly. After he was told that Koonty was his mother, Karna wrote her name too. And then, changing one letter at a time, he turned the name of Koonty into Dolly. He had had to take out the disc at first, to remind himself how to spell the name of the other mother then he worked his way from Dolly to Kolly to Kooly to Koonty. Then did it backwards ending up with Dolly again. Then tried it the other way round, doing Dooly, Doony, Doonty and back again until gradually Koonty became transformed into Dolly not only with letters, but in his imagination as well until at last the Koonty mother became in his mind indistinguishable from Dolly.

He did not tell the kigalis what these two names, Dolly and Koonty, meant to him for in the dangerous world of the Calcutta pavements, the less that was known about you the better. But because he repeated them so often the other little boys began to write them too. Soon the walls of Calcutta were scrawled with the names of Karna's mothers. The children wrote them in charcoal left over from pavement fires, they wrote them with dropped ball-point pens, they scoured them into whitewash with nails, using bits of broken glass they scratched them onto the bonnets of the cars of those who refused to pay for their guardian services and smeared the names with fingers dipped in rotten fruit pulp onto restaurant doors that had refused them food. One of the kigalis, a boy called Rishi, who thought of himself as an artist, tried to draw little portraits of Koonty and Dolly, but these for some reason made Karna furious. He scrubbed all over the pink faces with charcoal, at the same time yelling with rage at Rishi. People who saw the graffiti would wonder if this was some new political party of which they had not yet heard. Shall we vote for the Kooly Donty party? Or were these the names of gangs? And suddenly Kolly Doonty sounded dangerous.

Karna and his gang were stealing exhaust pipes ordered by the goondas when a loudspeaker car appeared, announcing, 'At the children's centre you'll get a bath, and nice food to eat and a game and a laugh. And if you don't come I'll chop you in half.' The kigalis were momentarily taken aback by these unexpected words but then they realised that the speed of this crawling car made it perfect for plundering. Bhima was giving the address and timings of the centre as Karna clung to the boot and gripped the legs of another boy who hung under the car and started to get the bolts undone. Bhima said, 'A new shirt for boys and saris for girls, and even some beads though we won't give you pearls.' The boys could make as much noise as they liked as they pulled off the exhaust pipe for no one could hear them over the sound of Bhima's announcements. 'If you are ill we'll have you made better, and with us you will read till you know every letter.'

Basu shouted suddenly, 'They are picking the parts off, Mem-sahib. Let us stop a moment and I will catch them and give them a thrashing.'

Bhima put aside his mike and, laughing, said, 'My goodness, Malti and Shivarani. Do you think we will be able to cope with such vigorous entrepreneurial urchins at our centre?'

'They're just a band of thieves. They don't deserve your kindness,' said Boodi Ayah sternly.

And then Karna saw Arjuna sitting in the car and let go his hold of the other boy's legs. The boy hit the ground with a crash and shriek of curses.

Inside the car Karna saw that Arjuna's hair was brushed and his hands clean. He wore a starched white shirt, a pair of flannel trousers and a tie. On his lap lay an open book. A bubble of bitterness arose in Karna, because this boy did not have to write words in dust, or read things from grease-stained paper but had a new clean book to read from. If Arjuna wanted a shirt someone bought it for him, if he wanted to go somewhere he was taken in a posh car.

Arjuna looked up, saw Karna peering in, gasped then glared. The two stared at each other grimly. Then Karna stuck out his tongue. Arjuna glowered and stuck out his tongue too.

'Hey you,' shouted Basu to Karna. 'Stop that and get your dirty fingers off the car.'

'I know that boy,' cried Boodi Ayah. 'He's the one that stole Koonty Memsahib's jewel.'

'It's the boy who said he was my brother, but my mother saw him and said he wasn't. He's just a dirty street boy and a thief,' said Arjuna.

'He's got Koonty's jewel has he? Let me to talk to him,' Shivarani said. 'Stop the car, Basu.'

'Arjuna Baba will catch something if that boy comes too near,' protested Boodi.

Outraged, Karna wriggled round till he had his back to the window, pulled his shorts down, flashed his bare bottom in Arjuna's direction, then lost his balance and fell. Malti began to giggle. Bhima was already roaring with laughter. Basu was outraged. 'Look what the filthy little kid is doing, Memsahib.'

'Koonty is my mother and she's supposed to be looking after me,' shouted Karna pulling his shorts up again. 'But she told her servants to chase me instead even though I've got a gold medal with her name on it.'

The car began to rock as the other boys took advantage and began swiftly to remove the rear lights.

'Let me see it,' said Shivarani.

'Tell my mother to come and find me and then I will show it to her.'

'I am her sister.'

'I won't let you see it. Only the Koonty Ma.' If Koonty really was his mother she would come for he remembered all the times Dolly had searched for him, calling out his name, asking people, 'Have you seen my son, Karna?'

'He has that medal. I saw it on his neck,' cried Boodi. 'You must take it back from the thieving rascal, even though now Koonty Ma is dead.'

'Koonty is dead?' gasped Karna.

'Yes,' said Shivarani. She was amazed at the expression of shock and horror that had come over the urchin's face.

'You're lying,' shrieked Karna.

'It's true.'

There was a long pause as Karna studied her face, then as he saw the truth there he let out a wild wail of grief because his mother had died all over again.

'Where did you get it?' asked Shivarani.

'It was round my neck when my mother found me.' Karna's voice was low and expressionless now, because he had just been bereaved a second time.

'Where did she find you?'

'In the river. She was a dhobi.'

Ah, that explains it, thought Shivarani. The dhobi woman had obviously found the gold chain in the river and put it onto her own child. Shivarani knew that no newborn baby could survive a journey from the Hatibari to Calcutta alone, and floating down the river. And also Koonty's child would have been a year older than Arjuna and this boy was shorter than him by half a head and looked a year younger. She said, 'So, since my sister is dead, let me see that medal, Karna, so that I know if you are telling the truth.'

Karna edged up the car, looked furtively from left to right, then pulled out the medal surreptitiously. It was the right one. Koonty's name glittered in the sun. Shivarani reached out, made a grab for it.

With a yell of fury, thrusting the medal back in, Karna leapt out of her reach.

'After him, Basu,' ordered Shivarani. 'Get my sister's medal back from him,' but Karna was running.

The chief minister came to open the street children's day centre and in his speech said how impressed he was with Malti and her two friends for making the lives of poor children a little easier. The Calcutta children had been cautious, fearing a police trap in which they would be gathered up and sent off to an institution or children's village. They had heard of such things happening to both children and adults during Indira Ghandi's emergency and their freedom was more important to them than any amount of food or clothes. They came in nervously, ready to run if needed and were greeted at the gates by Bhima. He had painted red lips on the side of his fist which looked like a talking mouth and as each child passed, the talking fist said, 'Hello, how nice to see you. What's your name?' The children, who had never been greeted by anyone before, let alone a talking fist, were unable to stop themselves from giggling. And they shouted with laughter when Bhima's fist mouth snatched a sweet and gobbled it. They grabbed at the sweets they were offered at first, because they were unable to believe that the gift was not a mistake. No one had ever given them anything in their lives. Whatever they owned they had to grab or steal and they snatched wildly when the clothes were handed out. When they were bathed and dressed in their new clothes, they were seated on the ground and given a tin plate. Malti, Bhima and Shivarani went round and doled out mutton curry, boiled rice, curds, vegetable curry and dhall which the children bolted down as though, if they did not hurry, someone would take it from them. 'You look like a good chutney server,' Bhima said to Arjuna giving the boy a jar and a spoon. 'Go round and give them each a dab.'

Shivarani thought that Arjuna had not seemed so carefree since his mother died. Perhaps since his father died. He danced joyfully behind Bhima as he gave out the chutney, asking the children, 'Is that enough? Shall I give you more?' Bhima had made him come alive again. After they had eaten Bhima taught the children to make a sun-catching cradle with a bit of string, then he taught them a nursery rhyme: 'The rain is falling, tapur tipur and floods have come in the river. The Lord Shiva has three wives, one chops and cooks, one eats, and one gets in a rage and goes home to her father.' He followed this with the word game, 'I have a frog. What frog?' Arjuna was at first amazed that these children, some of whom were years older than he was, had never before heard it, then he joined in eagerly.

All that day, no matter what she was doing, or who she was talking to, Shivarani's attention was on Bhima. This is how it was for her, these days. No matter what she was doing, her ears could not stop listening to the funny, silly things he said and even after she left him in the evening she would hear his voice inside her head. Bhima was in her dreams, she woke in the morning with thoughts of him. She realised with a shock, at one point during that day, that the chief minister had been talking to her for ages and she had not heard a thing he'd said because Bhima was telling the children the Mahabharata story of Arjuna and the parrot. Later, ordering the children to follow him and do everything he did, he led them round the yard, hopping on one leg, the children copying him or going on hands and knees, or waving his arms round like a windmill with Arjuna and a hundred pavement children windmilling their arms too. For the first time in days Arjuna was laughing and playing again and Shivarani thought, 'What a wonderful man Bhima is and what a wonderful father he will be.'

From then on increasing numbers of children came eagerly to the centre, till by the end of the week, when Malti arrived to open up there would be a mob already waiting to dash in the moment the gate was opened. After a fortnight there were so many children they hardly fitted into what had seemed at first like a generous space, and Shivarani and Malti were endlessly going round the countryside trying to raise funds or get people to donate rice, vegetables and clothes.

Shivarani at first told herself that the reason she was staying on, week after week, when she had so much more to do, was because she was waiting for Karna to turn up. She could not admit, even to herself, her true reason for staying on. She still looked out for Karna, though she was losing hope of finding him.

Swiftly the story of the wife of the Hatibari, who had wrapped a chain round her waist and drowned herself out of grief for her husband, spread around the countryside. The act had been almost suttee, people felt, and that made Koonty almost a saint. Pilgrims started arriving from other villages to see the place where the Hindu wife had died and to throw marigolds into the water. The misti wallah began to cook 'Koonty Ma shandesh' to sell to them. They sold out by midday. The darjees stitched Koonty's initials onto the clothes of children so that Koonty Ma would protect them from demons. The tea wallah was so busy he was forced to employ two extra boys. The garland wallah sold marigold garlands that he swore were exact replicas of the one Koonty Ma had round her neck when she went into the water. The owner of the arrak shop had to double his Calcutta order. Shivarani began to feel angry, accusing people of making profits out of her sister's sorrow, but the people of Hatipur were unashamed. 'You should be proud of Koonty Ma, who has behaved as the perfect Hindu wife and also is better off now, for the life of a widow is a terrible one in this country of ours.'

Shivarani's anger was partly from guilt. Koonty had often said, 'I could not bear to be a widow. I would kill myself if my husband died,' but Shivarani had become afraid that it would never have really happened if she hadn't told her sister that lie about the dead baby. It was only after Shivarani had told Koonty that she knew for sure that the baby died in the river, that Koonty had seemed to lose all hope.

DR Uncle felt guilty too and kept wondering why they had not noticed. 'At the moment of the goddess' immersion the boat gave a tremendous lurch. We all had to cling to the sides and were thrown about all over the place. At the time I assumed it was the wash from Durga's sinking, but now realise it must have been the moment that

Koonty went in too. It was only when we came to moor the boat that we discovered the chain was missing.'

'The whole thing comes from the way women are treated in this country,' Shivarani raged. 'My sister would be alive now if there was compassion for widows, instead of contempt.' She planned to devote herself from now on to the welfare of women, and in particular widows.

When Shivarani took Arjuna and Boodi Ayah back to the Hatibari she worried that Arjuna's sadness would return but the days in Calcutta had done him good, and he leapt from the car and rushed to see his cousins, hardly remembering to say goodbye to her. It was, thought Shivarani, surprised but relieved, as though the bad things that had happened had been erased from his mind. It was just before she left that she found him sitting alone on the front steps of the house, chiselling a stick.

'What is that?' she asked.

'An arrow. I need to know how to make them for the day I am big enough to humbelate Ravi like my mother told me to,' he said without looking up.

She drove away, her anxiety back.

Back in Malti's mother's house she packed and made her arrange-ments for the trip to the villages then went around to the YMCA where Bhima was staying. She found him in his room. He was lying on the bed, smoking a cigarette, looking at the ceiling, but he sprang up at the sight of her. 'My glorious Shivarani, how wonderful to see you.' He did a joking bow and an exaggerated motion inviting her to sit on the only chair. 'So you are off in the morning. How will we manage without you?'

'Come out with me,' she said. 'I'll give you dinner at Amber.'

'Shiv, Shiv. Don't tempt me. I haven't a bean at the moment.'

'I'll pay, Bhima. Please come.'

He shook his head. 'I will not be able to take you anywhere in return.'

'You don't have to.' But she could not persuade him. How stupid of her not to realise that he had no money, she thought later. The day would come, of course, when he would get a job, but now he was still a student and presumably his adoptive parents were not rich.

She left Calcutta for the villages early in the morning and as she slowly cruised past the children's centre, over the sound of children's laughter, she heard Bhima's voice singing them a story. She was possessed with a huge temptation to forget the women, to turn the car, go back to the centre and stay there forever.

Karna was practising making himself look more like the son of a zamindar so that the next time Shivarani Ma saw him, she would believe that he was Koonty's son. In the cinema he would carefully study characters who came from such houses as the zamindari and later practise the way they walked and arranged their features. He had lately mastered the gesture of twirling a moustache though it would be several years before he would have such a thing. He would stand before the posters of films, and study every detail of the clothes of the aristocrats. He had already bought a cream-coloured kurta with red glass buttons that looked so like rubies, that he thought no one would ever tell the difference. And a pair of curl-toed slippers and a large bright wristwatch.

That night, as he slept on the pavement in the snuggle of his kigalis, he dreamed that Shivarani looked out of the window of her black car and said, 'Now that you are wearing those curl-toed slippers, I know you are my sister's son and I am sorry I did not believe you at first.'

He woke suddenly with the feeling of her arms round him.

It was not Shivarani who held him so tightly, but a scarfaced goonda with a mouthful of golden teeth. Shocked at having been taken unawares, Karna, screaming, tried to struggle free. The other children woke too and tried to pull Karna from the goonda's grasp, but it was too late. The man already had the boy in his arms and leaping out of the scrum of sleeping children, began to run.

'Let me go, let me go,' Karna yelled and sank his teeth into the man's hand. The goondas were so ugly and wicked that they could not get women so stole kigalis and fucked them instead. Several boys had already been taken in this way and not one had returned.

People watched as the goonda rushed on, clutching the shrieking squirming Karna. A woman asked. 'What are you doing with that child?'

'He's stealing me,' Karna tried to shout, but halfway through the sentence Raki slapped his hand across Karna's mouth and said, 'He's my son and I'm taking him home.' The woman hovered, doubtful. Then shrugging as though not entirely reassured, turned away.

8

THE SONG OF THE GANDHARVAS

Helmed Arjun, crowned Karna,
met at last by will of fate.
Life long was their mutual anger,
deathless was their mutual hate.

Shivarani liked to arrive in a village when the men were absent, for otherwise the women became shy and would not speak but allowed their husbands to answer questions. Even when Shivarani asked a woman, 'Are you happy?' the husband, if he was there, would answer for her, 'Yes of course she is happy.'

She would go straight to the pond where, in the middle of the morning, the women would be washing their pots, bathing their children and exchanging gossip. They would look up, interested and curious, as she approached, but then wince with surprise when she suddenly shouted, 'When the government counted how many people there were in our country, they found that thirty-eight million women were missing.' Her words always made the listening women look worried and gaze around them as though expecting to see sisters, aunts, mothers vanish in a smoke puff.

'Where are these women?' Shivarani would demand and the women's expressions would turn from anxiety to guilt as though she was accusing them of carelessness. 'What has happened to them?' Women would look at one another, puzzled.

'They have been killed at birth because they were not boys,' Shivarani would tell them. 'But women, too, have a right to life.' A terrible shifting here. There were several mothers listening who had paid the midwife a little extra to snuff out the life of the newborn, unwanted female child. 'They have died in childhood because their mothers gave most of the food to the sons so that when illness comes, girl children are too weak to survive.' Another shiver of guilt here among the assembled mothers. 'They have been killed by husbands who have beaten them or in-laws who have not been paid the agreed dowry. Women, you have a right to stay alive and unharmed no matter how much dowry has been paid. When the men and boys become ill they are taken to the doctor but women and girls have to be nearly dead before that happens. Or they die without treatment at all. Women, you have a right to as much medical care as the men and boys. You have a right to education and only when you women are educated and properly respected can the standard of living in our country rise. It is up to women to take on the responsibility for health, hygiene and education of the family.'

'It is true,' the women would murmur. 'But what should we do?'

'Vote for the Communist Naxalite Party when the election comes. Vote for me, Shivarani Gupta. 'And stand together to claim your rights.'

When she got back to the Hatibari, Gadhari was upset. 'Something must be done about Arjuna, he is asking all kinds of questions, and I don't know what to say,' she told Shivarani, looking aggrieved and at the same time a little triumphant.

'What is the problem?' Shivarani asked Arjuna.

'Parvathi said that the Sun God put a baby inside my mother before she got married but I know it isn't true,' Arjuna told his aunt.

Parvathi was the maid who Gadhari had employed to look after Arjuna while Boodi Ayah had a holiday. She was a scrawny twelve-year-old with oiled hair tied back with a piece of coconut string and a length of dirty glass beads round her neck.

'This is the moment to tell him,' thought Shivarani. 'He is old enough to know,' and said, 'It is true, Arjuna, and it is possible that the baby was Karna.'

'You're a liar,' screamed Arjuna.

'It was the man's fault. He tricked your mother.'

Arjuna leapt up, sobbing. 'I hate my mother, I hate you, and I hate Karna and I'm glad you can't find him and I hope he's dead by now and I wish he'd drowned when my mother threw him away.'

The goonda's name was Raki. He was an undersized young man with a scarred face and a bad limp but these little physical defects were entirely outweighed by the splendour of his jewellery. He wore a gold bangle, gold earrings and round his neck a gold chain that was almost as thick as Karna's. On his fingers were rings in which were set precious stones and when he opened his mouth so much gold flashed out that you could hardly see any white teeth. Or perhaps Raki had no white teeth left. Goondas are ruffians who originate from the time of the East India Company when its moguls employed armed thugs, called paiks or lathials, to protect their huge fortunes. When the mutiny was over, the Company disbanded the dismissed paiks and lathials who continued to bully and rob on their own account. They evolved into the present-day goondas who are usually ill-educated young men of between twenty and twenty-five, living in the bustee, seldom homeless or dwelling on pavements, and often have started out as kigalis. Their favourite weapon is a dagger, though pistols are also used, as are bombs, the most simple being a bottle of soda water vigorously shaken before being thrown.

Raki summoned a rickshaw and held the kicking struggling Karna tightly as they got in. For the whole half hour of the journey Karna tried to fight himself free but Raki was much too strong for him.

'Why don't you want to come with me?' asked Raki, truly perplexed. Any other boy, he thought, would have felt it a step up to be taken by a goonda.

'You don't understand,' gasped Karna. 'I am not just a kigali. Go and get another boy.' He gave a surge and nearly broke free but the goonda needed a boy with fight and was more pleased than ever with his choice.

'Keep still, you worm,' Raki said. 'And if you bite me once again I'll whip your arse off. From now on I am your father and you must obey me in all things.'

'You are not my fucking father,' screamed Karna, his words muffled by Raki's gripping hand. 'My father is a zamindar and you are a stinking little fucker of your sister.'

'Ha, ha,' cried Raki, apparently amused and delighted. 'A zamindar, is he?'

The rickshaw took them to the heart of the bustee and when it stopped Raki hauled out the writhing Karna.

'Please do not pay me anything, sahib,' said the rickshaw wallah, who recognised the influential goonda.

All the way up the four flights of winding stairs Karna continued to fight for freedom though, exhausted, his struggles were only token ones now.

The goonda, with Karna under his arm, unlocked the padlock, opened the wooden door and plonked Karna in the middle of a barren room. 'Here we are,' said Raki. 'This is your home from now on.'

Karna gazed around him, at the tiny barred window and the walls that were stained and darkened from where oiled bodies had leant against them. The only furniture was a coat rack on which hung several pairs of men's outdoor pyjama and one solar topee. Against the wall were rolled some sleeping mats of straw. In one corner of the room were piled several cardboard boxes which apparently contained radios and television sets judging from the labels. And on top of these lay a heap of women's clothes and make-up. Karna felt a little reassured at these, for it meant a woman lived here and women, he knew, were kind to children.

When Karna had got his breath back, he leapt up and made a dash for the door. Raki got there first, and stood smiling, wagging an admonishing finger. 'Naughty boy. Do as Papa says.'

'I'll kill you,' screamed Karna. 'You just wait. I'll slit open your throat and cut off your head.'

'Oh, brave are you?' The goonda pulled out his knife, a razor-sharp Nepali kukri, and handed it to Karna. 'Go on, then. Let's see.' Snatching the knife Karna dashed at Raki. Laughing, the goonda dodged him. As though they were playing a children's game, Karna rushed this way and that, stabbing and chopping. Raki danced, hobbled and dodged, his lame leg not affecting his agility. Then Raki grabbed at Karna's ancient shirt, the last thing his mother had ever dressed him in and the fragile, filthy cloth shattered into shredded fragments and before Karna could put up his hands to hide it, the goonda had seen the gold medal and snatched at it. Wild with determination, Karna let fly, slashing at the goonda's hand but the man was too quick and in a moment had the blade tip between his fingers where it could do no harm. 'I want to look. I'm not going to take it from you. See these?' He gestured at his throat, his ears, his fingers and his wrists. He wore gold everywhere. The chains round his neck were thicker than Karna's and there were three of them. He stretched his lips and opened his mouth. Among the betel-red and black-stained teeth shone a dozen gold crowns. 'I have so much gold already, why should I want more?'

'Everybody says that first, then tries to grab it,' Karna said. 'The rich people chase me all over the town trying to get it.'

'Well, I won't.'

'Why not?'

'Because we are partners. I don't steal from my partner.'

'I'm not your partner. I don't want to be here at all,' said Karna. 'I want to go back to my friends. I want to be free. My mother said goondas were bad men.'

'Even if you don't like it, we are, and partners don't have secrets from each other, so come on, show me that thing.' Firmly Raki pulled the disc out and stared at it. After a while he asked, 'What is written here? Can you read it?'

'It says that my mother was called Koonty and was a zamindar.'

Karna felt angry and offended that this unknown person should be making free with his precious secret.

Raki laughed. 'So what are you doing in all these rags if your mother is rich? Why are you living in the park with the kigalis?'

'Because I was thrown away.'

'You should be glad that, even if your mother did not want you, as least I do,' chuckled Raki.

'What do you want me for?' cried Karna, tucking the disc back in. 'You won't be able to keep me forever. I'll get away in the end.'

'What's your name?'

'I won't bloody tell you.'

'Then I will give you one.' He was thoughtful for a while, looking at Karna with his head on this side then on that, as he made up his mind. At last he said, 'I think your name is Kamala.'

'Kamala is a girl's name. I'm not a girl,' shrieked Karna.

'What would you like to be called, then?' asked Raki. 'You can be called anything you like.'

Karna just scowled.

'Okay, you won't tell me,' said Raki. 'Now, listen to me, Kamala, I am offering you a job.'

'I'm not a girl and I wouldn't work for you, you banchod, if you paid me a hundred rupees.'

'You'll get more that that, even though you are a filthy little thrown-away urchin.'

'What job?'

'I need someone to collect merchandise.'

'I wouldn't collect your whatever that was because you are a stinking salah.' The toughness of his words were not echoed by his tone.

'Can you run fast?'

'You have seen,' said Karna grandly.

'And are you afraid of the police?'

'I am not afraid of anybody,' said Karna. 'Once I even fought off dacoits on the train because they were trying to hurt my mother. My real mother. The one who found me after I got thrown away. I beat them.'

Raki said, 'The other two who live here have been in the police station for three days. They might not come back but I need the stuff quickly. I will pay you to get it for me instead.'

'How much?' asked Karna.

'Two hundred rupees,' said Raki.

Karna stared at him, his eyes wide. He gave a little gasp, swallowed deeply, then said in a strangled voice, 'Three hundred.'

'Two hundred and fifty, then. Oh. You can keep the kukri. I have several other knives that are even sharper,' and he pulled from his pocket a flashing blade.

It was a cinema poster that made Shivarani suddenly realise that Karna was her sister's son. A poster advertising an old film version of the Mahabharata, with Dilip Baswani acting the part of the Sun God. She and Bhima were standing before it and Shivarani let out a gasp at the sight. 'I've made a terrible mistake,' she said. 'That boy who wore Koonty's chain looks exactly like this picture of Dilip Baswani. He must have been my lost nephew after all.'

'Yes, now you say it I think you may well be right,' agreed Bhima, examining the face in the picture carefully. 'We will have to find that boy again.'

Financial rewards were offered to anyone who could locate the child. Shivarani called up the kigalis and promised them handsome sums if they could lead her to their one-time fellow. When the weeks went by and there was no sign of Karna, Shivarani began to wish she had not rejected the goondas' help at the elections, for now, if she had friends among them, they might lead her to the boy she felt increasingly sure was her nephew. It was not only that he had the golden eyes of the Sun God, but she recognised the Pandava features in him, and even saw a likeness to her own father. But because she had rejected the goondas they not only would probably refuse to help but if they connected him with her, might do him harm to punish her. But in the end, she thought, she might have to allow them to beat up her opponents' voters, if it meant getting Karna back. Bhima accompanying her, she went round the bustees describing Karna, and asking if anyone had seen him. Although Bhima and Shivarani had put on their oldest clothes and hoped to be taken for locals, they were recognised at once. 'Come and see the sahibs,' went the shout along the lanes. 'Here is a big black one who has brought a babu with her.' People came running from every side and their already great enthusiasm increased more when Shivarani said, 'We will pay for any information you may give us that will help us find the child.' Instantly people appeared on every side who knew where Karna was. 'We need to see him first before we start paying out,' said Bhima. A moment later, twenty boys called 'Karna' pressed around them. 'I am Karna.' 'No he is not but I am.' People began to reach into the growing mob, pull boys out by their ears, drag them before Bhima and Shivarani, boys of every size and age and scruffiness. 'This is the Karna you are looking for and these other fellows are not called Karna at all.' Great scuffles broke out as the Karnas began to fight each other to shove each other away. 'It is me, Memsahib. It is me, Babu. I am the Karna you are looking for.'

'It seems to me that every mother in this bustee has called her son after the unlucky hero of the Mahabharata,' laughed Bhima to the crowd. 'Is there any boy here who is not called Karna?'

'It is hopeless,' sighed Shivarani as she and Bhima pressed on through the slimed and drain-wet lanes.

'Come on, Shiv. Don't give up,' cried Bhima. 'I'm sure we'll find him in the end. He can't just have vanished. We won't give up searching till we find him.'

Back in Malti's mother's house Shivarani felt defeated and told herself, if it had not been for Bhima she would not go on. How could I live without Bhima? she thought. He was always there when she needed help and yet she had never been able to do anything for him, however much she longed to. He was always so broke and she wanted to shower gifts upon him, to take him out to restaurants, to drive him over the countryside, to buy a plane ticket for him to take him on a foreign holiday. She wanted to buy him a new watch, a pair of cufflinks, new clothes, but of course all these things were unthinkable for Bhima would be far too proud to accept such gifts. She would have liked to invite him to come and live with her in the Hatibari bungalow instead of, as he was at present, staying in the YMCA. Other boys who had been in college with them already owned motor scooters and could afford to buy new clothes but Bhima's clothes were growing as tattered as Karna's had been the day he scrambled up the car and showed his bottom. Bhima's chappals had been repaired so often they were now more string than rubber. Shivarani wished Bhima would stop giving up all his time to charity and politics and instead earn some money so that his life could be more comfortable, but there was another reason too.

'I would like to get married,' he told her. 'But I can't afford to do that till I have a job, of course. What do you think, Shiv? Do you think I will make a good husband?'

'Yes, very good,' she had said, but really wanted to tell him, 'The best husband in the whole world.' She remembered again him playing with the children at the centre, and how she had imagined him being a father but she did not say that aloud either.

Raki heard of Shivarani's visit to the bustee and wondered if the name of his new messenger was 'Karna'. If so, he thought, it was lucky the child was out of the bustee that day for everyone had recognised the memsahib as Shivarani, the Naxalite politician. 'If you are that Karna and she gets a sniff of you and finds what you've been doing,' Raki warned the boy, 'then the police will beat you till you're pulped like a sucking mango. For this memsahib is a politician like the one who put my previous partners into prison.'

At first Karna did not know what to do. He had left behind him, among the kigalis, all the clothes that he had bought in the hopes of convincing Shivarani but all the same felt he ought to keep on trying for his mother's sake. On the other hand he had only promised his mother to get an education, and this was exactly what the goonda was giving him. He was giving Karna a salary too, which is more than his mother had ever expected. For a day or two he hovered this way and that between escaping from the goonda and presenting himself to Shivarani. But why should she believe him this time any more than before? She only wanted him so as to get the gold piece back, and he knew the goonda was right. And she might easily get him beaten up and imprisoned. Also he was starting to be happy with the goonda. He decided to stay where he was.

At first, after Sadas and Pashi were arrested, Raki was not worried, for he had paid up his due to the police with absolute regularity and down to every paisa. Unfortunately, though, the new Communist government was demonstrating its incorruptibility and instead of the two dealers being released after a few hours they had been incarcerated ever since. Raki was a member of a fifteen-goonda gang who gave protection to most of the main shops of the town. Protection was a profitable business for any firm that refused the goondas' services quickly regretted it. Their premises would be smashed up and their legs broken. But though Raki had offered every other goonda the jobs of Sadas and Pashi, he had not persuaded one. That kind of thing, they all said, was far too dangerous in this new Mr Clean Communist period and they preferred to stay with protection. It was in desperation that Raki had at last hit on the idea of getting a child to do his dealing.

Raki took Karna to meet his dealer, Nasrullah Amir Ahmed, a pot-bellied Muslim from the Punjab. Ahmed sat on embroidered satin cushions and leant against a sequinned bolster. His black beard was glossy and luxuriant, his kurta and churidars perfectly laundered and starched. He wore a long dark atchkan with diamond buttons and a richly embroidered rose-coloured cap.

'You are very smart, Nasrullah sahib,' said Raki, who even Karna could see was looking dishevelled in comparison, in spite of all the gold.

'This is because I am well looked after by my beloved bibi,' sighed Nasrullah. 'She is the best wife in the world and when are you going to get a wife for yourself, Mr Raki?'

Raki's lips did a bitter little twist. 'Who will give their daughter to a goonda with a limp?'

'What is the matter with you Hindus?' cried Nasrullah, throwing up his hands in mock despair. 'It is a pity you are not a Muslim, or I would give my own daughter to you for I would be happy to see her settled with such a fine rich fellow who is also in the business.'

Raki, not believing a word of it, smiled at the compliment, then gesturing to Karna, said, 'This fellow will work for me till Sadas and Pashi return. Go, go, Kamala, do namaskar to the sahib.'

'I am not a girl,' said Karna grumpily.

'Do you want to work for me or not?' demanded Raki. Nasrullah watched chuckling. 'Do as I say or I will fish in the heap for another boy.' Hastily Karna went over, and, bending, touched the Muslim's feet. 'Good boy, good boy,' said the dealer, patting Karna on the shoulder. 'Of course you are not a girl. Anyone can see that but all the same you are better-looking than those other two and I expect they will look even worse if, praise Allah, they are ever let out.' He examined Karna, then said to Raki, 'He's very small, though.'

'This is all I can get in such hard times,' said Raki morosely.

Raki went with Karna to start with, teaching him the principle of the job, though only selling ballpoint pens at first. At home Raki showed Karna the quick, almost magical hand movements required in the selling of the controversial products and taught him how to avoid the police. The situation had been much safer with Sadas and Pashi. They had worked together, one selling, the other standing nearby, ready to rush in defence if danger threatened. Raki's product was much more vulnerable now, with only a child selling and only himself guarding it, but what else could he do?

The boy was quick to learn and it was not long before he had mastered most of the tricks. Raki had been impressed from the start with the way Karna had fought him and if the child had put up less of a fight that first day, he probably would have dumped him and gone back for another. The child had courage, spirit and speed, three qualities required for the business and now Karna was proving to be clever too.

'Do not think for one moment of making off with my money,' Raki told Karna on the boy's first day in the business. 'For we goondas are involved in everything that happens in the town. We have contacts everywhere, from the poorest bustee to the richest bank, and will find you anywhere.'

Karna felt terribly pleased and proud on his first day of trading on his own as he stood with his tray of ballpoint pens slung from his neck and under it, the shelf of little packets which he could handle like a conjuror, bringing them into sight and out of it as though by magic. He knew what kind of person to sell to, how to let them test the product secretly, he knew how to take their money with no one seeing him. He would approach the likely customer, and before the foreigner or suitable desi person could rush on without a look at unwanted ballpoints, say in a special trading voice, 'I've got something very exciting. Would you like to see?' He had learnt to say it in Hindi and English. Raki and Karna had worked hard together at Karna's tone which was low and adult and did not come easily to the vocal cords of an unbroken voice. Then, when the potential purchaser's attention was engaged, Karna would show a fingertip smudged with white powder. 'Very high quality,' Karna would announce in his rich seductive whisper. How proud Dolly would be, he thought, that her son was earning so much money, and selling something so valuable that even rich people from Billaty bent down and tasted it. At last he had found a way of doing what she wanted and making something of his life.

Karna bought himself a new shirt with his first wages and carefully put aside the filthy old one on which were buttons his mother had once fastened, and a collar she had turned down. Later, when he found Raki using the rag to wipe up spilled milk, Karna became so furious that Raki, the proud goonda, who had never done dhobi work in his life, took it down to the pump and washed it with his own hands while the women looked on, jeering. What a sight, a goonda washing clothes. And what a tattered garment. Even our poorest people don't wear a bit of filth like that. When the fragment was dry, Raki brought it back up to the room and carefully folded it while Karna watched, thinking to himself, 'This is how a father would be,' and feeling something warm and trembly happen in his heart. The goonda said, 'There it will be safe,' and laid the little broken shirt with the female outfit, that, he said, had once belonged to Sadas' woman.

Karna decided that the next thing he would buy was reading and writing lessons, for Dolly had always wanted him to learn those things but had never been able to afford it. When he could read properly, she would not think she had spoiled his life by bringing him up as a pavement child. Karna felt sure that Arjuna was not making two hundred rupees a month, even though he did live in a grand house, went to a posh school and had everything bought for him. Arjuna, although only a year younger than Karna, was still an absolute baby and no one could imagine Arjuna selling heroin to tourists and managing day after day to escape being captured by the police or robbed by a drug-crazed customer. Arjuna would probably have been imprisoned or even murdered long before. Karna had in fact had a couple of near disasters in spite of all his care and Raki's training. As one man bent to sniff and taste Karna's white finger Karna had seen a policeman's shirt collar show under the kurta and was down the road and round the corner before the man was even straightened from his inspection. Then there had been the crazy foreign lady. Her very thin arms were covered in puncture marks and she had grabbed at his tray and, shaking it as though to rattle ripe mangoes off a tree, had started screaming words in English. He had not understood them but had known what they meant from the frantic desperation in her face. It was people like her, as much as Raki's warnings, that kept Karna from taking the magic powder himself. 'You will only need to take it once, and that will be your last day of trading, for you will lose your concentration and then be captured. So many goondas who have worked for me have lost the work like that and I would not like to see you coming to the end of such a promising career at your young age.'

Karna looked forward all day to that moment in the evening when he got back to the room in the bustee, dumped the money wads onto Raki's lap and waited for the goonda to pat him on the head and say, 'You are a clever boy.'

He could go to the cinema as often as he wanted, these days. Films were, and always had been, his greatest joy and now he could afford to sit in decent seats. His favourite actress was still Poopay Patalya. Karna wept when he saw her in her first grown-up part, playing a Harijan girl. She was acting with Zeenat Aman and there was a terrible scene in which thakurs wearing black leather jackets, dark shades and riding motorbikes, beat up Poopay because she had taken water from their well. That night and for many thereafter, Karna dreamt of rushing in to rescue Poopay and during the day he became absent-minded, working out the ways he would take revenge on the vile thakurs who had defiled his goddess.

The goonda protection gang met at intervals in Raki's room to discuss business over tumblers of arrak and on these occasions Raki insisted Karna slept in the corridor. 'Our discussions are private and also if you are to keep mind clear and body alert you will need proper sleep.' Sometimes the goondas would laughingly protest, when Karna was being sent away. 'Let the boy stay and drink a glass of arrak with us before he sleeps, for one day he will grow up and become one of us.' But Raki was adamant. 'This fellow must allow no drop of spirit to pass his lips for his full attention is needed for trading tomorrow.' So Karna would go out, wrap himself in a blanket and lie down on the concrete passage floor, whose hardness, each time, reminded him of being on the pavement by his mother. He would lie, listening to the muffled shouting voices of the drunken goondas, while his body and mind strained with the longing to have Dolly's arms around him and to hear her words of love. He would fall asleep wanting her, while the voices of the goondas became ever louder and more incoherent. Sometimes it would only be at dawn that the conversation ceased altogether and the gang felt into snoring drunken sleep.

Shivarani had paid to have posters put up in the town, with a description of Karna. 'He wears a gold medal bearing the name of his mother and anyone with information leading to finding him will get a reward of rupees ten thousand.' Karna saw them, and even read them but he did not believe a word of it. Why should these people want him now, when his mother was dead? It was some trick to get the golden disc back. He was amazed that such rich people should be so desperate for a little piece of gold, but he decided that trickers like them would probably not even pay out the reward if Karna was handed over. Or perhaps the Naxalite Memsahib was hunting for him because she knew he dealt in drugs. In that case if she caught him he would end up like Sadas and Pashi. He was not going to let that happen. Raki saw the posters too but he could not read and assumed that this was some new government rule, which Raki knew would not be obeyed or some new notice of traffic arrangement, that he knew would not work. It was Nasrullah who told him what the posters said. Raki had gone round to settle up for the month and the dealer, as he gathered up the money, said jokingly, 'Has that Kamala of yours got a golden disc round his neck?' then laughed till his belly wobbled at the unlikeliness of such a thing. Raki flinched with shock. 'Please tell me what you mean, Nasrullah Sahib.'

'Haven't you seen the posters?' The dealer was too pleased with his own funniness to notice Raki's reaction. Still laughing he said, 'My own boy has been circumcised so is clearly not a Hindu otherwise I might have tried to offer him to Shivarani Memsahib and claim the rupees ten thousand for myself, though, of course my young fellow does not wear this golden disc.'

'What is this about, Nasrullah Sahib?' asked Raki. 'Please tell me more.'

'They are offering the sum for the person who finds a boy wearing a golden medal that bears his mother's name.'

Flustered as he was, as Raki hurried out of the dealer's home and set off for the bustee, he began to add things up. And they all made sense. The Naxalite minister had gone looking for a boy called 'Karna' and even at the time Raki had thought that his new boy might be that very one. The boy said his mother was a zamindar who had thrown him away. Karna had a golden disc on a chain round his neck with what he said was his mother's name, and now there were posters round town offering a huge reward for such a boy. If the reward had been on offer two years ago, when Karna had first come to him, Raki would have rushed Karna off to the Shivarani Memsahib, to claim it, but things were different now. Karna knew too much about the business. He knew the dealer, knew where Raki lived and had met Raki's customers. Karna could identify them all and what use would money be if Raki was sent off to join the other two goondas in prison? Raki would be ruined if Karna was returned to Shivarani. But ten thousand rupees? But no, but no. Or yes, yes. Raki's mind rushed this way and that. All kinds of worries began to circulate in his mind. Just as he had caught sight of that disc two years ago, sooner or later someone else would too. And now anyone who saw it would not just try to steal it. They would tell the Naxalite minister and put Raki in dreadful danger. He decided the only hope was to get the disc off the boy's neck for without it, no matter what Karna said, no one would believe him.

That evening when Karna came home, Raki said, 'This week we have saved up rupees one hundred so let us celebrate.' And he brought out a bottle of arrak. Karna was surprised. 'But you are always telling me never to take anything that will slow my reactions and muddle my mind, Dada. I have seen people reeling and falling around the streets after drinking this stuff.'

'For this once, because I can see from how you have now become a grown-up man, we will relax that rule, and become like true brothers. Come, sit by me and we will drink together to our success.' He poured a thick glass tumbler full of arrak and passed it to the boy.

'What about you?' said Karna. Hastily pouring a tumblerful for himself as well, Raki took a took a carefully judged mouthful, not so little as to cause suspicion, not so much as to dim his alertness. He would need all of that if he was going to succeed in getting that gold off the boy's neck. When he had swallowed, he smiled, smacked his lips, and wiping his mouth with the back of his hand said, 'Wonderful. Now you, my dear Kamala. Go on. Take a sip. What do you think?'

Karna sipped, swallowed, and at once began choking and spluttering. 'Oh yukk oh yarr,' he screamed, sending spat sprays of arrak into

Raki's face. 'I'm not drinking that stuff. It burns my mouth.' Raki sighed and all the rest of the evening he tried to think of other ways of achieving his objective. Even members of his gang would claim the reward for themselves if they found out who Karna really was.

Raki tried a new tactic. 'I think it is dangerous, going out in the streets with that valuable thing round your neck. Why not leave it with me. I will look after it here while you are outside. I am worried for your safety.'

Karna, though moved at Raki's concern, refused firmly, but on an impulse bought an imported American baseball cap as a present for the goonda. Raki received the gift with an initial disbelief. 'This is for me? You have bought it for me?' Then he had put it on his head and examined his reflection in the cracked piece of mirror.

'You look like a very fine gentleman now,' said Karna.

'Thank you, Kamala,' said Raki.

After that, every time Karna saw the hat on Raki's head, he felt a flush of proud pleasure.

By now people were going round town catching boys as though they were fish in the Hoogly. They would put little medals round the boys' necks with the names of women on then haul the children off to Shivarani or snatch at the shirts of little street boys to see if there was a gold chain underneath. It was as though everyone was engaged in some enormous treasure-boy hunt. Jokes on the radio were made about the hunt for the boy with the golden disc, cartoons were drawn of him in the papers, the jewellers were doing brisk trade in writing on gold medallions, for how many female names could there be? Sooner or later someone must hit on the right one, then claim the reward.

Karna learnt to be alert all the time when living with Raki for after many hours of drinking with his fellow goondas, Raki would become violent and attack Karna, kicking his sleeping body or punching him with his fists. Once he even got his gun out and tried to shoot the boy, but was so drunk that he could not get his fingers round the trigger. Sometimes Raki would try to beat Karna when he was sober and then Karna would have to dart and dash and scuttle to avoid the flailing fists while Raki came after him, roaring, 'Why so little today?

Have you been playing with your kigali friends instead of working for me? Have you been giving my good money away to those no-good beggar people again?' This was a side of Karna that Raki had tried hard to eradicate. 'What is this, giving good cash to some female called Laika?'

'I only give her my own money, Raki Dada, I promise you,' Karna assured him. 'She wants to stop being a beggar and turn into a prostitute but her face is too ugly. She is collecting up for an operation.'

Laika got her skin graft and was able to open her eye and move her lips but her scars remained and she told him that sometimes men still shrank from her. Karna ran his finger along one of Laika's red lines. 'When I was little you told me these were a map of India's rivers,' said Karna.

Laika laughed. 'Did I tell you that?'

'There's the Ganges by your eyebrow and that's the Jummuna near your nose. The Hoogly flows beside your mouth. How can people not love somebody who has holy rivers on their face?'

'That is so sweet,' laughed Laika and, opening her choli, folded his face between her breasts.

Raki was outraged when a kigali was bitten by a rabid dog and Karna paid for his injections. 'What do you want to waste money on that kind of scum for?'

'He will die otherwise,' protested Karna.

'Why does that matter? There are too many of his kind around already. You are a very stupid boy, and I should have chosen a cleverer one, then,' raged Raki, whacking Karna in the stomach.

The goonda was unpredictable too. The first time Karna described how he had teased a couple of police constables, letting them get quite close to him then darting out of their reach just when they thought they had got him, Raki roared with laughter. But a week later when Karna did it again, this time letting the police get even closer before giving them the slip, Raki became livid with rage, and, taking the boy by surprise, grabbed him and beat him so hard and long that Karna could hardly walk next day. 'What? Why?' asked Karna, biting back sobs.

'You stupid little salah. Next time they will really catch you and then what will happen to all of us?'

But when Karna got back, his pockets tight with money, the packets all sold and Raki said, 'You are becoming better than Sadas and Pashi,' all the punches and the beating would be forgotten and Karna, who had never been praised for anything since Dolly died, would feel truly happy.

9

VANA-PARVA

'Arjun,' said the faithful Krishna.
'Arduous is thy cruel quest.
But thy foaming coursers falter
and they need a moment's rest.'

As he sat on the river bank, looking furiously across to the land
that belonged to Ravi who had murdered his father, and caused the
death of his mother and was being rewarded by ever greater riches
and acclaim, Arjuna was filled with anger at the way the good got
punished and the wicked rewarded. Ravi had been made a minister
by now and owned another house in Delhi. From the Hatibari river
bank you could see his marble palace, twice the size of the Hatibari
and growing bigger ever week.

To forget his anger and his loneliness and to avoid having to look
upon the injustice of Ravi's fortune, Arjuna began to go into the
village where the misti wallah pressed sticky sweets on him and the
rickshaw wallah begged him to step into his vehicle without charge.
The darjees would call out, as the boy went past, 'Come here and
be measured, Arjuna Baba, and we will stitch you the best shirt you
have ever worn.' Women would pluck mangoes off their trees and
press them into Arjuna's hands, girls would clamber out from under
the buffalo they were milking and offer the boy a mug of the thick
sweet white milk to drink there and then, hot from the udder and
salty from their fingers. They would hold the mug, then, to his lips
as though he was another baby calf, laugh with happiness as he drank
and let their fingertips trail across his white-frothed lip as they drew

the cup away. The people of the village felt guilty about Arjuna, as though it was their fault that the boy was now an orphan. The boatmen would take Arjuna for trips along the river, Arjuna sitting on the scarlet cushions where once his great-grandfather had leant. The river was filled with memories for Arjuna. Here his mother had waded along beside him, her thighs pale pillars glimmering in the water, her unfashionable bathing suit frilled out around his head as she tried to teach him swimming. Along this bit, and now Arjuna did not want to think it but the thoughts came all the same, the Sun God had come swimming to his mother. And this was the place where, before he was born, the hand of Durga had carried his new-born brother. He forbade the boatmen to take him near the house of Ravi though for he could not bear to look upon the place. The puntsmen told Arjuna stories of the places they were passing, 'That was once the house of Warren Hastings, and he and your grandfather would listen to music in that place. Dancing girls performed before them.' Or 'In that house your great-grandfather had a secret woman.' 'This is the place where your father, Pandu, met a girl called Shonali.' The village boys would set up games of cricket and nowadays they fought to have Arjuna on their side, because since he had been going to school he had become a champion bat. If he happened to cycle past the Hatipur primary school, the schoolmaster would rush all the children out into the yard and order them to chant, 'Good morning, Zamindar Arjuna.'

DR Uncle, worried that the boy was spending so much time with peasants and forgetting the dignity of his station, bought Arjuna a pony and hired a man called Piara Singh to come from Calcutta to teach him how to ride. 'All your ancestors could gallop towards a charging wild boar and sink a long lance into its shoulder. It will be a shame if, in this generation, the horsemanship skill is lost.' The pony was a little Katiawari mare called Janci whose ear tips met at the top so that Arjuna had to lean down and look through the ring they made, to see his way ahead. The teacher came every day for a month, first taking Arjuna round and round the lawns on a long rein, then progressing so that he rode on his own in the enclosure of the weedy tennis court until the boy was able to ride well. Then Piara took Arjuna galloping over the bunds, the little mud walls built to retain the water for the rice paddy in the growing season and ideal for jumping when the crop had been reaped and the fields were dry.

Raki feared he was growing soft, for lately he had started to feel affection for the boy, Karna. In the morning when he woke and saw the boy sleeping at his side, something warm and cosy would happen in Raki's heart which alarmed him. This kind of weakness was dangerous for a goonda, who must make self-preservation and the interests of the business his prime objective.

When Karna got home to find Raki waiting with a meal ready Karna would be filled with a kind of happiness he had not known since Dolly died. To Karna, who supposed beatings and unpredictability to be paternal characteristics and even signs of affection, Raki felt like a father to him. As he stood on street corners, watching out for customers, he would sing aloud, his tremulous renderings making passers-by smile. People with not the least wish for a ballpoint pen would stop and buy one, then linger on, intrigued, when the little singer of grown-up love songs began to whisper, 'I've got something very interesting here.' There might be one or two people in the world who are now addicted to drugs because of a Hindi film song.

Karna and Raki were sitting cross-legged on the floor, eating mutton curry and rice, when they heard someone or something coming up the four flights of cement stairs so slowly that the creeping crawling sound went on for half-an-hour. Then there came a scrabbling at the door which Raki and Karna ignored, thinking this was some arrak drunk who would soon go away. But after a while the door opened.

For a moment Karna did not recognise them as people at all. They crawled in, groping, unable to see because their eyes were hidden under purple and orange swellings the size of too-ripe mangoes and something had been done to their legs so they could not stand on them. Even Raki seemed taken aback. Sadas and Pashi tried to speak but when they opened their mouths, most teeth were missing, their gums were pulped and their words were incomprehensible.

'You see how careful you must be,' Raki told Karna, gesturing to his returned partners. 'If you let the police catch you or this Naxalite lady minister finds out where you are, this is what will happen to you.'

Neither Pashi nor Sadas would say what had happened to them in the prison, but if Pashi saw a piece of string he would shrink away whimpering and Sadas would let out screams of fear at the sight of a ballpoint pen so that Karna's merchandise had to be stored in the outside locked godown where Raki kept the bulk of his product and also all the weaponry required by the goonda protectors. Sometimes Raki would worry slightly that the boy should have easy access to all his most precious goods, but there seemed nothing else that he could do for the screaming and gibbering of Sadas made it impossible to keep it upstairs. For weeks Sadas and Pashi could not walk or eat or pee and Karna learnt to sleep through the sound of their yells and groans of pain and their screams of nightmare terror. Raki would pulp rice with milk and drip it through their crushed lips and even then it would take agonised ages before they could swallow.

The police were paying Karna ever greater attention and one day one of them almost caught him. For a moment Karna thought that he was done for as he ran with the policeman at his heels. But when he looked back and saw the overweight, sweating policeman lumbering along, and realised how easily he, Karna, could outstrip the fellow, the boy could not resist turning and with an insulting gesture, letting out a jeering laugh before sprinting on. He was enjoying his games with these two policemen more and more and revelled in the furious expressions on their faces when they realised that once again Karna had escaped.

'Don't make fun of the police,' Raki warned. 'These fellows can be very vengeful,' and as he spoke realised that he was definitely getting soft because he did not want Karna to get injured like Sadas and Pashi.

'They will never catch me,' boasted Karna. 'I am cleverer and quicker than any policeman.'

Raki went on feeling anxious, though. 'Don't tease them. It's a very dangerous thing to do.'

'Karna is not afraid of the police. Karna is not afraid of anything,' the kigali would tell each other. Karna had become their hero and their benefactor. In the winter when he found them shivering in the park he bought them shawls. And when Satish, a boy of his own age, had his hand crushed by a taxi he was catching, Karna set him up as a shoelace seller. Raki however was contemptuous of the kigalis and annoyed at Karna's helping them. 'Why do you waste your money on such trash? You save up and buy yourself a motor scooter and leave those dirty children to solve their own shit.' Or 'Hang onto all the money you can because although you are young now, one day you will need a woman and they are expensive.'

Sadas was the first one to start improving and a month later his words began to make sense.

'Hey, Kamala, come here, Kamala,' Sadas muttered one day, when Raki was out. Pashi leant against the wall and watched, grinning.

'I am a boy and not a girl,' said Karna.

'Come here, baby, come to me, Kamala, and let me hold you.' The battered goonda crept across the floor, his arms outstretched. 'I had a woman once, a real one. Oh, how I loved her, with what joy I fucked her. Come to me, Kamala, and let me fuck you too.'

Karna made for the door but Pashi leapt in front of it and blocked Karna's way. As he ran past Pashi to escape Sadas, the former put out his foot and sent Karna crashing to the floor, then Pashi threw himself on top of the boy and held him down while Sadas crawled over the room, to where the clothes were kept. Throwing aside Karna's little shirt, the goonda pulled out the clothes and make-up that had once belonged to his woman.

Then Pashi held Karna's head and Sadas painted scarlet on the boy's lips saying, 'This is the very one I put on my woman's mouth before I strangled her.' He could not stand without support but his arms were strong and his grip ferocious.

'You are a pig. You are disgusting,' screamed Karna, as scarlet smudged his teeth and tongue but each time he tried to get away, they punched him in the throat or stomach so that in the end he had so little wind left that he could not resist them. Then the goondas dressed Karna in the murdered woman's blouse and sari and thrust bangles on his wrists. They mascaraed his eyes and drew under them in lamp black. They put rings on his fingers and painted his toenails. They smudged rouge on his cheeks. Sometimes Karna would get away from them, and make dashes towards the door and they would watch, laughing, and catch him at the very last moment, just before he managed to escape. They had tossed aside his kukri, as they pulled out the woman's clothes and several times Karna almost managed to grab it. His struggles amused the goondas greatly. But Karna's strength and wind and hope were spent at last and when they tried to put earrings on him and finding his ears un-pierced, chopped large and bleeding holes in his lobes with a knife tip that was blunt, he could do nothing more than scream. And go on screaming as they pushed gold rings into the gout of blood. At last Karna lay very still and afraid because soon they would put necklaces on him and they would find the thing he already wore around his neck. In the end that was the only way in which the goddess blessed him. There were no necklaces among the dead woman's jewels.

Three hours later it was over. Sadas and Pashi looked at each other, and as though waking to reality, their expressions became worried. 'What will Raki say?'

'We should kill him and hide the body,' suggested Sadas. 'Then tell Raki that he ran away.'

As they spoke, Karna staggered up, grabbed his kukri and rushed at them. They were tired and he was young. He chopped wildly, slashing Pashi across the face and Sadas in the arm then made a dash for the door. As they tried to stem their bleeding, the pair made an effort to stop him but Karna was out, and racing down the stairs. Blood, from where they had cut his ears, mixed with the widely smeared lipstick. Mascara smudged across the swollen bruises on his face. One eye was closed completely. He ran staggeringly because of the things they had done inside his body. His own blood and the goondas' body fluids stained the silk cloth of the murdered prostitute's now tattered sari. Bangles shattered from his arms as he scrambled downwards.

Pashi and Sadas crept to the head of the stairs and watched him go. 'Bring back my gold,' screamed Sadas.

'Leave him,' said Pashi. 'He will have to come back, for where will he go to otherwise? Perhaps Raki will not believe him.'

Sadas said, 'If Raki could see what Karna looks like now, he would love us more than Karna, certainly.' Then he and Pashi crept back into the blood-and-semen spattered room.

Karna burst into his little godown and took out his pen tray. Then, bruised and bleeding, dry sobs racking his hurting body and with his kukri in his hand and the pen tray round his neck, Karna ran through the streets of Calcutta. He did not know where he was going, he was running to be as far from the filthy goondas as he could. As he ran, pieces of broken gold kept falling from his body but he never stopped to gather them. He ran as wildly and as mindlessly as the day his mother had been dying and he had tried to find a way to save her. Round his neck, his cardboard pen tray bobbed with ballpoints falling but he did not stop to get them. Underneath the little bags banged softly in their hidden drawer and Karna felt a little relief, amongst all the horror, that he had had the sense to bring along the valuable product, so that he had some means of living from now on.

Raki had been with the other goondas, in a distant village, providing political protection and when he returned that evening, he climbed the stairs feeling surprised that no delicious smells of simmering mutton korma was reaching his nostrils. Karna had become good at cooking lately, and Raki looked forward to the tasty meal after his long journey. But when Raki opened his door, he forgot all about the food in the shock at what he saw inside his room.

'It is that wicked boy Karna who has done all this,' Sadas and Pashi said as Raki gazed in horror at the shattered possessions, the blood-splashed walls and the wounds on the goondas. 'He has hurt us badly as you can see.'

'But why?' cried Raki.

'Look, look,' cried Sadas, pointing to where the women's clothes had been. 'He was stealing the gold jewels and when we tried to stop him he attacked us.'

'These boys from the streets are always the same. They are evil and treacherous and not to be trusted,' said Pashi.

'But he has been with me for more than three years. He has been like a son to me. He has never cheated me in the very smallest way.' Raki felt his eyes heat up with hurting tears.

'And he has been in the widow's godown. We saw him there. He has probably stolen all your stuff from there as well.'

'You should chase him now and put an end to him for he will be sure to betray us and then all of us will be done for,' said Sadas.

'You are right,' said Raki sadly. In all his life he had never met an honest person till Karna came to him. 'The boy seemed like my son but I know now what I must do.'

His chest was burning with the pain of disillusionment as he loaded his pistol. 'I am sorry that my boy did this to you,' he said as he went out.

Karna, who had always been so careful, who had traded in the darkest corners, who talked only in whispers when he was selling, who had slunk in daytime like a nocturnal animal, now ran in daylight in full view of all. Sometimes he would sink to the ground and crouch shuddering and sometimes he would scramble up and run again as though he was a dog with rabies. No one paid attention to the bloodstained child, who could have been a male or female. Such things were not unusual in Calcutta. But the police noticed him. They had been trying to track down Karna for two weeks and till this day he had always eluded them, letting them almost catch up with him, then suddenly vanishing, mocking them and shouting jibes.

'I'm sure it's the child dealer,' the constable said. 'This fellow may be wearing women's clothes but even with his face all beaten up, I think it is the same. I recognise that tray of ballpoint pens.'

'He is clearly an even more depraved child than we first thought,' said the second policeman. 'You can see from the state of him that he has been involved with some kind of filthy sex.'

Karna put up no resistance when they caught him. He was so numb with self-disgust and horror that he hardly minded it. They pulled him out of sight into a doorway, ripped the cardboard tray in bits and found the plastic packets in a moment. Then they set to work upon his body.

'You had better not do any more of that to him,' said one constable to the other after half an hour. 'We need him alive to give us the names of his associates.' But the other constable did not listen. He needed all the revenge he could take for the way this chit of a child had teased and outwitted him for so long.

The prostitute, Laika, who had managed eventually to get enough money together to pay for a skin graft that had made her sufficiently acceptable to achieve her ambition, was with a customer when she heard the screaming. And through the sound of the customer's grunts and groans Laika recognised the voice of Karna. Shoving the man away, she scrambled off the charpoy, and rushed out into the street, her hair wild and still pulling her sari back on. When she saw the policemen on top of Karna she began yelling, 'Stop that at once. Don't do it to him. Don't, don't, don't.' Her customer appeared, clutching his pyjama over his large erection and began shouting furiously, 'Come back at once, you bitch, and give me what I paid you for.'

The two constables were so engrossed in what they were doing that, at first, they were unaware of either the prostitute or her outraged client. After a while, though, one turned, saw Laika and, as if she was an annoying fly, gave her a swipe that sent her flying. With blood running from her nose where she had hit the ground, she began to run to the kigalis, her client coming after her, yelling abuse.

'They have got Karna. Come quickly, before they kill him,' Laika screamed.

The kigalis went racing to the alleyway that the girl had pointed out to them. The two constables were bending over something inert. One constable straightened and taking his gun from its holster, casually shot into the mob of oncoming boys. One gave a shriek and fell. The rest stopped abruptly.

Raki had heard Laika's shouts, seen the kigalis running and when he heard the gunshot, guessed what it might be. 'There, go there,' he told his rickshaw wallah, and moments later he was out of the rickshaw and at the other end of the alleyway. At first he thought, with dread, that it was too late, for the police already had Karna. But then he became a little hopeful that the presence of the kigalis might confuse the issue and that if he acted swiftly he would get a chance of doing what was needed.

The police still had their attention on the kigali mob. Raki saw Karna struggle to sit up. He had his kukri in his hand and, as Raki watched, Karna raised it to hack at the leg of Constable Two.

'That's my boy,' thought Raki, tears of love running down his face. 'My brave brave boy who never gives in. It is a shame that this courageous spirit should be extinguished, but all the same it must be done.' And he carefully aimed his pistol at Karna's heart, but at the very moment before pulling the trigger, Karna's kukri came down on the calf of Constable Two. The policeman staggered, began to fall, and met the bullet meant for Karna. Karna spun round, to see where the shot had come from, saw Raki standing there, and over the child's battered swollen face spread a smile of love because Raki, his goonda father, had come to save him.

Raki, sobbing, raised his gun again and carefully aimed it at Karna's heart. But Constable Two was quicker. He raised his gun, pulled the trigger, and Raki's chest exploded.

In the long moment of shock and silence that followed, Karna stood staring at the fallen body of the beloved goonda who had been about to kill him.

10

BAD OMENS

'At a distance,' Krishna answered,
'fiery Arjun fought his way,
Now he seeks the archer, Karna
and he vows his death today.'

'What do you think, Parvathi?' Shivarani asked the maid. 'Why will these women of India not listen to me?'

'Because you have no brothers or husband, Mem, you don't know the truth about women,' said Parvathi. 'They prefer male children as much as the men. It's the women who have let the men get the better of everything.' And Shivarani knew she was right, for you cannot subdue a whole sex, half a nation, without its compliance. She had written articles in any paper that would publish her, she had spoken on radio and had addressed big crowds in cities but there was always something more important than rights for women. Floods had drowned one bit of the country and drought was starving another part. The prime minister's son had taken bribes. Leading companies were smuggling money out. Leading crooks were smuggling goods in. Outrages from Shivarani's old party, the Naxalites – beheadings, tortures, bombings, stabbings. Scams and scandals are the stuff that news is made of, not the fact that a lot of Indian women seemed to be missing.

As Basu drove, she thought to herself, it is myths told by mothers, ayahs, grandmothers and aunts that have distorted thinking in our country, that have offered the prospect of unearned immortality and proposed uses and misuses of women as though they were the property of men. Even goddesses, she thought, are traded as though they were cows in the tales in the Vedas.

'What do you think when you hear such tales, Basu?' she asked her driver. 'Isn't it wrong that Parvathi, a goddess, should be a chattel to be traded?'

'Yes, Madam,' said Basu and added, 'I want to marry Parvathi.'

Shivarani was taken aback for a moment but then said, 'I know you will be a good husband to her.'

The car did a little swerve as though Basu was nervous then he said, 'My family will want to know how much dowry you will give her.'

'I am against the giving of dowry. It is one of the things I am trying to stop,' said Shivarani. 'I will do all kind of other things but I can't do that.'

The car moved along erratically for a few moments. Basu said, 'I beg you, Memsahib. I love her but my family will not let me marry her otherwise.'

'Come now, Basu. If you love her then go ahead. How can your family stop you?'

'They can't,' admitted Basu, 'but it will be so much trouble. For her as well as me if she has no dowry.'

A picture came into Shivarani's mind of brides doused in paraffin and set alight by their parents-in-law because the dowry had not been forthcoming, or insufficient. But she had pledged to stamp out the dowry system. She shivered. 'I can't do it, Basu, I am sorry,' she said.

Basu did not speak again for the rest of the two-hour journey.

That evening she met Bhima in Calcutta.

'You look sad,' he said. 'Is there something wrong?'

'It is difficult to combine my beliefs with my actions,' she told him. 'I long to give Parvathi a dowry, but how can I do it?'

'Oh, blow ethics, Shiv,' cried Bhima joyfully. 'I would always put people before morality.'

Shivarani sighed. 'I know you would,' she said, 'because you are braver and more foolish than me.'

'I like that, Shiv. I am a brave fool. I know I am, though one of these days I might surprise you by doing something clever.'

Shivarani did not ask what, but she felt something tremble in her heart at his words. She asked, 'What do you think I should do to get people to pay attention to my cause? Where have I gone wrong? Why won't the women of India listen to me? Why won't the men understand what they are doing?' She felt tired. She wondered if she could go on anymore. She looked at Bhima and his dear face was a beloved landscape in which she felt safe. Happiness began to bloom in her heart like a lotus opening as she looked into his dark eyes that always shone with laughter, his thick hair, the rich chocolate colour of his skin that looked almost black in the gloom. And the dream re-awoke ferociously in her heart. What did she care about all those other women when here, before her, was her very own chance of happiness. She would give it all up, she thought, for Bhima's sake. She would stop being a politician and become a wife, a lover. A mother. No more walking round the country, no more addressing crowds of gawping people who heard but did not care or understand. But marriage to a beloved person. She imagined herself permitted, at last, to caress that dark and darling body and her longing grew so huge for a moment, that she actually put out her hand to touch Bhima's and then withdrew it again. She could not make that move, it was up to him. She wanted to say to him, it doesn't matter about the job. Just being with you is all I want, all I've ever wanted, and I don't mind being poor if I am with you. I don't mind having nothing at all as long as I can share my life with yours. Even though lately the fame of her women's movement had begun to spread, funds to come in and the media was, for the first time, paying attention to crimes against women, she was ready to abandon it all. Shivarani had set up a Calcutta office with accountants to handle the money and several clerks to manage the details. She would give all that up for Bhima.

They were in the South Indian coffee shop. On the floor was a squashed cockroach, the walls glistened darkly with twenty years of oily fingering. The sole window, small and barred, was so thick with grime and webs that the light that filtered in was, though outside the midday sun was blazing, the same brown colour as the splendid South Indian decoction of coffee. This is where they always met when Shivarani was in Calcutta because Bhima could afford it and refused to go anywhere where he could not pay. He had refused to stay with Malti's family or even eat with them so often and so emphatically, that they had given up inviting him.

'What do you think, Bhima?' she asked again. He had not been listening the first time she spoke, but had his finger on his lips and looked at her with his eyes laughing, his other finger pointing at a large rat that was plodding its way through the café, making for the image of the Lord Ganesh seated on his vehicle mouse.

'Oh really, Bhima,' laughed Shivarani. 'In any other country a rat is considered the carrier of disease and here we are, coddling the creature with garlands and little feasts.'

'Isn't that lovely. Isn't that wonderful,' cried Bhima. 'Isn't that the most wonderful thing about our glorious country.' By now the rat had reached the god, and was settling down to eat the daintily set out food, a little slice of fresh coconut, a small dish of dahi and a steamed lentil cake called vadai.

'We treat rats better than we treat women,' said Shivarani trying to sound disapproving, but succeeding only in laughing. She could not be serious when she was with Bhima.

'To answer your question,' he said. 'What you need is a spectacle. You must do something even more dramatic than bribing the Prime Minister.'

Because Arjuna was at school and Gadhari was losing patience with Parvathi, Shivarani took her back to Calcutta with her, when she stayed in Malti's house. The maid had become glum and withdrawn after Shivarani refused to give her a dowry and Shivarani, who had at first been relieved at Parvathi's silence, began to feel guilty and wish that the chattering feckless Parvathi would return. So she felt almost relieved when Parvathi burst suddenly into the drawing room and announced that a rickshaw was standing at the front doors, in which sat a Calcutta prostitute and a beaten-up boy.

Though Shivarani said sternly, 'I keep telling you, you must not come into the room like this. You have to knock first. And there is no need to come troubling me with such matters. Tell the servants to get rid of them,' she was unable to suppress a smile.

Parvathi, looking almost like her old self, went on enthusiastically, 'But even though the boy is all over blood and bruises I think he is that dirty urchin who says you are his aunty. The kitchen servants have even threatened to give beatings but they won't go away and the prostitute keeps shouting that because this boy is the son of Koonty Mem and because you are Koonty Mem's sister, you must take him in.' Parvathi was breathless with excitement. Her eyes sparkled with suspicion.

'That's enough, Parvathi,' said Shivarani, swiftly getting up. 'I will talk to them.'

'And the prostitute is saying that Koonty Ma is a bad mother because she sent her servants to chase her son away. But why does she say that, Ma? Everybody is asking this question in the kitchens.'

'Enough, Parvathi,' roared Shivarani, hurrying to the door.

'But these are dirty people and you must never believe anything they say,' urged Parvathi as she followed Shivarani to the front doors.

Shivarani gasped with shock and horror at the sight of the beaten child in the rickshaw. 'They have hurt his mouth a lot, Ma,' Laika told Shivarani. 'So he is having difficulty in talking. But his goonda is dead and he has come to give you his piece of gold because, although you are so rich already, you want it so much.' A flicker of scorn crossed Laika's scarred face.

Karna pulled out his gold medallion and reluctantly offered it.

'That is not why I have been looking for you,' Shivarani told Karna seriously. 'I don't want to take that. It is yours and for you to keep.'

Karna stared for a moment, his mouth open, then at top speed, tucked it back inside his shirt again, all the time keeping his surprised gaze on Shivarani. Laika said, 'But you must get him education in exchange because that is what his mother, Dolly, wanted and he has no one else in all the world, now, to give him these things except for you.' At Laika's side Karna painfully nodded his agreement. 'This is a very good boy,' the prostitute went on. 'Even though the people of your house are rich and eat ghee with their rice each day and wear slippers of leather, there is no one in your house who is as kind and brave and good as this poor little boy. He is always helping people when they need it and you are lucky that such a boy wishes to come to live with you. And also, Ma, it is necessary that you take him, because as you see he has been beaten badly and for the moment till his wounds have healed up, he will have no way of living unless you feed him. And he is surely a member of your own family and not the proper child of Dolly because the dhobi woman was of a very black complexion and this Karna, as you see, has a skin that is as fair as your own.' When the prostitute had finished speaking she sat, waiting breathless for Shivarani's response.

But Shivarani's doubts were returning. How could this stunted ugly creature be the brother of the healthy handsome little Arjuna, and son of her pretty sister? As though reading her doubt Karna said, his voice muffled with pain and swelling, 'I swear, Ma, that everything Laika tells you is the truth.'

'Shall I call the policeman and ask him to come and give the pair of them another whacking for going around with such wicked lies?' suggested Parvathi.

'What do you think?' said Shivarani on the phone to Bhima. 'He does have golden eyes, and Koonty said that the eyes of the Sun God were golden. He has Koonty's medallion too.'

'Even though he is probably a fraud, from what you say he is badly hurt and needs medical treatment. And perhaps at the same time you can find some way, in Calcutta, of establishing his identity,' suggested Bhima.

'It will be a relief to know, one way or the other,' agreed Shivarani.

In the days that followed Karna felt inside him a hurt that might never heal because he had looked into the face of the person he loved, and understood that that person was about to kill him. It would have been better, Karna thought, if Raki's bullet had got him instead of the policeman for what had he got to live for now? Everything in his world was gone, and even its memories had turned bitter now, for those three years with Raki, his goonda father, had been wiped out in that single moment when the goonda raised his gun and pointed it at Karna's breast. Karna sometimes dared not shut his eyes, because when he did he saw the goonda wearing the baseball cap that Karna had given him and aiming his gun at Karna's heart. Karna did not want ever to think of Raki again and yet kept thinking of him all the time.

The crippled goondas, though, had damaged Karna in another and perhaps even more dreadful way. Their actions had altered his perception of himself and made him feel filthy, and unworthy of his mother. He wanted to tell Dolly, 'Before they did those dirty things to me I would have killed them both if I had had a gun.' He wanted her to come and cleanse him and because that could not happen his self-disgust went on scalding him and there was nothing that would ease it.

The general opinion of the Calcutta medical experts who examined Karna was that, though small and thin, he was probably about eleven years old. By the end of a month, during which Karna's face plumped out and health returned to his skin, there came moments when Shivarani thought the boy looked a little like Arjuna. Then Shivarani was told of a new test that was being used by some of the embassies on the children of prospective emigrants in which the DNA proved their identity.

When the results arrived and Shivarani knew for sure that Karna was indeed her dead sister's son, instead of feeling joy she was disappointed. While searching for Koonty's lost child she had imagined the little girl putting her arms round Shivarani's neck, gently kissing her, saying how happy she was to be back with her family again. But it was unthinkable that Karna should do or say such things. He was tough. He was too old for his years. He was not really a little boy at all, but a small and cunning adult.

When he was well enough she decided to take him back with her to the Hatibari where, she hoped, with gentler children to play with he too would gradually learn to exhibit sweetness. 'It will be fun for Arjuna to have a boy almost his own age to play with,' she told Bhima. 'He is often lonely in the holidays when the cousins are away.'

Gadhari was furious. 'Over my dead body will this filthy street urchin and bastard of Koonty come to defile our home.'

Even DR Uncle was doubtful. 'Don't you think, Shivarani, that the child will be better left among his own kind of people? Because he has always lived on the pavements he will find it very difficult to adjust to a civilised existence, I am sure.'

'He has nowhere else to go and the police will pick him up again if he is left in Cal,' pleaded Shivarani. 'Also he is the son of Pandu's wife. He is family in spite of his background.'

In the end even Gadhari had to agree that there was no alternative. 'Though he will have to eat among the servants and when I see him I will turn my back,' she said.

Before they left Calcutta for Hatipur, Karna insisted on returning to the goonda's room to retrieve his shirt.

'But you have a fine new one on already,' protested Shivarani.

'But all the same I must get back the one my mother gave me,' insisted Karna.

*　　*　　*

Later Shivarani would describe the scene in Raki's room. Blood everywhere, two filthy, half-starved crippled goondas creeping in their own excrement. The only reason the shirt was still there was because it was so ragged that even the desperate goondas had been unable to find a use for it. At the sight of Bhima and Shivarani with Karna, the two goondas cringed away and holding their hands to their heads, began to plead, 'Please, Sahib, Memsahib, we did not want to hurt him. We were only taking a little pleasure. There is so little pleasure in this life, that you cannot blame us for taking it where we can.'

Bhima stared at them with contempt, then said, 'These bits of filth are not even worthy of being punished.' To Karna he said, 'Get your shirt, little brother, and then let us leave these dreadful people to their sin and dirt.'

It was the morning that they were leaving for the Hatibari that the police came round.

'It has been brought to our attention that you have a boy called Karna on your premises.'

'Please leave the room. I need to speak to this officer in private,' said Shivarani to Parvathi.

II

UDYOGA

And the holy rite concluded, Karna ranged his men in war.
To the dreaded front of battle Karna drove his conquering car.
Morn to noon and noon to evening raged the battle on the plain.
Countless warriors fought and perished, car-borne chiefs were pierced
  and slain.

Arjuna went down to the stables where he expected, as usual, to find
his groom waiting with his pony already saddled. But Janci was still
in her stable, the groom was nowhere to be seen and the pony had
no water. He filled the pony's water bucket himself and as he was
putting it into Janci's box, the groom and Bika, Laxshmi's daughter,
emerged out of the straw. The groom looked flustered, Bika was
laughing. Both of them had straw in their hair and stuck to their
clothes.

Arjuna had not seen Bika for several months and the change in her
made him draw in his breath. 'Bika, what are you doing here?' She
was beautiful.

'You gave poor Prodosh too much work so I have come to help
him,' Bika said in a tone that made Arjuna know it was not true. Her
eyes were sparkling.

'But Sahib, please don't tell my mother that you have seen me
here for she does not like me to be near . . . horses and will beat me
if she knows.' Bika let out a scream of laughter and the groom tried
to stifle a giggle.

Riding his pony was the only thing that made Arjuna happy these
days. When he cantered through the Hatibari gardens, for a short

while he would stop remembering how his mother had wrapped a chain of iron round her body and drowned herself and forget the day a man called Ravi had killed his father. But all his joy vanished when Shivarani told him that Karna had been found and was coming to live at the Hatibari.

'I won't have that dirty creature in my house,' he yelled, his fists clenched, his face red. 'It's my house. I won't let him in.'

'It's not properly yours till you come of age,' said Shivarani. She tried not to let him see her anxiety and her doubt. 'Till then you have to do what your guardians say.'

'Then I will tell DR Uncle not to let him come,' screamed Arjuna.

'Perhaps Arjuna is right,' said DR Uncle. 'I think it is a bad idea to have this boy living here as well.'

Shivarani pleaded with the uncle. 'What will people say if they hear that the zamindar threw the child of Koonty onto the streets? And also this child is wanted for murder. What kind of reputation will this family get if they catch him and he is convicted?'

'Can he not go somewhere else?'

'Where?'

When it became clear that there was no avoiding the arrival of Karna, Gadhari retired to her bed of richly carved, hard, black jungle wood and stayed there saying, 'The very thought of Koonty's bastard makes me feel ill. I shall not get up again as long as the creature is in our house.' And she reached out and took yet another pill from one of the bottles that massed on her bedside table.

On the journey back from Calcutta, bringing Karna to live at the Hatibari, Shivarani tried to imagine the boy was her own, but could not. The thought, though, caused a dull ache to rise inside her heart.

The little boy sat stiffly upright and stared ahead as though wanting to pretend he was not here.

Cautiously Shivarani put her arm round Karna, hoping to comfort him, but her embrace felt inept and the child's body was stiff and unyielding.

During the three hour journey, for the whole of that time, Karna wished he had Laika at his side instead of the big black memsahib with the enormous teeth and the voice of a man. He tried to keep as big a physical distance as possible from Shivarani, but often when the car did a sudden turn, or stopped to avoid hitting a buffalo on the road, he would be flung against her body.

When she put her bony arm round him, Karna sat frozen with awkwardness and did not know how to respond. She reached out her hand, stroked his head and, trying not to notice his wince, asked, 'Are you happy to be coming home at last, Karna? Your troubles are over now. You will never have to sleep on the pavement again, or go hungry. From now on you will be happy and cared for.'

'When my mother was alive I slept on the pavement and often felt hungry but I was always happy and cared for when she was there,' said Karna stiffly.

'Yes. I am sorry,' said Shivarani and did not know what to say next.

As they reached the Hatibari gates, Karna remembered being here with his mother and had to squeeze his mouth tight to stop a sob coming out. Today, though, the durwan did not try to drive him away but put down his paper, sprang to his feet and did a smart salaam.

As the car moved along the drive, Karna saw where the malis had chased him across the lawn. And when they came in sight of the bend in the river where he and Arjuna had raced each other and Arjuna had refused to believe that Karna was his brother, Karna felt a flush of triumph.

The moment the car stopped before the house, Karna flung open the door and scrambled out without waiting for Shivarani.

Arjuna was standing at the top of the marble steps, his expression scowling, his fists clenched.

Karna recognised him at once. Scowling too and clenching his fists even tighter, Karna began to climb the steps. Trying to walk like a maharaja in a Bollywood film, pretending he had a crown on and that a cloak flowed from his shoulders, Karna marched up to where his furious half-brother waited. He felt regretful that he had only red rubber chuppals on his feet and that his New Market shirt was made of crimplene and not silk but after all, he told himself, grandeur comes from inside.

'This is your new brother, Arjuna,' said Shivarani hopefully.

'He is not my brother, and I am not letting him in,' roared Arjuna flinging out his arms, ready to block off the entrance.

Karna reached the top and standing in front of Arjuna so that their noses were almost touching, commanded, 'Get out of my way.'

'It it my house and I won't have you here, you dirty beggar,' yelled Arjuna.

'How dare you be so rude to me,' said Karna sternly. 'I am your older brother and you must call me Dada.'

Arjuna reached out and hit him in the face.

Shivarani shouted, 'Stop that.'

Karna caught Arjuna's leg and jerked it, cracking him to the floor, then he stepped over Arjuna's prostrate body and entered his home.

Shivarani tried to build some kind of relationship between Arjuna and Karna in the days that followed. 'You must try to understand Karna,' she begged Arjuna. 'He is your half-brother and you and he should be liking each other.'

'I hate him,' said Arjuna. 'I wish he had died in the river.' Arjuna could not bear to look at Karna. The constant reminder of what his mother had done sent waves of nausea through him. And now he thought about it, he could see his mother's face in Karna's.

The two half-brothers were unable to encounter each other without fighting. The Kaurava boys were delighted and would shout, 'Hit him, Arjuna.' 'Stick your fingers in his eyeballs.' 'Squeeze his neck until he strangles.' 'Let's see some blood,' as Karna and Arjuna punched each other.

Boys were trouble in every way, thought Shivarani. They were having dinner in the great dining hall. Arjuna was scowling at

Karna. Karna, as usual, was slurping and slopping his way through the food, eating like a pig from a trough. Red-eyed Parvathi was dashing breathlessly in and out, snorting like a gloomy pony through a blocked nose, bringing fresh chupatties blown up like beige balloons. Shivarani was reflecting on how much easier it was to deal with a thousand women than two young boys, when Karna asked, 'Why does Parvathi have to do all the work?'

Shivarani frowned and said, 'It's her job.'

'She is only a young girl,' said Karna. 'You should be sending her to school.'

Parvathi, fascinated, forgot her misery for a moment and stood, the dish pressed to her bosom, gasping with interest.

'Thank you, Parvathi. That's enough. You may go,' said Shivarani sternly.

'You keep saying all children should get education so why isn't Parvathi getting it?' persisted Karna.

'You shut up, you beggar. What do you know?' cried Arjuna.

Shivarani took a deep breath. 'Parvathi is a servant and you do not know what you are talking about.'

'And you keep saying that women must have equal rights with men,' pursued Karna.

'Like all boys should have equal rights with other boys,' sneered Arjuna.

'Shut up,' said Karna.

The Kaurava boys began to giggle.

DR Uncle said, 'Have some more chicken, Arjuna.'

'She is lucky to have this job,' said Shivarani. 'Without me she would have starved on the streets.' She paused, turned her attention to her mogali murghi for a while as though the roast spiced chicken might provide inspiration and tried to push out of her mind Basu's request for a dowry. She added, 'You are right in a lot of ways, Karna. But you will have to become older before you can understand everything. Life is just more complicated than you realise. Get out, Parvathi. What are you hanging around for?' and she slapped her bare palm on the table.

'Sorry, Memsahib,' said Parvathi, putting on an air of humble dismay and as Shivarani turned away, made a banana finger at Karna, whose support humiliated her, and made it seem as though he, a pavement child, and she who was forced to wait on him, were from the same group.

Shivarani caught the insulting gesture. 'Get out,' she roared and grabbing a chupatti from the plate she flung it at the girl who scuttled, laughing, out of the room.

At first Karna would wake in the morning just before the sun rose, and for a moment forget where he was. Then, when he remembered, he would feel hemmed in with walls and oppressed by the ceiling, which was where his sky should be. He would get up from the great carved Hatibari bed and sneak downstairs with bare feet, wearing only his pyjamas and go out to explore these village mornings which were something new for him. Each time he stepped into the Hatibari gardens he became amazed all over again at the silence. On the Calcutta pavements you could not sleep for a moment after the sun was up unless you were ill or dead. Calcutta was always noisy, but early morning was the worst. That is the time beggars hurry to their posts, rickshaw wallahs crawl from under the wheels of their vehicles, clear their throats of phlegm and ring their bunch of metal bells, mothers throw jugs of water over their screaming children's heads to ready them for school, crows hoarsely reclaim yesterday's territory, lorries and cars choke and cough into action, barbers shout invitations to shave or cut hair, little boys loudly beg to be allowed to polish shoes or catch taxis, women shrilly hold out fruit, ballpoint pens or shoelaces to workers rushing to the office, shopkeepers open up their stalls with rowdy clangs and clatters and fortune-tellers warn the rushing businessmen that they need to know what the coming day held for them.

Karna stood in the Hatibari garden and breathed in the heavy scent of flowers and waited for the first rosy, pearly flush of the rising sun and first experimental sound of birdsong. He would become almost breathless with pleasure as the rays began to pierce the branches of the orchard trees and turn the surface of the river scarlet. Once the gardener found him there, standing with his head a little on one side, listening to the sound of the river, smelling it. The old man laughed at Karna and told him, 'If you are going to be a zamindar, little boy, you will have to learn to lie in bed till midday.' He knew this was the boy who had jumped on the zinnias, but had been warned by DR Uncle not to talk about it. As the sun rose higher there would come the sounds of labourers' voices as they prepared themselves for work in their fields or on the zamindar's property. The milking cows in the village would summon their calves as they were driven to their grazing. Karna would go to where the carting bulls were being harnessed for mowing the Hatibari lawns and, stroking their sticky noses, watch as the men went over the bulls' humps for pressure sores, before putting the yokes on. Once, not knowing about Karna's background, the little boy who helped the gardeners came running up and began walking before Karna and whipping the dew drops off the grass with a long bamboo.

'You needn't do that,' said Karna, to whom no such thing had ever happened before. The gardener's boy was shocked. 'But, Sir, it is my holy dharma to ensure that your shoes do not get wet.'

Karna's good spirits would be a little spoilt when Arjuna cantered haughtily by on his pony, but when the rest of the family rose his happiness came to an end completely and he would be filled with an almost unbearable temptation to return to Calcutta though Shivarani had told him he could not do that yet for she was still sorting things out with the police. Karna felt uncomfortable when he was with the family – they always made him feel he was doing something wrong. At meals, though no one said anything, he would catch a sudden raising of eyebrows as though he had broken some unknown rule and the feeling made him want to splatter food, let the gravy dribble his wrists, let water spill as he drank from the glass. Even the way they all tried to talk to him kindly made him feel they were patronising, and making an effort to see good in him. Who cares about their princely ways? He came from real people who ate food to keep alive and walked because they were going somewhere. These people, thought Karna, made everything into some kind of puja, as though they thought they were gods. Even the evening walk was called a constitutional and then DR Uncle and Gadhari Aunty, if she was well enough, would dress up in outdoor shoes and wrap scarves round their heads as though they were about to climb the Himalayas, then walk very, very slowly, his hands clasped behind his back, hers holding her sari hem away from the ground, across the lawn and back.

He began to go to the village and chat with the boys there, drink tea and smoke beedis with the men, linger at the misti wallah's stall and talk about films. The people of Hatipur enjoyed Karna's company because he knew almost every film story and could sing most of the songs too. He would sit by the dobar and laugh with the girls over some comedy as they did their washing or swagger with the other young village men, copying a heroic actor and pretending to pull out guns or throw punches. As time went by Karna began to spend more and more time in the village and less and less in the Hatibari till he was hardly home at all and Parvathi would come back from the village with shopping and tell Gadhari, 'They say that that Karna was getting drunk with the misti wallah last night,' or 'I saw that Karna peeing in the open like a village boy.'

'Our family is being disgraced by the behaviour of this bustee child,' complained Gadhari. 'Here am I with my health gone, and what have I done to deserve this karma, that I am being asked to care for Koonty's bastard and that his presence is being a humiliation to myself and my family?'

DR Uncle tried to soothe. 'The boy is only here till term time. He will go to school with the others and after a term at Doon he will have learnt how to behave like a sahib.'

But Gadhari was not totally displeased and wished that Kuru Dadoo had been alive when Koonty's downfall became known. For everyone knew about Koonty and the Sun God now. Shivarani had thought it best to come out with the truth in a way that would let people understand that her sister's disgrace had not been her fault, for otherwise how would Karna's presence be explained? If Kuru

Dadoo had known about Koonty, thought Gadhari, he would have appreciated Gadhari's virtue and not have been taken in by a pretty baby face.

Parvathi had given up begging Shivarani. She began to feel despair. She was seventeen and would soon be too old for anyone. Basu was starting to say, 'If we get married,' instead of 'When we get married.'

'When I am rich,' began Arjuna, 'I will get a dowry for you, Parvathi, so that you can marry Basu.' He too had tried to persuade Shivarani to give Parvathi a dowry.

'I can't do it,' said Shivarani. 'Please don't discuss the matter any more.'

'Just give her some money as a present, then. Don't call it a dowry.'

'I may not call it a dowry, but the opposition will. All my credibility will be lost.'

There came a day when Karna thought he could not bear living at the Hatibari any longer, and determined to return to Calcutta no matter what Shivarani said.

'Just hang on a little longer,' she urged. She was having a terrible struggle getting the required money together and had even approached her parents in Canada for it. DR Uncle had done what he could but the murder of a policeman was an expensive matter and even he was having trouble in getting together such a sum without Gadhari finding out. 'You know how vengeful the police can be but in a few months I hope to get the last of the money to them,' Shivarani told Karna.

Parvathi listened with interest. 'Has he done a crime?' she asked eagerly.

'No, of course not,' snapped Shivarani.

'Why are they vengeful then?' Parvathi persisted. 'What were you paying them for?'

'Go inside this minute,' stormed Shivarani. 'What are you doing here? You are supposed to be helping with the cooking. How dare you hide there, listening to my conversation.' She seemed unreasonably angry, thought Parvathi, as she scuttled off.

That evening Parvathi found Karna setting off for the village.

'Mem must value you a lot to pay so much to the police,' she said. 'Why did you do it?'

'You shut up,' snapped Karna. 'All this is nothing to do with you. I didn't do it, anyway.'

'Why do they all say you did?' persisted Parvathi.

'I didn't even have a gun,' said Karna. 'So I couldn't have done it.'

Parvathi was starting to feel the excitement of a wild dog that has been on the trail of a sambhar deer for ages and has nearly caught up with it.

'Poor Karna. It is so bad of them to accuse you, for I know you would never do a thing like that.'

'Raki killed the policeman and though they say I was an accomplice, it was not true,' said Karna.

Parvathi gasped. She suspected that Karna had been involved in a bit of pick-pocketing or shoplifting. But murder of a policeman. No wonder Karna dare not go to Cal. In her wildest imaginings Parvathi had not thought of this.

'If I had had the chance I would have killed the policeman very slowly so that he hurt for hours,' said Karna. 'And then I would have killed Sadas and Pashi. And Raki. I wish it had been me who killed Raki.' When he said 'Raki' his voice had a choke in it as though someone had gripped him round the throat.

Shivarani stood before a full-length mirror and Parvathi knelt before her, arranging the hem of her sari folds. The maid, who was helping Shivarani to get ready to go to Calcutta for a press conference, said, without looking up, 'Have you thought any more about giving me a dowry so that I may marry Basu?'

'Stop that, I don't want to hear any more of the matter, Parvathi,' Shivarani snapped.

'That was a lot of money you gave the police for Karna,' said Parvathi, giving a small tweak to a fold of silk till it came in line with the rest.

'Keep out of this, Parvathi.'

'But considering he murdered a policeman, it is lucky that you did not have to give them more.' She rose and started to pin the silver Shiva brooch onto Shivarani's palu.

'Who told you that?' demanded Shivarani, really angry now.

'Karna.'

'He was lying. Why should he tell you such a thing?'

'Because it is true, Ma?'

'How dare you, Parvathi. This is outrageous,' said Shivarani to Parvathi's mirror reflection. Parvathi saw that her hands were trembling.

'But all the same,' said Parvathi, clicking the pin shut. She stood behind Shivarani, her legs apart, her chin up. Shivarani turned her head and glared at the maid for a long, long time and Parvathi glared back. Then Shivarani looked back into the mirror again and said to Parvathi's reflection, her voice shaking a little, 'You have been a faithful servant, so perhaps on this one occasion I will drop my principles and pay some money towards your marriage. Though we will not call this a dowry, but simply a sum to help set you and your husband up in life.'

'Thank you, Memsahib,' said Parvathi, and she did not feel she needed to sound grateful.

The press conference took place in the Grand Hotel. Shivarani was late because the traffic was extra bad and the candidates for the other parties were already seated. Later the journalists told each other, 'That must have been why Shrimati Shivarani was not quite her usual self.' When one journalist asked her, 'What are you doing to put a stop to the dowry system?' her answer had been so quiet that the man had had to ask the question a second time.

'Everything I can,' she repeated, in a tone that was almost mumbling.

And later, when the question of police corruption came up and she was asked, 'What steps will your party be taking to put an end to the bribing of our police force, Shivarani?' instead of booming out condemnation as they had expected, she looked flustered and there was a long pause before she answered, 'Many.' The journalists stared, amazed, for this was the question that always brought forth her most dynamic and most emphatic speech. Her great manly voice would usually boom and roar for ages when this was asked of her. After an even longer silence, Shivarani said, 'It will take time to put an end to it, though.' Her face had gone red and her tone was sad. She seemed to be hiding something.

Arjuna was outraged when he heard that Karna was coming to school with him. 'Everyone will laugh at me for having such a brother.' And when he heard that Karna's fees were to come out of the estate he became even more furious. 'Hatibari is mine. I inherited it from my father. I won't let my money go to pay for Karna's school.'

'Your uncle has power of attorney till you are twenty-one,' said Shivarani firmly.

Karna did not care what Arjuna felt, however. He was filled with happiness because after all these years he was about to fulfil his promise to his mother and get a proper education. He was going to go to the best school in India. In spite of everything that had happened to him, he was getting the chance to make something of his life at last.

Shivarani and Karna travelled alone on the train together because Arjuna and the Kaurava boys were required to get to the school a few days earlier

Shivarani had even brought a picnic meal for them and handed him sandwiches and a drink of coffee from a flask as though she was a mother. Or an aunt. He felt tongue-tied and was unable to respond when she tried to engage him in conversation. The journey seemed to go on for ever. During that night, as they lay on their bunks,

Karna could not sleep out of embarrassment, because he could hear the small movements of Shivarani's breath and body. He wondered what it would be like if the train was attacked by dacoits. Would he spring to Shivarani's rescue as he had done for his mother when he was seven? Would she be impressed with him like his mother was? Would she love him when she saw that he was unafraid of the dacoits and ready to die to protect her? But no dacoits invaded the train and Shivarani only saw the worst side of him, seated at her side – gauche, ugly, and shy.

Shivarani felt hurt, at first, at Karna's sullenness and ingratitude and shot hinting glances at the boy but he only sat hunched in his seat, answering her attempts at conversation with inarticulate grunts and accepting the food she had so kindly brought for him with barely a 'thank you' and certainly not a smile. She tried to imagine her sister, Koonty, holding this child when he had first been born and wondered how Koonty would be with him now. The boy looked so small and lonely and she wanted to hold him, to caress him but everything about him warned her off for Karna's heart was somewhere else. His love had already been given away. There was nothing left for the people of the Hatibari. She was filled with a pity that had no outlet and faced with a problem to which she had no answer.

He became aware of her scrutiny and flinched away.

'Karna, would you like some more gugni?' That was the only comfort she could find to offer though she knew that Koonty, Boodi Ayah, or even Gadhari would have found something more.

When Karna vanished at last into the school, Shivarani sat for a while trying to feel inside herself, and see what she felt. But she only had a sense of relief that the boy was now someone else's responsibility.

12

THE DIVINE CUIRASS

'This the helmet-wearing Arjun, sprung from Kuru's mighty race.
Pandu's son and born of Pritha, prince of worth and war-like grace.
Long armed chief, declare thy lineage, and the race thou dost adorn,
Name thy mother and thy father, and the house where thou wast born.
By the rules of war Prince Arjun claims his rival chief to know.
Princes may not draw their weapon 'gainst a base and nameless foe.'
Karna, silent, heard this mandate, rank nor lineage could he claim.
Like a raindrop-pelted lotus, hung his humble head in shame.

Shivarani got a letter from the women in the hills. It was written round the edges of a piece of newspaper and was so smudged and ill-spelt that it took her ages to decipher it. 'They are trying to cut our trees down and if the trees go, then the earth that we need for our food crops will start running down the hillsides like we have seen happen in other places. The rain will stop falling here if our trees go and also we will have no firewood. Help us please, Shivarani Ma.'

When the women of the cool mountain village saw Shivarani's car arriving, they came running out, crying to each other, 'Shivarani Mem has come to save us.'

'We must put our arms round the trees when the woodcutters come,' Shivarani told the women. 'And then they will have to cut through us, if they cut the trees.'

Shivarani stayed in the village for six weeks, spending most of the day with her arms round the trunks of trees, till every part of her inner arm knew the rough cool sensation of bark. Her hands and elbows ached for days after. Men came with chainsaws and threatened the women, but they held on. They tried to drag the women away, but there were too many and pulling women's bodies did not seem right to the men. The incident came to the attention of the media and there was such an outcry that the timber company was forced to withdraw.

By the time Shivarani got back to the Hatibari she found that Karna had been sent home.

He had been given a letter for his parents before being taken to the station.

'I don't have any parents,' he had said.

'If you were staying on you would have received a red card for that cheeky answer,' the head had responded. 'Give it to your guardian then.'

'Why do I have to go?'

The headmaster glared at the child. 'It is all explained in the letter. Your father . . . your guardian will read it to you.'

He was put on the train alone, with a message to his family that someone meet him at the station. After he sat down in his compartment he stayed quite still for a long time. His mouth was dry and his heart trembled. Then he took out the letter and stared at it, as though something about the sealed envelope would make sense of the catastrophe. If his mother had been with him, she could have opened the letter and read it to him. Quickly he had to suppress this thought, which woke wild and desperate memories of the train journey to the Hatibari with Dolly. His craving became so intense that his grief almost spilled over. Already other people in the compartment were looking at him with a mixture of curiosity and compassion.

He would not go back to the Hatibari, he decided. He could not go back. The shame would be too great. He could imagine how Arjuna and the Kaurava boys would enjoy his humiliation. But then he thought, 'Where should I go?' He would be arrested if he went back to Calcutta. He knew that. And he had promised his mother to stay with these people until he had been given a proper education.

When he arrived at the Hatibari, he stepped out grandly so that no one would guess at his shame . . .

'But why are you back? What happened?' his uncle kept asking, while Gadhari glared in the background.

'I did not like it there,' he said.

'Come on, Karna. Tell me the truth.'

'It is in this letter,' said Karna. 'But I have to give it to my guardian so I will wait till Shivarani Aunty gets back.' He dreaded his aunt's return.

'It seems that he is almost illiterate. We tried to give him special lessons for a while but in the end we decided it was not fair on the boy or on the school, and that it is too late for him to try to catch up now,' Shivarani read, two days later.

Karna stood before her, tense and shivering.

'I will think of something,' she told him gently and reflected that she had a better understanding of how to cope with a whole timber company than one little boy. Later she said to her brother-in-law, 'I should have been here. I should have been looking after him.' She was filled with remorse.

'It's not your fault. You just can't take a fish out of the water and expect it to thrive on land. I think you should let the boy go back to where he came from. He was very aggressive at school, apparently. Forever picking fights, particularly with Arjuna. And when he is around here, he and Arjuna fight so much that our heads are reeling with it. I think all this anger from these two boys might be at the bottom of much of my wife's illness,' DR Uncle said.

At half term Arjuna came back. 'The whole school is laughing because you have been expelled,' he told Karna. 'And they're all pleased, because nobody liked you. They all hated you, in fact.'

'I'll kill you, you salah,' said Karna through gritted teeth and went for his half-brother, grabbing him by the throat. Arjuna, who had been taught wrestling at school, siezed Karna by the legs and yanked him off his feet. Karna jerked Arjuna down as well. The pair lay on the ground, struggling, locked together hopelessly, each cracking in pain, grunts bursting unwanted from their throats. Arjuna's legs crushed Karna's spine. Karna would not loosen his grip. Sometimes Karna would manage to get a little advantage – a fist in the throat, an elbow in the jugular. Sometimes Arjuna would manage to grind a knee into Karna's groin or crush his free fist into his opponent's neck. To an onlooker they would have seemed like lovers. They might have lain there for days, till one or the other became weak from thirst and the battle was won without honour, if Shivarani had not come upon them and forced them apart.

'It is your fault for sending me to that school,' shouted Karna, turning on her. 'You should have known and paid for me to have some lessons before going there.' His face was red, his fists were clenched. Shivarani gazed down at him and wondered what to do.

'Karna,' she tried to talk gently. 'Perhaps we should think of another kind of education for you. Something more practical. Something that will help you find a career in later life.'

'Like a New Market porter,' he sneered bitterly.

'Oh, darling, don't talk like that. It's not what I meant.' She would have liked to hug him as she hugged trees, but trees don't wince away. 'Isn't there anything you really want to be?'

'A film star,' Karna said.

'Would you like to be a film star?' For a moment she felt hope, because here was something to work on, but then her heart sank again. What chance in the whole world had this hideous little boy of getting even the meanest film part? All the same she decided to make use of Karna's little flash of ambition.

'Then what about learning something that will be helpful for an actor?'

'Yes. Yes,' he said. He sounded eager.

'So where shall we start?' This was the most positive conversation she had ever had with Karna.

'I want a horse of my own,' he said. 'Arjuna has a horse and I want one too. All the movie stars ride horses in battles.'

Shivarani flinched. 'It takes a long time to learn how to ride well enough for that.'

'I can already ride a bit,' said Karna. His tone was almost pleading. For a moment Shivarani saw sweetness in his expression. 'Piara used to let me ride on his ponies when I was in Calcutta.'

Shivarani felt troubled. Arjuna, as heir to the Hatibari estate, had a substantial allowance. She was giving Karna pocket money from her own funds and because she refused to take bribes, was finding it difficult enough already to pay for everything.

'I just don't know what I should do,' she confided in DR Uncle.

'My dear Shivarani,' he said, 'If giving the boy a pony will put an end to all this fighting and quarrelling you go and find one and I will pay for it. Then perhaps we'll all have some peace.'

Karna gave a little shout of joy when Shivarani told him. He suppressed the sound instantly but it was too late. Shivarani had heard it. She smiled and thought, I have made him happy. Perhaps everything is going to be all right now. But a moment later her optimism was shattered by Karna saying, 'Because I am older than Arjuna, my horse must be bigger.'

On the way to the Tollygunge riding stables Karna peered out of the car window as though, by willpower, he could make the journey go faster. His knuckles were clenched so tightly with the intensity of his desire that they went white.

Shivarani, looking at him, thought, 'The police will not recognise him today, because they will never have seen him looking happy before.' But all the same she warned Karna, as they got out at the riding stables, 'Don't say anything that might let anyone guess who you are.'

Karna walked slowly past the lines of stalls, examining each pony's face until he reached a white mare, over whose stall was written, 'Devi'. Like a man who has suddenly been blown away by love, he stopped and stared silently.

Shivarani and the riding-school grooms waited.

'This one,' said Karna.

'We will buy Devi,' said Shivarani and to Karna, as the mare was loaded into the horse box, 'Now that the pony is yours, I hope there will be no more fights with Arjuna.'

Ignoring this, Karna said, 'I am going to call her 'Poopay'. All the way back to the Hatibari he insisted on sitting in the back of the horse box with his new beloved. Shivarani, in front beside Basu, kept looking back to see the boy gently caressing the pony's face, his lips moving as though he was murmuring love.

'Come on. Let's see you ride it,' cried Arjuna next day. Then stood watching, hands on hips, while Karna tried to get on. He had not ridden for many years and it took him several inept hops and scramblings before he managed it, during which he counted up the number of times Arjuna laughed, vowing to take revenge for each one later.

'Don't scoff,' chided Shivarani. 'Karna will get the knack of it soon. You weren't so good when you were first learning, either, I remember.'

Arjuna was furious when he heard the name of Karna's pony. 'It is an insult to the most pure and beautiful woman in the world, to call a horse after her,' he raged. 'You must tell the salah to give the horse another name or I will punch him in the mouth.'

'I can call my pony what I like,' said Karna. 'Why should he interfere? Was I allowed to choose the name for his pony?'

Every day for a week Karna trotted round and round the lawns, bumping up and down while Arjuna flowed gracefully and scornfully over the horizon on his golden Janci. And when, at last, Karna became able to ride round the estate on his own, if his path crossed Arjuna's, the boys would glare and try to slash at each other with their riding whips.

'I am definitely a better rider than Karna,' boasted Arjuna. 'Today I saw the sky between his bum and the saddle when he was cantering.'

'I can pick up a handkerchief from the ground at a gallop,' said Karna. 'I bet Arjuna can't do that.'

Piara Singh drew white targets on the trees and told the boys, 'See who can get a dart in the most targets at a gallop.' For an hour the woods were filled with the sound of galloping and the whack of darts in wood. Karna got forty-five and Arjuna thirty.

'Thought you were such a good rider?' jeered Karna.

'He's ruined my trees by jabbing the spikes in so hard,' complained Arjuna.

Piara had the blacksmith put metal blades in the end of long bamboo poles, hammered white-painted pegs in the lawn then taught the boys to pick them up on the blade of the lance. 'It is not a matter of beating each other,' he told the boys. 'Tent-pegging is a skill and the rider must learn the grace, balance and rhythm of a dancer as well as concern for the animal he is riding.' But even Piara was a little shocked at the ferocious way the two competed, teeth bared, expressions creased with furious determination. 'All the same this is better than beating each other up,' he told Shivarani. 'They are both good riders now. Why not let them come to Calcutta and race against each other on my horses?'

Shivarani agreed reluctantly and made another visit to the Calcutta police station, explaining the situation, and donating another substantial cheque to the police fund.

On the morning of the race Karna woke, shaking with excitement and apprehension and all the way to Calcutta he was very tense, telling himself over and over, 'I've got to beat Arjuna. I've got to beat Arjuna.'

A milky mist lay at knee level when they arrived at the racecourse. Hoopoes bounced along the rails. Piara Singh stood waiting with a couple of excited thoroughbreds.

A crowd of several hundred people was gathered at the side of the course, mostly disabled beggars and ragged little boys. There came small cheers and cries of welcome at the sight of Karna. A girl with a terribly scarred face pushed forward and hugging him, said, 'May Durga make you the winner, Karna.'

'Thank you, Laika,' he said. The boy that Karna had saved from rabies began shouting, 'Come on Karna, come on Karna,' even before Karna had mounted. Other people took up the cry. 'Come on, Karna.'

'Who are they all?' asked Shivarani.

'My friends,' said Karna stiffly. 'You see, here in Calcutta there are many people who love me.'

'There are people who are fond of you in the Hatibari too, Karna, if only you would let them,' Shivarani said.

Arjuna made a disgusted face.

'These horses go pretty fast and you can't stop them till you get right round the course,' Piara told the boys. 'It's lucky that the pair of you ride well, for I wouldn't lend out my beloved horses to just anyone.' Karna and Arjuna glared at each other, each wishing the riding master had said he was the better of the two.

Syces held onto ropes that were taut with eagerness, slung round the horses' necks. The horses were tense and showing the whites of their eyes.

Syces legged the boys into the narrow saddles, adjusted stirrups, tightened girths while the horses jibbered and pranced and sprayed white foam over their riders' knees.

Piara said, 'The men will hold on till you are ready to go.'

The oat-fed racehorse Karna sat on felt as jittery and insubstantial as smoke compared to his Hatibari pony.

'Do not worry about stopping, sirs,' said Piara Singh. 'When you come round the course, the syces will stretch a net across the track to catch you both.' He caressed Karna's mare's neck with a gentle hand and, smiling, said, 'Although you have not asked, her name is 'Draupadi'. She is called after the wife of all the Pandavas and I love her very much.'

Karna smiled. The wife of the Mahabharata heroes had been won by Arjuna in an archery contest. When the hero told his mother he had gained a prize, she, not knowing that it was a woman, said,

'Whatever you have got you must share with your brothers.' Thus Draupadi became the wife of all five Pandava brothers. Later one of the brothers played a game of dice and lost everything, including Draupadi. The man who won her tried to take possession of her publicly by pulling off her sari but the god Krishna performed a miracle, so that although the villain unwound and unwound the sari, the cloth never came to an end, and Draupadi's modesty was saved.

The sun was just rising and its rays were glowing, flame-coloured, through the brilliance of the mare, Draupadi's, mane. Karna suddenly didn't feel like fighting a contest but was tempted instead to canter away on this beautiful golden mare and forget about beating Arjuna. His gaze was lingering on the glowing distance, when a blue jay let out a loud screech and Draupadi shied wildly, nearly causing Karna to lose his seat. Arjuna shouted, 'Better not fall off just yet. Wait till the race has begun.'

'Right, go,' cried Piara Singh and the syces unloosed their charges which went off with the sizzle and whoosh of Diwali fireworks.

Karna had worked out a way of giving himself maximum advantage. He instantly took the rail, forcing Arjuna to take the slightly longer way round on the outside though to keep this position he had to stay so close that his boots rubbed the rail. As he rushed onwards, through the hiss of wind and the gasping of the horses, Karna could hear the roars from the crowd, 'Come on, Karna.'

Side by side the two heroes flew, while the sun rose higher and blue jays rose screaming. People kept yelling, 'Karna, Karna, Karna.' No one, Karna noticed, was shouting for Arjuna.

Karna began to feel triumphant when Arjuna dropped back. I am winning, he thought, and Arjuna is getting the full force of the dust thrown up from Draupadi's heels. Lumps of earth must be hitting Arjuna's teeth and filling his mouth. The thought made Karna pleased.

Then Karna was momentarily startled by Arjuna's roaring shout. The sound echoed and re-echoed round the racecourse. 'Ah ah ah,' like the bellowing of a wild tiger proclaiming its territory.

Karna's tiny flinch of shock shifted his weight slightly. Draupadi faltered. And in that moment, too late for Karna to do anything to stop him, Arjuna chiselled his horse into the tiny gap between Karna and the rails. Karna tried to shake him off by pressing till he was sure Arjuna's legs must be being crushed but Arjuna held on. Karna reached out his whip and slashed it backwards against Arjuna's face, catching Arjuna stingingly across the nose, but although Arjuna let out a yelp and yelled, 'You dirty double-dealer' he kept his place. But he was very pinched. Karna could hear his leg scrunching the splintering wood. Karna tried to strike out with his whip again, but missed and in the same moment felt Arjuna's toe strike the underside of his own boot, knocking it out of the stirrup. There came a clashing of metal as stirrups met. Karna slumped heavily sideways yelling, 'You bloody cheat.' Draupadi swerved and for long moments Karna, with one foot still in a stirrup, struggled to regain the other one. Then he fell. Arjuna, unbalanced too, fell on the other side at almost the same moment.

The crowd was silent with shock as the two un-ridden horses carried on round the course, racing each other, till Piara's syces caught them in the net. Then the heroes rose out of the dust.

'I will get you for this one day,' hissed Karna bitterly. His eyes and mouth were ringed with dark dirt mixed with sweat but when he looked down he was satisfied to see that Arjuna's boot was torn and blood ran from his leg. Karna hoped it hurt.

After they got home, because Karna had been humiliated on the racecourse in front of so many people who admired him, he was more frantic than ever to defeat Arjuna and shame him publicly. Whenever he thought of Arjuna, his nerves ached with longing. He would clench his fists and imagine a fistfight without gloves with Arjuna. He would dream of pressing his thumbs into Arjuna's eye sockets and crushing his fist down Arjuna's throat. He would dream of running Arjuna through with the tent-pegging lance. He would dream of driving darts into his brother's body as though Arjuna was a tree. Hurting, beating, humiliating Arjuna was the only thing he thought about.

★　　★　　★

'What shall I do?' Shivarani said to Bhima. 'You are so good with children.' They had met in the Calcutta coffee house. 'Do you remember when we were at college, and were working out ways of making society more harmonious? How we had said that the problem with our culture was that violence was the traditional way of solving India's conflicts?'

'I remember. We decided that it was because India's culture was built on a battle, the Mahabharata, and its religious thinking based on the conversation during that battle between a god and a soldier and that is why aggression is at the heart of all our country's problems.'

Bhima reminded her, 'And how we thought that if the aggression in men is channelled wisely, it has the potential to transform society and create and maintain harmony. Arjuna is presumably getting a good education at school and they are teaching him team games so that hopefully soon he will learn proper ways of competing. What about having Karna taught to fight graciously too? Why not have him trained in the fighting techniques of our tradition? Maybe his aggression could be channelled till it becomes useful and creative. Also training in dance and martial arts will give Karna the skills needed to become a film star, which is what you said he wants to be.'

When Shivarani told Karna that he was to be taught to fight, he glared at his half-brother, then looked eagerly at her, enchanted with the idea.

The first teacher who came to instruct Karna was called Markandaya. 'Before you can become a warrior you must understand the philosophy of our culture,' the old man told the boy. 'Do you know the story of Markandaya and the god, Vishnu?'

'I want to do fighting, not philosophy,' protested Karna.

'Listen to me,' said the old man. 'The holy man after whom I have been named spent his life in walking round the world listening to the thoughts and words of its people. But one day he fell out of the mouth of the sleeping god, Vishnu, and found himself in the infinite ocean of the Absolute. As he splashed around in the dark water he saw a luminous child playing alone in the endless dark waters. The babe seemed quite unafraid in this utterly solitary nothingness. The saint, accustomed to being hugely respected, was shocked when the child said, "Welcome, my child. Welcome, Markandaya." No one had called him "child"' for hundreds of years. He was offended.

'But the child was the giver of all the laws of nature. He was the essence of all creation. He was the potential of the Absolute wherein resides all possibilities. He told Markandaya, "Everything that does exist, will exist or did exist is already there and yet never there. I am the one who makes these things manifest and yet whose manifesting magic, which is known as Maya, cannot be understood." He told Markandaya, "There are three goals for human life, gratification of the senses, pursuit of prosperity and pious fulfilment of sacred duties and I am beyond all these." Then the god brought the holy Markandaya to his mouth again and swallowed him, so that the sage vanished once more into the gigantic body of the god.

'Markandaya was back in the world again but the experience had filled him with bliss so that he did not want to wander any more, but found a solitary place where, for the rest of his life, he listened to the sound of the God breathing.'

Karna was taught to dance the Bharat Natyam.

'You may find Karna a bit of a problem,' Shivarani told the teacher. 'He is always quarrelling with his half-brother and I suppose you need someone gentle for dancing.'

But the teacher said, 'Hatred is a great stimulator and the dance of Bharat Natyam requires passion.' The teacher taught Karna how to move his eyes, while keeping every other part of his face perfectly still. He learnt how to move one finger in a dance of expressive grace while keeping every other digit still as stone. He was taught how to slide his head from side to side on shoulders that stayed static.

You must dance like Shiva,' said Mr Nair. 'You must become the paradox, the naked ascetic yogi.' The teacher instilled in Karna the importance of using stillness instead of movement to defeat, and of expressing rage only through a movement of the eyes.

There followed circus people who specialised in bending Karna's body. They had moulded two-year-olds till they fitted inside water jars and made child limbs so flexible that legs and arms could be bent as far in the wrong direction as the right.

'Why do I need all these dancing and circus trick lessons? I want to be a film star,' complained Karna.

'You have to beat them all and for that you need an unusual training,' said Shivarani firmly. She was becoming quite optimistic. Karna's teacher assured her he was coming on well and she hoped that, after all and in spite of everything, he might in the end be discovered to have some talent.

Karna learnt how to hook his knees round his own throat and slide his body through a drainpipe. He was hammered and massaged till he could hang backwards through a hoop and light a cigarette from a candle using only his mouth and toes.

'He is not good,' said the circus trainer. 'But this will have to do for a child of his great age.'

Street performers taught Karna to stand on his head and pick up coins from the ground with his eyelids. He learnt how to juggle with seven burning oil lamps. 'You must learn to do it without the flames flickering let alone going out.'

Ascetics came from distant temples and tried to teach Karna how to put his body in a trance and then pass sharp spikes through his cheeks without pain or bleeding.

He was taught archery by an Olympic bronze medallist.

A yogi came and taught him to meditate. 'You must learn how to plumb into your powerful inner might and find the engine of the Cosmos,' the yogi said. 'Down here is an area which underlies all that exists. Move a little bit here and all the rest of the world will move for you.' He showed Karna how to sit in the lotus position, taught him a mantra then tried to lead his mind with his into the silence that is called the Absolute. Later when Karna opened his eyes he did not know if an hour had passed, or a minute, but he felt as though he was filled with sunshine. His hatred and agony had moved away and when he thought of Arjuna, Karna's feelings were friendly.

But the mood soon passed and the last training was the worst. An expert in the dance of Kathakali was brought from South India. The teacher told Shivarani, 'This boy is too old for training. Children must start at four or five years to be any good. The joints of the child must be supple as silk when I start or they may break down and then the child becomes disabled for life.'

Shivarani was worried but Karna insisted that he went through with it. A rope was fixed to the ceiling of one of the garden houses and Karna, with his naked body smeared with coconut oil, lay on the floor on his stomach. Holding the rope for balance, the teacher stood on the boy's body and massaged Karna's joints with his feet. Toes, heels and the man's body weight pressed into the tender parts of Karna till he could have screamed with pain. As though softening hardened leather, Mr Dhar slid his toes behind Karna's shoulder blades, into his knee sockets, between his ribs. For hours he slid his heels into the soft gaps behind Karna's hips and thrust his big toe against the boy's groin. He slithered his toes into the crevice behind Karna's buttocks and pounded the ball of his foot into his neck. Karna squirmed and sometimes screamed with pain but could not escape the oily squeeze of the grown man's feet.

At first, at the end of these sessions, Karna's body would hurt so much that he could hardly rise. He would walk staggeringly and force back moans. Sometimes he could not eat because of bruising to his stomach.

'I told you he was too old,' said Mr Dhar.

'I want to go on. I know I can do it,' said Karna. He was so stiff and sore that he thought he probably would be unable to pee, let alone beat Arjuna. There were times when he was so tired he did not have the energy to go to Dattapukur for the film.

By the time Arjuna came back from school on his vacation, Karna had completed his training.

He began to lie awake at night, going through every move for the wrestling match with Arjuna the following day. Or plotting his strokes all night long before a squash match with Arjuna at the Calcutta Club. As days passed he began to count up the wins and defeats in his head and sometimes became filled with panic because Arjuna was winning. On other occasions he would feel that he had actually beaten Arjuna more often. He began to lose count of who had won the most times. But in spite of all the lessons Karna was still motivated by rage and hatred. He would batter Arjuna with padded fists, or hurl his opponent again and again in judo throws, perform such sudden and strong karate chops that made Arjuna reel, winded.

Shivarani told Bhima gloomily, 'Each time I think things are getting better between Arjuna and Karna, they find new things to quarrel about.'

'What about giving them a chance to compete with other children,' suggested Bhima. 'It will get them out of this way of seeing only each other as rivals.' He arranged with a Calcutta school for Arjuna and Karna to come and first demonstrate their skills and then accept challenges from other boys. The headmaster was enthusiastic. What a lift for his school it would be when it was known that the boys of the famous Shivarani had performed there.

The whole school watched entranced as Karna and Arjuna fought it out and were awed by Arjuna's impressive, powerful swipes and the wild, sneaky, determined way in which Karna attacked. Long after any other boy in the school would have given in, Karna and Arjuna went on hammering blow after blow into each other's faces, till their breath was gone and their eyes swelled. When it was over, the head told his pupils that now they knew what real commitment meant and that when it was their turn they must compete with as much courage and determination as Karna and Arjuna had just done. But no one would fight with Arjuna and Karna. The other boys had seen the ferocious attacks of Shivarani's nephews and were too afraid.

But all the same, as time went on, Shivarani began to feel Karna's training had improved his attitude, and that he was starting to take more interest in perfecting his own strikes, lunges, punches and chops than in damaging Arjuna.

Karna was constantly challenging Arjuna. 'I'll race you to Dattapukur.'

Or 'I've learnt a new throw. See if you can defend yourself.' But Shivarani saw that Bhima had been right. Karna's training had taught him to fight with rules and to respect his opponent.

When Shivarani had lived in Naxalbari, a boy of thirteen had come to her in despair. 'When I look into my future, Madam, I see no job at all for me for the rest of my life, for there are even old men in this village who have never had work. And without work what am I? I cannot marry, I will never have children. Can you not please help me?' Shivarani had brought him back to Calcutta with her, had paid for him to continue his schooling out of her own pocket until she managed to get a scholarship for him, and eventually had persuaded the leader of the Naxalite Movement to give the lad a job. After a few years he had been made secretary of the party, had married, and now had five children and a nice house in Bombay. He had been hugely grateful to Shivarani, writing to her at each success, saying it was all because of her and telling her that he owed her many favours and that if there was anything he could do for her, she must only let him know.

She had not heard from him for some years, then she read an advertisement for a film school and realised that it was her Naxalite friend who ran it. She wrote asking him to take on Karna. 'He is my nephew and although he has not had a good education, having by unfortunate chance been brought up on the Calcutta streets, he sings beautifully and also he has had a most excellent training as a dancer and in the martial arts. Perhaps you will be able to start him off as a playback singer or stunt man, performing athletic, martial or dancing moves for less flexible actors.' She waited for the reply with a great certainly that she was on the way to securing Karna's future.

Lately Arjuna and Karna had been behaving better. Their contests had been formal, and it seemed to Shivarani that they were starting to hate each other less. She decided they needed a reward.

'I will take them both out,' she thought, 'for they are nearly grown-up men.' And told them, 'We will go to Firpos for dinner.'

Arjuna appeared wearing a cream silk shirt, beautifully cut white trousers and a silver tie. Shivarani had feared Karna might come in his gaudy Japanese nylon and was gratified that he wore an Indian black silk atchkan, a high-collared coat buttoned down the front, with tight white jodhpur trousers. He was a little too short and bore the signs of childhood stunting but there was a boyish flush of excitement on his cheeks that made him almost charming. She felt touched that he had worn clothes that he knew would please her.

Karna followed Arjuna and Shivarani through the long dining room. It was the first time he had been to a glamorous restaurant and he tried not to look too awed and thrilled by the glitter of candles, chandeliers, the shining weighty silver cutlery, glistening glassware and brilliant white starched linen.

The waiter who led them wore a towering pugree and a crimson silk cummerbund and for a moment Karna's happiness was tinged with a touch of sorrow because his mother, Dolly, had never in all her life eaten in a place like this. He felt a pain in his heart because she had lain on the hard pavement and felt so hungry for so long. How lovely it would have been, he thought, if he was coming to dine here with her, instead of with his enemy, Arjuna, and Shivarani who did her duty but did not love him.

Three girls at the adjoining table began to whisper to each other as the waiter came to take Shivarani's order. Karna took a sneaking peep and realised that they were watching his table with admiration. He tried to be taller and addressing Arjuna, said in a deep-voiced and important tone, 'Have you heard the latest cricket scores?'

Arjuna blinked quickly and then hastily took up the conversational opening.

Shivarani felt gratified to see the nephews talking formally and politely to each other and felt more pleased than ever because Karna's expensive training had been so well worth it.

As they reached the end of the meal, the girls at the next table began excitedly whispering to each other. Then one pulled a zinnia from the vase on her table, rose, and came across to Shivarani's table.

Karna saw her first and something about her made a catch come in his heart because she looked a little like Poopay Patalya. She held out the flower. Her face was shining with excitement. She seemed to be looking at him as she approached. Her eyes were wide and dark, her small red mouth was pouted with stifled laughter. When she reached their table she paused. Karna, feeling suddenly shy, could not take his eyes off her. His breath stopped. She gave him a laughing glance then presented her flower to Arjuna. She kept her hand cuddled in Arjuna's palm for a long extra moment.

Karna looked down at the table and the flush died away from his face.

'Go on,' smiled Shivarani to Arjuna. Arjuna rose, took the girl by the hand, and the pair made their way towards the dance floor leaving Karna and Shivarani alone at the table.

The film-school proprietor took so long to reply that Shivarani began to fear that her letter had been lost. She had not the slightest doubt that when he got her request he would eagerly do all he could to help so when at last his answer came it was a shock.

'Dear Auntie, How wonderful to hear from you after all these years. How much I would like to help your Karna but there is a long, long waiting list for this school and I am afraid we will not be able to fit your boy in. But it is probably for the best. You say Karna is illiterate and brought up on the pavements. I am afraid that if he studied here he would feel out of place, for all the other students are from rich families and have good backgrounds. Also I fear the parents of the other young people would be upset by their offspring having to mix socially with such a child. I deplore these snobbish attitudes, as you will remember from our time in Naxalbari, but what can one do? One must be sensitive to the requirements of the customer.'

He was no longer a Naxalite. He had recently become a supporter of the BJP, the Hindu party and it would be fatal to his political ambitions if it became known that he was helping the ward of a Communist minister.

Karna's face went red, and a shudder seemed to pass through his body when Shivarani told him that her friend did not have room for him.

'It is a lie, isn't it? I can tell from your face. He won't take me because my mother was a dhobi. I know that is the real reason.' He rushed from the house and did not appear for the rest of the week.

'Perhaps he has left altogether,' said Arjuna. He sounded almost regretful. He had come to need the rivalry.

Shivarani felt worried but did not know where to look for Karna.

'Who cares,' said Arjuna.

'Good riddance,' said Gadhari.

'He's probably gone back to his Calcutta ways,' said Uncle.

Karna, wearing an entire set of brilliantly coloured new clothes, came riding into the Hatibari estate a week later on a brand-new cycle with fourteen gears. He came to a gravel-spraying halt at the front steps and felt a thrill of delight at Arjuna's glare of envy.

'Where have you been?' asked Shivarani crossly.

'Bangladesh,' said Karna briefly.

'Why?' Shivarani's relief at his reappearance was being supplanted by a new worry.

'I've got a job,' Karna said.

'What sort of job? Tell me about it.'

'Oh, this and that,' he told her vaguely. 'I'm a sort of courier.'

Shivarani had a hopeful vision of Karna pedalling round the city delivering packages, which was swiftly followed by doubt. 'Don't give up on film school,' she said. 'I'm still trying.'

Karna appeared at intervals, after that, with bulging saddle bags as though he had been shopping. 'What have you got in there?' asked Shivarani. If the police caught him now, she did not think she would be able to pay them off again.

'This and that,' he repeated airily.

Karna seemed to wear new clothes every time they saw him. He would flaunt them, strutting a bit and relishing Arjuna's curiosity.

Karna had developed his own special dress style – back to front baseball caps, tight PVC trousers that emphasised the skinniness of his legs and skimpy nylon jackets with shoulders padded so high that he looked as though he was permanently shrugging. He began to walk with a swagger as though he had a gun in his belt and to chew gum until his jaws never stopped moving.

Arjuna asked Shivarani if he could have a baseball cap and a pair of PVC trousers too.

'I think Karna looks a freak,' said Shivarani. 'And you look very nice in your jeans and sweatshirt. Stick to that. In fact I would like to see you wearing our traditional India dress sometime. Shall I buy you khadi kurta pyjama?'

'But only foreigners and N.R.I.s wear such clothes these days,' protested Arjuna. 'Even bullock cart drivers wear trousers and shirts.'

'N.R.I.' ranted Shivarani. 'What is this N.R.I.? If you want to say Non Resident Indians, which I think is a ridiculously pretentious description anyway, just say it. How sick I am of all these abbreviations.' Exhaustion and worry about what Karna was up to was eroding her nerves. How she wished she could think of a way of getting him into film school.

Karna spent most of his time in Hatipur when he was around.

'What does he do there all the time, Arjuna? Do you know?' Shivarani asked.

'I'll go and see.'

'Don't go and spy on him,' she cried. 'I wouldn't like that.' But all the same she did not stop Arjuna.

Karna would see Arjuna coming from far off and make signals to his friends to hide the piles of watches, fountain pens and cigarette lighters on the tables. By the time Arjuna entered they were all sitting there silently and with virtuous expressions. It made Karna laugh inside, to see the disappointment on Arjuna's face.

'My brother thinks we are engaged in some illicit trading,' Karna would say, looking round the table. 'Whereas in fact we are just meeting here for a pleasant chat. Isn't that so, brothers?' And they would all laugh, making Arjuna's face go red.

Ever since the evening Shivarani had taken him and Arjuna to the restaurant and the beautiful girl had given Arjuna a flower, Karna had thought about women. He'd been in almost physical pain that evening, watching the way Arjuna put his hand on the girl's bare arm. He had burned with longing when she laid her head on Arjuna's shoulder. His skin had imagined, with hungry delight, the feeling of the girl's hair against Arjuna's neck and the warm soft moistness of her cheek. 'It is not fair,' he had screamed inside. 'It is not fair.' Shivarani had suggested he ask one of the other two girls to dance with him but they had not looked like Poopay Patalya. And anyway they would probably have refused him and then his humiliation would have been even deeper. He began remembering girls he had known in Calcutta and to think about pretty girls he had seen in Hatipur like Laxshmi's daughter, Bika, who would flirt and laugh with him till her mother came shouting with fury and dragged her away. He wanted to kiss Bika, he wanted to make love with her. He began to dream that women's hands were stroking his forehead and women's arms were around his body. He wanted the smell of women's bodies in his nostrils, and the sound of love words in his ears. It was not even sex he craved, though he longed for that as well. He wanted there to be a girl who caressed him with her hands. Even his pony did not soothe him these days. When he rode her, he would lie with his face against her mane, hug her round her neck and wish it was a woman's waist he held. He would talk to her, 'Poopay, you are my daughter and my love,' and his own words would increase his desire because she was not Poopay Patalya but just a horse. Once or twice he had tried flirting with Hatipur girls, but it was a small village and their mothers and fathers, even their grandparents, were always watching. Arjuna was one thing. This was only Karna.

But there was Laika.

Karna began to crave being clasped in Laika's great thighs. He wanted to be lost in her woman-perfumed dark. He wanted to wake in the morning with her smell of sex on him. He wanted her to love him in the Hatibari. He wanted to go down to the Hatibari breakfast knowing that he had been embraced by someone who felt he mattered. Even the servants in this house, thought Karna, mock at me behind my back and to my face do not respect me. Parvathi, the maid, had giggled when Karna, trying to be like Arjuna, had ordered her to bring a glass of water. He wanted Laika because she was rough, because her harsh voice stung his eardrums, because she would leave her blazing lipstick smeared over his face, because after he had had sex with her he would smell of her, fishy and cheap perfume. He wanted Laika because she reminded Karna of his childhood. And because he loved her more than any of the Hatibari people.

She had no phone so he tried a letter and wrote for days, but could not do it. Car number plates and the names of film stars are not enough when you want to send a message. He thought of asking Parvathi to help him, but could not bear the thought of her contempt. In the end he tackled Arjuna. 'It's a writing exercise I have to do.' He was taking lessons in the village.

'Funny sort of school work, Karna,' said Arjuna, with his pen poised. 'Is this what they are teaching kids these days? It looks more like an invitation to a whore.'

'Your mother is a whore, you salah,' shouted Karna, ripping away the paper. 'And more than that, she threw away her baby.'

But he managed it at last and met Laika at the station. She hugged him, keeping him pressed against her bosom for a long warm moment and as he leant against her, he felt comfort filling up his heart. He brought her in the rickshaw while the family were at dinner.

'Hush, Laika, don't make a noise,' he whispered. She was as wide and perfumed as a full-blown rose and he feared that they'd be sure to smell her. He could hear voices through the closed dining room door as he slipped up the stairs behind her swaying bottom. The people of the Hatibari never talked so happily when he was there, he thought. When Karna was at the table the family became tense and seemed to be always watching him and finding fault but now their laughter and cheery conversation sounded carefree and uninhibited.

After Laika started coming to visit him, Karna began to feel at peace and lost some of his need to fight. Sometimes he had the feeling that Arjuna was hanging around outside the room, presumably hoping to challenge him, and warned Laika, 'Be quieter or they will find out.' But Laika was a noisy lovemaker, letting out high-pitched squealing laughs as though she was being tickled at peak moments. Arjuna heard her in spite of warnings. 'I know about that girl,' he told Karna fiercely.

'What girl? You are a liar. No one will believe you,' hissed Karna, looking anxiously up and down the passage in case anyone was listening.

'When Shivarani Aunty finds out she'll send you back to Calcutta, to live on the pavement again.'

'You bastard. Don't you dare tell her,' said Karna. 'I'll kill you if you tell her.' He could not bear the thought of Laika being humiliated.

'Try,' laughed Arjuna. 'I'm an inch taller than you so just try.'

A silence fell while Karna tried to glare at Arjuna with self-righteous indignation but his mind was reeling. Arjuna might be right. He wasn't a helpless little boy anymore. Shivarani might send him back to Calcutta if she discovered he had brought a prostitute to his room and just when he had got his Bangladesh business going so nicely. At last Karna said, forcing his lips into the semblance of a smile, forcing his tone into friendliness. 'Look, why don't you come inside my room. We can talk about it there.' And when Arjuna hesitated, 'It's not a trick. I won't do anything, I swear. You can leave the door open.'

As he led Arjuna into his room he felt his heart begin to quake, because for the first time someone was going to know his secret.

He wished he hadn't been so stupid and would have liked to hustle Arjuna out of the room but already it was too late. Arjuna had seen.

Karna sighed and bowed his head, waiting for the mockery. But Arjuna was silent, and merely gazed round at the hundreds of dolls. They were every size and colour. Dolls in dresses, naked dolls, Barbies and Cindies, Cabbage Patch dolls and Cheerful Tearful. Some of the dolls were as large as a nine-month-old child and others the size of a man's finger. Then, to Karna's surprise, instead of laughing, Arjuna turned to Karna, questions in his eyes.

Karna shrugged, then said, as though pulling himself together, 'Hey, look at this.'

He took up two hideous little plastic dolls with thick orange limbs and dresses hacked from transparent shredded muslin. He held them out, one in either hand. 'I call this one Arjuna and this one Karna,' he said. 'Watch.' He went over the room and switched on his tape recorder. Then he put the little dolls on the floor, standing them upright. There was no reason at all why they should remain standing but they did. The pair wobbled for a moment on their lumpy feet, seemed to get their balance, then in time to the music began to fight each other.

Karna glanced at Arjuna. His brother was entranced, peering from side to side trying to discover the secret, watching Karna's hands. The two little dolls thumped each other, hugged each other, swayed from side to side, while Karna, like a sports commentator, kept up a monologue, 'Now here comes Karna with a strong left hook. Oh, Oh, Arjuna is over . . . no, no, he has managed to retain his balance. Now here comes Arjuna's straight left, a deadly punch. Will Karna be able to survive?' Suddenly, as though something angered Karna, he leapt up. The two little dolls collapsed to the floor and lay there looking exactly what they were, a pair of lifeless ugly toys. Karna put out his foot and began to crush them.

'Don't, don't.' Arjuna reached out, as though trying to prevent a murder. A moment later orange plastic splinters burst from under Karna's toes. He looked up and said to Arjuna, 'The girl's name was Laika. She is my friend and sometimes we make love, but if Shivarani Aunty finds this out and sends me away, all my hope of being a film star will have gone.'

He waited expecting Arjuna to say, 'You dirty pig, bringing such a girl into my house,' but instead, and perhaps because of the little broken dolls lying on the floor, Arjuna just nodded.

13

THE SUN AND THE MOON

Rain god Indra over Arjun watched with father's partial love,
Sun god Surya over Karna shed his light from far above.
Arjun stood in darkening shadow by the inky clouds concealed.
Bold and bright in open sunshine radiant Karna stood revealed.

Karna bought himself a car. While the Bangladeshi dealer waited impatiently, Karna got into the driving seat and pretended to be driving. Dazed with joy and wonder, as though he was still a little boy on the Calcutta pavement, Karna imagined taking his mother, Dolly, round the countryside in it. Or Poopay Patalya, he thought suddenly. He closed his eyes and pretended the beautiful film star was seated at his side. 'What a wonderful driver you are, Karna,' she would say. 'And what an excellent car this is.'

'How do you work it?' he had asked the dealer when he came out of his dream.

'I don't understand,' said the man.

'How do you make it go?'

The man looked disbelieving for a moment. 'You are saying you don't know how to drive but all the same you have bought it? How will you take it away?'

'You just show me,' said Karna impatiently. He could not wait to get going.

The man frowned. 'You can't just learn in ten minutes.'

'Oh, come on,' shouted Karna, burning with excitement.

★   ★   ★

That same afternoon, when Karna drove to the Hatibari, instead of Poopay Patalya at his side, he had a skinny Calcutta artist.

He arrived at the front steps in a judder of gears and a lot of unnecessary revving.

Almost the whole household, hearing the roaring of the ancient and incompetently driven engine came running out to look, imagining that an invasion was taking place, or some disaster had overcome the countryside. There came looks of astonishment mixed with mirth at the sight of Karna behind the steering wheel.

'There's a few bits missing,' said Parvathi. 'Where are the lights? And it hasn't got any door handles.'

'My Cal contacts are procuring parts for me,' Karna said grandly. A new generation of little kigalis were reaping them for him in Chowringee and Park Street at that very moment.

'Why do you need a car? Basu will drive you around if you want it,' said DR Uncle.

'I need it for my new business. I will have to be going back and forth over the border frequently from now on and the motor-cycle was too slow. Also I was not able to carry enough merchandise.'

'You don't even know how to drive it properly,' said Arjuna.

'This is Rishi,' Karna said, ignoring Arjuna and indicating the young man who was emerging, clutching paints and easel. 'He has come from Calcutta to paint my portrait.'

Rishi, a member of Karna's kigali group, specialised in painting pictures of tourists. They had to be done fast because tourists can't stay more than a minute or two standing on a Calcutta street.

That was long ago and Rishi had progressed since then and though sometimes he had sitters who complained that their portraits did not look like them and refused to pay, on the whole he managed to make a living from it. But all the time he felt dissatisfied and craved to be a real artist. He wanted to work with oil paints on huge bits of canvas, to swipe great swathes of colour with a hog-hair brush, to paint snowclad Himalayan peaks in the setting sun. He wanted to hold exhibitions and get reviewed in the Calcutta papers. But he could not even afford to buy a second pencil, let alone the material required for such a career.

When Karna commissioned his portrait, Rishi embraced Karna's feet with gratitude. 'This amount of money you are offering will make all happiness possible for me and in exchange I will make you look like the most handsome man in the world. I will take away every blemish from your face and make you look as chubby as a famous film star.'

'Come, Rishi, follow me. I will show you how I want my portrait done,' said Karna striding past the group of grinning people. He led his friend into the great hall where a full-length portrait of Pandu hung among the snarling boars' heads. It had been taken from a photo after the zamindar died and in it Pandu wears a starched white kurta, narrow jodhpur trousers, embroidered curly-toed slippers and a silken waistcoat. At Pandu's side is an antique sitar and he smokes a hookah.

'You must copy everything except the face,' Karna told Rishi. 'That, of course, must be mine. I wish to be seen wearing the clothes of the zamindar and also smoking the hookah. The only other change, apart from the face being my own and not zamindar Pandu, is that I would like my CD player by my side and not that old music thing that he has.'

When Arjuna learnt that Ravi was coming back to Hatipur to get married he became filled with excitement. Ever since Koonty had told Arjuna who had murdered his father, Arjuna had waited for his moment of revenge. He would have liked to kill the man, but he had made that promise to his mother. 'You must not spoil your life because of him. You must try to humiliate him but not kill him,' she had said.

When he heard about Ravi's wedding he saw his chance. It was going to be a very big occasion for Ravi was important these days. Daily Arjuna watched the magnificent preparations being made for his father's murderer's wedding and waited. Banana-tree arches, wrapped in fringed foil, were set up. Hooting lorries kept coming slowly in, heavily laden with food and equipment from Calcutta. Rickshaws jingled, weighed down with arriving guests and street tailors' treadle sewing machines whirred as sparkling wedding clothes flowed out of their needles. As the days went by the air became filled with spiced food frying, sharp with chilli and thick with the smell of raw onions and simmering mustard oil. Flour rose in pale flurries as chupatti dough was kneaded. A thousand people had been invited to the wedding of the misti wallah's son who once had worn ragged clothes and had no shoes, but today sported a big moustache, owned an imported Mercedes car and sat in the Lok Sabha. Ravi's bride had already been given so much gold jewellery by people hoping for political benefits, that if she wore them all at once she would not be able to stand up. The greatest people in the land were coming to this wedding. It was rumoured that even the Prime Minister would be there, though the zamindar of the Hatibari had refused the invitation.

As the guests were arriving, Arjuna went down to the river and, wearing only his pants, dived in. Daaks, balancing like yogis on their long red feet, ran away from him over the water surface. Buffaloes shuffled uneasily as Arjuna throbbed by. Women washing clothes straightened as he passed them and started clapping as though Arjuna was competing in a race. Once or twice village youths leapt in and swam competitively alongside but in moments they were soon forced to fall back, gasping. Local people recognised Arjuna. A young man watched the young zamindar with envy. 'Perhaps Arjuna is searching for a woman to love like the Sun God did,' sighed a girl. 'Keep your eyes away,' her mother snapped.

On the road that ran alongside the river, wedding guests passed in large imported cars. There were ministers from Delhi, big shots in business from all over the country, foreign importers, Indian exporters, the owners of airlines and railway companies, for Ravi was a person of great influence and high status these days.

Arjuna reached the other bank as the voice of Zeenat Aman crooned from the loudspeakers, 'Baat Ban Jaaye,' 'The never-ending language of love.' Half-naked and slimed with weed, he scrambled out of the water and stood dripping on the lawn. Women wearing glittering saris and weighted with jewels gazed, impressed and aghast. Men hurried towards Arjuna, preparing to do something but at the last moment thought better of it. After all, perhaps it was one of the local wedding customs to have a man wearing only underpants appear among them and anyway the fellow looked determined.

Arjuna strode towards the tent where the bridegroom sat and, sensing that something interesting was about to happen, guests began to follow him and stood crowding in the entrance of the sharmayana.

The bridal couple sat on a high dias at the far end and facing them were ranged hundreds of wedding guests on chairs. The bride's face and body were covered with so many layers of fringed silk and brocade that you had to guess there was a woman under there. The only part of her that was visible were her hands which lay on her lap like a pair of tiny rosy mice. They were meshed with golden chains and had been intricately decorated with scarlet henna.

Ravi wore the traditional helmet of banana pith wound round and draped with jasmine garlands that the village girls had toiled over yesterday. He was sweating heavily under his rich, embroidered silken kurta and heavier shawl. Round his neck he wore many garlands of marigolds and roses. His forehead was decorated with sandal paste and his face, or what could be seen of it through jasmine dangles, was red and sweating.

Ravi's parents, the misti wallah and his wife, sat in the front row and when they saw Arjuna coming, they got to their feet and looked around for help. 'It's Pandu's son,' the misti wallah shouted.

At his father's words Ravi tried to rise too and defend himself, but the clobber of clothes, jewels, garlands and the close proximity of his parcelled-up bride all hampered him.

Guests sat mutely. The entrances were entirely blocked with watching guests.

Ravi let out an inarticulate shout. The muffled bride stirred under her coverings and her fingers curled in anticipation of some unseen disaster.

Arjuna reached Ravi on his throne, then struck a ferocious blow right into the centre of the bridegroom's face and heard a crunch of nose gristle giving way. Ravi collapsed with a shriek.

The bride began to struggle wildly to escape from her coverings and see what was happening.

Arjuna turned and walked back through the rows of guests and out into the garden again.

Inside the sharmayana there followed a long and puzzled pause during which Ravi, fallen behind his writhing bride, let out small moans.

'I'm glad we don't have that custom in our weddings,' some of the male guests whispered. 'That punch looked as though it really hurt.'

When Ravi managed to struggle upright his nose was crooked and there was blood all down the front of his silken shirt.

As Arjuna went back to the river he caressed his fist and felt good because his parents had been in some way avenged. At the water's edge he crouched and wiped his bloodstained knuckles against the ground, not wanting to defile the holy water with Ravi's treacherous blood. When all trace of his father's killer was gone from his skin he dived back into the water and began to swim back, the remembered feel of his fist on Ravi's nose delighting him. He swam gently this time, feeling the water against his skin as he had not done on the way to the wedding. The wedding music had fallen silent so that he could hear the sound of water lapping at the banks and boats, the cries of water birds, the sound of banana leaves rattling in the breeze.

Arjuna began to feel happy. Perhaps he would stay in this artery of water for ever, moving up it like the needle in a vein, making his way, upstream, steadily, till one day he would reach the heart of the world. The place where Shiva lived. The place that was so cold and holy that you could see your prana stand before your face in a cloud of white. The place where silence was infinite and filled with bliss.

He became reminded of swimming his fingers through the hair of Parvathi when he had been little and she had come to kiss him goodnight after his mother died. His fingers had moved around her head like fishes and found cool strands there. She had shivered when he touched her ears.

By the time he had gone fifty yards, people were running to the riverbank. He swam on, their angry voices ringing satisfyingly in his ears. Behind him he heard one or two splashes. Some unfortunate servants had clearly been ordered to chase after him.

When Arjuna reached the Hatibari bank he looked back. Far down the water, two men were struggling to catch up with him. Arjuna laughed and swung round when his laughter was joined by others. Laxshmi's daughters stood there, watching him with admiration.

Other people were now appearing and began to cram round the dripping, panting Arjuna. The daughters of Laxshmi instantly gathered closer and leaned against him as though claiming him as theirs. He stood there, clothed in women, savouring the feel of them. They smelled spicy, smoky, fragrant. They smelled buttery, as though they had leant against cows. One held a small brass pot of pale thick milk.

Far away on the other side, there still came the shouts of anger from the wedding people of the palace. The two durwans in the water gave in and began to turn back.

One of the girls picked up Arjuna's thrown clothes, carefully folded them, and said, 'Follow me.'

'Come with us,' said another of the girls, taking Arjuna by the arm.

The girls began leading Arjuna towards Laxshmi's small hut. The milk that one daughter carried on her head sounded sloppingly in its brass pot. The procession moved very slowly because of staring people getting in the way.

The girls held him as though he was their cow. Followed by the heavy breathing crowd, they tugged Arjuna gently along a path through the trees and towards their home, a small thatched hut. Outside was tethered a couple of kid goats. A small cow had her nose tucked into a basket of boiled bran and sugar feed. Hens clucked and scratched. There was a little round haystack built on a pole to be out of reach of grazing animals. A TV aerial was fixed to the thatched roof.

'You are welcome to our house,' murmured one of the girls.

Another shouted, 'Ma, we've got him.'

Laxshmi came out, a short straw broom in her hand. 'Good girls, good girls,' she said. 'Now Bika will be saved.'

Laughter dimpled Bika's round cheeks. There was a naughty question in her wide dark eyes.

'Hello, Bika,' said Arjuna, feeling embarrassed to be standing before her wearing only his wet and muddy pants. 'Let me have my clothes,' he said to the girl who carried them.

The sisters shook their heads. 'You won't be needing them. You can have them later.'

Laxshmi said to her other five daughters, 'You can go now. You have done what I asked. Now get on with your duties. Is the kheer made? Has the calf been fed? Did you bathe the buffalo? Is the ghee cooked? Get on. Go away.'

The girls moved off reluctantly but the rest of the crowd continued to jostle for better views till Laxshmi rushed at them and threatened with her broom. 'Go away, all of you,' she shrieked. They began to back off nervously – they knew Laxshmi had once been Shivarani's maid but had had to leave because of her temper.

After war there comes peace. After battle the heart needs rest. After fighting the body needs love. After victory comes celebration. Arjuna, smiling inside and satisfied, followed Bika into the dark, saffron-smelling interior.

'Sit,' said Laxshmi. Arjuna sat on the floor while she and her daughter served him food as though he was a son-in-law. They laid before him a banana leaf heaped with rice, fish curry, dhall. They served him mango pickle, tomato chutney, chupatti, a little heap of chopped green chilli. And then watched him, their expressions satisfied, while he ate, pinching up the food with three fingers.

While Arjuna was eating, Bika and her mother hung garlands over the doorway. They mixed white rice paste and painted patterns on the ground as a mark of respect to Jamai Babu, the new son-in-law. While she painted, Bika kept peeping lovingly at Arjuna. The mother kept glancing at him proudly like someone who had captured a valuable wild elephant.

When he had eaten, Bika poured water over Arjuna's oily fingers while the mother waited with a towel.

At last the mother said, 'I will leave you two alone.'

As she vigorously swept a perfectly clean yard, the next-door-neighbour leaned from her doorway and said, 'So you have got the zamindar's son for your naughty daughter then?'

'God has been good to us,' said the mother piously.

'A pity the son is so skinny,' said the other woman, jealously. 'Skinny like a stick. The father was wonderfully fat.'

'Being skinny is the fashion of the moment. I have seen that on TV,' said Bika's mother, determined not to be done out of her triumph.

'But since your Bika is already pregnant,' said the neighbour, 'What need have you for Arjuna?'

'He does not know that she is pregnant,' said Bika's mother, sweeping steadily. 'And if you should tell him I will make sure this broom goes right down your throat and out the other side.'

'Lie down there,' Bika told Arjuna. The hut was cool and smelled of straw and mango. 'You are very beautiful.' A dove cooed sleepily and the melons on the roof creaked in a small wind. The river gurgled as if it was swallowing something.

When Arjuna rose from Bika's side, it was nearly midnight and inky dark in spite of the little oil lamps the mother had lit and set along the verandah.

Bika became agitated and the mother angry when Arjuna started moving towards the doorway.

'Where are you going?'

Arjuna blinked. 'Home. I can't stay here forever,' he said.

'Why not?' demanded the mother. 'Is that it?'

'What else should I do?' asked Arjuna. He stood waiting for Bika's mother to enlighten him, his neck bowed because of the marigold garlands they had hung over the doorway to honour him. He smudged his toes among the new rangoli patterns they had created for him as he tried to work out what he had done to make her angry.

'Don't you think you owe us something?' demanded the mother. 'You eat our food, make use of my daughter. Then walk away? Now don't you think you owe us?'

'I have brought no money with me,' said Arjuna, feeling he had understood. Feeling sad too. Disillusioned. 'But you can have my watch.'

Bika's mother burst out in a fury. 'Your watch? Who has asked you for money?'

'What else can you want?' asked Arjuna, now truly bewildered.

'Suppose you have made a child inside my daughter?' said Bika's mother. 'Who will care for it if the father does not?'

'What do you want me to do?' asked Arjuna.

'Marry her, of course,' said the mother.

Arjuna stared at her. 'We do not even know if I have made a baby,' he said after a long and amazed pause.

'Look at you,' cried the mother, gesturing his body up and down with a rice ladle. 'Is it possible that a great lusty healthy fellow like you fails to bring on a child?'

Arjuna, who had never thought about such things before, supposed she must be right and began to feel gloomy. 'But I don't think I could marry her right away,' he said. 'I don't have a job – I am only seventeen. Suppose you let me know later if she is having a baby or not.'

'I will surely do that,' said the woman grimly.

Arjuna dressed. All the happy feelings he had had with Bika had been driven away by the mendacity of her mother. As he began to walk away the mother shouted after him, 'And I am sure she is pregnant. Women can tell these things straight away.'

Next day, Arjuna returned to Calcutta. He asked Parvathi, 'Is it really true that women can look at a girl the moment she has made love and tell if she is pregnant or not?'

'Of course it's not true,' laughed Parvathi. 'Have you been making love then? And is the girl's mother trying to capture you?'

Arjuna thought to himself, how clever Parvathi is. She knows about everything that is worth knowing about.

'You must take condoms with you wherever you go,' Parvathi said. 'For a boy like you is sure to be led into temptation by every girl he meets and it's not only babies that girls give men these days.'

14

APSARAS

Thus spake proud and peerless Karna
in his accents deep and loud
And as moved by sudden impulse
joyous rose the listening crowd.

Shivarani was due to lead a group of women from Hatipur to Delhi to deliver a paper to the Prime Minister demanding three rights for women: the right to life, to freedom from violence and to education.

She had become very restless these days, as though something was on her mind.

'Don't you think you are overdoing things?' DR Uncle asked. 'Why don't you give yourself a rest?'

Shivarani would sit with him briefly, on the edge of her chair, looking tense and edgy. 'Is that chair uncomfortable, Shivarani? Shall I tell Parvathi to bring you some more cushions?'

It was not the chair that was uncomfortable. It was Shivarani's mind. When people talked to her, after a while they would realise that she was not listening but was thinking of something else. She did not remember things.

'What about getting me into films,' said Karna. 'Has anything happened?'

'Oh, yes.' She had forgotten even that. 'What about approaching your father? Perhaps he can help you,' she said vaguely.

Karna stared at her with his mouth open. 'My father? Have I got a father? I thought no one knew who he was.'

Shivarani sighed. Her mind had been far away or she would not have said anything. But it was too late. Karna had got the information and was shaking it like a mongoose with a snake. 'Who is he? Tell me? What do you know?'

'I don't really know. It's only a guess. It's probably not true.'

'You have to tell me. Go on.' He stood in front of her, his expression intense, his fists clenched. 'Who is he?'

'It was the actor who played the Sun God in the Mahabharata,' said Shivarani cautiously. Karna sat down again heavily. Of course. Dilip Baswani. He wondered why he had not realised sooner, for throughout his childhood people had compared him to the actor though as he grew older and deprivation stunted him, they had ceased to see the similarity. Dilip Baswani, Suriya, the Sun God.

That night, he piled all his possessions – his sports kit, his dolls and his posters of Poopay Patalya – into his car.

'Don't just go, Karna,' said Shivarani. 'That is not the way. I'll write to him.' But Karna was tired of waiting. The journey took three days and at night he slept in his car, curling up in his metal womb, with all the beloved things of his life close to him. He bought soda water, beedis and snacks of food from the towns and villages through which he passed and often in the remoter villages people would cluster round the sahib in his motorcar, so that Karna began to feel like a famous film star already.

On the long journey his mind would become filled with memories of Dolly. Arjuna's mother, who was so rich, had thrown him away as though he was a bit of unwanted debris and even when he came back to her, refused to recognise him. But when Dolly found him, though she was so poor, she had shared everything with him, going without herself so that he could eat. At other times his mind would dwell on Poopay Patalya, who, because of all the times he had seen her in the cinema, was now someone with whom he felt he had shared his life. Thoughts of her would make his heart swell with love and dedication. He planned all the things he would say to her when he met her which he felt sure would happen because he was heading for Bollywood.

He would let her know how in his darkest moments she had comforted him, how he had never truly felt alone even after his mother died, because thoughts of her had sustained him. He would tell her that if she was ever in trouble he would be there for her. He would let her know that if she needed it he would gladly die for her.

Sometimes he would think about Arjuna and feel triumphant because at last he had the advantage of his brother. Karna's father was a famous film star and Arjuna's was not. This time Karna was certain to win. He even had a little mental image of he, Karna, taking a leading role and out of kindness finding some small and subservient role for Arjuna.

When he arrived in Bombay, he found a cheap hotel, booked himself in, washed the grime of three days' travel from his body, then set about finding out where Dilip lived. It was not too difficult. Dilip Baswani was extra famous these days, it seemed, for although he no longer acted he was now making films. Everyone wanted to know him and get a part in one of his movies. The hotel doorman told Karna, 'You'll have to think of a pretty good line if you want to get in there. The place is like a fortress.'

The following day Karna polished his car till it shone like a jewel, put on his newest, most expensive and trendiest clothes and, keeping their Japanese labels trailing as though by mistake, set off.

As he drove up the road to the actor's house he began to feel both nervous and excited. He gave a little gasp as the house came in sight, not only because it was so huge and grand, but because beyond it was the sea, something he had only ever seen in films.

He arrived at bolted iron gates. An armed durwan dressed in a uniform that made him look like a soldier stood guard before them.

Karna, who thought he did not know fear, felt his heart hammering as he stopped.

The durwan looked up, glanced at Karna's unremarkable car and stayed sitting.

In the end Karna had to get out and approach the man. He said, in his most impressive voice, 'I am here to see Mr Baswani.'

'Have you got an appointment?' asked the durwan.

Karna shook his head and said, 'But when he knows who I am he will want to see me.'

'Name?' said the man boredly.

Karna was silent for a moment, while he considered, then he said, 'Baswani . . . I am a relation.'

The man's lip curled in an expression of scornful disbelief.

Leaning forwards Karna stretched his eyes wide. 'Can't you see the family likeness?' he demanded.

'No,' shrugged the durwan.

'Ring him,' urged Karna. 'Mention Koonty of the Hatibari.' Pulling the gold disc from his shirt he waved it before the man's eyes. 'Tell him about this,' said Karna, feeling his chances start to seep away.

'Whatever you are called, you still have to have an appointment,' said the durwan.

Karna felt in his pocket.

Instantly the durwan became more attentive.

Karna pulled a handful of notes out. The durwan raised his head slowly, his gaze fixed on the money.

Slowly Karna counted notes into the man's outheld hand.

'Wait there, I will call him,' said the watchman when his fist was full. Tucking Karna's gift into his shirt he went into his hut, where Karna heard his voice on the phone, 'The man says he is a relation.' He came out at last and told Karna, 'A body search is required. Mr Baswani has suffered a few assassination attempts while he has lived here.'

At last Karna was through. He felt as though he had entered the gates of Paradise. His car scrunched noisily along a pristine drive. It was winter and brilliant bedding plants had been laid out to represent the colours of the Indian flag, over and over. Fountains sprayed out of great ponds of clear water set in a blue grass lawn that gleamed like velvet and the marble house looked as though it had been carved out of the purest icing sugar.

Karna's heart soared as he reached the great front marble steps. He was about to come face to face with the hero of his youth, with the god of the sun, with Dilip Baswani. He was about to meet his glorious father for the first time in his eighteen-year life.

The doorman at the porch signalled Karna to take his car to the back. Ignoring the man's increasingly urgent and aggressive commands, Karna parked his dented car right in front of the marble portico, getting it as near to the steps as possible, then he got out.

'Please do not leave this car here, sir,' said the man hurrying up. 'Mr Baswani likes to keep his driveway clear of all but top-quality vehicles. Also other VIP visitors may be coming here.'

'I am a VIP visitor,' said Karna, pushing the man aside and climbing the steps.

When he turned around to give his car one last loving glance, he saw the doorman trying to push it out of the way.

'Take your hands off my car,' yelled Karna. 'Don't you know who I am?'

The man looked up, hesitating. He watched Karna doubtfully as the young man mounted the steps. He did not know who the fellow was but all the same decided it was better not to take the risk of antagonising some big shot, in spite of the fellow's youth and inferior transport.

Karna reached the front doors. The entrance was large enough for a Calcutta bus to pass through. Beyond the house Karna caught a glimpse of golden beach, walled round for privacy.

He followed the turbaned bearer into the great cool livingroom that was high and wide as a regal hall.

'What name shall I give Baswani Sahib?' asked the bearer.

'Tell him his son has come.'

The bearer looked worried.

'What?' asked Karna.

The man shrugged.

Karna smiled. 'He has other sons?'

'Exactly, sahib,' said the man, nodding. There was so much starch in his coat and turban that they crackled with the movement.

'I am another.'

'I will tell Baswani Sahib,' said the bearer. He left the room still looking troubled.

Karna sat there waiting for what seemed like ages. He got up and went round examining things to steady his nerves. Everything looks real and expensive, decided Karna. He did not know very much about art but the pictures on the wall were pleasing and touched his soul in a way he had never known before. 'When I am as rich as this,' he thought, 'I too will decorate my house with statues of shining black and green marble, have vases made of crystal with golden handles and on my floors have rugs that look like pictures and are made of silk.'

When Dilip Baswani came in, Karna at first did not realise it was the famous actor. This old man wore a rather grubby dressing gown, was fat and bald. His rosy cheeks and dark eyebrows were clearly the products of cosmetics. Even Dilip Baswani's mouth looked as though it had been brightened with lipstick. When he smiled he showed a row of shining white teeth that were clearly artificial.

But when Dilip spoke it was the voice of the Sun God, rich and thick as kheer. 'I am told you are my son.'

Karna said, 'Yes.'

Dilip Baswani laughingly scrutinised the young man. 'Well, dear young fellow, considering you are half my size in one direction and a good deal shorter in another, I fear you are deceiving yourself.'

'I don't think so,' said Karna.

'And who is your mother, dear boy?'

Karna pulled out the golden disc and showed it to the film star. 'My mother, Koonty, put this round my neck when she was fifteen, before throwing me into the river after my birth.' Karna could not keep the bitterness from his voice.

Dilip Baswani examined the disc then shrugged and said, 'I really haven't a clue who this Koonty is. There were fifteen-year-old girls all over India eager to make love with me and your mother might, or might not be one of them. And I have been to a million Indian villages so could well have been to Hatipur.'

'She was betrothed to the zamindar,' pressed Karna. It seemed important to him that the man remember his liaison with Koonty so that the existence of Karna should have some significance, rather than be merely the consequence of a trivial moment of self-indulgence.

'I really can't remember. Though I always tried to avoid seducing girls of good family.'

'What difference does family make? A girl is a girl,' said Karna.

The old man laughed. 'I suppose it was wrong but they all seemed to like it. I kept to the lower castes out of self-preservation. Families of upper-caste girls always made a fuss whereas those of the lower castes were positively honoured by my advances.'

'I am told she was very pretty.'

'That is the only sort I like,' said Dilip Baswani. 'But although your mother sounds delightful I am sure that if I had made love with a girl of a zamindar family I should have remembered it.' He summoned Karna to a colossal white sofa.

Karna subsided as though sinking into a bowl of paish and trying again, said, 'When I was a child people always noticed how much I looked like you.' He turned his face towards the film star, waited for it to be examined.

Dilip slumped down beside Karna, let out another laugh, and pointing said, 'Look in the mirror, my boy.'

Karna saw, in the vast and gilt-framed looking glass, himself and the aged star seated side by side, Karna so skimpy and big-headed that he was almost the opposite of Dilip Baswani in every possible way.

But then he remembered. 'Look at my eyes, aren't they the same colour as yours?' he said, almost pleaded. He opened his golden eyes as wide as they could go, and insisted the film star scrutinised them.

The eyes that looked back into his were heavily shot with blood and had dark bags under them. The gold, if it had ever been there, had become obscured.

'Beautiful eyes, very like mine,' joked Dilip Baswani. He squeezed Karna's knee with his fist and said, 'You might be my child. I am not saying you are not. There are probably a thousand other boys and girls under the age of forty who are my offspring. I conceived them wherever I went when I was young. It was one of my vices, though

I have had to give it up in my old age.' He paused, appeared to do a mental sum, then said, 'Isn't it ghastly? I might have children who are fifty-five years old. I started young you see. How old are you, my little man?'

'Eighteen,' said Karna.

'So what do you want from me? For I presume this is not just a visit of filial duty.'

'I want you to help me become a Bollywood star,' said Karna determinedly.

Dilip gave a short laugh. 'I might have guessed. That is the only thing they all want.'

'Who is all?' asked Karna.

'These boys and girls who say they are my children. So let's test you out. What do you know about me?'

'Everything,' sighed Karna. 'I have seen every single film you acted in. I saw you in that one where you were the gangster and the zamindar's daughter fell in love with you. Oh, and the one where you are a rickshaw wallah and the . . .'

'Yes, yes, yes,' interrupted Dilip. 'I have been all those. But these days the audiences demand lithe young men to take such parts. As you see I am not the shape any longer to leap about with maidens on the snowclad slopes of Kashmir but let us suppose you are my son, then it will be good to see you take over where I left off.' He surveyed Karna for a long moment then asked, 'You have a good rich talking voice. Can you sing?'

'Yes.'

'Well then,' said Dilip Baswani, 'Let it go.'

Karna threw back his head and let his voice soar out. He sang, in Hindi, a love song from a Dilip Baswani film, 'My heart goes dum dum dum when I see your eyes looking at me through the smoke of the fire. The leaves of our garden crackle when they feel the intensity of our love . . .'

There were tears in Dilip Baswani's eyes when Karna finished.

'Now a last question. But important. Have you ever been in love?'

Karna was about to say 'no', when the door opened and a girl came into the room.

'Ah, Poopay, meet Karna. He says he is my son,' said Dilip.

A great burst of roaring dizziness rushed over Karna at the abrupt, unexpected appearance of Poopay Patalya and the word 'yes' so nearly came bursting inadvertently from his mouth that he had to squeeze his lips together to keep it in.

Poopay wore a transparent gown through which flickered the most beautiful golden limbs in the world, enhanced by the smallest bikini. Even at the Tollygunge club swimming-pool Karna had never seen a girl wear so little. He had never seen a girl with such perfect breasts, such a small tight bottom, such a tiny waist. He had never seen such a glorious mouth, such dense eyelashes, such . . .

After the first swift glance he could no longer look at her but turned his eyes on the opposite wall as though Poopay was blazing with a light that was too strong for him. His heart was thundering so loudly that it obscured his hearing. He could not rise because of the weakness that had overtaken his legs.

And when Poopay said in a casual tone, 'Hi, Karna,' he could not answer either because thrill and shock had numbed his vocal cords.

Poopay, after one swift and unseeing glance at the person sinking into the sofa, said to Dilip, 'I'm having trouble with the lighting engineer, Papa.' She leant over Dilip, holding out photos. 'It makes me look fat from that angle. He won't listen to me when I tell him that this makes my face look so shiny. What do you think? Don't you agree?'

'I'll talk to him, sweetie,' said Dilip Baswani.

She became petulant while Karna sagged, feeling faint. She thrust out her lower lip and a tiny frown crinkled her forehead for a moment.

'You always say that, Papa, but when the moment comes . . .'

'I will tell him. Don't worry.' He reached out and patted the most gorgeous woman in the world, the most desirable woman in the universe, patted her on the bottom as though, as though . . . Karna felt as if he was choking.

Poopay glanced over at the sounds of spluttering and raised her eyebrows in surprise as if momentarily reminded of Karna's presence.

Dilip glanced at Karna too, then, as though understanding, smiled till his eyes nearly vanished into his rouged cheeks.

Poopay pulled out another photo. 'You'll know exactly what I mean when you see this one, Papa. Tell him it must be done the way I want. I won't go on otherwise.' Poopay left the room in a swoosh of some exotic perfume as Dilip was still assuring her, 'I will do it. I will talk to him.'

After she had gone, Dilip turned to Karna with laughter in his eyes. 'She calls me Papa so perhaps she really is my daughter.'

Breath was shocked from Karna's lungs. His heart seemed to stop. The blood froze in his veins.

'Do you still want to be my son?' joked the actor. 'What do you say, my little man?'

Karna stared at him and felt faint all over again.

'Come on, my boy. She calls me Papa, but who knows who is my child and who is not?'

'You mean she might not be?' asked Karna.

'You are looking hopeful,' laughed the old man. 'But consider it. Do you see a family likeness? To me this lovely girl is as unlike myself as you are. Now let us get down to business. You want to be a film star?'

Karna nodded, mute.

'Then you must start at the bottom. That is how most of us begin. You must go and try to get work as an extra. They are looking for young men in one of the films I am making at the moment. It's called . . .' He rummaged around among some papers. Then tossing them aside said, 'Oh, I can't remember the name. "Hug Hug Hug" or "Kiss Kiss Kiss" or something. I know I tried to get some sort of Western title. That's what goes down these days. But we have to keep it simple. Can't confuse the cinemagoing public with complicated foreign words. Perhaps we decided "Kiss" was too difficult.'

Karna thought of kissing Poopay and his lips began quivering and tingling.

Dilip Baswani said briskly, 'But anyway it doesn't matter. We'll probably change the name before it goes out.' He gave Karna an address. As Karna left, he called, 'And one day, when you are famous, you can come back and see me again. But not till then.' He thrust a paper into Karna's hand. 'Show them this and they will let you in.'

The door durwan at the film studio laughed when he saw Karna's chit, and turning told someone inside, 'Another of Mr Baswani's sons!'

A voice inside laughed too. 'How many is that then? Must be the tenth this month.'

Karna was hurried into a great tattered barren hall lined round with tiers of wooden benches, as though this was an arena for watching some game. All around, packed on the benches, sat men, some wearing expressions of despair, some hope, and some asleep. Several of them seemed to be trying out smiles, or arranging their faces to look moody, vicious or sweet. Karna squeezed himself between two men who were drawing heavily on beedies and sat. He kept his own face expressionless, not knowing which expression would be required. He wished he had found out more about the film from Dilip Baswani but the old man had suddenly lost interest in him and had him hustled out.

The air was dense with cigarette smoke that mingled thickly with dust that rose from the floor as soon as anyone came in. Men were appearing all the time, their feet stirring up puffs of dirt and causing some of the sitting hopefuls to choke a little into hands and handkerchiefs.

The man next to Karna, through a small fit of coughing, said, 'I have been here three days. I am hoping that today I will be chosen.'

'What are the extras wanted for?' asked Karna.

'Dacoits,' said the man and scrutinised Karna a little disdainfully. 'I don't know why they let you in. You don't have the physique.' Large muscles stood out on the man's dark-skinned arms.

'Unless you do a workout every day you never get into a film like this.'

'Don't you listen to him,' joked the man on Karna's other side. 'If he's so desirable why has he been waiting for three days?'

'Some people wait for weeks before they are chosen,' said the muscle man huffily.

After an hour, a man wearing a suit, glasses and carrying a folder came in and walked up and down the narrow path between the benches, scrutinising the faces on either side. Men who had been sagging listlessly sat up sharply. Winks and smiles and nods and scowls appeared on every side. Karna's neighbours both adopted expressions of such ferocity that he was reminded of the dacoits of his childhood. He himself tried a small cross frown, decided it was not his style, and waited to see what would happen.

The man with the folder began to point this way and that, saying 'You and you and you.' Men scrambled eagerly from their benches and gathered around him as he went on choosing. He would go out, and just when hope faded all round, return and choose some more. Several times his gaze fell on Karna and lingered there thoughtfully before continuing with selecting brigands. After Karna had been waiting there for four hours and had given up hope, the man returned and suddenly pointed a finger at him and said, 'You there. Can you dance?'

'Me?' Karna's heart leapt. 'Yes. Oh, yes.'

The man nodded. 'I may need dancers next week. Try again then.'

'I told you they wouldn't take a weedy fellow like you to do a dacoit,' said the muscle man.

'But he noticed you. That's the main thing,' said the man on the other side. 'If I was you I'd come back tomorrow all the same, just to keep your face in his memory.'

At last, after six hours, the choosing was done. The muscle man, much to his delight, got his chance but Karna's other neighbour did not.

Karna took the advice and arrived each day, sat there quietly and did not bother to offer fierce faces because he knew he would not be chosen as a brigand but might get a dance part if he played it right.

When, a week later, his great moment came and the finger pointed at him and summoned him down, Karna scrambled through the tiers feeling as though he was floating upwards.

Those chosen for the dancing sequence were gathered together in another shed, much like the waiting one, but without the tiers.

There were about two hundred men in a space rather too small. They milled around for what seemed like hours, people doing graceful leg stretches and wide arm movements in the hope that one of the selectors would come in and be impressed.

At last the waiting was over. Two men and a woman entered. The woman was small, middle-aged and dumpy. Her feet were bare and strapped to each ankle was a ring of dancing bells.

One of the men began to announce through a loud-hailer, 'I want groups of ten. No more. The first ten come over here. The rest of you stand back.' There was a rush and a scramble to be in the first group.

'Everyone will get a chance to show their skills but if there is any fighting I shall throw out the whole lot of you and start all over again.' The crowd shrank back meekly like children in the presence of a strict schoolteacher.

'He won't really throw us out,' the man standing next to Karna said. 'He says that every time but I have never known him to carry out the threat. They just don't have the time. He's got to have his dancers at the ready by this evening because they may have to start shooting tomorrow.'

Ten by ten the waiting men were lined up. A tape-recorder was turned on and Geeta, the little fat woman, stood before them and, her anklets ringing, demonstrated the steps. And all the while the man with the loud-hailer kept shouting threats, over the roar of Hindi pop, to the other hundred and eighty who had been crushed as far as they could go into a corner but who kept creeping out to watch the dancing.

Some of the dancers, in their desperation to be chosen, threw their bodies about so wildly that the people on either side were struck by flailing limbs and punching fists.

'Energy, energy,' urged the second man, who, Karna discovered, was the choreographer. And at the end of each trial one or two, or perhaps none would be chosen.

Karna was one of the lucky ones. The marvellous training that Shivarani had given him was not his only asset. He stood out with his golden eyes and flexible movements.

The departing disappointed looked enviously at the twenty chosen ones.

15

DRAUPADI'S SARI

Loud applauses greet the challenge
and the people's joyful cry,
But the thickening clouds of darkness
fill the earth and evening sky.

'I wish you could start your women's walk from somewhere other than Hatipur,' Gadhari complained to Shivarani. 'It makes us all look silly.' But all the same she came in her car to join the crowd of local people waiting to see the start of the march. All the women who could manage it were waiting to walk with Shivarani, even one or two of the married ones, though their husbands had forbidden it. Every one of the doll-maker widows was coming, among them Ravi's poor young bride. Her husband had been shot soon after his wedding by opponent goondas during an election campaign.

Shivarani was touched to see Gadhari there, in spite of her complaints. People began to appear bringing gifts, garlands and fruit, till the women's arms were full and they could not stop laughing. The village priest chanted prayers over the group and waved joss sticks at them and the village musicians beat drums and blew flutes as the women, their mouths full, set off for Delhi.

It took Shivarani and her followers four days to get to Calcutta and though she had tried to make arrangements for food, water and even shelter on the way, as the numbers grew, any chance of order gradually dissolved.

They reached Calcutta on the fifth day and in the afternoon passed the children's centre. Shivarani saw Bhima standing at the gates, knee-deep in cheering children. He smiled and waved for so long that even when she was out of sight she could tell by the laughs and smiles of those in the rear that he was still at it.

Maidservants began leaving their positions to join the gathering women, ayahs abandoned the children in their care, dhobi women dumped wet washing to follow Shivarani, brides-to-be ran away before their weddings, daughters discarded their duties to their parents, grandmothers threw away dignity and old age to join the Wives of Shiva.

At first people thought Shivarani's march of women was amusing, or even admirable. But gradually as the numbers of the women grew, their popularity diminished. Men who had laughed at first began to be afraid. Sometimes women living in smart suburbs would shout abuse as the procession passed by or order sweepers to throw buckets of night soil at it. They considered the protesters immodest and thought it was giving the country a bad name.

As the days went by the fear of the marchers grew because they needed so much water. Even in the biggest towns there was nowhere for several thousand women to slake their thirst and in the villages, people became afraid that their wells would be drunk dry by so many women so that in the end they had to rely on rivers. They would walk in dust and heat for hours, anticipating the moment of reaching cool and copious water where they could drink deeply.

At first they did not know where the rivers were and merely kept going in the hope of finding one, until someone discovered that the scars on the face of the prostitute called Laika accurately mapped the holy rivers. After that women would cry out, 'We are thirsty, Laika. Let us look into your face and see how long before we get our next bath and drink.' For the first time in her life people looked at Laika's face with pleasure instead of disgust and it began to make her prettier.

The women were almost always hungry. Their white saris turned red or grey depending on the colour of the dust they walked on. Their faces began to peel and blister in the sun. Dark women turned black, fair ones turned dark. Their hair, which could no longer be oiled, took on shades of red or developed streaks of yellow.

Sometimes a woman would fall ill, or become so tired that she could no longer walk and then her friends would pick her up and carry her. There was hardly anyone who could be persuaded to turn back at this late stage, no matter how ill they were. Some of the women had been pregnant at the start of the walk and gave birth at the roadside, attended by their friends, then, after resting for a little while, would be helped along by others. Some women died and their bodies had to be abandoned for relatives to find and cremate. Those who had no relations to give a proper funeral – widows who had been abandoned, girls who had disgraced and been thrown out, women who were for one reason or another quite alone, were carried to be placed in a holy river.

When the women had been walking for a little over two months, and were halfway to Delhi, the Prime Minister called a meeting. 'This "Wives of Shiva" organisation is de-stabilising the country.'

A deputation was sent to meet Shivarani. As the women came in sight, the men wondered if they were hallucinating, for, as far as the eye could see, far away to the horizon, there was nothing but women, all wearing white. It was like being in the snow of Kashmir. They halted the jeep in front of Shivarani and tried to make her stop and talk to them.

'You must walk along with me for we don't stop till night,' she said, and flowed around the jeep with the rest.

'If this continues,' the officials said, 'our country will be brought to its knees.'

'That's a good place for it to be,' cried Shivarani in a fury. 'On its knees and humble because of the way it has treated its women.'

The officials felt a touch of fear at being among so many aggressive-looking females but all the same persisted, 'The Prime Minister says this march is against the law.'

'What law? They must have invented a new one,' scoffed Shivarani, without pausing in her stride. 'I never heard that walking was illegal.'

The government officials returned and told the Prime Minister, 'She will not listen at all and there are so many women that it is impossible to stop them.'

'There are not enough jobs for the men, and if these women all start to demand equal pay and equal work, then where will we all be? Poverty will increase because of this obstructing female, Shivarani Gupta,' one of the ministers said.

'And also,' said another, 'while no one condones the murder of female infants what would happen to our country if it was stopped? Already the population is so high that there is not enough of anything to go round. Food, medicine, jobs, housing, transport, education. Imagine a situation with thirty million more females, each giving birth to an average of four children. You do not have to be a mathematician to anticipate the disaster.'

'These females must be returned to their homes before it is too late,' said the Prime Minister. 'This is top priority. We cannot have a civil war in this country with men on one side and women on the other. Soon we will be reaching the European state of affairs, with women demanding equality with men and then our country will become like those of the West, with broken families, children without fathers, young girls becoming pregnant. There will be sorrow and suffering everywhere.'

A new minister was sent to reason with Shivarani. 'If anything happens to these women it will be your fault,' he said. 'If they are injured it will be because of you.'

'This sounds like a threat,' said Shivarani. 'How can you injure us? Are you going to drop a bomb on us or something?' She meant it to be a joke, but the minister did not smile and Shivarani remembered Naxalbari.

The marching women at first thought the sound was thunder and that, though it was the wrong time of year, a storm was approaching. Some of them became invigorated, anticipating rain, planning to catch the water on their tongues. They began to leap and dance as they waited for a cool drenching that would turn their saris transparent and clinging.

Only Shivarani felt afraid. Laika, walking at her side, was laughing. 'They won't need my face today because they are going to get rain,' she joked. But Shivarani kept looking into the sky and did not answer.

The sound grew louder and Shivarani, gripped with a sudden panic, began shouting, 'Duck, get down, lie on the road.' But the women were dancing. Laughing. Did not hear her.

The bomber burst into view very suddenly, its black bulk blotting out light, its roar blotting out any other sound. It flew so low that the tree tops were bent with its passing. It flew so low that the suddenly silenced women could see the pilot looking down at them.

Later the pilot would say that he had been on a training mission and that the dropping of the bomb had been an error. An error that was never punished. In fact later he would be promoted.

Shivarani wrapped her arms round Laika, hopelessly trying to protect her as the bomb came twirling, gleaming towards them.

The women began screaming, scattering, falling, tumbling, running.

Later, when she thought back, Shivarani felt surprised at how slowly time had seemed to pass in what really must have been only moments. She remembered wondering if there was time to put out her hands and catch the bomb before it struck the ground. Then, with a blinding light and a terrible roar the road seemed to tilt up around her. Laika's body jerked wildly in Shivarani's arms and seemed to split in two in a jet of blood.

Shivarani knew no more.

Gadhari died while Shivarani was away. She had been ill for a long time, but DR was shocked all the same and for days after would be seen gazing at photos of her, with his eyes full of tears.

'She had a few faults, I know,' he told Arjuna, 'but which woman doesn't? And when people have been married as long as Gadhari Aunty and me, it is very sad to be left alone.'

Arjuna longed to think of something comforting to say, but could not find the words.

'It's all right, my boy,' DR Uncle said, and patted Arjuna on the shoulder. 'You must not feel troubled. But I am feeling lonely, so sit by me.' Then, to change the conversation, 'Have you given any thought to what you want to do with your life?'

'Yes,' said Arjuna eagerly. 'I want to be a film star.'

DR Uncle smiled for the first time. 'Cinema is the modern thing and we all should be up to date for the sake of our country's future. Also it will be a great joy to me in my old age to see my nephew taking leading roles in our great Indian epics. Let me hear you quote a few verses from Rabindranath Tagore to test your skill of acting.'

Arjuna did his best to oblige.

'It was May. The sultry noon seemed endlessly long. The dry earth gaped with thirst in the heat,

When I heard from the riverside a voice calling, 'Come, my darling.'

I shut my book and opened the window to look out.

I saw a big buffalo with a mud stained hide standing near the river with placid, patient eyes; and a youth, knee deep in water, calling it to its bath.

I smiled amused and felt a touch of sweetness in my heart.'

DR Uncle listened, his eyes glistening but also with his lips pressed together in an expression of disapproval . . . When Arjuna had finished he burst out, 'What is this bland way of talking? What is this English stiff upper lip attitude? Put more feeling into it, dear boy. Wave the arms around. Move the body. Let the features show deep depths of emotion. The eyes should fill with tears, the heart swell with feelings when such a poem is being recited. Perhaps you are not cut out to be an actor after all.'

Because Shivarani was away so long, DR Uncle took the responsibility upon himself and persuaded the Hatibari trustees to release some funds and arranged for Arjuna to become a student at the same Bombay film school that had rejected Karna.

When Shivarani returned, and DR Uncle told her he had sent Arjuna to film school, she became annoyed. 'He should have chosen a career in politics. The country will never thrive unless people like Arjuna, who have been well educated and have integrity, take a share of the running of it.'

But her anger vanished when she was given a message from Bhima.

'I have a job. Come and meet me in Cal. I need to talk to you.'

In a moment every pain that she had ever had in the whole of her life began to ebb away.

Bhima was already waiting in the coffee house. His eyes were shining with joy as he leapt up to greet her. He caught her by both hands. 'I had to tell you first, Shiv, because you are my best, best friend. Nobody else knows yet. I have got a job with the city bank and Malti has agreed to marry me.'

Shivarani's heart did a jerk. She stared at him. 'What?' she said. Her lips felt abruptly numb as though she had chewed strong paan.

'I am marrying Malti,' he repeated. He looked puzzled.

'What a lot of *m*s, there are in that sentence,' she thought, as she tried to make sense of his words. 'What a lot of *m*s.' Perhaps she even said it aloud, for she saw his puzzlement grow. At first she felt she was watching a Bollywood film and that Bhima was acting in a story. Soon the play would be over and everything would become real again but as his meaning seeped in and pain gathered like the poison from a cobra, strange things started happening to her body. Blood began draining out of her fingers, her toes and eventually her cheeks. A roaring sound started up inside her head. Her sight became blurred and everything began to spin.

Vishnu sleeps, floating in the ocean of the Absolute and in his dream he continually invents the Cosmos. All the worlds are merely the dream of the sleeping god, who will one day wake. And then everything will cease existing and only the Absolute will remain, infinite, inert and unchanging. This is a dream, thought Shivarani. God is dreaming. I am dreaming and will soon wake up.

She sat down very slowly because her legs had started shaking and she feared she was going to fall. She became suddenly aware that her hands were still held by Bhima's, who, after all was not going to be her husband, but was going to marry Malti instead. Feeling ashamed to be holding the hand of someone else's husband, she pulled her fingers away.

'What? Is something the matter?' he was saying. His voice seemed to come from far away as though she was recovering from an anaesthetic . . .

'No, nothing. I am glad for you.' The words came out strangled, as though she had something tight round her throat. Later she would wonder how she had managed to get those words out at all.

She leant back shakily and rested her head against the wall. It felt cool and rough and eased the dizziness a little. Avoiding Bhima's gaze she stared across the dingy café and instead of seeing chatting, laughing people, saw hope, happiness and expectation rush away like the dark current of a monsoon river. She wanted to wake Vishnu and end the dream but did not know how.

Karna's profits from his Bangladesh venture had earned him enough to rent a little Bombay flat which he had furnished with the kind of things he'd wanted for so long. It was new, bright, modern and showy. He would go round his lovely little home and explore his new possessions. His portrait, in which he stared rather glaringly, took up half a wall. He would run his fingers round the rim of his shocking pink Mellaware cups while he waited for his green electric kettle, that was shaped like an egret, to come to the boil. He would caress his telephone with its curled cable and big black numbers as though it was a pony, and anticipate, with shivers of joy, the moment it might ring. He would hold his cut glass tumblers to the light to make rainbows on the walls. He would walk with bare feet over the carpets till his feet tingled with nylon electricity. He would peer and stroke and sniff and hold in the way of someone who has a lifetime of deprivation to make up for. He would move from one piece of furniture to another, sitting on a plastic folding chair one moment, then the next sinking onto a polystyrene pouf, then jumping up and trying out his new sofa. He had arranged his collection of dolls around the rooms. They stood on mantelpieces and in glass-fronted cupboards. They sat on the coffee table and along the kitchen shelf, on the bedside table and leant against the walls. Karna did not mind that the dolls looked cheap and shabby compared to the pristine newness of the other things around them. The dolls were a celebration of his mother because no one had painted her portrait or even taken a photo of her. He had had his posters of Poopay Patalya put in golden frames and they covered almost all his walls. He had bought himself a music centre and in the evenings would sit listening to his favourite song, 'Papa kehte hain,' 'My father is talking,' the theme tune from the film 'Quayamat Se Quayamat Tak,' about a father and son who enjoyed a loving relationship. As Karna listened he would imagine himself enjoying such a relationship with his father, Dilip Baswani.

When Karna got the phone call he could not, at first, make any sense out of it. Thrill and disbelief turned him deaf and stupid while he listened to words that sounded like the talking of angels.

Dilip Baswani wanted Karna to act with Poopay Patalya in a chewing-gum advert. 'You will have to show her some Karate moves,' he said. 'The scene is only half a minute long but I want it to look convincing.'

The night before his session with the young actress, Karna felt so dazed with bliss that he did not sleep. It took him three hours to get ready the following morning and by the time he was dressed his room was scattered with rejected garments. By the time he set off for the studio he had squirted and sprayed himself with so many aftershave lotions and toilet waters that he staggered and felt gassed. He started up his car, trying to control his trembling and slow his breathing. As he reversed out he realised that the blue jeans and T-shirt he had ultimately decided on were quite wrong and wished he had bought a brand-new outfit before meeting the woman of his dreams.

He had seen Poopay Patalya from a distance a few times since the meeting in Dilip Baswani's house, but had never been close to her again. He drove carefully to the studio, praying all the way that he would not faint at the sight of her, or fall down in a stupor at her touch.

The film studio was busy when Karna arrived. Cameramen were balanced on step-ladders or crouched down low. A scriptwriter was working rapidly, his papers laid out before him on the floor. Engineers and electricians darted from one side to another, hauling machinery, swathing cables, arranging lights. A carpenter was finishing off a large piece of scaffolding and scene painters were wildly daubing. A group of dancers were performing in one part of the vast shabby hall and a love scene was being acted in another, while make-up people dashed from actor to actor dabbing on powder and wiping away sweat.

Again dizziness passed over Karna's sight for a moment and he had to lean against the wall to steady himself, when he saw Poopay Patalya. She was sitting in a canvas chair and reading a film magazine. She glanced up as he approached and a look of disapproval clouded her beautiful face. He felt a flush of horror all over again because her frown confirmed that he had put on the wrong clothes.

'I am Karna,' he said. He had to fight hard with his throat so as to keep his voice steady. And when she looked blank he added, 'Karate.'

'Oh, yes. You are late,' she said. 'I am making three films at once this week and am due at the next studio in an hour.'

'This is when I was told to be here.'

Poopay frowned again, said, 'No one has the least sense of time in this place,' then waving a hand she called out, 'The Karate person has arrived.' As people came running from various parts of the studio she told Karna, as though as an afterthought, 'I am Poopay Patalya.'

'I know,' said Karna, forcing his legs to stop quaking. 'We have met before, actually.'

She raised her eyebrows questioningly, 'Oh, really? Where?'

How could she not remember when to him it had been the defining moment of his life?

'In Dilip Baswani's house,' said Karna. He was going to add that he was Dilip's son, but already she was looking bored.

The choreographer appeared out of a flurry of glittering dancers and said to Karna impatiently, 'Come on, let's get started. I expected you yesterday. I was on the verge of finding someone else.'

Karna's heart felt touched with chill at the words.

The choreographer waved a camera into line and told Karna, 'You only get one take so get it right first time.' He told them swiftly what was required then said to Karna, 'Now get on with it.'

'We'll start with the *shudo* chop,' said Karna to Poopay Patalya. 'Get up and copy me.' His voice was cold and his throat tight. He was grateful to his body for remaining steady. Shivarani's tutors had taught him to slow his heartbeat and pierce his body so that it did not bleed or feel pain. These skills were coming in very useful now.

As Karna crouched before Poopay Patalya, showing her the moves, and the cameraman kept the film turning, he tried not to be dazed by the strange and wonderful smell of her.

Karna's lunges, feints and strikes became glorified because of the beauty that was mingling with him, his very essence reacting to the experience that was love. Love can make some men gauche and stumble. It can make them inarticulate and foolish. Karna became sharpened and speeded up by it. His body seemed to move with the swift whistling of a passing arrow. His brain was as still and clear as the water of a deep and pristine Kashmir lake. Poopay Patalya soared through his arms like the wild gander passing through akash. She poured over his neck as light and fluid as the running of river water. He swung and dipped and flipped, turned and rounded her as though he was being whirled, for a second time, in the current of a holy river.

'Shabash,' approved the choreographer.

After half an hour Poopay said she was tired and collapsed back into her chair, panting a little. There were beads of sweat on her upper lip. Her hair gave off the smell of foreign perfume. Karna stood waiting for her to get her breath back, pretending to watch the dancers, but really seeing her out of the corner of his eye. Her hair was thick thick thick and black black black. He wanted to bury his face in it.

A plump lady loomed up with a glass of water but Poopay waved her away and the actress's spot boy poured her cold nimbu pani from a flask, then wiped her forehead with a towel.

Karna could hardly bear to look.

'You are good,' she said to Karna out of the folds of the towel. 'I'm glad Papa suggested you for the act.'

Karna winced. How he wished Poopay would not call Dilip that name.

At the end of his second karate session with the actress, Karna asked her, 'What does "Poopay" mean?' He had often speculated on this and thought it might mean Glory, Greatness, Wonder. She was sitting before her mirror, and her ayah was brushing her hair. She said, laughing, 'Come on, you dope. Don't you know any French?'

Karna did not reply.

'Poupée. They spell it silly here, but I quite like it. Doll. It means "Doll". Can you imagine? I don't look much like a Dolly, do I?'

He felt winded, as though something had punched him in the stomach.

She teased, 'Your silence means you think I do look like a dolly?'

He shook his head mutely and realised he could no longer bring up his mother's face into his mind. Poopay's had got muddled there instead.

Poopay Patalya was intrigued by Karna. She had never met anyone like him. He was so cool, so efficient and her seductive presence did not seem to throw him as it did other men. She got the feeling that he did not like her much and this she found enchanting because all the other men liked her too much. She had grown accustomed to men who melted at her touch, who gasped and could not draw their eyes away when she looked into them. Karna seemed indifferent to her. As she followed the moves he demonstrated, she tried to charm him. She flirted with him and he remained brisk, businesslike and bossy. She was attracted to him because he was cool but also because he was funny-looking and she had grown bored of handsome men who all looked the same.

At the end of the karate session a pair of manicurists came and, resting Poopay's hands on their napkin-covered knees, one on either side, began to work on her nails.

Sitting with her hands held out, she told Karna, 'Bring me a Pepsi, darling. There's a fridge over there.'

Karna came back with the chilled bottle and then stood, uncertain.

'Come on, come on. I'm dying of thirst,' she laughed. Her hands were still trapped by the manicurists. 'Hold it to my mouth.'

The other Karna, the son of the Sun God, had been born wearing shining magic earrings and armour, which he had been warned he must never give away, or disaster would befall him. In that moment, as modern-day Karna raised the bottle to Poopay Patalya's holy lips, he reflected that he would have given them away and more in exchange for this shining glory moment and would not have cared at all about the suffering that such an action would later cause him. He held the bottle as devoutly as a priest would offer milk for the Lord Ganesh and through the thick, magnifying glass he could see Poopay's wide red lips puckering. She drank like a thirsty calf, with a childish gulping sound that made her throat quiver. Then, withdrawing her face she gasped, 'There, that's enough.' Her lips were wet and jutting out her chin she said, 'Wipe it off, darling, would you. There's a tissue there.' She indicated the box with a nod of her head.

Wrapping the tissue round the tip of his forefinger Karna gently dabbed the smudge from the goddess' skin with the unemotional efficiency of a doctor treating a patient.

Poopay felt a little piqued and wondered if Karna was gay for this was the first man who had touched her glorious lips without trying to follow it up with a kiss.

Poopay did not kiss. She thought the act was both boring and unhygienic. So wet and sticky. So utterly pointless. If you wanted to please your mouth eat a gulab jaman. But all the same she felt challenged by Karna's indifference to her and as she sat at her dressing table she could call, 'Hey, Karna, look here. Have I got a spot? No, no, look closely.'

'Your skin is perfect,' he told her briskly and turned his face away, unable to endure the closeness of her wonderful perfumed heartaching presence.

To Karna, Poopay was without flaw. He did not have to fight a temptation to kiss or make love to her. Other women were for kissing, for fucking. This one was Karna's perfect goddess. It did not even occur to him to try to kiss her or to tell her that he loved her. Perhaps even her name was hindering him from seeing her as anyone with whom he could have a sexual relationship. In some strange and lovely way Poopay and his mother were becoming entwined. This beautiful film star was filling the dry hurting gap that had been left ever since Dolly died.

Poopay began to take Karna with her when she met her friends, young actors, actresses and other movie people who came from all over the country and talked English interspersed with swathes of Hindi or the other way round. They met in each other's houses because it was difficult for most of them and in particular Poopay, to go out without being recognised.

To the people of India, Poopay Patalya was a goddess, no less. And there is no way that a goddess can walk the streets like an ordinary mortal. Her face was known by every man, woman and child in the land. Even if there was anyone who had not seen her in a film, there she was on the hoardings, thirty feet high and twenty feet wide. Poopay Patalya was the most famous person in the sub-continent and when she moved about the countryside she had to wear dark glasses and travel in a car with darkened windows, because she would be mobbed if she was recognised.

To Karna, Poopay was a whole continent. Her veins spread through his consciousness like rivers through the land, watering and flooding and receding so that he could almost smell them, fish and water, mud and the oldness of stone that has been stroked for ten thousand years. Her tendons and her ligaments, the beating of her heart, the rise and fall of her pristine lungs, the marrow of her bones were infinite spaces in which his senses roamed. His years on the street had sharpened his senses till he was as acute as a wild animal and was on the edge of seeing through things. His nostrils quivered like a dog's from a nose that was narrow as a pencil. He could sniff out fear or opportunity in a moment. He could tell the mood of a person before they knew themselves what they were feeling. But the hugeness of Poopay Patalya, who seemed to Karna to fill the Cosmos, made it impossible for him to take her in smaller parts. He could not sip her, but could only swallow her whole like a greedy god guzzling up the river of infinity. It was as though she was spread as widely as the Ganges when it flooded. He could only see the map of the universe and was unable to focus on any single constellation. Her words left him dazzled as though through her he could experience Himalayan snow and the icy caves of Shiva. Her moods took him to areas beyond the range of human breathing. Her feelings left him experiencing the density of the deepest part of holy rivers. He was dazed with the glory of her. She was the goddess. She was Kali, black, fierce and terrible, who dances with a necklace of skulls and her tongue hanging out. She was Uma too, who is mild and beautiful. Karna, with his nose sharp like the sniffing of a jackal, knew that all these were Poopay Patalya.

16

A MOON-SHAPED ARROW

Towering high or lowly bending,
on the turf or on his car
With his bow and glistening arrows
Arjun waged a mimic war.
Targets on the high arena,
mighty tough or wondrous small
With his arrows still unfailing
Arjun pierced them, one and all.

'Bhima and I have been forbidden to meet till the day of the ceremonies,' laughed Malti. 'So I want you to act as a go-between, Shivarani.' Then, when Shivarani did not answer, she asked, 'What's the matter? You looked suddenly sad.'

'I'm fine,' said Shivarani and tried to make her lips smile. 'And I am really happy for you.'

In the days that followed, trying to keep her voice steady, Shivarani would tell Bhima, 'Malti says, she can't bear to wait so long till she sees you again.' Then go to Malti with the message, 'He loves you.'

Shivarani wondered if she could endure any more. She did not like going to Calcutta these days and spent more and more time at the Hatibari.

One evening Parvathi suddenly began to scream with excitement. 'He's on the TV. Come and look, Memsahib.' Shivarani came reluctantly and for a moment, as she glanced at the screen, she did indeed think that it was Arjuna, hurling Poopay Patalya and at the same time chewing-gum. It was another moment more before Shivarani realised that the actor was really Karna.

'I always knew Karna would become famous one day,' chortled Parvathi. 'And Poopay Patalya beats him in the fight. Who would imagine that someone would one day beat Karna, let alone a woman.'

'It's only a story, Parvathi. Don't be so silly,' Shivarani chided.

Parvathi was very pregnant with her second child when Karna returned to the Hatibari. Her hand shook as she offered him the dishes of aloo sag and mangsho jhol. Because she had seen him on the screen she was so awestruck that she nearly dropped the dishes. 'To think that I should be in the same room with a famous actor,' she sighed.

'It was only an advert for chewing-gum,' snapped Shivarani. 'And look what you are doing. The juice is running all over the floor.' Parvathi hastily straightened the dish and gazed upon Karna with one hand across her eyes as though the sight of him dazzled her.

'Bring more chupatties. Why are you standing there?' snapped Shivarani.

Parvathi hesitated, seemed about to speak, then waddled off reluctantly. She thought that if she made some mention of the value of keeping silent, Memsahib would allow her to stay and listen to the conversation. She had become good at getting what she wanted out of Memsahib these days. She had asked Memsahib to invest in a pension for Basu. 'For when he retires or when he gets ill or something. Like he would get if he was working in a company.' She had heard that company drivers were given such things. 'Now he's got family and everything so I thought you might like to put something aside for us, you know, just to thank me for keeping my mouth shut.'

'That is called blackmail, Parvathi,' Shivarani said grimly. But all the same she told Basu the next day that as he had worked for her so long and loyally she was setting up a little trust for him in case anything should happen to him. And that when he retired he would receive a pension from it.

'Thank you, Memsahib,' said Basu and going down on his knees, touched his kind employer's feet in a gust of thankfulness. He could never understand why his wife seemed so unmoved by the new and marvellous generosity of a once slightly parsimonious employer. 'Is there something I don't know?' he asked Parvathi later.

Parvathi smiled, kissed the top of his head, and said, 'Lots and lots, my love,' as though it was a joke.

However this time Parvathi decided to say nothing. Her power over Memsahib must not be wasted on trifles, she decided. There would surely come the day when she, her husband or her children needed something big – dowries, college fees, even a little car of their own. She would keep her threats for then.

Arjuna was shocked when he saw the chewing-gum advert. How could such a thing have happened? How could his hideous and common brother get such an opportunity while here was he, Arjuna, still studying and with the chance of getting a part years away? Perhaps he would never get one, for it seemed to him that since he had been in Bombay, every second person was in competition with him. Then, just when Arjuna was feeling something very near to despair combined with huge jealousy, a producer came to Arjuna's film school. 'Your brother, Karna, says you know how to ride a horse.'

A breakthrough, thought Arjuna with excitement. A pity that it had to come through Karna, but anyway, a start. 'I have ridden for years and I'm pretty good.'

'Oh, you don't need to be good,' laughed the man. 'All you need to be able to do is stay sitting on your horse. I need some more mounted soldiers for a battle scene. It's an advert for Amul butter.'

'I will do it,' said Arjuna. 'Is Karna in it too?'

The producer laughed. 'He was okay in the chewing-gum advert so we are having him in this one also.'

'What part is he playing?' asked Arjuna, starting to feel glum.

'The king of the opposing army,' said the man.

'And I will be one of the soldiers,' said Arjuna in a gloomy voice.

The director did not hear the gloom. 'That's right. I expect it will be fun for you taking part in a film with your brother.'

'Actually I am a far better rider than Karna,' said Arjuna. 'He only started learning to ride a few years ago. I have ridden all my life.'

'He's good enough for the part,' said the producer.

'Him the king and me the soldier,' sighed Arjuna morosely. 'Him with the main part and me an extra.' But all the same he told the man, with what smile he could muster, 'Okay. I'll do it and tell Karna, "thanks".' As the man left Arjuna was already vowing to make a fantastic success of his pathetic role and become recognised.

In the advert, Karna was to eat a slice of bread and butter, then say, 'There is nothing like Amul after a hard day's fighting.'

'We are trying to get Poopay Patalya to take the part of the princess who hands it to him, but she is so busy these days appearing in three or four films at once, that she may not be available.'

The advert was to be shot on the Maidan of Calcutta. This was an area on which had once stood the village of Govindpur but in 1758 the British threw out the residents, destroyed their houses, built a massive and impregnable new fort costing two million pounds and cut down the dense surrounding jungle to give their cannons a clear line of fire. It was now a public expanse, three kilometres long and one wide, bounded by the racecourse and important streets on two sides, the river on a third and a stream called Tolly's Nullah forming its southern boundary.

It was a very popular place and the makers of the advert had a difficult time finding space to film. All day and all night Calcutta's residents used the Maidan – performing yoga exercises, walking their dogs, flying kites, playing cricket. On the day of the Amul Butter battle a large crowd of onlookers mingled with the dancing bears, performing monkeys, jugglers, fire-eaters, puppet shows and contortionists, to see the filming. Film extras jostled with stilt walkers, magicians and children being given pony rides. There were grown-ups practising tent-pegging and in the distance, an elephant. Actors in tin and cardboard armour hung around stalls drinking sugar-cane juice or eating samosas while people pushed through the throng of brightly bridled cinema horses to get their fortune told by parrots or to buy paper dragons.

Shivarani told Basu to park the car and stay with it. 'In a crowd like this there will be nothing left if it is unattended for a second.'

She knew it was her duty to support her nephews but the whole thing depressed her. She could not imagine what Koonty's reaction would have been to the sight of her two sons taking part in a trashy advert. It must be her fault, she thought. Because she had no children, she had not known how to set Karna and Arjuna on the right path. By now, she thought, any other boys would be following proper careers as lawyers, accountants or politicians.

Although there were a thousand other thrilling things to see, the appearance of Shivarani always attracted a little crowd. A group of children followed her, doing a mocking Shivarani walk and whispering, goddess Kali, goddess Kali. She would swing round on them suddenly, at the same time pretending to look furious and spreading her hands as though trying to catch them. And then she would watch and laugh as they fled with frightened giggles.

Karna arrived in his car and almost before he was out the dresser was pulling a glittering cloak, baggy jodhpur trousers and a chain breastplate made of nylon rope over his tracksuit. The whole thing had to be done very fast because there were more than a hundred people to dress and only ten minutes to do it in.

'What about make-up?' asked Karna.

'No time for anything like that,' the man said. 'No one will see your face anyway. Here's your horse. Get on quick. Shooting should have already started.' They put a crown on Karna's head. A narrow white horse with the inward-turning ears of a Katiawari was led up and Karna was legged into the gold-tasselled saddle. Karna's horse had flared nostrils, an arched neck and prancing feet. It constantly whisked its tail and snapped on its foam-covered bit while Karna sat back in his saddle, looking haughty, holding a scarlet leather rein with a casual hand, as though he had been brought up riding fiery stallions instead of a pony mare called Poopay.

Then Karna saw Arjuna gazing at him with an expression that was almost awe and certainly envy. Sitting tall and straight as though he was a real king and with his heart singing, Karna inclined his head slightly in Arjuna's lowly direction. This moment, Karna felt sure, made up for all the humiliations and sadnesses of his life. Looking down, he announced to those around, in his new, irritating, grand voice. 'Meet my younger brother who is following in my footsteps though why he has to compete with me in everything I do, I have no idea.'

There came a gust of sympathetic laughter at the comment.

Arjuna flinched.

All the while film people rushed around shouting orders, arranging cameras and dashing at the watching crowd, threatening them with dreadful punishments if they did not stand back.

The producer began shouting instructions, 'Common soldiers to your places!' and the rest of the riders began mounting and flowing into the field.

Karna, who was not one of the common soldiers but their king, restrained his mount which started stretching out its neck and fiddling with its bit. As he waited, he saw someone rush up to Arjuna and ask, 'Are you a rider extra?' and heard Arjuna answer glumly, 'Yes.'

'What the hell are you standing there for then?' shouted the man, tossing Arjuna a cloak. 'Here, fling this over your clothes. You'll be at the back so it hardly matters what you wear.'

Karna felt gratified to hear Arjuna mutter, 'Sorry' as he wrapped himself in the tinsel nylon.

'And get on that horse there,' ordered the man.

Karna watched anxiously and breathed a sigh of relief to see that Arjuna's small brown horse had ears that hung like a depressed rabbit's.

★　　★　　★

Shirvani, who had seen the whole encounter, felt dispirited and wondered where it was all going to lead. There seemed no place on earth these two boys could be, and not make a fight out of it.

As Karna went riding by, she called out, 'Good luck.'

He waved and grinned. 'Thanks for coming,' he said.

'I wouldn't have missed it, darling,' she told him. She thought she saw a little flush leap into his cheeks because she had called him, 'Darling'.

Shivarani watched him go and wished that her relationship with him was as relaxed as with the local children.

The commander of Arjuna's army sat on a large, thickset black horse and was wearing the golden turban and floating robes of a Sikh warrior. His expression was haughty and his posture grand. In his hand was a curved and bejewelled sword which winked in the bright sunlight.

As Arjuna trotted up on his dull gelding, the Sikh shouted, 'You are too tall. Go right to the back where you don't show up. And be sure to keep your T-shirt covered with that cloak at all times just in case the camera catches you.'

Arjuna shrank to the rear of the battlefield and for the first time properly understood true disgrace.

For a while Arjuna, T-shirt and jeans concealed by six yards of ladies' tinsel and handloom, hoped to restore his dignity by perking up his horse. He pressed his heels into its side, took a firmer hold of the bit, rearranged his weight, even shouted encouragingly at it. But nothing worked. The horse seemed to hardly notice, and did not even bother to prick its ears. Arjuna's humiliation was complete.

At last the two armies were in place, facing each other across the plain, with the producer moving between the two on a motor scooter and shouting out orders through a megaphone, the gawping crowd being forcibly restrained by bamboo whackings. The only creature to be spared a beating was a huge Himalayan fighting bear that stood with his owner, towering so alarmingly over those around him that when the crowd controllers reached him, they edged away. He was known to be harmless but all the same it was best to be on the safe side when dealing with a creature that weighed as much as three grown men and had claws as long and sharp as plough spikes.

The crowd was a constant problem and the producer already regretted having chosen the cheaper option of filming his battle scene in this public place. A balloon seller had been paid not to sell during filming but unfortunately several adults and children who had already purchased released their strings. The sky was now dotted with bright colours, making it hard for the cameramen to get the shots they needed without the inclusion of twentieth-century gas-filled plastic.

The bear lived with his owner in a small hut in the bustee. They slept side by side on charpoys, the bear's being reinforced with iron bars that the owner had pilfered from the railway line when the wood frame had started cracking. The bear had a large appetite for arrak though a rather weak head and it adored stuffed paratha so the pair ate and drank together like friends. The bear's function was to put on a performance of fighting and attacking his owner. The more ferocious the attack the bigger the crowd and the greater the revenue. Unfortunately the bear found it almost intolerable to show aggression to someone he loved so much. For a while he would prance around rattling his claws, wrinkling up his snout, letting out murderous growling sounds, giving his beloved little pretend shoves with his paws. But suddenly, often just when the crowd was starting to gasp with horror, fearing the man was about to be mauled to death in the midst of the most furious clinch the bear would be seized with emotion. Flinging his arms round his owner, the bear would kiss and kiss his cheeks with enormous lickings.

Human activities interested the bear because he thought he was one and now he was finding the activities on the plain before him absolutely fascinating. He was very sensitive to his owner's moods and because the man was so excited by the throng of horses and riders, the bear felt excited too and could not take his eyes off the ranks of glittering soldiers.

*　　*　　*

There came a shout from the director. The gold-turbaned commander waved a hand to say he was ready. The cameras began turning and the horses ahead of Arjuna went galloping off in a cloud of yellow dust, a bounce of whisking tails and quarters, a clatter of armour, a roar of yelling and a burst of thrown clods.

But Arjuna's horse stood still. 'Go on, get going, you idiot,' shouted Arjuna, digging in his heels. Still the horse did not budge. In fact Arjuna wondered if it had gone to sleep for its head was hanging low and its ears still drooped. 'Get moving,' yelled Arjuna, kicking hard. He was going to miss the battle altogether in a moment. He craned longingly after the rest of the army and dug his heels even harder into the side of his reluctant mount till at last the horse raised its head a little and set off at a shuffling trot. Arjuna kicked again and the pace increased slightly but they were rapidly dwindling back. Soon Arjuna would be left behind for the gap between him and the rest of the army was widening every moment. The air was now filled with shouts, clashes of metal, of people beating dekchi lids, and the thudding of hooves. Two of the horses had been trained to fall and the cameramen dashed alongside, filming them both from every angle for the many shots to be inserted later, giving the impression of a dozen terrible tumbles.

Arjuna began to feel desperate at his horse's unenthusiastic gait. Looping his reins he whacked the side of the horse's neck with them, at the same time shouting exhortations, implorings and furious threats. The horse speeded up a little and he heard liquid sloshing in its stomach as though it had recently drunk a lot of water. Arjuna slapped, shouted and drummed his heels into the animal's side and the horse toiled into a slow canter.

There came a roar, followed by screams. Then three of the horses ahead of Arjuna turned in mid-charge and began rushing back towards him and towering over them he saw the vast dark figure of a Himalayan bear.

Arjuna's horse changed its character in a moment. Suddenly its ears pricked up and its body seemed to bunch together under Arjuna's in a spasm of terrified muscle. More riders were now flying towards them, their turbans unwinding, their faces filled with horror, as they leant back in their saddles and pulled desperately on the open mouths of their terrified mounts.

Ahead of Arjuna, horses tumbled, reared, threw their riders, crashed to the ground. Some were going one way, some another, but the bulk of the army had become trapped in the melee. And in their midst was the great bear rearing to his fullest height, letting out frightful roars and growls and raking at the air with his six-inch claws. He had always been aware that his master was disappointed with his feeble shows of violence so now, in this crowd where there was no loving master to kiss he seized the chance to put on the best performance of his life.

He snapped his teeth with frightful snarls, and warriors, frantic to escape, began getting tangled up in each other's stirrups and were pulled to the ground. He raked the air with his claws and nearby horses went lunging backwards, crashing into each other, falling on top of others already fallen. Several more horses burst out of the fray and came rushing towards Arjuna, then past him.

Arjuna, keeping the firmest grip possible on his horse's mouth, making full use of its mindless, terrified bolting, rode straight towards the turmoil, and in the way that horses rush back into burning stables, the gelding charged in panic towards the very thing that panicked it. Arjuna held its head steady and would not let it turn. This crazy horse was giving him a chance not only to catch up with the army, but to go ahead of it. If only he managed to keep this horse moving on a straight course, he might be the only soldier left to charge the enemy. The dingy cloak that had been thrown over him to hide his twentieth-century clothes began slipping off and eventually fell to the ground to vanish under milling horses' legs and fallen warriors. It was a relief to no longer have it tangling up in his hands and getting wrapped round his face.

He did not give the bear a thought. He had come here to fight a battle and bears had not entered into it. All his attention and his only aim was to get to the front line and defeat the enemy. And if there was a bear in the way he hardly noticed.

As they plunged through the crowd Arjuna had a glimpse of the great bear, claws extended, teeth bared, then they were past it. He nearly fell when they were brought up sharply short by the heap of writhing struggling fallen men and horses but regained his balance instantly. Then as though he was in the Hatibari and was faced with one of Piara Singh's little bushes, he leant back, gathered up his mount, and with a thrust of his heels, urged it over the squirm of fallen soldiers. The horse leapt with a snort and a surge of muscle, and Arjuna saw, as they flew through the air, the Sikh warrior king lying below. His face was creased with agony, his golden turban had fallen off. Behind Arjuna he could hear, over the human screams, the roaring of the bear. Through the megaphone came the increasingly furious voice of the producer yelling, 'Stop the action, stop the action.' And 'Will the owner of the bloody bear remove it at once before any more damage is done.'

Arjuna drove his horse onwards, thrusting through the mob till they burst through what had once been the front line of his army. There the horse stopped as suddenly as it had started, nearly tilting Arjuna over its head. As it stood staring dazedly around, its syce rushed up, took it by the bit, and began lovingly and consolingly to stroke the white foam from its trembling withers.

Across the plain, the enemy king, Karna, still waited on his white horse, surrounded by his soldiers who were milling around as though they did not know what they were supposed to be doing.

At the appearance of Arjuna, Karna stood up in his stirrups, waved his arms and began yelling, 'Get to the back, Arjuna. Your T-shirt is showing.'

The bear's owner had been running round the fringe of the dishevelled army ever since the animal had first gone diving into the battle. But till now excitement had been roaring so loudly in the bear's ears and the clamour around him had been so great that he had not heard. Suddenly his master's voice reached him and there was displeasure in the beloved's tone instead of admiration. All the bluster left the animal in a moment. He dropped back on all fours and began to waddle toward the voice. He emerged from the crowd, cringing, to be greeted by his master's fury.

People were already running into the crowd, catching horses, helping riders up, getting warriors back into their saddles.

A motor scooter appeared out of the dust and the producer leapt off and began dashing up and down yelling orders, instructing everyone to take up their places again. The sikh commander's black horse was led out, but there was no sign of its rider.

There came shouts. 'Come here. The leading man is badly injured.' The producer dived into the crowd and moments later Arjuna heard him shout at someone among the fallen soldiers, 'Get up at once. What are you doing lying there? We have to complete the filming before sundown,' and the Sikh commander chokingly reply, 'I can't even stand, so how do you expect me to get on a horse? I need medical treatment.' His voice was very weak.

'Where am I going to find a man of your shape to play your part?'

'I don't care,' moaned the Sikh. 'I am probably dying and all you can think about is your filming.'

The producer let out a snort of furious aggravation and emerged, his face scarlet with frustration. 'Bring a stretcher,' he shouted. Then, seeing Arjuna out at the front on his gasping bay he said, 'You'll do.' He got back onto his motor scooter and beckoning Arjuna to follow, began to slowly chunter back to where the director sat. As Arjuna followed the motor scooter on his exhausted horse, he passed the bear creeping humbly behind its angry owner, back to its place in the crowd.

First-aid people went by with the stretcher on which lay the Sikh commander, his face grimacing, his head bare. He was letting out high-pitched moans of pain.

Ten minutes later someone was handing Arjuna a heap of glittering garments. The producer said, 'Put these on and don't waste time. I've only got forty minutes left to finish the shoot and then it will start getting dark. We can do the close-ups in the studio tomorrow if the real actor is up to it.' Baggy silk jodhpurs were pulled over Arjuna's jeans and his head was hastily wrapped in a golden turban.

Arjuna had been transformed from an invisible too-tall warrior at the rear of the army into its commander. Thrills raced through his body like electric tinglings. The Sikh commander's great black horse was led up. It pawed the ground impatiently with wide hooves and let out a snort like the blowing of a trumpet that sent flies shooting like arrows from its vibrating nostrils. This horse had not been panicked by the bear. This was a king's horse, a war horse, a regal horse. Arjuna mounted it, thrilled because he was no longer a hidden hijra in a woman's dress, but a king, a maharaja, a leader of armies.

'I don't want any heroic stuff,' said the producer to Arjuna. 'Your function is to do nothing and look decorative. Do you understand me? Now this horse is a different matter altogether to the donkey you've just been riding, so keep a good hold on its mouth. You know how to do that, don't you?'

Arjuna nodded, mute with joy.

It took fifteen more minutes for the whole enemy army to be rearranged and by that time the producer was scarlet with fury and frustration. However in the end most of the horses were up and most of the riders managed to mount again.

'Let those who are bleeding or who think they may have broken something keep out of line of the cameras till after the battle. Then they can moan and wince as much as they like. The more the better in fact,' shouted the producer. 'Real injuries will make the scene all the more authentic.'

Arjuna rode to the front of his army and sat waiting for the producer's instruction for him to give the command to charge. The horse chomped on its bit and pawed at the ground, sending up a little flurry of dust.

Across the field Karna sat calmly on his tall white horse, a bright streak among the bays and browns of his army. Arjuna leant back too, in a kingly posture, to looked haughtily down his nose and languidly swung his jewelled sword. When Karna raised a mailed hand, Arjuna raised his too.

'No need for all that,' the producer shouted to Arjuna. 'Just keep that creature under control. This will only be a short shot and Karna will be the one in view. Just do as I say and let's bloody get on with it.'

At Arjuna's back his army murmured with the suppressed moans of the injured and the gasping of recently panicked horses.

Then the order came. Arjuna raised his sword, yelled, 'Forwards, my men. Into the battle. Charge,' and loosing his grip on the reins, dug his heels into the horse's sides and cantered towards Karna, the enemy.

Karna came charging at Arjuna, his billowing cloak making it seem as though he filled the whole horizon.

'Kill, kill kill,' yelled Arjuna and he pulled out his sword and brandished it. 'Death to you, you varlot,' he roared.

Karna pulled his own sword out. 'Say your prayer for your last moment is here, Arjuna,' he shouted.

The cameras whirred. It looked as though the two commanders were going to be involved in a head-on collision. Their plastic swords seemed about to run each other through. This was going to be the best bit of the film.

As the horses met, Arjuna flung away his sword and reaching out, grabbed at Karna's throat. Karna flung away his sword too and grasping Arjuna's hands tried to pull them away, while the two mounts skidded and reared. Alongside, the cameras worked furiously, cameramen ducking and dodging for every angle.

The horses heaved and swayed as the two heroes, groaning and grunting with the effort, hauled and thrust at each other's bodies, each trying to throw the other from his horse, while all around them the two armies clashed swords, clanged shields, and shouted war cries.

There came a cry from the crowd of onlookers. 'Come on, Karna, do it for Poopay Patalya.' Everyone had seen the famous karate scene by now.

Karna's concentration wavered momentarily. He whispered, 'Poopay' as he fell.

Around Shivarani the crowd had been shouting, 'Come on, Karna' but Shivarani, her own voice inaudible in the din, had been shouting, 'Stop that, Arjuna, stop that, Karna. You'll hurt yourselves.' If she had been at home, she would have ordered the pair of them to behave themselves and it was frustrating now to look on helplessly.

Quite soon Karna rose, apparently uninjured, out of the dust. He was crownless and dishevelled, but none the less alive. She could not understand, though, why he should look so furious, as though once again Arjuna had beaten him in a hard-fought contest.

Later the producer congratulated Arjuna saying, 'Well done, young man.' The story had been revamped. The advert would not show the king eating Amul butter but, instead, the Sikh commander.

Thanks to the Amul advert, Arjuna, limping and stiff, arrived back in Bombay a hero. His class rose and cheered him as he came into the room and his tutors all smiled, looking pleased and gratified. He received an invitation to a party from the director, Dilip Baswani.

Shivarani's rich friends, with whom Arjuna stayed in term time, lived on Malabar Hill. They became worried when Arjuna told them he was trying to buy a car to drive to the Baswani party. 'Those film people are such snobs,' his host said. 'You should allow our driver to take you there.' Arjuna's hosts were like grandparents to him.

Nothing would persuade Arjuna, though. He wanted to arrive in his own car, as Karna had done.

Although Karna had been extra cold to Arjuna since this episode, all the same Arjuna decided to approach him and see if Karna, who knew everyone and could get anything, could get him a loan, or even a car on credit, till DR Uncle could be found. Arjuna approached his half-brother with trepidation. But when Karna heard what Arjuna wanted he laughed. 'A car? Of course. I can easily get you one.'

Arjuna was surprised and delighted. Karna, in spite of his sulky ways, was at heart a good sort after all. He did not seem at all resentful, anymore, about the unfortunate battle.

'In fact,' said Karna, 'I am thinking of selling my car and buying something else. Would you like to try it?'

'Don't worry about paying me. Let me have the money whenever you can,' said Karna cheerily later. 'There's no hurry at all.' Arjuna began to think he had misread his half-brother from the start.

The car petered out five kilometres before the Baswani estate. First it became quieter, then slower, then stopped altogether and nothing would start it. Arjuna turned the key, pressed the accelerator and even tried shouting to the car, as he had shouted to Draupadi. Nothing would produce the smallest sign of life from it.

Arjuna knew nothing about the workings of cars and after half an hour managed to flag down a lorry. The lorry driver opened up the bonnet, peered into Arjuna's engine and muttered something incomprehensible, but which Arjuna eventually understood meant that some vital part of the vehicle was missing and that there was nothing the lorry driver could do.

Arjuna arrived in the turnip lorry an hour later. His starched white front was grimed with dust, his shiny black shoes hopelessly blurred. The durwans at the gate were at first reluctant to let him in even when he flourished his written invitation, and in the end Mr Baswani was sought out.

'My dear boy,' he cried, laughing at the sight of the dishevelled Arjuna. 'Can this really be the same shining hero that unseated the king in the butter advert? Come and meet my daughter, Poopay Patalya.' He gestured to where a small slim girl wearing a black sweatshirt and tights, her mass of blue-black hair held in a band, was laughing with a group of friends.

Arjuna recognised her instantly and gasped with delight. Around Poopay were women gleaming in gold silken saris, mouths were bright with lipstick, eyes were ringed with mascara and throats glittered with jewels. Poopay had not dressed up at all, wore no make-up and was, Arjuna decided, more beautiful than any woman there.

Poopay turned from her friends and called, 'What are you saying about me, Papa? I can hear you.'

'Poopay always calls me "Papa",' explained Dilip Baswani to Arjuna.

'Does she? Oh really?' cried Arjuna, enthusiastic. 'In that case may I have your permission to marry her?'

Dilip smiled. 'If I thought you were serious and if she really was my daughter, I might say "yes".'

'Is she or isn't she?' demanded Arjuna.

'Do you really want to know?' teased Dilip. 'Everyone tries to make out that I am their father. Even your brother, Karna.'

'Karna?' The statement temporarily winded Arjuna. He said, 'Karna' again, in an almost despairing tone. He sighed. He felt a little gulp of nausea rise in his throat. He said miserably, 'Then you must be the man who destroyed my mother's life.'

Dilip smiled and patted Arjuna's elbow. 'Karna and I have already had that out and we have come to the conclusion that, because of my predilection for girls of the lower castes, it could not have been me.'

'Oh,' said Arjuna, feeling relieved.

'Poopay, come and meet Arjuna,' called Dilip. 'He wants to marry you.'

Poopay came over, laughing and showing a lot of small bright teeth.

'I've seen all your films. I think you're absolutely marvellous,' Arjuna breathed.

'Thank you,' said Poopay and she gazed on Arjuna's face as though as thrilled with him as he was with her.

They were standing like this, staring at each other, when Karna appeared.

'Oh, you two have met, have you?' he said gruffly. And to Arjuna, 'You are bloody late. Where have you been?'

'Your car broke down,' said Arjuna crossly, dragging his gaze from Poopay with difficulty.

'I can't understand that,' said Karna. 'It was always very reliable. I never had the least trouble with it. You must have done something wrong.'

Karna was shaken by the sight of Arjuna who, he thought, would have been certain to arrive too late. But it had not all been bad. He looked very smart and tidy and Arjuna was a mess, though when he came upon Poopay and Arjuna looking at each other, there had been something in Poopay's expression that worried him.

17

UNITY

Peerless Karna, lead us onward
To a brighter happier fate,
For thy arm is nerved to action
By an unforgotten hate.

Karna wrote, inviting Shivarani to stay with him in Bombay.

Shivarani read the letter twice over, and felt moved. It was badly written, wrongly spelt, but graciously worded. She wondered if, for the first time in nine years, some kind of intimacy would develop between them when she visited him. For her sister's sake she had always tried to do her best for Karna but somehow it had never really worked. She often had a sense that she had failed him, but now he had written this letter. 'Dear Shivarani Aunty, I have a flat of my own in Bombay. It is rather small but all the same it would be very nice . . .' She tried to imagine herself in a rather small flat with Karna, and could not. After she read on she understood better why he had written, even why he had asked her to come. 'I have been offered the leading role in a new Mahabharata. I am to act the part of Arjuna,' he said. She could almost feel the shiver of joy that had gone through him when he wrote the words. 'The training you gave me, all those dancing lessons and martial arts have paid off.' He was trying to thank her.

'Dear Karna,' she wrote back. 'I would love to. I will come by train.' Because he was almost her child, she had a piece of news that she felt he ought to know. But as soon as the letter had been posted, she began to have second thoughts.

On the journey there, she went over in her mind, once again, the conversation with DR Uncle.

'I am lonely,' he had said, 'and I think you are too. Will you marry me?'

She had caught her breath. A shock of pain had pierced her.

'I am sorry, I should not have said anything.' DR Uncle touched her hand. 'Forgive me. The matter will not be mentioned again.'

'May I think about it?' said Shivarani quickly.

'Will you? That will be good,' smiled DR Uncle.

She would marry DR Uncle, she decided now. It would solve a lot of problems. Ever since Bhima had told her he was marrying Malti, Shivarani had tried to find a way of banishing him from her heart. Perhaps this would be the way.

Karna was waiting for her at the station. He came towards her smiling then touched her feet. 'My car is waiting,' he said a little grandly.

He drove her through Bombay, pointing out the sights, telling her of places where a film had been made, pointing towards the sea. 'That's my father's house.'

'And that's where Poopay Patalya lives,' he said, and became suddenly so silent that she thought she could see into his heart.

'Tell me about this film part you have been offered.'

He said shyly, 'It is the most wonderful thing that has ever happened to me.'

She leant back, feeling soothed because, after all, though she had made many mistakes, things were turning out all right. Bombay flowed by glitteringly. Karna's driving seemed to have improved a little, his gear changes now often worked first time. She was relieved to see that he could manage an emergency stop. The sleeping buffalo should be grateful too, she thought.

Karna was chattering childishly, making Shivarani feel that he was experiencing proper childhood for the first time in his life. Perhaps, despicable though these trashy films were, they would all the same give Karna the things he had so far lacked. At least, she thought, he should be able to gain enough self esteem and money from it so as not to have to resort to crime again.

He said, 'After this I won't ever mind anything again.' He glanced at her swiftly and added, 'Dilip Baswani, my father you know, arranged for me to play the part. He was impressed at how I handled the adverts.'

Shivarani was brought up short. It was at her suggestion that Karna had sought Dilip out, but all the same he was the man who had seduced her sister Koonty and ruined her life. It was because of Dilip Baswani that Koonty was dead. Shivarani did not want to have to be grateful to him. But she only said, 'That's wonderful, Karna. Really wonderful.'

'And also, in spite of never having been to film school, I got the lead, not Arjuna.'

'Good for you,' said Shivarani, feeling glum because even now, in his moment of triumph, Karna could still not stop the rivalry.

Karna brought his car to a tyre-shattering halt in front of a large grim-looking apartment block and told her proudly, 'My home.' It was pitch dark inside the hallway. Karna said, 'Electricity seems to be off again. We'll have to feel our way up.' He paused and even though she could not see his face, she sensed that he was trying to pluck up his courage to say something that embarrassed him. At last he muttered, 'Shall I hold your hand or something? The stairs are a bit broken.'

'No, no, thank you. It's all right,' smiled Shivarani.

They had to climb nine flights to reach his flat, Karna giving frequent warnings, 'Be careful here, there's no banister.' And 'This bit's rather tricky because two stairs are missing.'

They got there at last and Karna grandly unlocked and threw open his door. Shivarani flinched at the sight of the clutter and the tiny room. Karna, unaware, led her round. 'There are my cups and plates and things,' he said, waving a hand. 'And in there is my bedroom.' He flung open a door. 'I thought you should sleep there.'

'What about you?' Already Shivarani was wishing she was home again.

'I'll be on the sofa,' said Karna. 'And this is my portrait. Did you ever see it after Rishi finished it?'

'Goodness,' said Shivarani.

'The eyes follow you all round the room, wherever you go,' Karna said.

'They certainly do,' said Shivarani. She looked around.

'Do you ever see Arjuna?' She did not hold out much hope here, presuming that the relationship was as bitter as ever. But Karna said, joyfully, 'Oh yes. I see him quite often as a matter of fact. I've been helping him quite a lot and he's grateful to me, I think.'

'Good,' said Shivarani and could hardly believe what she was hearing.

'We have to get on nowadays, you see, because I managed to persuade Dilip to give him a minor part in the Mahabharata too. We'll both be acting in the same film.'

'How nice of you to be so helpful, Karna.'

'At the moment, Arjuna and I are engaged in a mammoth squash contest. It has been going on for two weeks. We are going to play our final game tomorrow. Why don't you come and watch?'

'I'd love to,' said Shivarani.

The squash tournament had been vicious. Squash balls had burst like eggs under the gigantic blows. Racket handles had shattered. The brothers had already worn through a couple of pairs of gym shoes each and chunks had been knocked out of the plaster walls, where they had crashed against them. This was the final and deciding game.

But when Karna and Shivarani arrived next day, Arjuna was not there.

Karna, who felt sure he was going to win because everything was going his way these days, began to feel jittery. Then a bearer came and said there had been a phone message from the film studio and that Mr Pandava had been detained.

★   ★   ★

'Don't take it so hard,' Shivarani tried to console. 'It must have been something unavoidable. I bet he'll be there tomorrow. I will definitely come and see it then. I'm looking forward to it.'

Gradually, as they returned to his flat, Karna's dark mood began to lift, and by the time they arrived he had become quite cheerful. He told her, 'Today we are getting our scripts. I've got to go round to the studio to collect mine.'

'I will do some shopping while you're away,' said Shivarani. It seemed the right thing to say, and shopping the sort of thing people do when they come to stay in Bombay, but all the same she laughed at herself for she was not at all a shopping sort of person.

Karna arrived to find the studio oddly empty.

'Where is everyone?' he asked. Usually at this time the place was humming with activity, engineers up ladders fixing bulbs, painters getting the back boards up, make-up people dashing round with palates of grease paint . . .

'There's been a change of plan,' the stage manager said. He looked shifty and uncomfortable.

'Where is Arjuna?'

'He has gone away with Mr Baswani.' The stage manager's nervousness seemed to increase.

'I've come for my script,' said Karna.

'Oh, yes.' The stage manager pulled out a wedge of papers and handed it to Karna.

Karna looked at it then handed it back. 'Hey, this isn't mine. This says "Karna", I'm doing Arjuna.'

'This is what Mr Baswani told me to give you,' said the man looking miserable.

'But this is ridiculous. Where is Mr Baswani? I need to talk to him. There's been some ludicrous mistake.'

The manager sighed heavily. 'They have gone to the airport.'

'To the airport?' Karna kept his tone steady. 'Who has? Why?'

'They are flying to some mountain village. Mr Baswani heard that there was some good snow at the moment and he did not want to miss it.'

'Why do they want snow? Who wants snow? Who has gone to the airport?'

'All of them. Mr Baswani, Miss Poopay and Arjuna Pandava. Mr Baswani wants to do a quick snow scene before starting on the big one.'

Karna stared at the man in silence.

The manager had been warned to expect a scene. Mr Baswani was a great one for last-minute choppings and changes. 'Mr Arjuna left a letter for you.'

As Karna ripped it open he had to keep an icy control on his hands to stop them trembling. 'I'm sorry about the squash,' wrote Arjuna. 'We'll play the match when I get back but Dilip has asked me to play Arjuna and we are off to do some of the filming in the Himalayas.'

Karna stared at the letter in silence for what, to the manager, seemed like ages. Then at last he said in a voice so quiet it was almost a whisper, 'What time did they go? Which road did they take? What time does the plane fly?'

Shivarani waited in Karna's flat for hours and when by afternoon he had not come, she went herself to the studio.

'He has driven off to the mountains, I think,' one of the lighting people told her. 'Something to do with the filming of the Mahabharata.'

'When will he be back?'

The man shrugged. 'You can never tell with filming.'

Irritated at Karna's lack of concern in not sending her any message, hurt because she had been hoping that something good might come in her relationship with Karna on this visit, she packed up her things and returned to Hatipur.

★　　★　　★

Arjuna sat in the back of the gleaming purring Audi with Poopay Patalya at his side. He kept looking at her. Each time he turned away he would think, she can't really be as beautiful as that, and then have to have another look. He and Poopay were to spend three days dancing, singing and flirting with each other in a remote snowbound Himalayan village.

They were hurrying through the night to catch a plane that would take them to a place where snow lay. Arjuna did not remember any snow in the story of the Mahabharata and had no idea what this bit of film was about but if it meant staying near to Poopay then he was not going to ask questions.

Sometimes during the hours that followed, Karna thought he must be catching up on them. The script of Karna's part was at his feet and its open pages flopped about his shoes as he thrust the accelerator on to yet greater speeds.

Dilip Baswani was relieved to have put a distance between himself and Karna for the moment and hoped that by the time they got back to Bombay, Karna would have got over his anger. Although Baswani had been perfectly within his rights to change his mind, he had flinched from telling Karna face to face. If Karna still made a fuss when they got back he would explain to the young man that he had purposely given Karna the more difficult and subtle part because he was a more experienced actor than Arjuna. And that was true. Surely when it was explained to him Karna would see the sense of it. One thing Dilip could not stand was emotional scenes.

Arjuna, Poopay and Dilip Baswani arrived at the hill station at midnight. The air was cold and thin, and they breathed heavily as they climbed into the waiting car, then coughed because the cold rasped their throats.

At the hotel where they were staying people came running to meet the car. A young man held out a fleecy blue coat to Poopay.

'This is your new spot boy,' said Dilip as the boy snuggled Poopay into the sleeves. 'He will look after you while you are here.'

Another young man began wrapping Arjuna in a woollen coat as well, as Dilip went waddling off to his room.

'Why does he only wear a thin shawl and fix us up in these huge great jackets?' laughed Arjuna.

'It's a shahtoosh shawl,' said Poopay. 'Just as warm as the stuff he's got us into, though ten, a hundred times the price. He's a show-off and wants us to admire his ability to endure the cold. But really he's just as allergic to the cold as we are.'

That night Arjuna could not sleep. Through his mind whirled thoughts of being with Poopay, up here in this snowy place.

He woke next morning and saw a sparkling white landscape and the snow clad peaks of Shiva's mountains made rosy red with the light of the rising sun. A man went cantering by on a small white pony. His heart was singing. At the first chance he would climb alone and explore these beautiful mountains where, he felt sure, God lived.

They began to film at midday. The sun was in exactly the right position, said Dilip Baswani. Poopay wore only a chiffon choli and pyjama that left her midriff bare as she started dancing though the dancing mistress who crouched before her, demonstrating the steps, was wearing a large wool jacket.

'You must be quick,' said Dilip. 'She mustn't be outside like this for more than a minute. This cold will make her ill.'

Between takes the spot boy wrapped Poopay in the coat and brought her cups of hot soup. Arjuna was impressed, for she did not even get goose pimples in her exposed midriff.

'She's not human, that's the truth of it,' one of the camera-men said.

Arjuna who was only marginally more warmly dressed than his partner, followed the dancing mistress' instructions as best he could and decided to wrap Poopay with the whole of his body if she made the smallest shiver.

When they got back to the hotel, Arjuna's cheeks were red where the biting winds had scalded him. Others were trickling in now. One of the camera crew, pouring coffee said, 'I hope the mist lifts in time for us to do some real good shooting.'

Poopay's spot boy, Raj, said, 'Has anyone one seen Miss Poopay's fleece jacket?'

A murmur of 'no' and 'no' went round till the spot boy pounced shouting, 'How dare you wear it. It's hers.' And dragged the blue jacket off the back of a furiously protesting backdrop man.

The filming took three days. They had to stay an extra day after that because there was no flight back. There were groans of aggravation at the news, but Arjuna told the others, 'I am going out to explore.'

'Do be careful,' he was warned. 'These mountains are treacherous and you are not used to the height or the cold.'

As Arjuna began to climb the lower slope he felt surprised at how quickly the cold increased and he was glad of the great padded coat. He reached a little noisy stream and stood for a while, collecting his breath and looking down at the bubbling sparkle that was pure as diamonds. Around him the mountains glowed and sparkled, birds hung on the thermals, love and success waited for him down there in the valley and Arjuna was filled with the powerful sensation that it was possible for everything in the Cosmos to become right, good, beautiful and happy. A profound joy began to fill him. Then moments later, the atmosphere began to change. The mountains became less lovely, the cries of the birds took on a note of harshness and Arjuna got a vision of the polluted river that this pristine stream was fuelling. He looked around him, trying to work out where the negativity was coming from, but the sky was still as clear and blue and the peaks as rosy. He sat down by the little stream and waited, because he knew that his karma was catching up with him.

It had taken Karna three days to get to this place. The plane had left by the time he got to the airport so he had driven all the way instead. He had neither eaten nor slept in that whole time, but instead, round and round inside his mind, he worked out what to do when he got there.

At first he had thought out the things he would say to Arjuna, even planning to plead with him. But he knew, as soon as he had the thought, that he could not do it. It was not in his nature. He briefly considered threats but knew almost at once that that would be no good either, for threats had never worked with Arjuna.

Then he thought he would go straight to Dilip Baswani and have it out with him. Perhaps Dilip had not understood Karna's need for this part or even had forgotten he had given it to Karna. 'You are my father,' he would tell him. 'And also my acting skills are more subtle and wide ranging than those of Arjuna so I will be clearly better for the part.' As soon as he said this, Dilip Baswani would say, 'How foolish of me, Karna, my son. What could I have been thinking of? Of course you must act the part of Arjuna.' Karna began to feel drowsy and fell into a dreamy state in which he forgot the film and began to anticipate soon being once more close to Poopay. But then he jerked awake with the thought of Arjuna who might refuse to give up the part, make a fuss and threaten fights with him. Then perhaps Dilip Baswani would decide that both he and Arjuna were giving too much trouble, and find another actor altogether, for after all both Arjuna and himself were young and inexperienced, and there many others who Dilip might decide in the end would do it better.

Karna had gone so long without sleep by the time he reached the mountain village that he started hallucinating, seeing Poopay Patalya standing taller than the tallest peak and taking up the whole horizon, like Shiva's wife, Uma, the maid of the snows. Or opening his palm and finding her smiling face there, as small as a mango stone.

He snuggled down into the anorak that he had bought for the trip and felt increasingly hopeful and warm all the way to the hotel where, he was told, the film people were living.

One of the film crew emerged in response to Karna's knock and took his coat. It seemed Dilip Baswani was on the phone upstairs.

'Would you mind waiting for him in the passage as Miss Patalya is in the front room being interviewed by a journalist for a major paper,' said the man, leading the way. Karna followed asking, 'And Arjuna? Is he here?'

'He has gone for a walk,' said the man. 'He said he won't be back till evening.' He laughed and added, 'He says he's going to find the source of the Ganges. No good all of us telling him that it's not here. He won't believe us.' He led Karna along the passage and indicated a chair. As Karna sat down, he heard Poopay's voice through the closed door. After the man had gone, Karna leant back, listened to her voice and felt his soul start swaying as though he was about to faint.

Closeness to Poopay sharpened his senses and he could smell her perfume through the closed door, and hear every word that was said. The journalist asked, 'Our readers will want to know, have you got someone special at the moment?'

'Yes,' said Poopay. 'I have found the man of my life. We looked into each other's eyes and I knew that was it.'

Karna's heart began to beat fast. Hope and worry started mingling.

'Is it who we think it is?'

Karna gripped the back of a chair to steady himself and felt his legs trembling.

Poopay giggled. 'Go on. Have a guess. Of course it's Arjuna.'

When the man came to tell Karna that Miss Poopay's interview was over and that he could go in and see her now, he discovered that Karna had gone and had not even waited to take his coat.

'He must have gone walking off into the cold with only his T-shirt and his jeans,' the man told Poopay.

'I can't imagine who he is, but he sounds very silly,' Poopay laughed. 'I bet he remembers his coat quite soon and comes back for it. Otherwise he'll die of cold.'

But Karna did not come back.

*   *   *

Arjuna had walked quite a distance up the mountain when he saw the flicker of a dark figure that swiftly hid itself behind a rock. He shuddered and a little chill of apprehension ran through him. He peered through the bright white for a long time but the figure had vanished. Perhaps it was a hallucination. Or some mountain animal. But then the figure reappeared, much higher this time, moving furtively. Slinking like something wild.

Crouching out of sight so as not to be seen himself, Arjuna kept watch as the dark figure crept slowly upwards, sometimes vanishing for ages, sometimes appearing briefly, having run out of cover.

After a while the approaching person even began to look like Arjuna's self, so that he wondered if exposure to so much snow and holiness had affected his mind and was making him see visions. Sometimes the figure would vanish for so long that Arjuna would decide it definitely was a hallucination, but then would reappear, nearer each time.

It was only at the very last moment that Arjuna realised it was Karna.

He went on waiting. Perhaps, after all, Karna must have been required for these snowy shots and Dilip had had him urgently brought here. But in his heart he knew that Karna had come after him in anger.

Then Karna was there, standing yards away and Arjuna rose from his squatting position and faced him, braced for fury. Even physical attack. But Karna just stood, his cheeks scoured with the cold, panting from hurry and the thin air. He was wearing only a pair of cotton jeans and a black T-shirt. He licked his lips as though he was about to speak, but no sound came out. He was shivering.

Arjuna said, 'I am on a pilgrimage.'

'I will come with you,' said Karna. His voice was harsh, as though his words were grating in his throat. Then he asked, 'Why are you looking at me like that?'

Arjuna shrugged and said quickly, 'I thought you might be angry with me.'

Karna let out a laugh that had no humour in it, and said, 'I wonder why you should have thought that.'

Another silence fell. Arjuna pointed at the stream. 'Dilip Baswani told me that this runs into the Ganges. I am climbing up to find where it starts.'

A shudder of hatred went through Karna's body. 'Dilip Baswani is a liar so it probably is not so. Shall we start walking?'

'You can't possible come with me. In those clothes you will die of hypothermia.'

'It will not be for long,' said Karna.

Arjuna shrugged and set off up the path. Karna strode quickly after him and began walking on the inner side, a little higher so that they were shoulder to shoulder. They walked without talking, the silence broken only by the shuddering breath of the shivering Karna. Then Arjuna pulled off his anorak and, thrusting it at Karna, said, 'Let's take turns with the warm clothes.'

Karna, without accepting it, asked, 'Have you heard of Man Bahadur?'

'Who is he?'

'My mother read about him to me from an old newspaper cutting she had kept from a few years before,' said Karna.

'He was a thirty-five-year-old Nepali who made a pilgrimage up the Himalayas wearing totally inadequate clothing. He was caught in an avalanche and lay under the snow for three days and survived.'

'You are not a Nepali,' said Arjuna, still holding out the anorak. The cold was starting to pierce his body too, so that he was shivering as well.

'But I am also making a pilgrimage,' said Karna.

Arjuna peered at him through eyelashes that were crusted with ice. 'Are you?' Perhaps there was another side to Karna after all.

'There are pilgrimages, and pilgrimages,' said Karna. After five minutes Arjuna said, 'At least borrow the gloves and scarf.'

Karna waded on and said nothing.

'Don't be stupid,' said Arjuna.

'Put your coat back on,' said Karna.

Arjuna suddenly tossed his coat over the edge. It floated down, turning and turning, its sleeves waving like arms pleading for help. He tore his gloves off, unwound his scarf, and sent them whistling after the coat. The gloves fell separately and landed, scarlet dots like blood, on the white landscape. The scarf twined itself around a bent and leafless tree where it fluttered like the flag of a victorious mountaineer.

'Idiot,' said Karna.

'We'll just have to hurry now,' laughed Arjuna who felt free because now he and Karna had become equally disadvantaged. They had become the same height too ever since Karna began to walk on the higher ground.

Arjuna and Karna now went in step, like equals. Arjuna looked down and realised it was hard to tell which foot was his and which was Karna's.

Karna wanted to hurry to keep his blood from freezing but the cold was slowing his legs. Arjuna was labouring too. Side by side they struggled upwards, heading towards the solution to the most ancient problem in the world. The rivalry of siblings.

Arjuna felt his breath running short as his lungs grew cold. He began not only to confuse feet, but hands and thighs as well. Perhaps there was no difference at all between him and Karna. Perhaps they had always been the same person.

'I have heard that Yogis come up here, strip off their clothes and wrap themselves in wet sheets then have a race to see who can dry the most frozen layers with the power of their minds,' Arjuna told Karna.

'If we had sheets then we could test each other,' Karna said.

'You have to be a yogi.'

'Perhaps we are,' said Karna, the words coming out oddly because his jaws were rattling. 'Do you remember the rishi that Shivarani got in to teach us?'

'He said that everybody has an inner sun and it's just a question of finding it,' Arjuna remembered.

'Can you find yours?' Karna wondered what his life was going to be like after his rivalry with Arjuna had come to an end. Perhaps, when Arjuna was no longer there he, Karna, would step into the young man's shoes in every way so that soon he would grow to look entirely like Arjuna and no one would remember the taller and more handsome brother.

The narrow path was now merely a scratch on the mountainside, a way made by the sharp hooves of ibex and not designed for the fleshy feet of men. The young men sometimes lost the silver thread of water and had to drag themselves over rock ledges to find it again. The water was becoming thinner and colder and now carried chips of ice and pompoms of snow in its tiny current.

They rounded a boulder and jostling together on a pinnacle of sparkling ice they saw a tiny jet of water shooting from a crevice.

'A boulder the shape of Vishnu's toe,' thought Arjuna, knowing as soon as he saw it that this, whatever Dilip Baswani thought, was clearly the source of the Ganges. A river shaped from anger. A river made out of fury. The sage Kapila had cast an angry glance on the sixty thousand sons of King Sangara, went the story, and they were all burnt to ashes but the saint Bhagiratha prayed that Ganga should flow from the toe of Vishnu and purify the ashes of the princes.

'And shaped like hair in this place,' thought Arjuna touching the rock. Its surface was harsh, the water slipping over it seeming almost to fizz as though with mineral, as though it still effervesced with Ganga's anger . . . In her rage at being brought down like this she had descended heavily and would have drowned the world if the god Shiva had not stood under her and caught her on his brow. She became divided up into several streams, or rivers, as she flowed through Shiva's matted yogi locks of hair. Arjuna imagined the madman of the moon-crowned hair standing here, ash-smeared and crazy dancing, holy ascetic, creator and destroyer, with the water of India thundering through his matted tresses.

But the river was not safe yet. A sage had been at prayer and was disturbed as Ganga rushed out of Shiva's hair, so the holy man drank her up in revenge, leaving the earth dry. The gods implored him to relent and in the end Jhanu allowed Ganga to flow out of his ear.

Arjuna started to feel as though he had drunk the intoxicating juice of Soma, had become the river itself with the blood running through his veins turned into the waters of India. Bliss began to swell in him until he felt that one such moment as this was better than a whole lifetime of ordinary happiness. Perhaps, he thought, this is what the gods felt like when they drank the Soma, the milky-sapped lord of creeping plants. Arjuna had drunk nothing but the cold pure air of the god-filled Himalayas but the golden joy that surged through him and seemed to be filling and swelling in the Universe, felt like Soma in its most holy form. Radiance started to warm Arjuna's body and he turned to ask Karna, who knew about drugs, if he had ever tasted Soma.

But before he could speak, something rushed across his sight and tightened round his throat.

Karna had bought the scarf from a stall in the village. He had shouted at the salesman who had kept asking him what colour scarf he wanted and had replied angrily, 'Any colour.' The scarf seller had never had such a customer before.

Karna now flung the purple rumal round Arjuna's neck and hauled it tight. Their feet slipped and slithered on the overhang of rock as Karna tried to get purchase and Arjuna fought to save himself. His tongue began to swell, his eyeballs to bulge, as he fought for breath and frantically tried to free himself from the strangling cloth.

Arjuna coughed, choked and staggered then lost his balance, toppled at the edge and grabbed out at Karna. Moments later both young men were plunging down the sheer drop of the mountainside. They seemed to fall for ages, cracking against a rock on this side, smashing headfirst into a tree on that, breath being knocked out of their bodies, sense out of their heads. Sometimes their bodies would briefly pause and proceed again on their downhill rush, tumbling, smashing, stifling. And all the time grasping each other as though they were still battling for dominance in the air.

At last the pair punched into the ground in a puff of snow.

★   ★   ★

Karna did not know how long he had lain unconscious. His first sensation was one of agony in a hundred places on his body. His back, his shoulders and his legs felt terribly cold. It was a long time before he could open his eyes, and when he did he could make out nothing at all apart from white. Whichever way he looked, only blazing white.

After a while he became aware that there was something under him that was warm, and he wondered if it was a woman he had been making love with, though his body felt more as if it had been beaten with lathis than enjoying sex. The cold was frightful, it scalded round his head and through his legs. His hands and feet had lost all feeling. His buttocks were jabbed with chill. It was gnawing into the back of his neck so that he feared his spinal cord would freeze, grow brittle and then snap. Only his chest and stomach continued to stay warm because of something he lay on. He snuggled closer to it and knew that he would be dead by now if it had not been there. But perhaps he was dead for otherwise what was this glaring whiteness? He lay like this for a long time, vague thoughts wandering through his mind. Sometimes he would fall into a half dream in which he was lying face down on the hot body of his galloping white horse and beating Arjuna round the maidan. Sometimes the dreamy state would place Poopay Patalya underneath him and then he would wake with a jerk of guilt and try to shift away before he degraded the goddess with an act of sex. Sometimes he would dozily imagine he was lying on the bonnet of the car and the warmth was coming from the running engine.

It was a long time before his mind became sufficiently engaged for him to realise that the whiteness was snow and he was burrowed into it. Then, through the veil of snow he thought he saw the outline of a human head. His body was very stiff and when he tried to move, shoots of pain rushed through him. He forced his joints to move and with numb fingers clawed the snow away and revealed the face of Arjuna. There was a deep gash across his forehead. He was quite still and even when Karna touched his cheek he did not stir. The cheek was warm though. Karna gazed on his brother's closed-down body. He could not make out what they were doing here. Had the pair of them gone walking through the mountains and had a fall? Why were they not wearing suitable clothes? Neither he nor Arjuna was even wearing gloves.

Then he saw the rumal round Arjuna's neck and started to remember.

Arjuna began to stir, making Karna shift away, embarrassed at the close proximity. The moment he lost contact with Arjuna's body, the terrible cold seized him, making him shiver violently so that he could hardly breathe. His teeth clashed together audibly as he watched Arjuna slowly open his eyes, Arjuna asked in a voice muffled with bruising and blood, 'Who won?' Then, when Karna did not answer, Arjuna put his hand to his neck and felt the rumal there. 'It looks as though you did.'

Karna stared away over the mountains.

'You can just go and leave me here,' said Arjuna. 'I've sprained or broken something and I can't walk so I won't have a chance. You don't have to do anything more.' He felt sorry that his life was over and that he would never act the part of Arjuna or see Poopay Patalya again.

'Tell me how to be warm and I will help you,' said Karna.

'I don't want your help. Why should I want that?'

Karna squatted down. 'This is not the way it should end,' he said.

Arjuna tried to shrug, let out a yelp of pain, and said, 'It never is. Go.'

'I can't go,' said Karna. 'Because heat is coming from your body and without it I will die.'

Arjuna said, 'There is a sun inside you. That's what the yogi told us.' He felt tired and comfortable. 'After you have found it you will be able to leave me.' He closed his eyes and waited for Karna to go.

Half an hour later Karna was painfully climbing down the mountainside with Arjuna in his arms.

Down below in the village he could hear faint cries, perhaps of people calling Arjuna. Karna tried to shout back but the bruising of his fall had drained his lungs and only a whisper would come out. Karna arrived with Arjuna at two in the morning. It had taken him six hours to carry his half-brother down from the mountain.

By the time people came running out at Arjuna's calls, Karna had gone.

No one could understand why the two young men had not died. No one really believed that Arjuna and Karna had been out there for eighteen hours, wearing only their jeans and T-shirts. There must, everyone secretly thought, be some other explanation. The story passed round gently of some pretty Nepali girls who had entertained the naughty brothers until some romping incident had caused an accident and Arjuna had had to be brought home on the back of Karna.

18

COSMIC CONSCIOUSNESS

Little recked the dauntless Karna
if his foe in anger rose.
Karna feared not face of mortal,
dreaded not immortal foes.
Nor with all his wrath and valour
Arjun conquered him in war
Till within the soft earth sinking
stuck the wheel of Karna's car.

The pony looked out of her stall and neighed at the sight of Karna and he felt shocked because she had become small and old without his noticing. He had not been to see her for a long time. He felt guilty for he knew that he would never ride her again because these days he only rode tall white horses that bucked and pranced. As he rubbed his nose against the pony's whiskery one, he remembered how furious Arjuna had been when he had called her 'Poopay'. He fed her a piece of sugar cane and as she scrunched it, he wondered sadly, 'Why did I save Arjuna on the mountainside? If Arjuna had died, then Poopay would have fallen in love with me. And if there was no Arjuna, then Dilip Baswani would have given me the part of Arjuna again.' He had so nearly managed to do it. One more moment with the rumal. Or leaving Arjuna to die after they had fallen. But, as the pony munched and dribbled sugar juice, some part of Karna felt glad that he was not the murderer of his brother because if he had done it he would no longer have been worthy of Poopay Patalya and his mother.

'I was headed for greatness,' he told the pony. 'I was nearly there until Dilip Baswani gave the part to Arjuna, but now I have thought of another way of becoming great.' He was going to enter politics.

Because his face had been seen on TV and he was now becoming known, people would vote for him. He would stand in Hatipur at first, he decided, because there was not much competition there and also because he knew so many people who would support him.

Shivarani turned away as he came into the Hatibari.

'You seem annoyed,' he said.

'Of course I am. Why didn't you tell me you where going when I stayed with you in Bombay?'

Karna stared at her. He had forgotten that she had been staying with him. He had not thought of it again till this moment. 'I'm sorry,' he said.

'I was going to tell you something,' she said.

'What?'

But suddenly she could not bring herself to tell him that DR Uncle had asked her to marry him. Why should Karna be told, who did not behave like her child at all, but like a stranger.

She had been avoiding DR Uncle lately, because, although she had made up her mind to agree to marry him, she could not bring herself to say it.

'Oh, nothing. I have forgotten what,' she told Karna, adding, 'You think of no one but yourself.'

'When I become a politician, I will be thinking of other people all the time.' He said it meekly but his words made Shivarani crosser than ever.

'That's the thing about you, Karna. All you ever think of is your own glory.'

Karna gazed at her. 'You were always trying to get Arjuna to go into politics. Why is it different if it is me?'

'What do you expect to be able to do then?' she demanded.

'Open hostels for pavement dwellers to sleep in,' he said hopefully. 'Provide free hospital beds and medicine for people who can't afford it.' He paused, and said sadly, 'My mother would still be alive today if there had been such things available for her.'

She tried to go on being grumpy but instead felt touched with pity.

When Arjuna arrived at the Hatibari and was told that Karna was one of the Hatipur district candidates in the coming local election, he began to laugh at first. 'Karna standing for election here? What on earth does he think he's playing at? This is my ancestral place and nothing to do with Karna at all.'

'You ought to stand too,' laughed Parvathi. 'Because it would be funny if Karna became MLA when you are zamindar.'

'Me?' Arjuna was taken aback. Then grew thoughtful.

'But I won't know who to vote for,' Parvathi giggled. 'None of us in the village will, because you'll both be famous film stars by then.' She was terribly excited about the filming of the Mahabharata, the battle scene of which was taking place on the Calcutta maidan in the following month.

Something fluttered inside Arjuna's stomach. Here was another chance to compete with Karna. Here was yet another way of making Poopay proud of him. He and Karna fighting it out at the polls. The thought filled him with excitement.

Quite quickly, although there were other candidates and other parties contesting the election, the Karna Party and the Arjuna Party, as they were popularly known, became the only two that anyone considered in the area. Both candidates had had badges distributed and now most people for miles around had pinned to their clothes either a gold plastic button in the shape of a K or a silver steel pin in the shape of an A. The other candidates might not have existed for the attention the people of this area gave them.

Arjuna commissioned the village carpenter to build a scaffold on his car and fix great posters to it showing himself dressed in his film role, in silver and white and holding a bow and arrow. He put on the costume he would wear when he acted in the film as well, then, with a loudspeaker attached to the roof, he toured Hatipur with a silver flag bearing his logo streaming from the bonnet of his car. Children pressed their faces against the hero's windows leaving snotty marks on the glass. Hatipur residents struggled to get near. The misti wallah forgot that this was the man who had punched his son on his wedding day and could only see the glittering figure of Arjuna of the Mahabharata.

Arjuna was only into the first ten minutes of his speech when another loudspeaker was heard, roaring so loudly that it obliterated Arjuna's voice. Coming towards him till they met in the middle of the main street was Karna's car. Beside Karna and at the back sat his friends who were acting as his bodyguards. They were boys who had been in his kigali gang and had now become goondas. They carried mobile phones and cradled AK-47 guns which Karna had managed to obtain from his Bangladesh contacts. Karna had instructed them on how they must behave in Hatipur, forbidding beatings no matter how provoked. 'Also you should smile when you talk to these villagers,' he added. Two of the goondas had to be taught this skill, never having performed it before, but the other two were eager to show off their gold stoppings, which, if Karna got in, they hoped to add to.

The street was not wide enough for overtaking. Karna and Arjuna met face to face and for a while shouted speeches that no one could hear. For a while the two loudspeakers blared, wiping each other out, till at last the politicians laid down their microphones and, leaning from their open car windows, began to shout at each other with increasing fury, demanding withdrawal. The crowd gazed with open-mouthed delight. There was one bad moment when a goonda bodyguard suddenly thrust a gun butt out of Karna's car window. There followed a brief tense moment as the gun trained on Arjuna's chest, then some word from Karna persuaded the man to withdraw his weapon. The two cars were shoved this way and that by the excited crowd. They rocked and bounced as the people heaved and pressed against them, but neither was able to progress.

Arjuna had an idea. He would continue his speech from the middle of the river. Half an hour later he was holding forth from the great Hatibari boat, with the crowds thronging the banks to hear him.

DR Uncle was taken to the riverside and sat in a chair that had been brought for him. He needed to be near, because his hearing was fading. 'Bravo, bravo, Arjuna,' he shouted shrilly.

Arjuna was in mid-speech when another boat appeared, being punted swiftly along, carrying Karna surrounded by his goonda bodyguards. They looked incongruous with their long pony-tails, dark glasses, drainpipe trousers and menacing weapons.

Bridges, banks, trees and rooftops had never been so crammed since the day the Sun God had swum into the Hatibari.

'I am of the family of zamindars,' shouted Arjuna. 'For generations my family has looked after this place. We are bred to care for you. Karna cannot even read. I will be far better at looking after this village and its people than the illiterate son of a rickshaw wallah and a dhobi woman.'

'Quite so, quite so,' agreed DR Uncle.

'See how he despises us poor people,' shouted Karna. 'I know your needs because I have been poor myself. I am the only one that can help you.'

'Quite right, Karna. Bravo, bravo,' cried DR Uncle who could not hear anything but felt his nephews needed encouraging.

It was growing dark. People began to light little lamps of wick and oil, and set them floating on the water as though it was Diwali.

'Do you want someone who despises dhobis to be your minister?' bellowed Karna, 'Or me, who respects you, will listen to your troubles and understand your problems? I do not scorn people who have been denied education. I pity them. And as for the zamindars, my mother was poor but she was a much, much better person than any one of them. She was kind, gentle, never told a lie in the whole of her life and did not despise anybody. Unlike these zamindars.'

Mosquitoes started to fly. People began to scratch, but could not drag themselves away from the riverside.

'Karna talks of morality and goodness,' shouted Arjuna. 'But he dealt in drugs and was a thief.'

337

'And Arjuna is a cheat. If he had not cheated me I would have had the leading part in the Mahabharata instead of him. If he had not cheated me I would have been the one to eat the bread and Amul butter.'

Karna and Arjuna were vanishing into the night until you could only tell where they were by their voices. People looked from one hero to the other, persuaded by the first, then by the second. Then by the first again.

'What do you think?' Arjuna asked Shivarani next morning. 'Do you think they'll vote for me or Karna?' Karna had already gone back to Calcutta with his goondas.

Shivarani sighed. 'Will your rivalry with Karna ever end? Do you think the two of you will go on fighting for the rest of your lives?'

'Perhaps there will come a day when we are too old for hatred.'

'There is no such day,' sighed Shivarani.

'Perhaps a day will come when one of us beats the other so convincingly that there is nothing more to fight about,' suggested Arjuna.

'That is a good idea,' said Shivarani. 'For as long as you and Karna are imprisoned in hatred you will never know freedom.'

'What should we do then?' asked Arjuna.

'You have answered that question yourself. Set up one final competition that will finish your rivalry for ever. Have one last great contest and then get on with your own lives without thinking about each other for like this neither of you can ever truly know happiness or even love.'

All the way back to Bombay, Arjuna kept going through this idea in his mind.

When he next met Karna, he told him. 'Do you think Shivarani is right? Is it possible that we could have a contest which ends all contests? Do you think it is possible that one of us can beat the other so convincingly that we never need to compete again?'

'I don't know what you are talking about,' Karna said coldly.

'I have been thinking ever since the time on the mountain and the way that you saved me, that it is time we ended our rivalry.'

Karna stared at Arjuna bitterly. 'It is you who keep it burning.

You have stolen my part and the woman I love. You have cheated me out of every win.'

'Come on, Karna, it was not my fault. Dilip made that decision not me. And as for Poopay, can I help it if she finds me attractive?'

'Swine,' said Karna. 'Bastard.'

'Hush. Now listen. I have an idea. We are grown up. This bickering is not suitable for men of our age. Let's race each other from Bombay to Calcutta to arrive on the first day of filming. If you win I will go away. I will not be there to play Arjuna. I will never see Poopay again.'

Karna gazed at him in disbelief. 'Why should you do that?'

Arjuna shrugged. 'There are other women. There are other parts. I might even give up films and become a full-time politician. Do you accept the challenge?'

Karna shrugged. 'How can I trust you? You cheated before.'

'Things are different now. May the goddess curse me if I break this promise.'

'OK,' said Karna, hope starting to fill him like sunshine after rain.

'But you must swear that you will go away if I win, as well.'

'I swear on the head of my mother, Dolly. How shall we race?' Karna visualised swimming, riding, running. Already his muscles were tightening for the contest.

'In our cars?' suggested Arjuna.

'Which cars? Will you buy a new one?'

'We will stay as we are. You in yours and me in mine.'

Karna smiled. He owned a brand-new Triumph Herald and Arjuna only had the old Ambassador.

These were cars that had been manufactured in India after the Indian government stopped the import of foreign goods and for thirty years had been made from the original Morris Oxford template. Slow and reliable, they were the only car available in the country apart from a few fragile Western cast-offs and much later, the Fiat 1100. They were also almost indestructible but all the same, thought Karna, even before he had tinkered with the one now owned by Arjuna, it had not had much life left in it.

That he might lose the race was a thought that Karna could not allow to enter his mind. He knew with a desperate certainty that he had to win.

Arjuna employed a mechanic who specialised in preparing cars for the Himalayan Rally. The man knew every trick and agreed that Arjuna's was the best kind of car for this competition. 'In all India there is not such a strong car as the Ambassador of this period and also you can get parts for such a car anywhere. It has a simple engine so that, with a little instruction from myself, you will be able to replace most parts yourself. Though once I have lightened the body and speeded up the engine, this vehicle will probably get you from Bom to Cal with nothing going wrong at all.'

Karna, too, was souping up the engine of his new Triumph Herald. The kigalis of Calcutta reaped parts off the parked cars of Park Street and New Market and sent them to him, until Karna and his mechanic had transformed his family runabout into a formidable racing car.

The brothers decided that no one should find out about their race. Certainly not the media, who would undoubtedly make the most of India's two up and coming Bollywood stars, setting off to beat each other in a frightful dash over the countryside, the prize being the part of Arjuna and Poopay Patalya. Both knew the sort of thing Poopay might say when she found out. Karna and Arjuna kept the race absolutely secret.

The only people to see Karna and Arjuna leave Bombay in their final competition were their respective mechanics who carefully checked the opponent's cars. Everything was minutely looked over, from the steering to the brakes. They even examined the cars' undersides to ensure that no explosives were fixed there before allowing the two combatants to set off.

The pair left Bombay in the early morning, before most people were up.

Karna's new car was quicker off the mark – almost at once Arjuna was overtaken but he was not worried. There were many hours and miles before them. Arjuna felt relieved that they had prepared their cars in Bombay and not Calcutta where Karna had so many friends and acquaintances of the underworld. At least he did not have to worry about some drastic damage having been done to his car. In Calcutta, one of Karna's goonda or kigali friends, on hearing of the race, would probably have cut through Arjuna's steering rod or tampered with the braking system. They would not have worried about maiming or even killing Arjuna if it meant that their hero, Karna, would win the race. Luckily Karna did not know that kind of person in Bombay. But all the same Arjuna felt a touch of uneasiness if there came a slight change of tone in the engine and a throbbing sound that might have come from a loose nut startled him.

Karna drove very fast, passing everything on the road, trying hard not to make errors. As he hurled bumpily along the rutted surfaces and left the town, a jumbo jet filled with people travelling off to England, Europe or America, moved over his horizon. He was touched with a sudden scald of loneliness at the thought of the people up there, excited and carefree, while he sat alone fighting for the only things that would make his life worth living. But then the thought came to him that soon Arjuna would be gone, he would be famous and rich and then he and Poopay would often sit on aeroplanes, sipping gin and travelling to America and London. He was grim with determination as he flew up through the gears. He had so far been rather unlucky – Arjuna always got the luck and Karna never did. But this time, he assured himself firmly, it was not going to turn out like that.

Karna was far ahead now but Arjuna knew that all he had to do was keep steadily on. Arjuna had visited Karna's mechanic secretly. A large sum of money had changed hands and the mechanic had made a small adjustment to one of the tyres and to the spare of Karna's Triumph Herald. Hopefully, when Karna got his puncture, it would be in some unpopulated area. It would take Karna some time to discover that the spare had been dealt with too and even then Karna, who was so clever and resourceful, would find a way of mending the puncture in the end. But by that time Arjuna should have got himself a good head start.

Arjuna did not feel guilty. After all, Karna had tampered with the Ambassador before selling it to him. All's fair in love and war and he felt sure that Karna too would have taken any advantage he could. The little damage he had caused to be inflicted on Karna's tyre would not put the other in physical danger, whereas who knows what lengths Karna, who had already tried to murder Arjuna, might have gone to if he had been among his criminal friends.

By evening, Karna's eyes started to sting with staring but he thrust on through the velvet black of the Indian night. He dared not stop to sleep, in case Arjuna, who sometimes seemed superhuman, managed to overtake him.

He had been tempted, several times during the previous week, to find some way of tinkering with Arjuna's car, but this race was for something much, much more important than the part of Arjuna. It was for Poopay Patalya. It was for Dolly. Karna wanted, when he won this race, to feel that he had been worthy of his success. Worthy of the two women he loved so much. He wanted to become, once more, worthy of Dolly, his mother, who never did dishonest things. He had forgotten, for a while, the wonder of Dolly's glorious honesty but now could not stop remembering how, even when she was so poor that she was starving, she had refused to cheat or steal or lie. Perhaps, he thought, he had brought bad karma on himself by tinkering with Arjuna's car the last time. Perhaps, if he had left things alone Poopay would not have looked at Arjuna in that special way at Dilip Baswani's party and she would not have told that journalist that she was in love with Arjuna. But this time he had done it right. He would win because of his driving, his courage and his strength. He would beat Arjuna because he would not need to sleep or eat or rest for two days and nights. He would win the race because he knew the roads and people of India, and understood the inside of his car, whereas Arjuna, who had been brought up as a sahib and zamindar, had been sheltered from all these things. Karna would win because he was better than Arjuna and not because he had tricked him.

Sometimes dogs or drunken people staggered across the road before him and he was forced to hurl the car up against the verge or rush towards those coming in the opposite direction. Great insects beat against the windscreen then died there in a splat of black blood. Owls rose from the road and went winging off, so silent that it made Karna feel his urgency was something almost contemptible.

At every turn of the road, Arjuna expected to find Karna stranded with his puncture. The mechanic had assured Arjuna that he had shaved a patch on the inner tube so thin that it would certainly give way as soon as the tyres heated up. He hoped the man had not tricked him as he pressed his foot down on the accelerator. He leant into the night and felt a little touch of regret because this was going to be his last contest with Karna. After this Karna would have to go away forever, set up a life somewhere else and leave Arjuna without a challenger.

Karna nearly crashed into an over-turned lorry that was spilling ghee and wove with screaming wheels among the crowd of men, women and children who wildly tried to gather up the golden oil before it sank beyond reach into the dust. Women were dabbing at the ground with their sari ends and men had taken off their turbans and were pressing them into the pools of fat then squeezing the precious butter oil into tins, brass jars and terracotta pots. They were so absorbed in reaping this luxury harvest that they hardly winced away as Karna whirled among them.

When Arjuna dodged the ghee gatherers half an hour later he was thinking about all the other times he and Karna had competed with each other. Those days when, as little boys in Shivarani's garden, they had tried to see who could pee the furthest. That thrilling race on the Calcutta course. How they had walked together up the Himalayas, seeing whose breath ran out first, seeing who collapsed first of hypothermia. Whatever happened from now on, thought Arjuna, he would never again find an opponent as worthy and as exciting as Karna.

Karna thrust past long processions of bullock carts, hay toppling house-high, little paraffin lamp swinging from each axle. Often the driver was asleep. The bulls knew their way home. He was feeling increasingly confident. By now he must be so far ahead that Arjuna did not have a chance and he wondered at Arjuna's foolishness in choosing to race in the slow old Ambassador.

Then there were all those times when Karna had been belittled, thought Arjuna. There had been that cricket match at the Hatibari. Boys from Doon School had come to stay and they had tried to get a team together but had been one man short.

'Let's ask Karna,' Arjuna had suggested. 'He's frightfully good.'

'Who is Karna?' the friends had asked and when Arjuna had explained they had decided it would be better to play one man short than have such a person on their team. Why had Arjuna not insisted? Karna must have known the discussion was going on, and must have realised why he was not invited to play.

And in spite of this sort of thing happening again and again throughout their boyhood, Karna, himself injured, had carried Arjuna down the mountainside, struggling in the freezing cold to save Arjuna's life.

At midnight driving suddenly became difficult. Karna switched the windscreen wipers on, thinking it was raining, although it was January and the monsoon was over. But then he realised it was because he was crying. How odd, he thought, as he tried to push the tears aside and see the road. He did not remember ever crying but now the tears were rushing down so thickly and swiftly that it was as if all the weeping of his life was flowing out.

An idea came to Arjuna. Suppose, when he came upon Karna, he said, 'You don't have to finish this race after all. You can be the winner.'

Karna wondered if there had been tears on his mother's face when she died. Perhaps as she lay dying she had wept like he was doing now. Perhaps she had lain there desperate for him to return and had died crying because she would never see him again and had not had a chance to say goodbye to him.

Arjuna was starting to feel regretful at what he had done to Karna's tyres. It would have been so much better, he realised now, if he had managed to win the race by his driving skills alone. But Karna was always so tricky and he had not thought it possible to beat his half-brother in any other way. And when he had seen that Triumph Herald transformed into a racing car with all those expensive stolen parts, Arjuna had felt that Karna had already cheated him. He decided that when he came across Karna struggling with his puncture, Arjuna would stop and help him. Then, when the tyre was repaired, the two would start the race from scratch and this time it would be a fair one.

What was the purpose of tears? Karna wondered. When people see you crying do they give you back your part? Do they say to you, 'Oh, you are crying, so please play Arjuna after all?' Do they say, 'Oh, you are crying, so please understand that it was only a joke. Poopay and me are not really in love. She loves you, Karna.' Do people say things like that? No.

★   ★   ★

Definitely, thought Arjuna, when he found Karna, he would suggest they abandon the race altogether. For he saw now that this was not the way to solve their rivalry.

Up there, in the Himalayas, there had been a time when Arjuna had thought that he and Karna had become equals and that in the future they would support each other and enjoy the friendship of being brothers. Perhaps this was still possible. The two of them would drive on to Calcutta in the Ambassador, and on the way they would work out a more sensible and satisfying way of sorting out their relationship.

Karna had reached the place on Laika's nose where the river bent. He was starting to feel smug and successful. It had been absurd, from the start, that Arjuna should have expected to beat Karna in that old tin can. Then there came an explosive sound so that, for a moment, Karna thought that he had been shot at. He visualised Arjuna leaning from the window of his competing car, aiming a pistol. The car began to skid crazily. He clutched the steering wheel, gripping with all his might but it kept swirling wildly. The car began to slide with a scream of tyres, skidding this side, that side. Lorries thundered by heavily, blowing their horns at him, narrowly missing him.

When he came upon Karna, Arjuna could say, 'I have always admired you, admired your courage and resourcefulness. Even though you are not my father's son, but only my mother's, I will give you money from the Hatibari estate for it is not fair that I should have so much and you so little.'

Karna could not regain control. The car thundered down a long steep slope, rolling over and over, so that Karna kept cracking from floor to roof and back again. It hit the riverbank with such force that Karna was hurled though the windscreen in a shatter of glass. The car bounced and fell again, this time into the river. With a great surge of water and a screaming rush of daaks and egrets, the bonnet punched mud and Karna's car rocked there, like a fat dart in a soft target . . .

Arjuna thought, 'When I inherit the Hatibari I will ask Karna to come and live with me there. He and I together will restore the tennis courts and we will play great tournaments till we get too old to run. And when we get the stables once more filled with Katiawari horses we will set up tent-pegging in the grounds and see who can take up the greatest number of pegs on their lance, just like my grandfathers and great-grandfathers used to do. Karna and I could live together in the Hatibari in a joint family situation, he with his wife, I with mine, our children being brought up together just as I was brought up with my cousins.' He imagined his and Karna's children skidding over the flooded paddy fields, punting themselves in banana logs, heard their happy laughter as they played in the Hatibari gardens and felt filled with a warm hopefulness at the thought.

'Or should I hand the Hatibari over to Karna, because although he is not my father's son, he is my older brother?' wondered Arjuna. 'And ask him to let me and my family join his?'

When Arjuna arrived in Calcutta without having encountered Karna on the way, he decided that, since all was lost he would not go to the maidan at all, but drive directly to Dumdum airport, abandon his car and take the next plane out of India. But then he thought, suppose he had passed Karna on the road and had not seen him. He decided, after all, to face the humiliation of defeat though as he drove towards the Calcutta maidan he knew Karna had beaten him.

At the maidan huge crowds had already gathered, much larger than usual and swelling all the time. Buses were arriving with so many clinging to the outside that the bus itself was invisible. Bullock carts trundled through the traffic, squashed tight with villagers. Lorries arrived, crammed with peasants, motor scooters piled with complete families poured in, taxis were disgorging twenty passengers at a time. People were arriving in rickshaws, on foot and there was even a crowd of people swaying along on the back of an elephant. Kigalis, goondas and pavement dwellers, people who had never been seen at the maidan before were flocking in having heard their hero, Karna, was performing here today. There were also very large numbers of beggars creeping, hobbling, or pulling themselves along on little wheeled platforms, coming to see Karna who had always helped them when he could.

Karna woke and did not know how much time had passed. He did not know where he was or what had happened at first. It took him some time to understand that he was hanging head down on the bonnet of his car with the rest of his body inside it. Karna tried to get up but something had happened to his body so that it would not move and he could not feel his legs.

Almost everyone from the village of Hatipur was at the maidan. The few who were too poor or sick or old to make the train journey to Calcutta were left in the village feeling sad and bitter at being deprived of the sight of their own young zamindar, in his hour of glory. There was some confusion as to who exactly would be playing the part of Arjuna and who of Karna. The street people of Calcutta had definitely heard though, that Karna was to play Arjuna. Fights and brawls had broken out all over the town in the past days, disputes concerning the playing of Arjuna, but the people of Hatipur had no doubt at all that their hero was the man.

Everyone had heard of the wonderful excitement of the last film battle that had taken place here and since news had gone round town and countryside that the Mahabharata was to be made here this day, there were a hundred times as many people present, anticipating excitement and profit. The air was a dazzle of multicoloured paper kites and gas balloons. There were people selling every kind of food and drink from hot samosas to chilled sugar-cane juice. There were fortune-telling parrots and dancing monkeys. There were puppeteers, contortionists and snake charmers. The bear was there, rattling his claws, snarling cheerfully and vaguely remembering some previous triumphant moment when he had rushed around growling till horses reared and riders fell. He was long on nose and claw and short on sense and memory and would have rushed in once again if Dilip's goondas had not described to his owner all the painful ways they knew of murdering bears. The man now held his animal tightly on a new steel chain clipped to its nose ring.

Piara Singh, the pony man, was there with his jockey wife and daughter, as well as his whole stable of ponies including the two race-horses. If one of the film ponies was put out of action, Piara Singh was ready with a replacement, though his racehorses were highly strung and had never pulled a cart before. And if a rider fell, then the women of his family were prepared to don Hindu warrior's clothes, stick on an artificial beard, take up a bow and arrow and drive a chariot. Film producers were renowned for being generous in a crisis and Piara expected to make a good profit today. He was also doing well with the pony rides, shouting, as he ran the children up and down, 'It was I who taught the heroes, Arjuna and Karna, how to ride.' And when the jogged and breathless children were returned to their parents, he charged double his usual rate which was paid without argument. Later the parents would tell their friends, 'My child was taught to ride by the man who taught the heroes of the Mahabharata.'

There was something wet under Karna's cheek, and at first he thought it must be river water that had splashed up there or that his tears were still falling. But then he saw that the liquid pooling over the red paint-work of his car was red blood. He tried to put his hand up to see where it was coming from, but his arm would not obey him.

* * *

349

It was as though the biggest fair had come to town and everybody was attending it. In a cordoned-off area stood ornate golden chariots, shaped like wings and shaded over with tasselled silken parasols. The teams of ponies harnessed in gilt and scarlet, tingling with bells and glittering ornaments, were tethered waiting, while their syces administered a touch-up to the grooming, wiped the flies from their eyes and painted on another layer of tarry gloss to their hooves.

Bearded kings, long-haired princes and foot soldiers dressed in hessian sat in the shade wearing ornate golden armour and helmets, and drinking Thumbs Up. The elephant that had been hired for the day had been dressed up in embroidered fringed satin and wore jewels on her head. Her turbaned mahout sat cross-legged on her neck smoking a beedi and behind him, standing in the howdah, the warriors waited, gleaming in silver foil and holding bows and arrows.

Carpenters were carrying out last-minute repairs to cracked chariots, mechanics were working to get wheels turning, bearers ran among the actors with flasks of water and paper tissues. Around and among all these scurried make-up people with large paintbrushes and tubs of powder, hairdressers reaching on tip-toe to give a wind-swept actor yet another brush-up and darjees quickly mending some rip in a robe or replacing jewels on a headdress. The cameramen waited on bamboo scaffolds for their order to start shooting. The filming could not begin because the leading actor had not yet arrived.

Dilip Baswani, though convinced that the battle scene of the Amul Butter advert had worked so well because of the location, knew about the unruliness of the Calcutta crowds so had had a fence of bamboo and rope erected in the early morning and an army of goondas defending it. His goondas also passed the word around that those who flew kites during the filming would be beaten up instead of paid. Dilip had discovered, in his many years of filmmaking, that the stick worked much better than the carrot in this kind of situation.

*   *   *

Because Karna's car was nose down in the water the top of his head was in the water. He could feel the river running loudly past his ears and through its sound he started hearing Dilip Baswani's theme tune of the Mahabharata. He realised he must be further down Laika's nose than he had first thought, perhaps by her right nostril which meant he was very near the maidan and had probably won the race if he could only get out of his car. He was starting to feel cold and he felt a terrible pain in his throat.

DR Uncle was sitting in his car waiting for the arrival of his nephew, as news of the hero's arrival had been preceding him ever since he reached the outskirts of the town. And when Arjuna's car appeared, DR Uncle's eyes filled with tears as he said, arms outstretched for embrace, 'My dear boy, you cannot imagine how proud we all are of you.'

Karna tried to raise his head out of the water but his neck would not work either. Or his legs. Or any part of him expect his mouth and eyes. Sometimes the current sloshed against his lips. He wondered if Durga would come again and put out her hand for him to lie on. He wondered if she would rescue him once more.

Shivarani rushed at Arjuna. 'They have been phoning me all night.'

'Who phoned?' he asked. He felt dazed, exhausted and was looking round for Karna.

'Dilip Baswani rang me ten times yesterday, saying that they were shooting the Mahabharata battle scene early because the weather was right and that you must come here the moment you arrive.'

Arjuna was hardly hearing her as he got out.

'What a damn-fool idea driving here from Bombay when you could so easily have come in the plane like the rest of them.'

Shivarani raged on, then staring with horror at the car she cried, 'And are you telling me you have come all the way in that? It was even breaking down when Karna had it, so what could you have been thinking of to use it for such a journey? You might have been killed, making such a journey in that old car.'

By this time Arjuna had been recognised and people were gathering round, struggling to catch a glimpse of the hero.

Arjuna blinked and felt confused. 'How did you know I was coming? How did you know I was here?'

'How did I know?' said Shivarani. 'Everyone in Calcutta knows. Do you think that, now you have become a great film star, you can continue to rush round the countryside like an anonymous person? See how these people are all running over from every side to take a look at you.'

Over the river sounds and the noises coming from the maidan, Karna heard cars passing. A little flock of goats went pattering past. Occasionally he got the feeling that people were looking down into the river, seeing his car, wondering if something should be done about it. Sometimes he heard people's voices and tried to call out, but no sound except for a bloody bubbling would come from his throat.

'But what about Karna?' gasped Arjuna. 'Where is he?'

'Hurry,' Shivarani said as she struggled with the jostling craning people who were reaching out to pinch at Arjuna's clothes so that they could say later, 'I touched the hero, Arjuna, with these very hands.'

'Dilip Baswani is going crazy, wondering where you have got to,' Shivarani yelled through the din. 'All the other actors are there already.'

When no one came and Durga did not put out her hand a second time, Karna realised that after all the goddess had abandoned him. She was no longer Mother Durga but had taken on the form of Kali and was dancing, her tongue hanging out and blood-filled skulls hanging round her neck.

Parvathi, followed by her toddlers, was now emerging from Shivarani's car, letting out shrieks of delight, yelling, 'make way, make way,' and shunting the children before her. She thrust herself through the tightening crowd and threw herself at Arjuna's feet. Clasping his ankles she ordered the children, 'Do namaskar, children, and when you are grown-up you will be able to tell everyone that you touched the feet of the great hero, Arjuna.'

'What's all this?' demanded Arjuna, trying to pull his toes away in embarrassment.

Parvathi struggled to her feet and began shouting to her husband who was still sitting in the driving seat of Shivarani's car and looking awkward. 'Come on, Basu. Why are you still sitting there? Come and honour our great holy hero.'

Basu emerged, looking nervously from scowling Shivarani to joyful Parvathi, unsure which of these two powerful women he ought to be pleasing. He could not understand why Shivarani, who used to be so strict, seemed to allow Parvathi to get away with absolutely anything these days and had not argued at all when Parvathi insisted on coming to see the filming of the Mahabharata and bringing her children. His son had puked all over the front seat on the way here, his daughter had dropped her fizzy drink and Memsahib, although looking cross, had said nothing. She made no protest as Basu joined his wife and bowed to the new hero.

'Go on, hurry and see Dilip. He does not even know you are here,' Shivarani ordered Arjuna.

A bus churned heavily past, creaking over the rutted road and belching out petrol fumes. A mongoose came daintily down to drink and leapt back in panic when it saw Karna.

*   *   *

Dilip Baswani burst out with smiles of relief at the sight of Arjuna. 'My dear fellow, what a fright you gave us. I was even starting to worry that you had decided not to act in my film after all. Come along now, Poopay is ready and you know what she is like. She has three other films to perform in and if we keep her waiting any longer she will be off with the wind.'

'And Karna? Where is Karna?' Arjuna felt afraid to even mouth the name in case his brother manifested himself.

'Karna? Don't worry about Karna for the moment,' said Dilip. 'You and he will have to come here tomorrow. That's the scene where he gets his chariot wheel stuck in the mud and you cut his head off. It can't be done in all this clamour, though. I'll have to have it shot separately. Over there is your chariot. Get your costume on, get in, and get started.'

Arjuna swiftly pulled on the plumed silver helmet and wide-shouldered armour.

'There, now you look exactly like the real thing,' cried Dilip in delight, leaning back to get the best possible look of his new hero in full costume.

Arjuna cautiously eyed the ornate but unsteady-looking cart to which was harnessed a set of prancing and decoratively harnessed ponies. He asked, 'Am I supposed to drive that thing?' Somehow these acts of daring lost their spice when it was not a competition with Karna.

'Don't be silly,' cried Dilip. 'Haven't you read your Mahabharata? Your charioteer is the Lord Krishna. Him.' Dilip pointed to an actor in golden armour, his face and hands painted blue. 'This man is a syce who is taking the part for today because the real actor is afraid of horses. But I hope this fellow knows how to drive a cart. Do you?' he demanded of the man.

'Yes,' said the costumed syce, getting into the chariot, while another syce held the head of the leading pony.

Dilip called a cameraman over and gestured to the charioteer. 'Make sure you don't get this fellow's face in the shot. Only his back or blurred shots of him.' He said to Arjuna, 'We'll do the conversation scene between you and the real actor later, after the shooting of the battle scene is done. We'll get the pair of you to act standing in the cart, but without the ponies. I'm hoping I'll be able to hire the elephant again,' and then to the stand-in Krishna, 'Where's your crown?'

'I've got it here, sahib,' said the man. 'It's a bit tight and gives me a headache so I'll put it on at the last moment.'

Dilip nodded. Still standing the man took up the reins and told Arjuna, 'You can get in now, Arjuna Sahib.'

Arjuna climbed in and stood behind him, feeling relieved that, after all, he had not been defeated and would not have to go into exile.

The Krishna syce put on his sparkling crown with its peacock plumes as the ponies were led onto the battlefield. The cart trundled heavily and an odd sound seemed to be coming from one of the wheels making Arjuna hope it did not fall off during the filming.

The commanders gave their signals to charge.

The syce loosed Arjuna's lead pony, Krishna whipped up his team and they set off at a canter towards the enemy army.

Dizzily Karna began to wonder if his body had become the property of someone else and that was why it disobeyed him. Vague fantasies began to wander through his mind that he was both a man and a woman and that all he needed to do was to unite the two and then he would be able to move again, get out of the river and be freed of pain.

In a moment the air was filled with dust, the shouts of antagonists, the rumble of iron-shod wheels, the clatter of harness and hooves and roars from the satisfied onlookers.

Arjuna had problems with balance at first but eventually found a way of bracing his knees against the wooden side of the unsprung cart and raised his six-foot-high bow to shoot rubber tipped arrows.

At first Karna thought that night was falling because it had grown so dark. But then sight returned and he realised that the river water round him was red from blood. And as time passed and his blood kept slowly running out and mingling with the holy river he began to look into the face of death.

As Arjuna stood pulling back his bow with tin-clad wrists, while his cardboard cart clattered in a cloud of yellow dust over the bumpy grass, the sensation of being the true Arjuna from the Bhagavad Gita stole through him.

'Are you all right, Arjuna Sahib?' asked the charioteer. He looked back anxiously at his passenger, who appeared to be fainting against the cart side.

Snatching up his bow and hastily firing, Arjuna assured the man, 'Yes, yes, I'm okay.'

At the end of the filming there was still no sign of Karna. 'Could he have had a crash?' Arjuna wondered to Poopay.

'He drove too?'

'We were having a race,' he muttered guiltily. He would tell her the whole story one day but not now. Not now.

'Surely you would have seen it. Don't keep worrying about Karna. He is the one person who knows how to look after himself,' she laughed. 'I'm sure he will turn up in entirely unexpected circumstances as usual. We need to celebrate so come on, let's find somewhere where we can be alone together.'

Karna saw Dolly coming. At first he wondered why she came walking over the water like an apsara but then he remembered she could not swim, so had no other way of getting to him. She looked exactly the same as she had done thirteen years ago. The only difference was that she was not dead any more. Although she was walking on the water, her sandals and even the hem of her sari were perfectly dry.

★　　★　　★

The crowds kept such a close watch on Poopay and Arjuna that although they were heavily protected by gangs of Dilip's goondas, they could not find anywhere to be alone. Even in Arjuna's car, with the goondas running round and whacking anyone in their path, there were people clambering at the windows to have a look.

The excited couple tried to drive to the Grand Hotel, but they were stopped by mobs. Eventually, protected by Dilip's goondas, they crept into Poopay's van on the maidan, where for the first time they kissed, feeling as though they were in a small boat in heavy seas because of the way the crowd kept thrusting and shoving and scrambling up the sides.

The sun sank, owls began to swoop low over the water and the river became lost in darkness. Karna heard a bullock cart creaking by and caught a sideways glimpse of its swinging lamp. Some men went by carrying burning brands and shouting to each other for confidence. It was pitch-dark by now, and Karna could no longer see the trees or the bushes. The riverbanks and the water that ran between them was lost to his sight but he did not mind all that because Dolly was with him and she was smiling.

The battle was over. Shivarani stood looking over the littered battlefield, and although there were no bodies of dead soldiers on it there was other debris. As far as could be seen, among the empty Thumbs Up tins, popcorn packets, green coconut shells, lay bits of broken cardboard chariots and the tattered pieces of paper harness and rubber from men's armour. The rubbish-littered battlefield and its tawdry debris seemed to symbolise the hollowness of life and the falseness of its promises. The great and roaring battle, that would look so real on film, was only an illusion, like the happiness of life, thought Shivarani. She felt so tired, her mind and body ached and she wished she could go and live in Canada with her parents, where snow muffled sound in winter, and the nearest neighbour was twenty miles away. But she had to stay here, for it was her dharma to keep on working on behalf of women, most of whom had all the things she longed for. It hurt to go to other women's weddings or be asked to cuddle other women's babies but she knew she must keep doing it because that was her duty. In the morning she was interviewing candidates for the job of manager for a loan system she was setting up for women who needed capital to start a business. In the afternoon she flew to Kerala to dissuade Christian families from sending their daughters to Italy to become nuns when they were too poor to give the girl a dowry or an education. They saw taking the veil as a way of giving their daughter a future but Shivarani would tell them, 'It will be better for your daughters to be poor, uneducated and even unmarried here than far from home, in another culture and without the language.' She would have preferred to be able to say, 'You do not need to offer a dowry and she will be educated free,' but things had not progressed so far as yet. One day, one day, thought Shivarani, if I still have the energy. She sighed. She was forty-two, the only man she had ever loved was engaged to marry someone else, and now there was no hope for her anymore. She would have liked to weep but like all the other things inside her, her tears had dried.

She began to walk across the maidan towards the river, trying to get away from noise, the people, the pointless celebration, for in this city there were too many people and too much going on. She wished that the bomb had killed her in the road that day. Or better still she had died in Naxalbari while Bhima held her and before she understood that she would never have happiness.

When she reached the river she stood listening by the water, but even here there came the sound of the city clamour. She heard someone walking towards her and felt annoyed that even here she was not left alone.

She turned to face the approaching person, frowning, ready to explain her need for solitude, to request whoever it was to go away, to leave her for a while. The sky behind the intruder was glowing with city lights and a white mist was rising from the ground, so that the oncoming person was hardly visible, and she could not even see if it was a man or a woman.

When the person came close to her, however, she did not ask him to go because it was Bhima. He did not speak but came and stood beside her. For a while the two of them stood, staring silently at the dark water, then Bhima said, 'I could not stand the bank job.'

'I am sorry,' said Shivarani.

'I want to be working with the children. I want to help people. I could not bear it inside there, insulated from them all.'

'I understand,' said Shivarani.

'So I left the job.'

'Oh,' said Shivarani.

'And now it is over between Malti and me,' he said.

Shivarani waited. She did not know what to say.

After a long time Bhima added, 'We are not getting married after all.'

'I see,' said Shivarani and kept staring out at the river. There was something odd in the water. It looked as though a car had crashed in.

Then she understood. Gasping she pointed. 'Bhima, that's Karna's car.' She went leaping down the bank, with Bhima following her. She began shouting, 'Karna, Karna,' but there came no answer. She scrambled into the river and waded through it till she could see the car. 'Bhima, quick, go for help. He's badly injured.'

As Bhima went running back, Shivarani scrambled through the mud. The car was jammed nose down in the water and Karna's head and shoulders protruded through the shattered windscreen, and hung down so that water lapped his forehead. His eyes were closed, there was a terrible gash in his throat, and blood ran over the sides of the bonnet continually staining the water red. She ripped a strip off her sari end and tied it round Karna's throat in an attempt to staunch the bleeding then, putting her arms round him, tried to hold him up. 'It's going to be all right, Karna. Bhima has gone for help.' He opened his eyes and looked at her blearily. She smiled at him. 'I'm with you. Don't be afraid.'

Karna whispered, 'Ma, even though I never got the luck, I did my best. I tried my hardest to make you proud of me, but it never worked out.'

'I know, Karna, I know,' his mother said. 'I have been so proud of you.'

The last thing Karna heard on earth was the voice of Dolly saying, 'I know, Karna. I know. I have been so proud of you.' He knew everything was all right then and that he had not let her down after all. She did not look at all like Poopay Patalya but was more like the goddess, Durga, very tall and with a beautiful dark face. He knew it was Durga because she had risen out of the river and instead of offering just her hand, put her arms round him and eased his pain away. Then the goddess lifted Karna from his broken car, very gently carried him down to the bottom of the river and holding him in her holy arms, took the world away.

Because Karna was dead, Arjuna won the election. Dilip Baswani wanted to throw a party to celebrate Arjuna's success but Arjuna refused. 'No one knows which one of us has really won.' He added, 'I did not realise when he was alive that I would miss him.' So Dilip threw an engagement party for Arjuna and Poopay Patalya instead, to which anyone who was anything was invited. It was even grander than the one to which Arjuna, all that time ago, had arrived on foot because Karna had caused his car to break down. All the most famous Bollywood stars turned up and the most powerful politicians too. Even the Prime Minister of India accepted the invitation.

Bhima was there. He and Shivarani had met a week before at Karna's funeral but had not had a chance to speak because of the hundreds of people who had come to mourn their hero. Beggars, goondas, kigalis, prostitutes, smugglers, dealers, and people from Bollywood and Hatibari too, everyone that had ever met or heard of Karna seemed to be gathered round his funeral pyre. The only thing Shivarani had had a chance to say to Bhima was, 'His little pony, Poopay, died on the very day that Karna did, as though she knew.'

He handed Shivarani a glass of champagne then took one himself. 'Look,' he said, balancing his own on his head.

'Oh, Bhima,' Shivarani laughed as the glass crashed in a stutter of spilled drink. Nearby ladies glared at him and leaping out of the way, dabbed at their precious silk saris.

'Usually I can do it,' he laughed. 'And I can balance it on my nose if I am feeling really steady but today I am feeling wobbly.'

'Why?' she asked.

'Because I am to get a salary for my work at the children's centre. I have a job again, Shivarani.' He studied her face. His dark eyes shone. Another glass toppled, spraying both of them with champagne.

'The Prime Minister is looking,' said Shivarani, and tried not to laugh.

'Sometimes I can even balance a filled glass on my tongue,' said Bhima.

'Bhima, I have to tell you something,' she said suddenly.

He raised his eyebrows. Drops of champagne fell from them.

'DR Uncle has asked me to marry him.'

'You can't do that,' laughed Bhima.

'Why?'

'Because you are marrying me.'

Poopay wore a clinging blue chiffon sari trimmed with gold and round her neck an uncut diamond on a heavy chain that was Arjuna's engagement gift to her.

She looks so beautiful my eyes can hardly bear it, thought Arjuna, as he watched his wife-to-be over the rim of his champagne glass.

Dilip called him. 'Come with me, Arjuna. There is someone here who wants to talk to you.' He led Arjuna to a small private sitting room, with Poopay following. There stood a little boy, flanked by Bika and her mother, Lakshmi.

Laughing, Dilip gestured to the boy. 'Come on, tell him.' The boy, who looked about six, came towards Arjuna and, standing before him, did a gracious namaskar.

'My name is Abhimanyu,' he said.

Arjuna stared and into his mind sprang the memory of a young man emerging from Janci's stable, followed by a straw-tangled Bika. Turning to Bika he said, 'Then you are married to my groom, Bika? I am glad,' he said. 'This little boy looks exactly like that charming young man.'

The boy frowned slightly. 'I am *your* son,' he said.

Bika's mother rushed forward. 'What he tells is true. Everyone says Abhimanyu looks just like you and not like any pony syce. Come, Bika, tell him.'

'Every day I would think, after that love we made together, you would call for me,' said Bika.

'It took her six years to realise that you had forgotten her,' said Lakshmi. Her tone was bitter.

Bika had started crying. 'For six years she has tried to make me come to you, but I would not do it because I thought that somewhere inside you, you must feel love for me as I feel for you and that when you were ready you would come.'

Poopay let out a sound that was only half mirth. Bika glared at her then said to Arjuna, 'But now I can see you have forgotten me entirely and that night meant nothing at all to you so I have come to you to demand you take responsibility for this child who is your son.' She suddenly burst out sobbing. 'I can't do it, Ma. This kind of tricking is wrong no matter what he has done.'

'Silence, Bika,' roared her mother.

'You see what it is like to be famous,' laughed Dilip Baswani. 'Your children will be cropping up every single week from now on.'